ADRKABLE

By Sarra Manning

Nobody's Girl
Guitar Girl
Let's Get Lost
Pretty Things
Fashionistas Series
Diary of a Crush Trilogy

AD♥RKABLE

SARRA MANNING

www.atombooks.net

ATOM

First published in Great Britain in 2012 by Atom
Reprinted 2012 (twice)

A CIP catalogue record for this book
is available from the British Library.

ISBN 978-1-907411-00-7

Typeset in Bodoni Book by M Rules
Printed and bound in Great Britain by
Clays Ltd, St Ives plc

Papers used by Atom are from well-managed forests
and other responsible sources.

MIX
Paper from
responsible sources
FSC® C104740

Atom
An imprint of
Little, Brown Book Group
100 Victoria Embankment
London EC4Y 0DY

An Hachette UK Company
www.hachette.co.uk

www.atombooks.net

AD♥RKABLE

The Ad♥rkable Manifesto

1. We have nothing to declare but our dorkiness.
2. Jumble sales are our shopping malls.
3. Better to make cookies than be a cookie-cutter.
4. Suffering doesn't necessarily improve you but it does give you something to blog about.
5. Experiment with Photoshop, hair dye, nail polish and cupcake flavours but never drugs.
6. Don't follow leaders, be one.
7. Necessity is the mother of customisation.
8. Puppies make everything better.
9. Quiet girls rarely make history.
10. Never shield your oddness, but wear your oddness like a shield.

1

'We need to talk,' Michael Lee told me firmly when I stepped out of the makeshift changing room at the St Jude's jumble sale, which was actually four curtained rails arranged in a square, to have a good preen in front of a clouded mirror.

I didn't say anything. I just stared back at his reflection, because he was Michael Lee. MICHAEL LEE!

Oh, Michael Lee. Where to begin? Boys wanted to be him. Girls wanted him. He was star of school, stage and playing field. Enough brains to fit in with the geeks, captain of the football team so all the sporty types bowed down before him, and his faux-hawk and carefully scuffed Converses also pulled in the indie crowd. If that wasn't enough, his dad was Chinese so he had an exotic Eurasian thing going on; there was even an ode to his cheekbones on the wall of the second-floor girls' loos at school.

He might have been all that and a bag of Hula Hoops but,

as far as I was concerned, if you were one of those popular types who got on with absolutely everyone then you couldn't have much of an edge. To be all things to all people, Michael Lee had to be the least interesting person in our school. That took some doing because our school was bursting at the seams with mediocrity.

So I couldn't imagine why Michael Lee was standing there in front of me insisting that we needed to have a chat, chin tilted so I had a great view of his poetry-inspiring cheekbones. I could also see right up his nostrils because he was freakishly tall.

'Go away,' I said in a bored voice, wafting my hand languidly in the direction of the other side of the church hall. 'Because I can guarantee that you have nothing to say that I'd want to hear.'

It would have sent most people scuttling back from whence they came but Michael Lee just gave me this look as if I was all hot air and bluster, then he dared to put his hand on my shoulder so he could turn my stiff, cringing body round. 'Look,' he said, his breath hitting my face, which made me flinch even more. 'What's wrong with that picture?'

I couldn't concentrate on anything other than Michael Lee having his football-playing, prize-essay-writing hot fingers on my clavicle. It was just wrong. Beyond wrong. It was a whole other world of wrong. I screwed my eyes tightly shut in protest and when I opened them again, I was looking at Barney, who I'd left in charge of my stall, against my better judgement, talking to a girl.

Not just any girl but Scarlett Thomas, who happened to be

Michael Lee's girlfriend. Not that I held that against her. What I held against her was that she was vapid and had a really annoying voice, which was breathy and babyish and had exactly the same effect on me as someone crunching ice cubes. Scarlett also had long blonde hair, which she spent hours combing, spritzing, primping and tossing so if you stood behind her in the lunch queue there was a good chance you'd get a mouthful of hair.

She was tossing her hair back now as she spoke to Barney and, yes, she was grinning a vacant grin and Barney was smiling and ducking his head, the way he did when he was embarrassed. It wasn't a picture that made my heart sing, but then again ...

'There's nothing wrong with that picture,' I told Michael Lee crisply. 'It's just your girlfriend talking to my boyfriend—'

'But it's not the talking—'

'About quadratic equations or one of the many other things Scarlett doesn't understand, which made her fail her Maths GCSE and have to retake it.' I gave Michael a flinty-eyed look. 'That's why Ms Clements asked Barney to tutor Scarlett. Didn't she mention it?'

'She did mention it and it's not them talking to each other that's wrong, it's how they're not *really* talking at all. They're just standing there and gazing at each other,' he pointed out.

'You're being ridiculous,' I said, even as I surreptitiously glanced back to where Barney and Scarlett were indeed gazing at each other. It was obvious they were staring at each other because they'd run out of things to say and it was awkward, nervous gazing, because they had absolutely nothing in

3

common. 'There is *nada*, nowt, not one thing going on. Well, apart from the fact that you and Scarlett are slumming it at a jumble sale,' I added, turning my attention back to Michael Lee. 'Right, now that we've cleared that up, feel free to go about your business.'

Michael opened his mouth like he had something more to say about the utter non-event of Barney and Scarlett gurning at each other. Then shut it again. I waited for him to leave so I could go about *my* business, but he suddenly moved closer to me.

'There is something going on between them,' he said, bending his head. His breath ghosted against my cheek again. I wanted to bat it away with an irritated gesture. He straightened up. 'And nice dress, by the way.'

I could tell he didn't mean it from the almost-smirk on his face, which made me wonder if Michael Lee might actually have some hidden depths buried way below the surface of his bland exterior.

I sniffed loudly and contemptuously, which made the quirk of his lips blossom into a full-blown smirk before he strode away.

'Jeane, my love, don't take this the wrong way, but he was being sarcastic. That dress doesn't look at all nice,' said a pained voice to my left and I looked over at Marion and Betty, two volunteers from the St Jude's social committee who manned the cake stall and policed the changing room. One of their stern looks would scare off even the most determined perv. I didn't doubt that they'd pelt peeping toms with rock buns if the stern looks failed.

'I know he was being sarcastic but he was also being very mistaken because this dress is made from all kinds of awesome,' I said, stepping back so I could get my preen on, though my heart wasn't really in it now.

The dress was black and I didn't normally do black because why would anyone want to wear black when there were so many fabulous colours in the world? People with no imagination and Goths who hadn't got the memo that the nineties were over, that's who. But it wasn't just black; it had these horizontal patterns all over it – yellow, green, orange, blue, red, purple and pink squiggly lines that made my eyeballs itch – and it fitted so well that it could have been made just for me, which didn't happen often because I have a very odd body. I'm small, like five feet nothing, and compact so I can fit into children's sizes, but I'm sturdy with it. My grandfather used to say that I reminded him of a pit pony – when he wasn't telling me little girls should be seen and not heard.

Anyway, yes. I'm sturdy, stocky even. Like, my legs are really muscly because I cycle a lot and I'm kind of solid everywhere else. If it wasn't for the iron-grey hair (it was meant to be white but my friend Ben had only been training as a hairdresser for two weeks and something went badly wrong) and the bright red lipstick I always wore, I could have passed for a chubby twelve-year-old boy. But this dress had enough nips and tucks and darts and horizontal lines that at least it looked as if I had some kind of shape because me and puberty hadn't got on very well. Instead of womanly curves, it had left me with a general lumpiness.

'You'd look so pretty if you wore a nice dress instead of all this nasty jumble sale stuff. You don't know where it's been,' Betty lamented. 'My granddaughter's got lots of clothes she doesn't wear any more. I could sort you out some things.'

'No, thanks,' I said firmly. 'I love the nasty jumble sale stuff.'

'But some of my granddaughter's old clothes are from Topshop.'

It was very hard to restrain myself, but I didn't immediately launch into a rant about the evils of buying clothes from high street chains, which peddled the same five looks each season so everyone had to dress just like everyone else in clothes that were sewn together by children in Third World sweatshops who were paid in cups of maize.

'Really, Betty, I like dressing in clothes that other people don't want any more. It's not the clothes' fault that they've gone out of fashion,' I insisted. 'Anyway, it's better to reuse than recycle.'

Five minutes later, the dress was mine, and I was back in my own lilac-tweed, old-lady skirt and mustard-coloured jumper and heading to my stall where Barney was leafing through a stack of yellowing comics. Thankfully, Scarlett and Michael Lee were nowhere to be seen.

'I got you cake,' I announced. At the sound of my voice, Barney's head shot up and his milk-white complexion took on a rosy hue. I'd never known a boy who blushed as much as Barney did. In fact, I hadn't even been certain that boys *could* blush, until I met Barney.

He was blushing now for no good reason, unless ... No, I wasn't going to waste my precious time on Michael Lee's crackpot theories, except ...

'So, Michael Lee and Scarlett Thomas, what were they doing here?' I asked casually. 'Hardly their scene. I bet they've gone away to disinfect themselves from the stench of second-hand goods.'

Barney was now so red that it looked as if someone had plunged his head into a pan of boiling water, but he hunched over so a curtain of silky hair covered his burning face and grunted something unintelligible.

'You and Scarlett?' I prompted.

'Er, what about me and Scarlett?' he asked in a strangulated voice.

I shrugged. 'Just saw her checking out the stall when I was trying on dresses. I hope you gave her the hard sell and offloaded that chipped "Rugby players do it with odd-shaped balls" mug that I can't shift.'

'Well, no, I didn't have a chance,' Barney admitted, as if he was confessing to something shameful. 'And that mug is really chipped.'

'True. Very true. Not surprised you didn't get round to it,' I said, cocking my head in what I hoped was an understanding manner. 'You two looked pretty tight. What *were* you talking about?'

Barney flailed his hands. 'Nothing!' he yelped, then realised immediately that 'Nothing' was not a suitable reply. 'We talked about Maths and stuff,' he added.

I'd been sure that there wasn't anything going on with Barney and Scarlett apart from some compound fractions, but Barney's apparent guilt was forcing me to rethink that theory.

I knew I could winkle the truth from Barney in nanoseconds,

and that the truth was that Barney had a crush on Scarlett – being easy on the eye and untaxing on the brain, she was considered quite a catch. There was no point in getting upset about it, even though I'd raised him to be better than that, and it really wasn't worth talking about any longer. It was far too boring.

'I got you cake,' I reminded Barney and watched his eyes skitter from side to side as if he wasn't sure whether my abrupt change of subject meant that the topic of Scarlett was over and done with or if it was a sneaky tactic to catch him out.

For once, it wasn't. I handed over a huge slab of cake, which was obscured by a napkin. Barney took it warily.

'Well, thanks,' he muttered, as he uncovered his prize and I watched his face go from deep pink to bedsheet-white. Barney was so white that he was only a couple of shades down from albino. He hated his skin almost as much as he hated his orange hair. At school, the lower years call Barney 'the ginger minger', but Barney's hair *isn't* ginger. It's actually the colour of marmalade, except when the sun is shining and it becomes a living flame, which is why I've forbidden him from dyeing it. He's not a minger either. When his face isn't obscured by a thick fringe, his features are delicate, almost girlish, and his eyes, which were fixed on me imploringly, are pond-green. Barney is the only boy I've ever met whose signature colours are white, orange and green. Most other boys are blue or brown, I thought, and made a mental note to explore this colour theory on my blog later in the week. Then I turned my attention back to Barney, who had puckered up his face and was thrusting the napkin and its contents back at me.

'This is carrot cake!'

I nodded. 'Carrot cake with cream-cheese frosting. Yum.'

'Not yum. This is, like, the anti-yum. I ask you to get me a cake. A CAKE! And you come back with something made out of carrots and cheese. That is not cake,' Barney snapped. 'It's non-cake-food disguised as cake.'

I could only stand and stare. I'd seen Barney petulant before – I was usually responsible for it – but I'd never known him quite so snippy.

'But you eat carrots,' I ventured timidly under the weight of Barney's ferocious scowl. 'I'm sure I've seen you eat carrots.'

'I eat them under duress – I have to have meat or potatoes with them.'

'I'm sorry,' I said and I tried to sound like I meant it. Barney was in a very unpredictable mood and I didn't want to trigger another explosion. 'I'm sorry I sucked at the cake selection. I obviously need to work on that.'

'Well, I suppose it's not your fault,' Barney decided magnanimously. He looked at me from under his fringe, a mere glimmer of a smile just hovering on his lips. 'You do really suck at choosing cakes, but it's good to know you suck at something. I was beginning to wonder.'

'I suck at loads of things,' I assured Barney, as I decided that it was probably safe to stand behind the stall with him. 'Can't turn cartwheels. Never got the hang of German and I don't have strong enough facial muscles to arch an eyebrow.'

'It's genetic,' Barney said. 'But I think you can teach yourself to do it.'

I pushed up my right eyebrow with my fingertip. 'Maybe I

should tape my eyebrow up every night and hope that my muscle memory kicks in.'

'I bet there's an instruction guide on the internet,' Barney said eagerly. It was just the kind of obscure, random thing that he liked to research. 'I'll put my Google-fu on it, shall I?'

We were friends again. I mean, boyfriend and girlfriend again. I got Barney a slice of chocolate cake, then spent the rest of the afternoon adding to the list of things I absolutely sucked at, which made him laugh.

It was good. We were cool. Though I wondered why I had to run myself down in order to make Barney feel better about our relationship when I was a card-carrying feminist. Like, seriously. I had the word 'feminist' on my business cards. But for once I took the easy option because I couldn't bear the thought of three hours of Barney moping about. I didn't even yell at him when he spilt Dr Pepper on the 'Adorkable' hot water bottle cover it had taken me ages to knit.

2

I hate Jeane Smith.

I hate her stupid grey hair and her disgusting polyester clothes. I hate how she goes out of her way to make herself look as unattractive as possible but still wants everyone to notice her. She should just wear a T-shirt with 'Everyone! Pay attention to me! Right now!' printed on it.

I hate how everything she says is sarcastic and mean and sounds even more sarcastic and mean because of the flat, toneless way she speaks. As if showing emotion or excitement is way too uncool.

I hate the way she shoved her fugly face into mine and jabbed a finger in my chest to make her point. Though, now I think about it, I'm not sure she did do that, but it's the kind of thing she would probably do.

But mostly I hate her for being so obnoxious and such an out of control bitch that even her boyfriend can't stand to be around her and has to start looking for an out. Especially when that out is my girlfriend.

I knew that Barney fancied Scarlett. It was a given. She was really fit. Really, really fit. Whenever we went into town and got within fifty yards of Topshop she was mobbed on all sides by model agency scouts.

But Scarlett never went to see the agencies because she said she was three inches too short to be a model and she was far too shy. Before we started dating, I thought Scarlett's shyness was sweet. But, after a while, shyness isn't endearing and doesn't make you want to protect someone, it makes you secretly grind your teeth in frustration.

The thing about shyness is that it seems a lot like not trying, the same way that Scarlett wasn't even trying to make our relationship work. I was putting the effort in, calling her every night, thinking of cool things to do on our dates. I bought her presents and helped her set up her BlackBerry and in all ways I was an excellent boyfriend. Whether it's football or A-level Physics or dating, what's the point of doing anything if you're going to do it in a half-arsed way? And I don't want to sound bigheaded but I could go out with pretty much any girl at our school – in fact, any girl at any school in our borough. The fact that I *chose* Scarlett should have given her a huge shot of confidence and she could have shown a little gratitude too.

So when I saw Scarlett and Barney together, it made me furious. All I ever got from Scarlett was a lot of hair-tossing and a few wan smiles but Barney got longing looks and giggling. I couldn't actually hear the giggles but I imagined them as tiny, silver daggers aimed right at my heart and, when I turned my head away, I saw a short, squat, grey-haired girl preening in the mirror.

Jeane Smith is the only person at our school that I've never spoken to. Seriously. I hate labels and cliques and all that bullshit about blanking people 'cause they're not into the same music as you or they're crap at sports. I like that I can get on with everyone and always find some common ground to talk about, even if they're not that cool.

Jeane Smith doesn't talk to anyone, apart from that Barney kid. Everyone talks about her, or about her revolting clothes and the arguments she picks with the teachers in every single one of her classes, but no one talks *to* her because if you try to, you find yourself on the business end of some serious snark and a superior stare.

That was what I got when I tried to explain my suspicions about Barney and Scarlett. About halfway through my first sentence, I realised my mistake, but it was too late. I was committed to having a conversation with her. And I don't know how anyone could manage a dead-eyed stare that also promised unimaginable pain but somehow Jeane had mastered the art. It was as if her retinas had been replaced with laser pointers.

Then she was sticking out her chin and being a bitch, and suddenly whatever whacked-out thing that was going on with Barney and Scarlett didn't matter as much as having the last word.

'Nice dress, by the way,' I said, cocking my head at the horrible multi-coloured mess of a dress that she was wearing, and it was a low blow and completely beneath me, but at least it got Jeane Smith to shut up. But then she smirked and she was one of those people who could make a smirk say a thousand words and none of them good ones.

By the time I'd finished that unpleasant little exchange, Scarlett and Barney had finished their silent flirting. She hurried over to me, her face more animated than I'd ever seen it.

'Can we go now?' she asked, as if it had been my idea to go to a jumble sale full of tatty old junk and stinky clothes that wouldn't have been accepted as donations at the crappiest charity shop in the world. But Scarlett had wanted to come and as she never suggested interesting or fun things to do on dates, I'd seen it as a real sign of progress in our relationship.

Now I suspected that Scarlett had only wanted to come because Barney was going to be there. Normally I'd have come straight to the point and asked Scarlett what was going on, but something made me hesitate. If I couldn't make it work with Scarlett, what did it say about me? It said she preferred a mumbling ginger kid over me, which just ... no. That couldn't be possible.

So I just said, 'Cool. This place smells like someone died in here.'

Scarlett murmured in agreement but, just as we reached the door, she turned her head and looked back at the corner where Barney sat. He wasn't looking longingly at Scarlett but at Jeane, who, from the way she was standing with her hands on her hips and a belligerent look on her face, was giving him a hard time.

'God, I *hate* that girl,' Scarlett said, her voice murderous and low. I stared at her in amazement. It was the first time I'd ever heard Scarlett express an opinion. 'She's so mean. She made me cry in English once because she, like, actually stuck her hand up in the middle of me reading from *A Midsummer Night's Dream* to complain about my delivery. At least I don't sound like a stoned robot.'

'Well, she is kind of annoying . . .'

'She isn't kind of anything. She *is* annoying,' Scarlett informed me icily. She was full of surprises this afternoon. She even glared at me as I held the door open for her as if I was a Jeane Smith proxy.

'Why are you getting so worked up about her?' I asked, as we walked up the steps that led to the street. I already knew the answer – Scarlett was hating on Jeane, because Jeane was dating on Barney. I was sure of it.

'"I am Jeane Smith,"' Scarlett intoned in a mechanical voice, which made me smile reluctantly, because this worked up, ranty Scarlett was approximately one thousand times more fun than the Scarlett I'd been dating. '"I have a million followers on Twitter and I am a blogging genius and my disgusting clothes and old lady hair are actually the last word in cool and if you don't agree it's because you are not cool. In fact, you're so uncool that I can't even bring myself to look at you, in case you infect me with your nasty, uncool suburban germs." Ugh! She's so up herself.'

'She has a blog? Big deal. *Everyone* has a blog.'

'You haven't seen her blog,' Scarlett muttered darkly. 'The stuff she goes on about – it's unbelievable.'

'How come you're cyber-stalking her anyway?' I asked, my voice getting so squeaky that I choked on the final syllable.

'I'm not.' Scarlett's voice, on the other hand, was fading into its usual whisper. 'I *have* to read her blog, otherwise I wouldn't be able to join in when people are talking about her at school.'

'Don't you Year 12s have anything else to talk about that isn't Jeane Smith?'

Scarlett didn't reply, but looked up and down the road then gave a sigh of relief. 'There's my mum's car. I've got to go.'

'I thought we were going to get a coffee.'

'Well, yeah, my mum texted me and said that she was, um, like, in the area.' Scarlett squirmed unhappily. 'While you were looking round the jumble sale. I mean, that's when she texted me.'

I should just end this, I thought. Because this, *us*, we were going nowhere and yes, Scarlett would give me her sad face that looked like a baby seal just before it got clubbed to death but I'd seen Scarlett's sad face so often in the last few weeks that I was immune to it.

'Look, Scar, I've been thinking . . . ' I began, but Scarlett was already backing away.

'Got to go,' she yelped, as her mother tooted the horn. 'See you tomorrow or something.'

'Yeah, see you,' I said, but Scarlett had already started running to where her mother's Range Rover was blocking the traffic and there was no way she could have heard me.

3

All too soon it was five o'clock and the jumbling hordes started thinning out.

I'd had a good afternoon and sold most of the heavy items, including a mouldy collection of pulp fiction novels, a hideous framed painting of a clown that had given me the shudders every time I looked at it, and an art deco statuette of a black cat, which had a light fitting shoved on top of its head and an electrical lead and plug where its tail should be.

It meant packing up the stall and loading my plastic crates into Barney's mum's massive petrol-guzzling four-wheel-drive didn't take too long and we didn't have to pile things up on the back seat like usual. Barney had only passed his test a couple of months before and it sent him into a sweating, shaking tizzy when he couldn't see out of the rear window.

Even though his field of vision was completely clear, Barney still needed absolute silence while he was driving, but as we got nearer to where I lived it got harder to keep quiet.

I waited until we stopped at a traffic light. 'So, do you want to hang at mine for a while?' I asked. 'Or we could go and see a film. There's that one with Ellen Page that we talked about. Or how do you feel—?'

Barney hissed in annoyance because I was still talking as the lights changed from red to amber. 'Sorry,' I muttered, sinking back on the seat as he tensed every muscle in anticipation of the lights turning green and having to drive off again without the car stalling.

I tried to keep still and quiet, and not even breathe too heavily, until Barney had pulled slowly and carefully into the kerb outside the redbrick mansion block where I lived.

'So, do you want to do something now?' I asked. 'For a couple of hours.'

'I can't. You know my mum likes me to spend Sunday evening at home so she can check that I've done my coursework and that I've washed behind my ears and sharpened my pencils and I have enough clean T-shirts to last the week.' Barney wrinkled his nose in disgust. 'I bet even when I'm at university she'll drive down on a Sunday afternoon to check up on me.'

'I'm sure she wouldn't do that,' I said, although I thought Barney's mum would do precisely that if Barney didn't have a younger brother who needed just as much, if not more, supervision than Barney. There wasn't much love between Barney's mum and me – she thought I was a bad influence on her son and had much preferred the days when he stayed at home and didn't have a social life. But I was careful never to raise this topic with Barney because I didn't want to be the sort of girl who came between a boy and his overbearing mother.

'Yeah, she would.' Barney unclipped his seatbelt. 'I'll help you get everything inside, but then I have to go home.'

Once we'd ferried all the crates and boxes and bags into the foyer, then into the rickety lift up to the sixth floor and *then* dumped them in my hall, Barney took a deep breath and waited for me to hang up my jacket.

I could see his anxious face reflected in the hall mirror and it was a perfect match for my own. I hated this part. The good-bye kiss part.

I took two steps forward as Barney craned his neck a few centimetres towards me to show willing. When we were practically nose to nose, he screwed his eyes shut and pursed his lips tightly until they resembled a cat's bumhole. Apart from the lack of visual stimulation, when I pressed my lips against Barney's they didn't feel very kiss-shaped. His mouth wasn't relaxed, his lips weren't soft and pliable, so we ended up kissing the way we always ended up kissing, mashing our mouths against each other furiously as if the effort made up for the lack of passion.

There were no hands cupping or fondling. Barney kept his arms at his sides and I placed one hand very decorously on his shoulder and there was absolutely no tongue. The first time I'd tried to introduce it, Barney had freaked out so much that I'd never dared repeat it. I counted, 'One elephant, two elephant, three elephant' in my head and when I got to 'fifty elephant' I gently disengaged our lips.

19

'We're getting better at that,' Barney remarked, even though he had this pained look on his face as if he was longing to use the back of his hand to erase the phantom feeling of my mouth. 'Don't you think?'

'Definitely,' I agreed, but we both knew it was a lie. Or I did and surely Barney couldn't be *that* deluded to think that the fifty seconds we'd spent with our mouths grinding against each other was an improvement.

Barney was funny and kind and he knew lots and lots of useful things about computers but we had no sexual chemistry at all. I wasn't sure that any amount of kissing practice was going to change that. You either had sexual chemistry or you didn't and we *so* didn't.

'Well, I'd better get going.' Barney sighed, and it was a slight sop to my ego that he sounded completely unenthused about leaving me. 'My mum was making lentil soup when I left. Guess I know what's for dinner.'

Maybe it was more that he just didn't want to go home. 'I bet that carrot cake's sounding pretty good right now,' I said lightly and Barney grinned.

'You're so lucky living on your own, Jeane. No one to tell you what to do. You can eat what you want when you want, stay up as late as you like, spend so long on the internet that your eyes go blurry and—'

'And if something gets broken or stops working, I have to figure out how to get it repaired all by myself. I have to do my own cleaning and my own cooking and get myself up for school—'

'Oh, don't try and make out that it's awful,' Barney scoffed.

'It's not like you ever do any cleaning and you live on Haribo and cake. Just think about me going home to be nagged to death by my mother as I eat her disgusting lentil soup and her really chewy homemade bread. It's grey,' he added with a shudder, as he headed for the door. 'She says it's just the wheatgerm, but it's still no colour that edible bread should be.'

I followed Barney out because he could never work the latch and as I leaned in for a friendly goodbye peck on the cheek, he jerked his head back like I'd been about to lunge for his mouth with tongue unfurled.

'I'll see you tomorrow,' Barney said heartily to hide the fact that he'd reared away from my lips like they were infected with flesh-eating bacteria, his face flaring up for about the seventeenth time that day. 'Gotta go!'

I listened to the soft slap of Barney's sneakers on the parquet floor, the scrape and creak as he pulled back the metal grille and stepped into the lift, then its whirr as it travelled between the floors. I could even hear the distant slam of the front door. It sounded so final, so definite.

After my parents had got divorced and I'd moved into a flat in a mansion block with my older sister, Bethan, I'd been thrilled. It seemed so exotic after spending my first fifteen years in a semi-detached house with a garden, garage, double glazing and fitted wardrobes.

Living in a mansion block which smelt of beeswax and had a black and white tiled floor in the lobby – even the fact that it had a lobby – made me feel like a girl in a book written in the 1920s who bobbed her hair and said, 'Gosh, thanks awfully' when men held doors open for her.

Bethan and I had even talked about learning to tap-dance so our tap shoes would make the most splendid sound as we soft-shoe-shuffled (or whatever it is that you do when you tap-dance) along the hallways. But that was last year, and this year Bethan is doing a year's residency at a specialist paediatric hospital in Chicago and I'm living on my own in a beautiful flat, which isn't quite so beautiful any more because, well, life's too short to vacuum or dust or pick up after myself.

There was a vaguely clear path from the front door to the open-plan living room. I crunched over magazines and sweet wrappers to get to the table and switched on my MacBook.

It took a huge effort but I didn't check my email, or my Twitter or my Facebook, but started to read my Business Studies notes.

I always have homework on a Sunday evening. Not because I'm a slacker who leaves everything to the last minute but because Sunday evening is the loneliest evening of the week. Everyone else is hunkered down with mums fussing about packed lunches and clean clothes. Even my real, grown-up friends say they get that back-to-school feeling on a Sunday night that can only be quelled with a cheesy film and a tub of ice cream.

I don't have a mum fussing about me, or a dad for that matter, so I always leave some homework in reserve so I don't have a chance to start wallowing. You can't really wallow when you're painstakingly adding financial data to spreadsheets for your Business Studies coursework.

It didn't even help that the company I'd created for Business Studies was my actual real-life company. Adorkable was a geek-championing lifestyle brand and trend-spotting agency that I found myself creating after my blog (also called Adorkable) started winning loads of awards and I kept getting asked to write pieces for the *Guardian* and take part in live dicussion panels on Radio 4. The actual figures I was cutting and pasting from one document to another showed the actual money I'd made in the last six months from consultancy work, public engagements, journalism and selling Adorkable-branded products on Etsy and CafePress. It still didn't make Business Studies fun. Not one bit. I was just sighing in relief as I got to the end of the last column when the phone rang.

My mum called at 7.30 every Sunday evening so it shouldn't have been a surprise and my heart shouldn't have stumbled like it did. Maybe it was because I spent the rest of the week repressing the memory of our Sunday evening phonecalls so it was always a shock when she called and said my name with that same note of trepidation that she's been using for as long as I can remember.

'Hi, Pat,' I said. 'How are things?'

Things were fine in Trujillo, Peru, although the power had been out during the week and she was running low on clean clothes because ...

'Do they even have washing machines in Peru?' I asked distractedly, because her voice was crackly and there was a weird time delay and even when we'd lived in the same house we hadn't had much to talk about.

'Of course they do, Jeane. I'm running out of clean knickers because I haven't had a *chance* to do any washing. Peru isn't the Third World. They have washing machines and hot and cold running water and yes, even Starbucks. Though that says more about globalisation than—'

We'd only been talking for two minutes and things were already frosty. 'You were the one who said the power had gone out!'

'Well, that's because, as you know, I spend Monday to Friday outside the city in a very remote region of—'

'Oh yes, how are the Peruvian women prisoners?' I asked pointedly, disdain curling round every syllable.

'Do you have to be so flippant about everything?'

'I'm not being flippant,' I said, although I was. Not that she could ever tell either way. 'Really, I want to know. How are they?'

I knew the Peruvian women prisoners would keep her talking for a good ten minutes. After all, they were the reason, or the flimsy excuse, she'd given for packing two holdalls and a wheeled suitcase and hotfooting it over the Atlantic so she could spend two years writing a research paper on The Effects of a Tree-Hugging, Happy Clappy Approach to Incarceration on the Homicidal Tendencies and Behaviour of Long-Term Female Inmates in the Peruvian Prison System. I'm paraphrasing because the actual title of her research paper would make anyone fall asleep before they finished reading it.

Pat waffled on and I just 'Hmm'ed every now and again as I thought about what my first tweet of the evening would be. Usually I tweet at least once every five minutes, but Barney said it was really antisocial to keep prodding at my iPhone when we were together and I was now experiencing severe Twitter withdrawal.

'Anyway, Jeane, how are *you*?' Pat had got to the end of extolling the virtues of teaching violent, serial-killery women how to meditate and was now ready to get on my case about, well, everything. 'How's the flat?'

'I'm fine,' I said. 'The flat's fine too.'

'You are keeping it tidy, aren't you? And you are doing the washing up and cleaning the kitchen floor because otherwise you'll get ants—'

'We're on the sixth floor. I don't see how any ant would be able to climb up that many flights of stairs, unless they took the lift.' Pat sucked in her breath. 'Everything's very tidy.' It wasn't as if she ever looked at my blog and saw that I'd set up a DustCam (which was my old laptop trained on a patch of sideboard) to try and prove Quentin Crisp's theory that, after four years, the dust didn't get any worse.

'Well, if you say so.' I could tell she didn't believe me. 'How's school? Ms Ferguson has been emailing me. She says everything seems all right.'

Ms Ferguson and I were tight and unless I suddenly marched across the school grounds spraying people with gunshot, she wasn't going to spill to my mother my lesser crimes of arguing with my teachers, setting my iPhone with an alert and ringtone only audible to sensitive teenage ears so I could receive emails in class, and the battle of wills I was currently locked in with Mrs Spiers, my A-level Art teacher, over my refusal to paint a boring life study of some twigs. Y'know, the usual stuff.

'That's because everything is,' I said. 'So, I should probably let you go.'

'Wait! Have you heard from Roy?'

'Yeah. He's coming to London soon and we'll get together then,' I told her, gazing round at the mess and thinking about the time in the not-so-distant future that I'd have to clear it up before my father saw it.

'And you've spoken to Bethan?'

'Yes.' I was starting to sound a little exasperated. 'We Skype each other all the time. You could Skype me. It would be cheaper than calling.'

'You know I'm not very good at computers.'

'There's nothing to be good at. You just download the app and click on install and your computer does the rest. It's easy. Even you can do it.'

'Jeane, don't start.'

'I'm not starting anything. I'm just saying that I'm online all the time and if you had Skype, you could just get in touch whenever—'

'Well, I'm not online much. There isn't an internet café on every corner.'

'You said they had Starbucks, which all have free Wi-Fi so I don't see what the problem is.'

'No, you never do.' She gave a bitten-off sigh. 'Why do you always have to turn every conversation into an argument, Jeane?'

'It takes two people to have an argument, Pat,' I reminded her, because when I did have an argument, I never backed down. Even when I knew I should. I was born to be ornery. 'I have to go now.'

'Will you at least say goodbye properly?' she demanded.

'Goodbye properly,' I drawled, which was mean when Pat couldn't help what she was any more than I could help being a snarky little cow. 'Look, I'm sorry. I still have a ton of coursework to get through and the thought of my Business Studies spreadsheets is making me cranky.'

'Well, I'm relieved that it's not me that's making you so cranky,' she said in a slightly less huffy voice. 'But you promised you wouldn't leave your homework to the last moment.'

It wasn't the last moment. The last moment would be filling in columns as the register was read out. 'I know,' I gritted out. 'Sorry about that.'

There was another two minutes and thirty-seven agonising seconds of content-free conversation before Pat finally rang off.

I stretched my arms over my head to ease all the aches and pains in my neck and shoulders that always occurred when I talked to Pat, then I double-clicked on Firefox, then on TweetDeck, and connected my iPhone to my computer so I could upload the pictures I'd taken that afternoon.

My fingers flew over the keys as I wrote my first tweet of the evening. Then I hit return and within ten seconds someone had replied.

And, just like that, I wasn't alone any more.

4

I love Sunday evenings. The other six evenings of the week are
so crammed full of homework, football practice, school council meetings, debating society business and doing admin work
for my parents that even going out with my friends feels like
one more thing to be ticked off my to-do list. Besides, my parents are adamant that I need ten hours' sleep to prepare me for
the week ahead so I'm strongly discouraged (some people
might even call it forbidden) from going out on Sunday
evenings.

My mum was bathing my little sisters and as I padded up the
narrow stairs to my attic bedroom I could hear Melly complaining bitterly about sharing a bath with Alice. 'She's five, I'm
seven. I need my dignity, Mum.'

I grinned as I shut my bedroom door and carefully placed
my laden tray on the desk. On Sunday evenings my mum
expects me to clean out the fridge of all the food that's left over

from the weekend before the supermarket delivery arrives on Monday morning. Also we're not meant to eat what they call 'rubbish' Monday to Thursday so it's the last chance to stuff my face with greasy, sugary food.

Munching on a cold spring roll, I switched on my computer so I could finish my Physics homework. *They* think I finish all my assignments before I go out on Friday night, but they couldn't be more wrong.

Mum knocked on the door as I was jotting down the last of my formulae. 'Michael? Everything all right in there?'

She wasn't allowed to come in unless she had my express permission since the time she'd caught me with Megan, my girlfriend before Scarlett, in a compromising position on my IKEA rug.

There'd been a week of long, excruciating discussions about personal boundaries and getting girls into trouble. Now, whenever Mum put my clean clothes in a laundry basket outside my door, there were always packets of condoms stuffed into the pockets of my jeans. I had ninety-three condoms still in their shiny foil wrappers at the last count.

'Yeah, everything's cool,' I called out. 'I took the last of the chocolate chip pancakes Dad made yesterday, was that OK?'

'Better in your mouth than on my hips,' Mum said. 'What are you doing in there anyway?'

Sometimes I thought back with fondness to those halcyon days when she used to barge into my room without knocking. It was almost preferable to the way she stood outside my door and bombarded me with questions.

'Just mucking about on the computer,' I said vaguely.

'Well, Dad and I are about to watch a DVD if you want to join us,' she persisted. 'Nothing too chick-flicky.'

'No, it's all right,' I ground out, 'Really, Mum, I'll be down later.'

'If you're sure ...'

I didn't answer, just grunted, because if I carried on talking she'd be there for ever. Eventually I heard her tread on the stairs – she was the only person I knew who could make her footsteps sound reproachful. I turned back to Facebook. Scarlett was online but as soon as I logged on, she logged off. Or turned her status to 'invisible' so I'd think she'd logged off – either way, it didn't look good for the limping, bleeding beast that was all that was left of our relationship.

Almost as if my fingers were acting independently of my brain, I saw them type 'Jeane Smith + blog + Twitter' into the Google search box. I didn't know why I was bothering when the five minutes I'd had of Jeane Smith that afternoon were enough to last me the rest of the decade and anyway, there had to be *thousands* of women called Jeane Smith who had blogs. Even if it seemed like a really poseurish thing to do, to stick an e on the end of your name so it sounded French or something and ... oh!

The very first link of the 1,390,000,000 search results directed me to her blog, Adorkable.

There was a picture of Jeane, so I knew I'd come to the right place. Underneath were the words, 'I have nothing to declare but my dorkiness'. Well, she'd got that right.

Jeane Smith lives in London and is a blogger, a tweeter, a dreamer, a dare-to-dreamer, an agent provocateur, a knitter and an iconoclast in training.

One day, a few years ago, she started a blog called Adorkable, so she'd have somewhere to talk about the many, many things she liked. And also the many, many things that gave her conniptions. Then people started reading this blog and a year after its creation it was voted Best Lifestyle Blog by the *Guardian*, as well as winning a Bloggie Award, and has since been featured in *The Times*, the *New York Post*, the *Observer* and on the websites Jezebel and Salon.

Your humble and articulate blogmistress also made it to number seven in the *Guardian*'s '30 People Under the Age of 30 Who are Changing the World' list and is also considered to be a social networking and social trends expert (whatever the hell *that* is) and consults for all sorts of trendy companies with offices in Soho and Hoxton. Her journalism has appeared in the *Guardian*, *The Times*, *NYLON, i-D* and *Le Monde* and she's spoken about youth trends at conferences in London, Paris, Stockholm, Milan and Berlin. Jeane also writes a style column for the Japanese teen magazine *KiKi* and has a regular stall at several very well-attended jumble sales in the Greater London area.

As well as being a blog, lifestyle brand and trend-spotting agency, Adorkable is also a state of being. On our own we're dorks, geeks, misfits, losers, weirdos, the downtrodden – but together we're heavy. Oh yeah.

What*ever*, I thought to myself because it was all so much bollocks. *Obviously*. She was just a seventeen-year-old girl with serious attitude problems – and people who went to school and lived with their parents and had to stick their hand up and ask permission to go to the loo in the middle of a study period did not change the world or have wanky consultancy gigs. They just didn't.

Jeane Smith was full of shit and I didn't even know why I was still staring at her blog and something called a DustCam. It seemed as if she updated her blog at least once a day so she must have a lot of downtime to kill when she wasn't sourcing smelly second-hand dresses and being an iconoclast in training. I scrolled down lots of pretentious posts about getting in touch with your inner dork and the entries she made at 8.15 every morning so she could show off that day's colour-clashing ensemble with running commentary:

Swirly patterned frock: donated by Ben's grandma
Stripy tights: GapKids (Shouldn't I have outgrown the
    children's department by now?)
Cherry blossom sneakers: jumble sale
Candy necklace: from my local newsy

I didn't get why Jeane was so proud of her truly appalling sense of fashion. OK, I wasn't rushing out to buy a copy of *Vogue Pour Homme* each month but I bought my clothes from Hollister, Jack Wills and Abercrombie & Fitch so I obviously knew what looked good and swirly patterns and stripes on fusty old clothes didn't. Anybody that had two working eyes in their head could see that.

At least the Jeane striking a variety of exaggerated modelly poses (she gave her poses names like 'PoutyFace' and 'Oldtime PoutyFace' and even 'Oooh, my sciatica') was a bit happier-looking than the snarling version I'd seen that afternoon, but apart from that I didn't know what this whole exercise had proved. Well, other than that Jeane Smith was even more up herself online than she was in real life and it was no wonder that Barney was sick of her. I was all ready to find a corner of the internet that didn't have Jeane's dumb dork agenda all over it when I came across a YouTube link and clicked on it without thinking.

I reared back in my chair with an alarmingly girly shriek as Jeane appeared in shiny tights, leotard and with a towelling headband strapped across her forehead. She looked ridiculous but very pleased with herself as she was joined by two older girls, at least a head taller than her but wearing the same stupid workout gear.

Then I heard the unmistakeable hook from 'Single Ladies' and the three of them started doing the dance. The Beyoncé dance. There was even the hand flick, which didn't make up for the fact that Jeane insisted on going left every time her backing dancers went right, resulting in giggles and a lot of good-natured pushing and shoving. I couldn't help sniggering too because watching someone you didn't like make a tool of themselves was always comedy gold but soon my sneering became smiling because ... I don't know ... Maybe it was the way Jeane swung her non-existent hips and sucked in her

33

cheeks and was absolutely unself-conscious, unlike every other girl I knew. They were always checking their hair and thrusting out their tits like everyone was watching them, even when nobody was.

Finally, Jeane attempted to leap in the air and knocked into one of the other girls during her very shaky landing. The pair of them collapsed on the floor. The last girl standing struggled on but she was laughing so hard that when Jeane hooked her foot round her ankle, she gladly sank down on the pile so all I could see was a gangle of shiny-tighted legs. The song stopped and before the screen went blank, I could hear a voice saying, 'Jeane, you are such a muppet.'

I skipped past the link to her Etsy and CafePress shops (was there any part of the internet that she hadn't got her sticky paws on?) selling branded mugs, T-shirts and tote bags that said stuff like 'I Heart Dorks' and 'Dork is the New Black', so I could go directly to her Twitter page.

It didn't make much sense. But Twitter didn't make much sense to me. All those people posting about what they'd eaten for breakfast or how much they didn't want to do their German homework all seemed a bit too self-indulgent. Like, every single random thought had to be tweeted for posterity. Obviously they were all total losers who didn't have any friends, so they went on Twitter and talked bollocks with a whole load of other social rejects who didn't have any friends.

OK, I *was* on Twitter, like I was on Facebook and MySpace and Bebo, but apart from one tweet ('So, what happens next?') I'd never bothered with it. From the look of Jeane's Twitter, I'd been right to leave the tweeting to other people because her Twitter feed was mostly replies to other tweets and it was like reading thirty in-jokes that weren't that funny.

I also didn't find it funny that Jeane had over half a million deluded fools following her tweets. How was that even possible? Were her tweets sprinkled with magic dust? There were actual proper celebrities who were on TV and in the papers who had fewer followers than she did.

As I was staring in disbelief, the page updated itself.

adork_able Jeane Smith
Can this really call itself a cake when its main ingredients are cheese and carrots?

I clicked on the link to see a picture of a slice of the moist and delicious carrot cake I'd eaten earlier at the jumble sale.

Jeane spent the next five minutes debating the finer points of carrot cake and cake in general with the multitudes hanging off her every tweeted syllable.

adork_able Jeane Smith
I'm not adverse to a smidgeon of chilli in my chocolate (quite yummy) but not sure where I stand on rosewater cupcakes.

I was automatically logged in as @winsomedimsum (all combinations of Michael Lee and my date of birth had been taken) and I was leaping into the fray before I had time to come up with a million and one reasons why it wasn't a good idea.

winsomedimsum is yum

@adork_able How do you feel about parma violets?

She shot back a reply instantly.

adork_able Jeane Smith

@winsomedimsum I like the idea of them more than the reality of them. They taste like the smell of old ladies' handbags. You feel me?

I knew exactly what she meant. When my grandmother came to stay, she was always asking me to fetch her reading glasses or her spare handkerchief or 'fifty pence to get yourself something nice' from her handbag and it smelt all powdery and faintly floral and musty, just like a tube of Parma Violets.

winsomedimsum is yum

@adork_able Anyway, once you've eaten water chestnut cake, carrot cake is for lightweights.

adork_able Jeane Smith

@winsomedimsum OMAG! I so want to try that. And what's the red stuff in Chinese buns? It's muy moresome.

winsomedimsum is yum

@adork_able Red bean paste. It's kind of an acquired taste.

adork_able Jeane Smith

@winsomedimsum Oh, I've definitely acquired it.

Then we talked about how we both hated milk, 'except in tea, of course,' which led to talk of yoghurt and cottage cheese, which a friend of Jeane's called Patti swore blind they dyed red and used as gore in horror films.

An hour had raced by and Jeane and her friends were now tweeting about a band they were all going to see the following weekend. I'd never heard of the band but I was pretty certain they'd be the kind of band that I wouldn't like, either all fey and jangly and singing about holding hands in ice cream parlours or so loud and jarring that they made your ears bleed.

I also wasn't sure about correct Twitter etiquette. Did I say goodbye before I logged out like I did when I was in a chatroom? Or did I just go because they were all still wittering on about some band called The Fuck Puppets and wouldn't even notice?

In the end I was saved by the bell. Or by my mother calling from the foot of the stairs about staying on the computer for too long or about the DVD they wanted me to watch with them or possibly the dangers of eating too much cold dim sum this close to bedtime. It was hard to tell.

I texted her to say I'd be down soon, even though I knew that drove her mad, and then made the startling discovery that in the time I'd been tweeting, I'd gained over fifty new Twitter followers, including Jeane herself. I suppose it was a big deal.

37

Jeane might have over half a million followers but she was only following a mere thousand people herself, which made me special. It made me one in five hundred, apparently.

My mean inner voice crowed triumphantly, 'Ha ha! Fooled her.' I tried to ignore it. I hadn't fooled anyone; I'd just exchanged tweets with a girl who was friendlier on the internet than she was in the flesh. There was no more to it than that. I followed Jeane back, then turned off the computer so I could go downstairs and see what all the yelling had been about.

5

I watched Barney and Scarlett closely over the next few days. Except they had no idea they were being watched because I was very, very stealth-like. Barney and Scarlett, however, were entirely un-stealth-like.

Now I knew what to look for I saw evidence of their treachery everywhere. It's like when you discover a brand new word, and by the end of the day you've heard three other people on three separate occasions say this previously unheard word, because the word had been there all the time but you just hadn't realised it. (And can I just say if Barney and Scarlett were a word it would be something clunky that felt wrong as you tried to sound it out like rambunctious or discombobulated?) Anyway, I digress: I was talking about REAL evidence of Barney and Scarlett's crimes.

For instance, Scarlett commented on every single one of Barney's Facebook status updates, even though they were very boring. 'Thinking of eating an apple. Should I have a red one or a green one?' he'd type, and within five minutes Scarlett would have commented with a 'ROFL'. Except she didn't even capitalise it, she used all lower case, like she was too stupid to figure out the shift key. She was also fond of 'lmao' and 'lol' and was obviously so stupid that I wondered how she managed to get to school without being run over.

There were other signs, too, that suggested Barney was doing more than guiding Scarlett through the minefield that was GCSE Maths. He was meant to tutor her for one hour after school on Tuesdays and Thursdays but I noticed that actually he was nowhere to be found on Tuesday and Thursday evenings at all. He wasn't on Twitter or Facebook or Google Chat and he certainly wasn't answering his phone.

When I asked him casually on the Wednesday morning, 'Were you screening my calls last night?' Barney stammered and stuttered his way through a torturous denial that involved his Physics class finishing early and having to get a permission slip signed in the school office and the planets realigning in some mysterious way that caused him to leave his phone in his locker. I wasn't buying it.

And I certainly wasn't buying the way that Scarlett and Barney tried to ignore each other. He was 'tutoring' her so there was no reason for her to pretend that he wasn't standing right behind her in the lunch queue. Especially when he looked as if he was sniffing her hair at one point.

Biting my tongue and not saying anything was really hard – usually I spoke first, tweeted second and thought last. The evidence was piled high against them, but when I wasn't at school or scowling at Barney's status updates and Scarlett's inevitable lolz, I started to doubt it. Because really, Barney and Scarlett? It made no sense. They defied all laws of God and man. I'd raised Barney in my own image: he was on my side, on the side of the dorks, on the side of all that was good and pure. Scarlett was strictly darkside all the way.

That was the conclusion I'd come to by lunchtime on Wednesday as I sat in my favourite secluded spot behind the language lab knitting furiously and listening to a podcast about the fair trade coffee industry, rather than doing the reading on the fair trade coffee industry. I was just getting to grips with a tricky bit of moss-stitching on circular needles when a shadow loomed over me.

'Go away,' I muttered without looking up, because I could see boy feet in a pair of off-white Converses and the only boy I talked to at school was Barney and he knew better than to wear off-white Converses like every other boy in Years 12 and 13, so it was no one that I wanted to talk to. 'You're in my light and this is my special spot so go away.'

'You're the rudest person I've ever met,' said a voice that I recognised, even over the heated debate about fair trade farming in Peru. Yes, bloody Peru. With a put-upon sigh I looked up at Michael Lee. 'Why are you so hostile?'

'Why are you still in my light?' I said, putting down my knitting so I could unhook my earbuds because he was still blocking the weak rays from the late-September sun and showing no signs of moving. Obviously we were going to have to chat this out. 'What do you want?'

I was pretty certain I knew what Michael wanted and part of

me wanted it too. Because thoughts of Barney and Scarlett (or Barnett as they'd be known if they were celebrities) were going round and round in my head and I had nobody I could talk to about it. I had friends. I wasn't some sad-sack Betty-No-Mates, but I didn't like to overshare when it came to deep stuff. I had no problem with oversharing about undeep stuff though.

I'd used to talk to Bethan about the deep stuff but it was different over Skype, especially when she was working eighty-hour weeks and always sounded so tired. My frustration at my current lack of a confidante had to be written all over my face, making me even more scowly than usual, because Michael took a hurried step back even as he said, 'Oh, I was just passing and I thought I'd come over and say hi.'

'Why the hell would you want to do that?' I asked very coldly. 'Did you think that because we had one unpleasant conversation at the jumble sale we're now on hello terms? We're not. We have nothing to talk about so just, like, go away.'

Michael narrowed his eyes. He really was ridiculously pretty for a boy. It was another reason why I was harshing him – he was so used to girls going swoony in his presence (I once saw someone from Year 9 walk into a tree rather than tear her eyes away from him) that I didn't want him to think that I was, too. That was the deal with the really good-looking boys: they automatically assumed you were pining and panting for them and wouldn't be satisfied until you'd had their babies, no matter how ugly their personalities might be.

Apart from narrowing his eyes, Michael didn't react in any way to what I'd said. I decided we were done and so I picked up my knitting again and began to retrace my stitches.

'Look, I was just trying to be friendly,' he suddenly said.

'Is this part of some lame-o student council outreach programme?'

'It's funny but I'm starting to figure out what this whole deal with Barney and Scarlett is about,' Michael remarked casually. Then he had the nerve to sit down next to me on the wall. I tried to ignore him. 'If I was going out with you, I'd be looking for an exit strategy too.'

'And if I had the incredible bad luck to be going out with you, my exit strategy would involve running into oncoming traffic,' I snapped. 'Now, why don't you go and share your paranoid little delusions with someone who actually gives a toss?'

Michael jumped up from the wall, knocking into me so I dropped about twenty more stitches, and muttered something under his breath that sounded like the word 'Bitch' said ten times, really fast. I kept a cool smile pinned on my face because I knew it would enrage him further, though I didn't know why the need to take Michael Lee down a peg or fifty had suddenly become my life's vocation.

I watched him stride across the scrubby patch of grass where the stoners often sat and when he rounded the corner by the bins I got to my feet, stuffed my knitting and iPod into my bag and marched off to English.

Scarlett was sitting at the back with her little posse of friends. They all thought they were perched on the cutting edge because they bought their clothes in American Apparel and went to gigs on school nights. They weren't evil per se, but they sure had a lot to say for four girls who wore exactly the same clothes, listened to exactly the same music and had the same opinion about everything. Apart from Scarlett – she wouldn't know an opinion if it moved in next door and played death metal all night long.

I always sat at the front because I always got to class too late. Besides, it was easier to keep an eye on the teacher and berate them loudly if they were trying to stick us with extra coursework. As I pulled out my chair, I made sure to catch Scarlett's eye and give her my most blank-faced stare. Always worked better than a glare – it let the recipient know that they weren't even worth the trouble it would take to scrunch up your facial muscles.

Scarlett went as red as her stupid name and shook her head so her hair fell over her face (a move she could only have learnt from Barney), as Ms Ferguson shut the classroom door, smiled at us all brightly and announced that we were going to have a debate about the two novels we were studying for A-level: *The Great Gatsby* and *The Fountainhead*.

There was a collective groan as I reached into my pocket for my iPhone. The chances of a rigorous literary debate were slim and if I arranged my books just so on my desk, I could probably do some tweeting without anyone noticing. Ms Ferguson was cool, but she wasn't *that* cool.

I let the chatter buzz around me. It wasn't a debate, just a rehashing of the plots of both books, though I heard someone say incisively, 'That Daisy Miller, she was really up herself.'

It was almost worthy of a tweet, but I had an unwritten rule that I would never badmouth anyone I knew in real life on the internet. We also had an unspoken rule in class that everyone's opinion deserved to be heard, no matter how rubbish and misinformed it was.

'So, Scarlett, which book did you prefer?' Ms Ferguson asked gently. All the staff treated her as if she was made out of spun glass.

There was a reedy whisper from the back of the room, like wind whistling around the chair legs.

'I'm sorry, Scarlett, I didn't quite catch that,' Ms Ferguson said, her jaw moving even after she'd spoken, as if she was grinding her teeth.

'Well, see, hmm, I didn't really understand what the guy in *The Great Gatsby*, not Gatsby but the other one, um, what he saw in Daisy.' I swivelled round in my chair to watch Scarlett look pleadingly at her friends, until one of them, Heidi or Hilda or whatever her name was, whispered something to Scarlett. 'Yeah, like, well, Daisy: it didn't even sound like she was that pretty.'

I actually heard Ms Ferguson's swift intake of breath (another reason why I sat at the front – you really got to sniff out a teacher's weaknesses) then she caught my eye as I grimaced at Scarlett's extreme moronitude.

'Jeane,' Ms Ferguson said, and she sounded a little desperate. 'Why do you think Nick Carraway is in love with Daisy?'

'I wouldn't say that he's necessarily in love with Daisy,' I said slowly, my eyes still fixed on Scarlett, who squirmed unhappily. 'He idealises her and imagines she's his perfect woman, even though it's obvious that she isn't. I think what Fitzgerald is showing is that nobody ever knows what someone else is like. Not really. They just end up projecting all this crap on to the other person. And, yes, people might say that Daisy didn't ask for his adoration but she takes advantage of it all the same, you know?'

Scarlett was staring at me blankly and it was pretty obvious that she didn't know. She was the Grand Poobah of not knowing. 'OK,' she said, looking down at her hands. 'OK.' She sounded a bit gulpy and I wondered if she was going to cry. 'I don't really know what you mean.'

'Have you actually read *The Great Gatsby*, Scarlett,' I said, 'because Nick's unrequited love for Daisy is pretty much the cornerstone of the book?'

There was a deathly hush in the classroom. Even Ms Ferguson seemed to be holding her breath, instead of jumping in and telling me to back off.

'I know that,' Scarlett said a little huffily, which was the first time in six years I'd ever seen her exhibit some backbone. 'I just, well, I get it mixed up with *The Fountainhead*. They are kinda similar.' There was a murmur of agreement around the room. I felt like banging my head on the desk.

So, in my defence, when I said, '*The Great Gatsby* is about the death of the American dream and *The Fountainhead* is about the theory of objectivism and the strength of the individual. They couldn't be more different unless you're completely retarded,' it was directed at the whole class, not just Scarlett.

Scarlett bent over so her face was entirely obscured by her hair and burst into tears hard enough to make her shoulders shake. 'Oh, Scarlett, I don't think Jeane's bad mood is worth crying over,' Ms Ferguson said dryly, as Heidi/Hilda and another girl rushed to throw their arms around Scarlett and coo at her. My lips curled with contempt as Scarlett got to her feet and ran from the room, ricocheting off desks as she went.

'See me after class, Jeane,' Ms Ferguson sighed, then set us a thirty-minute writing exercise on the themes of loss and longing in *The Great Gatsby*. I could feel twenty-eight pairs of eyes shooting laser beams between my shoulder blades.

'That was totally uncalled for,' Ms Ferguson said, once the class, including a still-sniffing Scarlett, had trooped out. 'It's hard enough to get Scarlett to contribute, without you eviscerating her when she does.'

'I was including the entire class in that last comment,' I pointed out and Ms Ferguson rested her chin in her hands and rolled her eyes.

Usually when she rolled her eyes it was more conspiratorial. I'd roll my eyes too and we'd share a look that said, 'God, what are we doing here?'

Ms Ferguson, or actually Allison as I call her outside of school, was an almost-friend. I saw her at gigs and art shows in Hoxton and we followed each other on Twitter. That said, what happened outside school stayed outside school. I even knew she was in a band called The Fuck Puppets and it was a secret I'd take to my grave, which must have been why she was finding it so hard to give me the bollocking that I sort of deserved.

'I shouldn't have said "retarded",' I conceded. 'Because it's offensive and, er, disablist, but how can anyone get *The Great Gatsby* muddled up with *The Fountainhead* if they've actually read both of them? It's like muddling up monkeys and daffodils or baked beans and Pez dispensers or—'

'Yes, I get the idea,' Ms Ferguson snapped, then she folded her arms and tried to stare me down. I obediently lowered my eyes so I looked a little contrite. 'I expect much better of you. You let yourself down.'

I hate it when people give you the whole 'I'm not angry at you, I'm just disappointed' speech. It was so predictable and, quite frankly, *I* expected much better from Allison. But that wasn't the point right now. 'I'm sorry,' I said, though my usual monotone delivery made it sound as insincere as it did in my head.

'It's no use saying sorry to me. You have to say sorry to Scarlett. In front of me, and, Jeane, I want an unambiguous apology that isn't some clever play on words that could be misinterpreted. OK?'

She knew me so well. 'OK.'

I shoved my folder and my dog-eared copies of *Gatsby* and *The Fountainhead* in my school tote bag, which I'd made myself and had 'I Dork, Therefore I Am' embroidered on it, because I thought we were done, when Allison made an awkward choking sound.

'Everything's OK, isn't it? With the whole living by yourself deal because if there's anything you need to talk about, you know that I'm he—'

'No, no,' I said quickly, standing up. 'Everything's fine. It's better than fine. It's absolutely dandy.'

Allison actually followed me to the classroom door. 'We could talk *outside* school,' she murmured meaningfully. 'If you like.'

'I have to go. I'm going to be late for Business Studies,' I said, and it wasn't just to get her off my back: I was horribly late and I hadn't managed to listen to all of the podcast because Michael Lee had interrupted me.

I tried to keep my head down for the next forty minutes but the lesson took an alarming turn when Mr Latymer decided to drill me to within an inch of my young life about the positive effects of fair trade farming in the developing world. There was only one thing to do and that was to launch into a skin-stripping rant about the negative effects of so many corporate owned coffee chains taking over Britain's high streets.

It turned out most of the class preferred to argue over who did the better Frappuccino – Starbucks or Caffè Nero – than about fair trade farming. It got very heated very fast and I could sit back and tweet to my heart's content as Heidi/Hilda threatened to wallop Hardeep when he tried to introduce Costa Coffee's Frescatos into the debate.

The bell went as Mr Latymer was trying to restore order and I could quietly slip out of the classroom, while all around me people were being given detentions and shouting things like, 'I don't care if there are five hundred calories in a Double Chocolate Frappé made with skimmed milk. Why do you have to ruin everything for me?'

All I had to do was get my bike basket and pannier out of my locker and I'd be free of this hellhole that reeked of cheap disinfectant and failure until 8.40 the next morning.

'Jeane,' said a grim voice, as I was head first in my locker. For a second I thought it was Michael Lee and, in my alarm, I banged my head as I emerged from the metal cubby hole, only to see Barney standing there.

'Oh, it's you,' I said. 'I thought you were someone else.'

Barney didn't say anything even though he was working his mouth furiously like he was chewing a massive wad of gum, which was something he'd never do because he had an irrational fear he'd swallow it and clog up his insides for ever. He

49

obviously wasn't going to form actual words for some time so I continued to search for my rosebud lipsalve.

'How could you?' Barney finally asked.

'How could I what?' By now I was rummaging in the furthest reaches of my locker amid Tupperware containers that hadn't come home in weeks.

'Scarlett had to leave Maths halfway through because she was crying.'

I sneered to myself. 'She's *always* crying about something. Honestly, she's wetter than a ... a ... well, something that's really, really wet.'

'You called her a retard, which is wrong on so many levels.' Barney sounded properly angry. Almost as angry as the time he'd been deep into *Red Dead Redemption* and I'd tripped over and pulled out the power cord on his Xbox.

I found my lipsalve and carefully extricated my head from my locker. 'I didn't call *her* a retard. It was aimed at the whole class and I promised Alli ... Ms Ferguson I'd apologise so don't get all up in my face about it.'

'You were totally out of order,' Barney persisted, his face red. 'Saying mean things about people isn't cool, it's just mean. She can't help it if she's not good with words and she doesn't like talking in class. Have you any idea how frightening you are, especially when it takes a lot of courage for someone to take part in a class discussion anyway and you just—'

'Barney, I *know*,' I said gently. If I hadn't been entirely sure that there was anything to know before, now I was certain. Barney was defending Scarlett's honour and her right to say idiotic things in class like his life depended on it. 'I know about you and Scarlett.'

For a second, Barney's mouth hung open in surprise. Then he shrugged. 'There's not that much to know.'

'Do you want to try that one again?' I hissed, because I couldn't do gentle for very long. 'Don't even try to pretend that there's nothing going on between the two of you.'

Barney sighed. 'Nothing has happened but we like each other. A lot. But it's complicated because she's seeing Michael and, well, there's you.'

'What about me?'

'She's terrified you'll kill her.'

'Like I'd lay a finger on her.' I snorted derisively.

'It's not your fingers she's worried about. It's why I didn't say anything. I mean, I tried, I wanted to, but every time I bottled it,' Barney admitted, and for once he wasn't ducking his head, or biting his lip or hiding behind his fringe, but looking me straight in the eye. 'You're very intimidating.'

'Intimidating? What's so intimidating about me?' I demanded, hands on my hips, and Barney was right: there wasn't much to choose between my normal face and my fight face.

'It's like there's no room for me,' Barney said. 'You're always ten steps ahead and I'm always lagging behind and it's like nothing I do or say is ever cool or clever enough for you.'

'I don't expect you to lag behind me,' I spluttered helplessly. Now it was Barney's turn to lean back against the lockers all free and easy because his big secret was out and the world hadn't ended. Whereas I was standing there with my nostrils flaring and it felt as if my eyes were about to bug out of my head. 'I try to include you in everything I do.'

'Yeah, but I don't want to wind your wool at sponsored

knit-a-thons or wander the streets of Hoxton so you can take photos for your trend-spotting reports. And honestly, Jeane, I can't work out what's going on when you drag me to roller derby, but you never hear the word no.'

I couldn't believe it! I'd let Barney into my life. I'd taken a chance on him, decided that maybe there was more to him than there was to the other cretins who lolloped along the corridors at school like they'd only just mastered the art of walking on two legs, and he repaid me by choosing Scarlett. Scarlett? She was so stupid she was practically brain-dead.

Barney lost the nonchalant slouch as soon as I started shouting at him. He tried to argue back but I just shouted louder until the sound of my voice drowned out his bleating.

I didn't care that there were still a few last stragglers milling about, or that they'd all stopped milling in favour of standing and watching and even pointing and sniggering as I flayed the skin off Barney's worthless two-timing body with the pointy end of my tongue.

'You were nothing before me,' I screamed finally, as Barney cowered where he stood. 'And you'll be nothing again, just a spotty geek immersed in *World of Warcraft* with no social skills. Just as well that Scarlett isn't people but pond life, isn't it?'

Then I shoulder-bumped Barney so hard that he rocked on his feet, as I stormed off. And I knew it was wrong and it wasn't the right reaction to have in the circumstances but I was already composing the blog post I'd write about Barney and his perfidious, treacherous, morally reprehensible, snake-like behaviour as soon as I got home.

6

I was shaking, actually shaking, for a good ten minutes after my argy bargy with Jeane. It was my own fault, I thought to myself, as I sat in the Chemistry lab during my free period. I should have been making notes on molecular formulas, but all I could think about were the things I should have said to wipe the superior look off her stupid, ugly face. I'd forgotten all about the horror of our first encounter at the jumble sale. I'd forgotten all about her well-earned rep as the rudest girl in school and I'd forgotten that everyone pretends to be someone else on the internet and that Jeane's friendliness was only Wi-Fi-enabled. '*Oh, I was just passing and I thought I'd come over and say hi.*' Every time I relived that moment and the piss-and-vinegar look on Jeane's face, I died a little inside.

The bell rang and as I was heading to Computer Science I bumped into Scarlett's best friend, Heidi, who was bustling down the corridor with a fistful of chocolate bars, a can of Diet Coke and a wad of tissues.

'Oh. My. God. Shit's just got real,' Heidi announced, though she needn't have bothered because she was carrying all the items necessary to soothe any teenage girl's frayed nerves. Except ice cream, though the student council had looked into the possibility of a vending machine that dispensed miniature tubs of Ben & Jerry's.

'What kind of shit?' I resigned myself to being late for Comp Sci because Heidi always took several minutes and OMGs to get to the point.

She rolled her eyes at me. 'Scarlett is, like, literally in pieces. For real.'

'She's not *literally* in pieces,' I said, because it annoyed me how Scarlett and Heidi and their whole gang misappropriated the word 'literally' until it literally lost all meaning. 'What's she so upset about?'

'Jeane Smith made her cry. I mean, she literally tore Scarlett apart and now Scarlett's hyperventilating in the loos. And the only paper bag we could find for her to breathe into smelt of ham and pickle sandwiches so then Scar started retching as well and it was, y'know, just wrongness.'

Heidi stopped but I knew it was only to let in oxygen and she'd start yammering again if I didn't seize the moment. 'Why did Jeane make her cry? Did they have an argument about . . . ?' I paused because I didn't want to mention Barney, but Heidi noticed a gap in the conversation and crowbarred her way back in.

'Would you believe it if I said Jeane had a go at her about our

A-level English texts? I mean, like, what? Then Jeane totes called Scar a retard.'

'So, has Scar stopped crying?' I asked and my perfect boyfriend halo was slipping because the news that Scarlett was weeping in the girls' loos didn't make me want to rush to her side. It just made me think, *Oh God, now what?* Though calling someone a retard didn't seem like Jeane's style. It was low even for her. 'And don't you have a lesson to be in?'

'The circs are beyond extenuating.' Heidi wriggled her shoulders in annoyance. 'Don't even think about reporting me. Scarlett *needs* me.'

'Well, let's just pretend that we never had this conversation,' I said. 'And tell Scar I'll see her after school and I hope she's all right.'

'If you were any kind of boyfriend, you'd come with me and make sure she's all right,' Heidi said, widening her mascara-caked eyes at me. 'Did I mention that she's literally fallen apart?'

'Yeah, you did, but Scarlett is in the *girls'* loos and I'm really late for Comp Sci and probably going to have to put myself on report so I'll be all boyfriendly and caring when I give her a lift home, OK?'

'Whatevs.' Heidi was already walking away and trying to tug down her short skirt where it had ridden up. There had been a time, the summer before last, when I thought that Heidi and I might become something. We kept getting off with each other at parties but when we weren't getting off with each other we'd had nothing to talk about, and then I met Hannah and all other girls just seemed something less in comparison.

I had a sense memory of Hannah sitting on the stairs at a

party that summer, her blonde hair shining in the muted candle-light as she told me about her favourite Sylvia Plath poem; her voice had got all choked up and she'd had to wipe away one single, solitary tear that slowly trickled down her cheek. Then she'd laughed and said, 'God, I'm every teen angst cliché, aren't I? Crying over Sylvia Plath on the stairs at a party.'

And then I thought about Scarlett crying her eyes out in the girls' loos because someone half her size and twice as ugly had been mean to her and really there was no comparison between her tears and Hannah being moved to tears about something she really cared about and actually I was pleased to go to Comp Sci and learn about database theory – women are far more complicated than database theory.

When the final bell rang, I headed to the staff car park, where as head of the student council I was allocated a parking space for the rusting, held-together-with-gaffer-tape-and-chewing-gum, ancient Austin Allegro that I'd inherited from my grandma. It was where Scarlett should be but there was no sign of her.

She couldn't *still* be crying.

I pulled out my mobile but, although I had seventeen messages, most of them to do with the debating society's upcoming battle against the local posh school, the football match on Saturday morning and a party on Saturday night, Scarlett was not one of the many people that had texted me because she needed me to do something for her. Even my mum wanted me to buy a bag of red onions and some garlic on my way home.

Feeling entirely put upon, I walked back into school to track down Scarlett. There wasn't a gaggle of Scarlett's friends hovering anxiously outside any of the girls' cloakrooms, clutching cans of Diet Coke and texting frantically, but I eventually tracked her down to the Year 12 common room. It was half the size of the Year 13 common room and smelt faintly of fish and old gym kits, which was why most of Year 12 preferred to shiver outside come sun, rain and blizzard, but there was Scarlett huddled on the windowsill and, sitting next to her, his arm round her shoulders, was Barney.

They both looked up when I bounded into the room, Scarlett brushing what *had* to be the last tears from her face, Barney leaning down to whisper something to her. And the weird thing, weirder than Scarlett and Barney tucked away in a smelly room with his arm round her, was that I felt like I was doing something wrong just by standing in the doorway and intruding on whatever the hell it was they were doing.

'Are you ready to go, Scar?' I could barely squeeze out her name. 'I've been looking everywhere for you.'

Scarlett frowned. 'Well, I have stuff to do so I don't need a lift, but, like, thanks.' She didn't say anything else. Instead she gave me a pointed look, which was something I hadn't known she could do.

Mind you, it was nothing compared to the look that Barney was giving me. I'd only ever spoken to him a couple of times – once I'd said hello to him at a gig and once I'd had to write him up for texting in the middle of a Maths lesson – and both times he'd stammered and blushed and stared at the ground. But now he looked at me like he had every right to be sitting next to Scarlett, so close that from shoulder to knee they were touching. He gave me a tight smile.

'Actually,' he said, 'me and Scar were having a private conversation.'

'Fine,' I said, like I really was fine with this distinctly unfine situation, but I wasn't going to be the guy who lost his temper and let loose a torrent of angry words that I'd regret later. *Be the bigger person*, my dad always says, *even when someone is trying to make you look small*. I could do that. Or I could at least try. 'Well, I guess I'll see you tomorrow.'

'OK, or I'll text you,' Scarlett said weakly, and I think all three of us knew that she'd do no such thing.

On the way home, I knew for certain that I had to end things with Scarlett ASAP. By rights she should be the one to do the dumping, but instead she was being indifferent and unreliable and hanging out with the geeky ginger kid who was tutoring her in Maths so she could *force* me to be the bad cop. The thing was that I'd never had to dump someone. Yeah, I'd broken up with girlfriends before but it was more a mutual decision that we weren't into each other any more. Then there was Hannah and that had been a case of, 'You know I love you, right, but you also know my dad works in the Foreign Office and I'm being shunted off to boarding school in sodding Cornwall to do my A-levels because he's being posted somewhere where there's a good chance that he and my mum might get kidnapped by rebel forces. For fucking real.'

We'd talked about long-distance relationships and how we could Skype every night but in the end Hannah was in so many tiny pieces about her parents that I didn't want to be one more thing for her to worry about. The break-up was awful. I'm not going to lie: I cried. Hannah cried. Even our mums cried and

I still have a Post-it note in my wallet that Hannah gave me just before she left on which she'd written: 'Even when I'm a grey-haired little lady I'll always think of you as The One Who Got Away.'

Thinking about Hannah and how she was the only girl who'd ever reduced me to tears, apart from Sun Li in kindergarten who'd spurned my amorous advances only after I'd given her a tube of Smarties, made me so distracted that I overshot a red light and nearly crashed into the back of the car in front of me.

Somehow I managed to get home without mowing down any stray pedestrians. Then I had to go out again, on foot, to get garlic and onions after a bollocking from my mother about shirking my responsibilities and it wasn't until she was making a lasagne that I was able to go to my room and begin to brood properly.

After the first five minutes of 'Woe is me' I decided that brooding was boring. I switched on my computer but I didn't want to go on Facebook because before I knew it I'd be cyber-stalking Scarlett, so I drifted over to Twitter at exactly the same time as Jeane Smith, who wanted the world to know that she'd just posted a new blog. I was already in that mindless internet haze that had me clicking on the link without really register-ing what I was doing and then I was rocking back in my chair and nearly upending myself in the process.

Barney's gone and got boy disease
When I started this blog, I made a solemn vow to myself that I would never blog about people I know. I would not talk shit about people I know. And when people I know do crummy, mean things, I will not call them on it. Not on this blog. No, sir.

Except for now, because I'm outing The Boy. Regular readers will know all about The Boy, I mention him often. He's part boyfriend, part sidekick, part kiss-buddy. Well, he *was*, and I always called him The Boy to protect his privacy and to, well, protect him, but he's not worthy of my high regard or my protection any longer.

HIS NAME IS BARNEY AND HE'S A TOTAL NO-GOOD, TWO-TIMING RATFINK! Worse, I was training him up to be a sensitive, well-rounded, free-from-macho-bullshit boyfriend (I even bought him a 'This is what a feminist looks like' T-shirt) but you can't train up someone when it turns out they're the MOST LOW-DOWN SNAKE IN SLITHERTOWN so now I'm breaking all my blogging rules and I'm USING SHOUTY CAPS AND I HATE SHOUTY CAPS!

Before he met me, Barney was pretty much a cultural embryo. He'd been nowhere, experienced nothing, never had a single, solitary adventure until I made space for him in my life. I introduced him to people and places and tastes and sounds that expanded his world (which wasn't difficult when his world was a TV screen hooked up to an Xbox).

Before me, Barney hadn't even *heard* of roller derby. He'd never eaten sushi or chilli-infused chocolate. He'd never been to a jumble sale or listened to Vampire Weekend or The Velvet Underground and cried during 'Pale Blue Eyes'. Never seen a foreign film. Hadn't stayed up all night and climbed to the top of a really big hill to watch the sun rise. Still let his mum buy his clothes and, worst thing of all, he downloaded music off the internet and *never paid for it*.

He leeched my cool like he was trying to jump-start a car battery, and how does he repay me? By mooning over another girl. Having wrong thoughts about another girl. Wishing he wasn't with me, but with this other girl.

People fall in and out of love the whole time and it's not like Barney and I are *Romeo and Juliet* Redux (though I'm quite sure his mother would love it if I drank some poision and, like, died), so if Barney wanted to fall in love with someone else, there's not a whole lot I can do about it.

But it turns out there's been something going on for *weeks* and I had to find out, from, like, one of *them*. You know, one of the anti-dorks. Even then I refused to believe it, because Barney would never do that to me, because I'd made him listen to Sleater-Kinney and Bikini Kill and added the F-bomb to his Google Blog reader and showed him in a million other ways that he had to be cool and treat me with respect in order to make amends for centuries and centuries of patriarchal domination and boys thinking they're better than girls just because they have a lump of flesh dangling down between their legs.

What he did was extremely not cool. Even if there hasn't been actual physical cheating, which I guess would be hand-holding and kissing and all that other mushy stuff, there's been emotional cheating, and if Barney had closed down the space in his heart that he'd let me rent out then he should at least have had the decency to tell me. Right? Of course, right!

Also, another thing that's speeding me on my way to a total rage blackout is that even the geeky boys with the flicky fringes and the need to fumble adorkably in their long-fingered way with guitar picks and mix CDs and Moleskine notebooks will always throw over geeky girls in favour of the easy option, especially when the easy option has long blonde hair, size-eight skinny jeans and zero personality.

I'm not saying that all size-eight blonde girls have zero personality, of course I'm not, and, hello, do you not know about my out of control girl crush on Lady Gaga? And I'm not girl-bashing, not even on this particular girl, rather I'm asking: When will being independent and strong and not following the pack and daring to be different and being brave in my opinions, my fashion choices and my hair colour be enough?

Aren't those all admirable qualities for a girl to have? They are when you're a boy with no confidence and no ability to stand out in a crowd until a girl like me drags you into the limelight. And I *liked* Barney. I liked having him in my life and I'm trying to be philosophical, though it's hard when I can taste anger and disappointment in the back of my throat and it tastes the same as licking a battery – and let's not go into why I know what licking a battery tastes like.

Mostly I'm mad and ranty because there's nothing I can do. 'Cause Barney's so blinded by love that all he can see in me are all the ways that I'm not like this other girl.

Actually there are lots of things I can do. Sixty-five of them would get me arrested, forty-seven of them would reflect badly on me, so all that's left is declaring right here, right now that Barney never deserved me and he's a traitor to dorkdom.

And no, outing Barney and turning the hurt into words hasn't made me feel even a teensy bit better.

To start off with I was pissed off to be side-swiped as an anti-dork, like that was a bad thing. Then I wondered why someone had to document their every last thought and feeling for total strangers to pick over and, when I was done with that, I thought about Jeane.

Before I'd thought of her as Barney's bossy girlfriend who made his life such a living hell that he had to sniff around Scarlett, but now I could see that they'd been a proper couple. OK, she was still really bossy and it seemed like their whole dynamic revolved around Jeane giving Barney a crash course in her brand of loser cool, but they still had something between them: friendship, affection, a crappy taste in music.

I'll say one thing for Jeane though: when she was hurt and upset, instead of being all 'Like, whatever,' or 'I wasn't really into him anyway,' she wasn't afraid to get real, even if getting real meant getting messy. I had to respect that because I was always worried that people would start to hate on me, or lose respect for me, if I was anything less than perfect. Being perfect isn't always easy.

Back on Twitter, instead of holding court like I expected, Jeane was fielding off all enquiries.

 adork_able Jeane Smith
It's all in the blog. I have nothing to add, unless you want to send me chocolate or pictures of dogs in amusing outfits.

I could kind of empathise with what Jeane was going through, because I was kind of going through it too. Also, when I thought about it, Jeane didn't have anyone at school to hang out with, apart from Barney. Besides, who doesn't love a picture of a dog in a comedy outfit? I could do better than that though.

 winsomedimsum is yum
@adork_able Dogs on surfboards totally pwn dogs in amusing outfits

I tweeted Jeane with a link to pictures from the annual dog surfing competition in California, which I had saved in my bookmarks for when I needed a laugh.

Then I went downstairs because it was time for dinner and a lively family discussion about Al-Qaeda, if it would be possible to clone Alice so cloned Alice could go to school and real Alice could stay home and watch CBeebies, and why both Melly and Alice were too young to have mobile phones. I made my escape once Melly started crying because apparently she was the only seven-year-old in her class who didn't have an iPhone.

I headed straight for my computer because I had a Comp Sci essay that wouldn't write itself and was amazed to find that I had over a hundred emails. I wondered if my spam filters had broken until I saw they were all Twitter follow notifications though I wasn't sure why.

Then I checked Twitter and I knew exactly why. Jeane had retweeted my tweet, as well as replying to me.

adork_able Jeane Smith
@winsomedimsum Oh dear Lord. I have seen
the light. There is nothing funnier than a pug
on a surfboard.

Then she tweeted the masses:

adork_able Jeane Smith
Thx for puppy pics. Still waiting for chocolate.
Too overwrought for Twitter. Will be adding
songs to a break-up playlist on Spotify.

I settled down to make some sense of the notes I'd taken in
class but it was hard because my focus was not on database
theory. It wasn't even on Scarlett and what I was going to do
about that whole sorry situation. No, I was clicking refresh on
my Twitter feed and trying to pretend that it had nothing to do
with Jeane Smith.

7

It took me a long time to fall asleep, not just because my entire body was still thrumming with rage, but because I had to file my monthly trend-spotting report with an ad agency for 8 a.m. Tokyo time.

I must have slept because all of a sudden I was woken by the triple threat of alarm clock, iPhone and computer all beeping merrily at precisely 7.43 GMT. Before I even sit up, I always check my email and, snuggled up in my inbox, was something from Bethan.

Just read your blog, little sis. Remind me never to piss you off. Are you OK? Let's Skype after school. Love you longtime, Bethan xxx

It was one of the best ways to wake up, except it reminded me all about the day before. I couldn't reread my blog until after I'd showered (when was someone going to make a handheld device that was totes waterproof?) but, as I was brushing my teeth, I managed to and then I read the comments. Ninety per cent were in the 'You go girl, kick his sorry arse to the kerb' camp. As ever, the other ten per cent called me a man-hating, lesbian feminazi who needed a good shag and a beating, and when I read my blog for a third time, I did wonder if maybe I'd gone a little too far. Going a little too far was a habit I just couldn't break.

As I photographed my morning ensemble (stompy motorcycle boots, bright orange tights, plaid knee-length shorts, long-sleeved green T-shirt and prim, floral short-sleeved blouse) I contemplated deleting the blog. I contemplated it for the whole time it took to shove two raspberry pop tarts in the toaster then scald my tongue because I was too impatient to wait for them to cool down.

I decided that I wasn't going to delete anything. Yes, I'd given Barney a bashing, but he had deserved it, and everything I'd written and posted was how I really felt. They were my feelings and I had the right to express them in any way that I wanted to. People were so scared of telling the truth because the truth was chaotic and complicated and decidedly uncool, but uncool was the way I rolled. Or it would be if I used tired old phrases like 'That's the way I roll', which I so don't.

I wasn't going to cut and delete, but I could still make things right.

It was a measure of how sorry I was that I marched up to Barney's front door and rang the bell, even though I knew it would be answered by his mum.

That woman hates me. Like, she *really* hates me. She opened the door, looked at me and said, 'Oh, it's you,' except she made it sound like, 'What primordial swamp did you just crawl from and why can't you just leave my son alone, you horrible, badly dressed little tramp?'

'Thought Barney and I could walk to school together,' I said in the face of some truly malevolent glaring. I stared right back at her.

'He's already left,' she finally said, though he obviously hadn't because I could see his parka hanging from the banister.

Not even I could call Barney's mum a liar to her face, but then Barney came tripping down the stairs, falling down the last two as he caught sight of me.

'Oh, I thought you'd already gone,' said his mum without any attempt to sound sincere. I had to admire her barefaced rudeness. 'Jeane's here.'

'What do *you* want?' Barney demanded, as he picked himself off the carpet, then grabbed bag and parka. 'You've got a nerve.'

'I know,' I said, standing aside as Barney brushed past his mother, who tried in vain to kiss him goodbye. 'Bye, Mrs M. Lovely to see you again,' I cooed, because I knew it would piss her off. Then I climbed back on Mary, my bike (named for Mary Kingsley, famous Victorian explorer), and pedalled after Barney, who was running down the road.

'You can't get away from me that easily,' I said, as I steered myself into the road. 'I know you're really pissed off with me, though I'm not sure if it's about what I said yesterday or if it's because you read my blog, or—'

'Or because you never listen to what I'm saying because you're too busy making everything about you.' Barney shook his head in disgust. 'There's so many reasons why I'm pissed off with you that it's hard to pick just one.'

'Well, if it helps in any way, I'm sorry for all of those things,' I assured him, then I had to pause to do an illegal left turn. 'It's very hard to be a good listener when you talk as much as I do.'

'Will you take down the blog?' Barney asked. He didn't seem like he was ready to forgive me, but at least he was still talking to me.

'No, I can't do that. I'm entitled to have those feelings and blog about them, but I will take your name off the post,' I conceded. 'I don't ever self-censor. This is huge for me.'

'Yeah, well, the stuff you wrote was well out of order.'

'And what you did was out of order too,' I pointed out. 'I had to find out from Michael Lee. Michael fucking Lee. If you'd told me from the start, yeah, I'd have given you a hard time, but I wouldn't have turned into a complete ranting maniac. So for that, I'm sorry.'

'I heard you the first time,' Barney snapped. I was forced to slow down as we were a couple of streets away from school and the road was clogged up with people who were too lazy to walk and got lifts everywhere from their doting parents, then dared to complain about global warming. 'Fine, I accept your apology.'

Part of me wanted to remind Barney that he should apologise too but that would only lead us into another argument. Besides, there was another part of me that was hugely relieved that we'd never have to kiss on the lips for the count of fifty elephants ever again. Barney would make a much better friend than a boyfriend and I just had to suck up the humble pie.

'So, are we, like, cool now?' I asked.

Barney came to a halt. 'If I say we're not cool, you'll just badger and harass me until I change my mind, won't you?'

'I wouldn't say harass, exactly.' I had to admit defeat and get off my bike because there were too many cars at a standstill for me to get through. 'But I won't rest until I've made you see the error of your ways. You need me in your life because I'm a really good friend. I'll make you mix CDs and cupcakes and find amazing comics in second-hand bookshops and … and … and I'll even be nice to Scarlett. I'll be the measure by which all other friends are judged and found unable to compare to my superior friend skills. What do you reckon, Barnster?'

'Since when do you call me Barnster?' Barney asked sourly, but he was wavering, I could tell. It was something in his eyes.

'It's the kind of nickname friends give each other.' I tried out a cheeky grin, though there wasn't much to grin about. I was still mad at Barney, not for crushing on Scarlett but for being such a dick about it, but I needed to get over it, because when he wasn't being a dick, Barney was good people. 'You can give me a nickname too.'

'How about, um, Rage Against The Jeane?'

We'd arrived at the school gates now and Barney had fallen into step alongside me, so I could elbow him in the ribs. 'That's not a nickname, it's a really bad pun and it doesn't exactly roll off the tongue, does it?'

Barney wanted to smile – his lips were stretching and contracting like he had some weird facial tic. 'Why is it impossible to stay mad at you?' He shrugged. 'Fine, we're friends, but you're on probation and don't ever blog about me again.'

'And I *will* be nice to Scarlett,' I vowed magnanimously. 'I won't make any snide remarks or say anything to her that in any way could result in snivels, let alone tears. Honestly, I want you two to be happy. People should be happy.'

Barney tagged along with me to the bike sheds and stayed while I chained Mary up. 'We're not together, you know,' he said morosely, hands shoved into the pockets of his parka. 'She's scared to break up with Michael.'

I snorted. 'You'd think she'd be glad to be shot of that over-bearing idiot.'

Barney nodded vigorously. 'Yeah, you would, but Scar doesn't like confrontations or hurting people's feelings and she's terrified of having the wrath of every other girl in the school rain down upon her. You can't dump Michael Lee with-out serious repercussions.'

I turned my head so Barney couldn't see that I was rolling my eyes so hard that I was sure one of my retinas had just detached itself. I tried to make sympathetic noises but Barney looked at me sceptically like he wasn't buying it for a second.

'Oh, Jeane, you are *so* full of shit,' he said, and he smiled at me properly for the first time in days. 'It's what I like most about you.'

It wasn't until lunchtime that I was able to hunt Scarlett down. Her and her boring friends always headed for the high street to visit the salad bar in Sainsbury's so I trailed behind them, pausing only to buy spicy Nik Naks and Haribo, then followed them back to school as I waited for an opportunity to

71

get Scarlett on her own. The four of them didn't appear to function singularly.

Luckily Scarlett had a hair emergency and a free period so she was forced to leave school on her own and, as I'd been banished from my A-level Art class for a week after telling Mrs Spiers that I'd rather poke my eyes out with a paintbrush than have to draw a landscape, seascape or anything else pertaining to nature, I seized the opportunity.

I let her buy her hair gloop first, because I'm nice like that, then fell into step beside her as she dawdled along the road. As she glanced to the side, she caught sight of me. Her eyes widened in terror and her face drained of all colour. It was the perfect time to launch into my apology.

'So, I'm sorry, right. I'm sorry about what happened in English, though I didn't mean that *you* were a retard. I was talking about the whole class but I shouldn't have used that word in the first place and I shouldn't have had a go at you about our set texts as a sneaky way of having a go at you about this whole business with Barney, OK?'

It wasn't an elegant apology but it came from the heart and that had to count for something. Scarlett didn't seem to think so. She tried to duck past me, but I swiftly sidestepped so I was facing her full-on. I don't think I've ever seen anyone look so terrified, not even when my friend Pam Slamwich (so obviously *not* her real name) realised she was the only member of her roller derby team who wasn't in the penalty box and she was just about to get thrown off the track by four blockers.

'Please leave me alone,' Scarlett said in a pained whisper.

'I can't do that until you at least acknowledge my apology. I don't expect you to forgive me, but I've said I'm sorry and I meant it.'

Scarlett shook her head. 'Whatever,' she managed to say, but it wasn't in a jaunty, fuck-you kind of way. More like it was the bravest thing to ever come out of her mouth. She was so wet that I wanted to wring her out.

'So, does that mean you accept my apology?' I persevered and Scarlett shrugged and pursed her lips and generally acted like she was in ungodly amounts of agony.

This was going to take for *ever*. And I didn't have for ever. I was too busy for for ever. And what Scarlett was too stupid to realise was that she had all the power, so I was going to have to point that out for her and also run to keep up with her as she suddenly dashed across the road.

'Listen, Scarlett . . . will you just listen to me?' I grabbed hold of her arm and she stopped instantly as if my touch had paralysing properties, which would actually have been very cool.

'OK, I'm listening,' she mumbled.

'Scarlett! You might think that I'm just an uppity, shouty, badly dressed girl who's made you cry on two separate occasions and if I'd just disappear then your life would automatically be one hundred per cent better, but guess what?'

'What?' I definitely had her attention now.

'My future happiness is in your hands,' I told her, grabbing the limp, lily-white hands in question and giving them a little shake so she'd appreciate the urgency of the situation. 'I like Barney and you like him too.'

'Well, look, about that . . . ' She tried to pull her hands free but I hung on for dear life. 'It's not what you—'

'You probably like him a lot more than I do and he likes you way more than he likes me, especially right now 'cause he's mad at me, but we were a disaster as a couple, so the two of you have my blessing.'

'Oh,' she said. 'Oh, right. Well, I wasn't expecting that.'

'I'd much rather have Barney as my friend than my boyfriend but that's only going to happen if that's all right with you,' I told her, and it was hard to admit that someone as blah as Scarlett had a say in my destiny. It stuck in my throat like a piece of dry chicken, but she was the kind of person that needed to have everything spelt out for her. In fact, I should have prepared some flash cards just to make this whole exercise a little more humiliating than it already was. 'If you two do get together then Barney isn't going to want to hang with me unless you say it's OK.' I paused. 'Which is kinda wrong because people aren't personal property, they should be able to do what they want and be mates with who they want regardless of what their special friend thinks, but not everyone is as enlightened as me.'

Scarlett certainly wasn't. Maybe that's why she was frowning. She was a very hard person to read when she wasn't cowering in fear. 'But we're not together, Barney and me,' she said. 'Not right now anyway.'

'You prefer Michael Lee to Barney?' I asked incredulously, because anyone who'd spent more than ten minutes in Barney's company would infinitely prefer him to Michael Lee if they possessed more than two working brain cells. 'Then what the actual *hell* have you been playing at?'

'No, no! You don't understand.' We were blocking a path for two tutting mothers who were brandishing their Bugaboos at us.

Scarlett sighed as I took a step to the right just as the mums veered right so I was almost tangled up in the pram wheels. She yanked me to safety and the weirdest thing happened: Scarlett Thomas and I were suddenly sitting on a garden wall and talking about boys. Or she was talking about two boys in particular and I had no choice but to listen. Barney was going to owe me big-time for this.

'. . . and I really like Barney, like, really *really* like Barney, 'cause he gets me, which is weird because you wouldn't think he would and now that we've been hanging out a lot, I think he's actually quite cute, but I'm with Michael and I don't know how to not be with Michael, you know?'

'It's simple. You just, well, dump him. Say, "You're dumped," but maybe you want to find a slightly nicer way of putting it,' I advised her. 'Like, "You're an all right person as persons go, but let's not do this any more."'

'I couldn't say that!' Scarlett gasped. 'It's way too mean but whatever I say there'll be an argument and he'll get angry and when people get mad at me, I start to cry. I wish I didn't but I do.'

I did squirm at that, just at little. 'It's impossible to get through life and never have anyone get angry with you. Usually I can't go an hour without someone wanting to kill me, but it's just ten unpleasant minutes that you'll have to suffer before you can get to the good stuff.'

'Hmm, I didn't think about it like that,' Scarlett mused, before her face squinched up again. She'd have been much prettier if she didn't keep crinkling and scrunching and creasing her face. 'And it's not like Michael would shout at me, because he's too nice to do that, but he sighs and he gives me

75

this look like I'm being really lame and I have been lame because I thought that if I was a rubbish girlfriend then he'd break up with *me*, but he hasn't. He just sighs even more. It's, like, so stressful.'

The time for tact was over. 'For God's sake, Scarlett, stop being so pathetic!' I snapped. I was being cruel to be kind because if she could face my wrath then she could easily face Michael Lee's sighing, which sounded strictly amateur hour to me. 'You have this amazing opportunity to seize happiness. You like Barney loads, he likes you loads back and the only thing standing in your way is your own lack of guts.'

'Yeah, but . . .'

'Here's what's going down. You're going to go back to school and you're going to find Michael Lee and tell him that he doesn't make you happy but Barney does and you need to follow your bliss. You got that? Follow your bliss! Think of it less as breaking up with someone and more changing the course of your future, right?'

'Right!' Scarlett nodded jerkily. 'Yeah! Like, I totes deserve to be happy. And it's not Michael's fault that he's kinda boring and doesn't make me happy, but it's not my fault either.'

'Now you're getting it.' I patted Scarlett's arm and took a moment to revel in my own power. I would make an amazing motivational speaker. Let's face it, I would totally kick all kinds of arse as a public figure, say an MP, or even Prime Minister, or even staging a *coup d'etat* and becoming a dictator, but a benevolent dictator, which would make a great blog post. 'Come on! Let's go back to school so you can follow your bliss!'

Scarlett jumped to her feet and had even taken three

purposeful strides before she came to a halt. 'Um, Jeane, could I follow my bliss by dumping Michael via text message?'

'No! What is wrong with you?' I punched her on the arm, very lightly, but she still jumped back and rubbed her bicep reproachfully as if my fists were made of reinforced concrete. 'Remember, breaking up with him will only take you ten minutes out of your whole entire life.'

'Well, I s'pose . . .'

I could tell Scarlett was wavering again so I spent the whole walk back to school whipping her up into a state of near hysteria. It wasn't just about dumping Michael Lee, it was about taking control of her own life, no longer standing in the wings but being the star of her own movie.

As soon as we marched through the school gates, Scarlett was all, 'He should just be getting out of Maths now. Right. I'm going to find him and then I'm going to tell him that he's getting in the way of me and my bliss. I am my own leading lady, aren't I?'

'You *so* are,' I said, and I'd never admit it to anyone, especially not Barney, but when she was all riled up and indignant, Scarlett was almost fun. 'Good luck!'

'I don't need luck,' Scarlett called over her shoulder as she strode down the corridor. 'I make my own luck.'

I still had doubts that Scarlett would follow through. The moment she was in front of Michael Lee and his cheekbones, she'd crumble and she and Barney would never get beyond the what might have beens and he'd still be mad at me.

To take my mind off things I engaged Mr Latymer in a lively debate in Business Studies about bankers' bonuses and big corporations scrooging their way out of paying taxes. We were meant to be talking about globalisation but I hadn't done the reading, so I could buy myself some time and, as an added bonus, it was always funny when he got worked up and his face went bright red and spittle started flying out of his mouth.

We'd been going back and forth about exactly how much the national debt would be reduced if everyone paid the right amount of tax when I realised that the rest of the class weren't paying attention, but instead of the disinterested muttering that usually happened in these circumstances, I could hear people giggling behind me. For one moment I wondered if Rufus Bowles had stuck a rude note to the back of my chair again – 'Jeane Means Whines' had been his finest moment – but no one was looking in my direction. I glanced over my shoulder to see everyone in the class, and I mean everyone, looking at their phones and making no attempt to hide it.

'Right, Jeane, enough of this.' Mr Latymer took advantage of my distraction to clap his hands. 'I don't want to hear another word out of you for the rest of the lesson.'

My plan had worked, because my plans always did. Now I could lean back in my chair and hiss at Hardeep, who always sat next to me in Business Studies because he got to class even later than I did: 'What's going on?'

'Scarlett's dumped Michael Lee,' he hissed back. 'By the Year 13 lockers. She was acting like a total mentaller, kept shouting at him about being in the movies or something.'

'You shouldn't use words like that,' I said automatically, even though inwardly I was punching the air in triumph. Sometimes I almost feared my own power.

'Says the girl who called her a retard,' Hardeep snapped and then Mr Latymer was snapping at both of us in a way that promised detention if we didn't shut up.

So I shut up and while they debated globalisation I did the reading on globalisation that I should have done the night before and even made a start on the next chapter.

All in all, it had been a very successful Business Studies lesson, I thought as I made my way to the bike shed. And Barney was probably ordering me a muffin basket at this very moment due to my stellar work on Scarlett and her self-esteem issues.

There really was no way that the day could get any better.

Then I saw Michael Lee waiting by my bike, waiting for *me*, if the pissy look on his face was any indication, and all of a sudden the day had got a lot, lot worse.

8

Jeane Smith walked towards me in yet another eye-hurting outfit of stuff that didn't go together and orange tights. Why did anyone ever think it was a good idea to design and sell orange tights and why did Jeane think it was a good idea to buy them?

A couple of Year 8s rushed past and almost knocked her off her feet, because they were bigger than her, and I wondered how someone so small could cause so much trouble. She was a wrecking ball in human form.

'I know you've come to yell at me,' she said crossly once she was in earshot, 'so just do it now because I'm on a schedule here.'

No one but Jeane Smith could make me feel like I wasn't that big of a deal. Even if I rescued small children and puppies and kittens from a burning building with no thought for my own safety, Jeane still wouldn't be impressed. That thought made my top lip curl up like a Quaver.

'What the hell did you say to Scarlett?' I demanded, as Jeane reached my side and started attaching her pannier to the back of her bike.

'I was apologising to her,' Jeane said haughtily. 'And then we got talking about girl stuff. I wouldn't expect you to understand.'

'I definitely didn't understand when she started screaming about following her bliss and starring in movies, but I managed to decipher enough of it to know that I've been dumped.'

Jeane smiled serenely. Actually, she smiled smugly. 'Look, if it's any consolation, she'd been wanting to do it for ages . . .'

'No, it's not,' I ground out.

'You knew there was something going on between her and Barney . . .'

'You're singing that tune now, are you?' I couldn't believe what I was hearing. 'I taught you *that* tune.'

'Whatevs.' Jeane shrugged. 'You and Scarlett weren't making each other happy, that's what she told me, and her and Barney will make each other very happy, though God knows what they actually talk about, and I'm sure you'll find another girlfriend to validate your existence by the end of next week, so, really, what's the problem?'

'You! You're my problem. You had no right—'

'Excuse me! You were the one who told me I needed to do something about Barney and Scarlett, so I did. You should be thanking me.'

It was bullshit. She hadn't cast her dorky spell over Scarlett in the name of girl power and sisters doing it for themselves. I'd read her blog the night before when she'd been baying for Barney's blood, and it was obvious she'd decided that if she was going to be miserable then I was, too. She absolutely hated me, though I couldn't imagine why. I'd done nothing to Jeane, but my mere existence seemed to really piss her off.

'Why should I be thanking you? There was no need for you to get involved; I was dealing with it.' The only way I'd been dealing with it was by delaying the inevitable dumping but I wasn't going to tell Jeane that and see her face light up with spiteful glee.

'The reason why you're mad at me is because this is obviously the first time in your life that things haven't gone your way,' Jeane informed me. 'This whole sitch will help you to build character and anyway, *we're at school*, it's not like Scarlett was your one true love and you were going to get married and have children. You're totally overreacting.'

'Look, whatever problems Scarlett and I had, they were *our* problems. No one asked you to stick your fat nose in them.'

'Well, actually, you did.' Jeane reached up to touch the tip of her nose. 'And my nose isn't fat, it's big-boned,' she added, and I wanted to laugh because it was one of the best comebacks I'd ever heard, but I would never, ever give her that satisfaction. 'Look, are you going to bang on much longer, because I have a ton of stuff I need to do this evening? Scarlett was right when she said you were boring. You're like a CD that keeps skipping – you never get to the end.'

'But ... But ... But ...' I couldn't believe I was standing there blustering and 'But'ing and at a loss for words because, yes, Scarlett had dumped me, but I'd known we were well on the outs and though it had been humiliating, it wasn't the end of the world. Still, there was a right way and a wrong way to dump someone. 'Why did you have to get Scarlett so mad? In fact, *how* did you manage to make Scarlett lose it like that?'

'It's one of my superpowers,' Jeane said. She crouched down to unlock her bike. 'I can't say it's been fun because it hasn't but I've got to go.'

She climbed on her bike and she was about to go even though there were many things I had to say, though I couldn't remember what they were at that exact moment. 'Well, we should really *not* do this again sometime,' she said jauntily, and she stood up on the pedals and moved forward and I grabbed hold of the back of her bike because I'd just remembered that I wanted to tell her that she was an insufferable, stuck-up cow …

It seemed to happen in slow motion. Jeane went pitching right over the handlebars. I watched helplessly as she seemed to stay airborne for several long moments then she hit the ground with a dull thud, arms and legs at horribly weird angles like she'd broken all her limbs. *I'd* broken all her limbs.

She lay there silent and still, which would have been a relief at any other time, but not when I was sure I'd just killed her. *Oh God! This is going to seriously screw up my Cambridge interview* was the immediate thought that popped into my head before I remembered that I was a trained first aider. Partly because my dad was adamant that everyone should learn basic life-saving skills but also because my mother had been equally adamant that it would look good on my UCAS form.

I needed to check that Jeane was still breathing but to do that I had to turn her over and she really shouldn't be moved. Or should she? Was I meant to be putting her in the recovery position?

'Heavens to fricking Betsy,' she suddenly groaned and rolled over. She wasn't dead and I wasn't going to be charged with manslaughter. Maybe aggravated assault, because her tights were shredded and there were steady streams of blood running down her legs, which made her orange tights look even worse. 'My phone? Is my phone all right?'

Jeane wasn't yelling at me, which was good, unless she was saving her energy for when she called the police. I picked up her bike – the front wheel was completely buckled – and set it on its kickstand. 'Where was your phone?' I asked her hoarsely.

She frowned or else her face creased up in pain, it was hard to tell. 'Maybe it's in my pannier.'

I unbuckled the flap and pulled out her bulging 'Dork is the New Black' tote and placed it in front of her. Jeane sat up and groaned before she began to root through her bag, so at least her arms weren't broken, which just left legs, ribs and possible concussion because Jeane was too much of a rebel to wear a safety helmet.

'Maybe you shouldn't move?' I suggested. 'You might have internal bleeding.'

'I *need* my phone,' she insisted, looking up at me with plaintive eyes that made her seem more Bambi than battleaxe. 'I can't find it.'

'Are you sure it was in your bag?'

Jeane looked around the yard and I even squatted down and looked under a few parked cars until she gave a yelp. I turned round so quickly that I nearly fell over because it sounded like a pained yelp but it was actually an I-found-my-phone yelp.

'It was in my pocket,' she said, then she actually kissed her phone and rubbed it against her face until she realised that her cheek was grazed.

'Are you all right?' I asked her, because the way she was acting made me think that she was suffering from shock, though it really wasn't any more crazy than how she usually acted. 'Does anywhere hurt?'

'I'm a little winded,' Jeane said, and she was taking this much better than I'd ever expected. She hadn't screamed or said anything bitingly sarcastic so maybe she did have a brain-bleed. 'Everywhere's kinda stinging a bit.'

'I *am* sorry. I didn't mean to do what I did. It was a moment of madness. I'll pay to get your bike mended.'

Jeane gave her bike a cursory glance then turned her attention back to her phone. I'd never seen anyone type so fast. 'It's all right,' she said. 'It's only a bike. No bones broken.'

'Are you sure?'

'I think I'd know if my bones were broken,' she mumbled. 'And the bike is just a thing, things can be replaced.'

I stood there, arms hanging uselessly down by my sides. I wasn't used to feeling useless and not knowing what to do next. Should I make Jeane stand up? And after she was upright, should I offer her a lift home? And sometime after that, should I beg her not to file an official complaint against me that would in any way impact on my choice of university?

'Well, you should probably stand up . . .'

'Yeah, just finishing my tweet. I've spent all day totally tweet-blocked so this is a bit of a blessing in disguise,' Jeane said, and then she looked up and then she looked down and then, only then, did she scream.

It was a horrible, piercing sound that rent the air, scaring a flock of pigeons, which were scavenging by the bins, into flight.

'You utter, utter bastard! Look what you've done to my tights!' Jeane pointed at her shredded tights. 'They're ruined!'

They were and, quite frankly, it was an improvement. 'You just said that things can be replaced.'

'Not my orange tights. It took me *years* to find a pair in the right shade of orange and I got these in a shop in Stockholm and they were the last pair.' Jeane clenched her fists and I really thought she was going to cry. Or punch me. 'You shouldn't go round tipping people off their bikes. You're head of the student council; you're meant to set an example.'

'I know, I said I was sorry and I am sorry about your tights but they are only tights.' I looked at them again and wondered why Jeane wasn't more concerned about her cuts and grazes and then my eyes wandered down to her left ankle and stayed there. 'Oh my God.'

'I'm glad you appreciate the severity of the situation,' Jeane snapped. Unbelievably she was reaching for her phone again. 'I'm going to try and find an inferior pair of orange tights on eBay and you're paying for them.'

'Jeane!'

'Now what?'

I pointed a shaky finger at her ankle, which didn't even look like an ankle any more. It was the size of a football. 'How can *that* not hurt?'

'*What?*' She looked down and then her eyes rolled so I could only see the whites and she lurched backwards so I had to rush to her side to stop her bashing her head on the concrete. She opened her mouth to say something but all that came out was a weak little whimper.

'Does it really not hurt, Jeane?'

She clutched on to my arm. Her nails were painted with wonky candy stripes. 'Now I come to think of it, it hurts like a bitch,' she gritted. 'I think I might vom.'

I patted her hand, which was icy cold, as if she was in shock. I took off my leather jacket and placed it around her shoulders. 'Look, I'm going to take you to hospital so you can have it X-rayed.'

Jeane shook her head resolutely. 'No! I hate hospitals. I *think* I can feel my toes. Would I be able to feel my toes if it was broken? Shall I ask Twitter?'

'I have no idea.' I forced myself to look at her ankle again. It was bulging over the top of her sneaker. 'And rather than wasting time tweeting maybe we should take off your shoe before it cuts off your circulation?'

'No! It will hurt too much!' Jeane lay back down on the ground. 'I'll have to stay here for *ever* and I have so much stuff to do tonight.'

Now that Jeane had reverted back to type, I felt easier. She was even more of a drama queen than Alice, but at least Alice had the excuse of being only five. Still didn't have a clue what I was going to do with her though. 'You *can't* stay there for ever and you can't walk and your bike's all mashed up so I'm going to give you a lift. To hospital.'

'I'm not going to hospital,' she protested. 'One whiff of industrial floor cleaner or seeing an elderly person with yellow skin and varicose veins on a drip and I'll throw up all over you.'

'Don't be such a baby,' I said sternly. Then I had an idea. 'My dad's a doctor. Will you deign to see him?'

Jeane's face twisted with indecision. 'What kind of doctor?'

'A GP. Head of his own practice. Twenty years' experience and if you're really well behaved he'll give you a sugar-free lollipop.'

'What's the point of a sugar-free lollipop?' she groused. 'Well, I suppose I could see your dad, as long as he promises not to hurt me.'

I chained her bike up while she insisted on taking a picture of her mangled leg and tweeting it to her followers, and then with much wincing and flinching I helped Jeane to her feet, or rather her right foot because she couldn't put any weight on her left foot. Then, clutching on to my arm, she tried to hop to my car. Every time she made contact with the ground, her breath caught, like the impact was jarring her ankle.

'I could carry you?' I offered half-heartedly. 'You can't weigh *that* much.'

Her eyes narrowed to piggy little slits. 'You even try to carry me then you can forget about ever having children,' she hissed. 'I can manage.'

In the end I drove my car as close to the bike shed as I could and soon we were on the way to my house, without me giving much thought or consideration to whether I wanted Jeane anywhere near my house.

Jeane had been glued to her iPhone for the entire five minute journey but as I pulled into our drive and parallel parked next to my dad's Volvo, she looked up and gave a long, low whistle. 'Swankerama,' she said with a slight sneer to her voice like it wasn't cool to live in a big house.

But we didn't live in a mansion set in fifty acres with a duck-pond, an ornamental lake and a croquet lawn. It was just a big, rambling Victorian house with a roof that leaked and sash windows that rattled in their frames. And the basement and most of the ground floor were taken up with the doctor's surgery but Jeane still looked disapproving.

My dad always finished early on Thursdays and as I ushered a hobbling Jeane through the side door, he was just coming out of the surgery.

'Oh dear,' he said. 'Someone's been in the wars.'

I expected Jeane to launch into a detailed account of how I'd crippled her, but she just leaned against the doorframe so she could hold out her hand. 'I'm Jeane, do you accept walk-ins?'

'I think I can make an exception,' Dad said calmly, like he wasn't at all phased by a seventeen-year-old girl with iron-grey hair who was dressed like a freak. 'Michael, will you tell Agatha that she can go home then make sure that Melly and Alice don't put CBeebies on?'

Jeane waggled her fingers at me as I headed up the stairs to relieve our au pair. 'So, do you think my foxtrotting days are over?' she asked Dad. 'And do you mind if I live-tweet my medical examination?'

Half an hour later, I had Melly and Alice sitting at the kitchen table doing their homework but mostly arguing about who was the queen of Disneyland Paris and I was making a start on dinner. Thursday night was always stir-fry night, which involved chopping up a huge amount of vegetables.

I'd just started on the peppers when I heard a heavy thump and drag on the stairs and the sound of voices. I looked up in time to see Jeane enter the kitchen on . . .

'Crutches!' she exclaimed happily, as Alice and Melly both

stopped arguing in favour of staring at Jeane with wide, confused eyes. 'I'm *so* guaranteed to get a seat on public transport.'

'It's not broken?' I asked nervously. Dad had followed Jeane into the kitchen and he didn't have the look of a man who was going to ground me and give me a looooonnngggg lecture on good manners and not tipping people much smaller than me off their bikes. But no: he was smiling indulgently at Jeane, who was clutching a bouquet of sugar-free lollipops in one hand.

'It's just a bad sprain,' he said, as he opened the freezer and pulled out a bag of frozen peas, which were only used in a vegetable emergency. He gestured at one of the kitchen chairs and Jeane sat down and propped her pasty white leg (now devoid of torn orange tights) up on the chair next to her. 'Now keep this iced for a little while and then I'll bandage it.'

Alice nodded. 'RICE,' she noted. 'Rest, ice, compression, elevation. If symptoms persist, please consult your doctor. Who are *you*?'

'I'm Jeane, who are *you*?' Jeane stared right back at Alice, who couldn't take the pressure and hid her face in her hands.

'She's Alice,' Melly said. 'I wouldn't pay her any attention, she's only five. I'm nearly eight.'

'You're not nearly eight,' Dad reminded her. 'You only turned seven two months ago.'

'Yes, but I'll never turn seven again,' Melly insisted. She gave Jeane an appraising glance. 'Are you one of Michael's girlfriends?'

'No,' I said shortly. 'Jeane goes to my school and don't ask personal questions.'

'Is Melly asking personal questions again?' Mum wanted to know as she came through the door. She dumped handbag, briefcase and laptop bag on the table, took off her coat, slung it over the back of a chair, kissed Dad, then caught sight of Jeane who was eyeing her with interest. 'Hello, who are *you?*'

Introductions were made. It was like watching two dogs circle each other warily. I'd never seen Jeane look less sure of herself. 'Well, I've rested and I've iced,' she said, staring at her foot. 'Is it time for compression yet?'

'Why don't you stay for dinner?' Mum suggested. Mum's suggestions always sounded like a direct order.

'Well, I do have rather a lot to do this evening,' Jeane said, staring at the worktop where Dad was making a marinade. 'What are you having?'

'Turkey and tofu stir-fry,' Alice said. She shuddered. 'I never eat the tofu; it's yuck.'

'Why don't you phone your parents and let them know where you are?'

I looked at my mother in horror. She knew me. I was her eldest child. Her only son. She'd raised me and nagged and chivvied me to do my coursework on time and not eat between meals and we even watched subtitled Danish detective TV shows together so she had to know that Jeane was not someone who was my friend and certainly not someone who I wanted to stay for dinner.

At least Jeane and I were in complete agreement for once because she was looking equally horrified, especially when she saw Dad cutting up huge chunks of tofu.

'No, it's OK,' she said. 'I don't need to call my parents. I'd *love* to stay for dinner.'

9

Jesus wept.

There were so many reasons why I shouldn't have been having dinner at Michael Lee's house but his dad had been really nice as he picked bits of grit out of my bloodied flesh with a pair of tweezers *and* he'd given me lollipops, even if they were sugar-free. Besides, it had been *ages* since I had a home-cooked meal, probably not since Bethan had gone to the States. But the best reason for staying for dinner was the look of utter panic on Michael Lee's face, like his entire reality was about to come crashing down.

It was payback for my sprained ankle and my ruined orange tights and it was another lesson for him on how life felt when it wasn't going your way.

And to start off with it was fun. I totally bonded with Melly and Alice and while the stir-fry was being stirred and fried they took me up to their room, which was rammed full of pink princess paraphernalia but also a metric arseload of Lego and Beyblades so I didn't have to lecture them on the evils of gender stereotyping. Not that it would have done any good.

Alice and Melly were sweet and made it clear that they much preferred me to Scarlett and that my approval rating was very high with the under-tens. Melly even offered to lend me her favourite pair of stripy tights but they were too small, which was a pity because Melly's favourite pair of stripy tights were pink and green and completely awesome.

I could have stayed on Alice's bunk bed for the rest of the evening being entertained with tales from the primary school frontline but, all too soon, it was time to sit down to eat the infamous turkey and tofu stir-fry, which was actually delicious. I mean, even the tofu was delicious and there were soba noodles, which I absolutely love, and it would all have been great if Michael's mum had let me just shovel the food into my face in peace.

His mum (she said I could call her Kathy but made it sound like she'd stab me if I tried) is a lawyer and she cross-examined me like I was in the dock on ten counts of assault with a deadly weapon. She wanted to know why I'd thrown off the shackles of parental responsibility at such a young age and what I was doing for A-levels and whether I had a part-time job and why my hair was grey.

I could tell that she didn't like me. People's mothers never do and it wasn't like I cared whether she liked me or not – I was never going to see her again – but when someone gives me attitude, I can't help but see their attitude and raise it.

So, instead of being polite and simply answering her

questions with monosyllabic replies like any normal seventeen-year-old would, I got really, really defensive. When I wasn't being all TMI.

'My mum's in Peru being touchy-feely with women prisoners. She's trying to teach them how to meditate,' I said. 'And my dad's moved to Spain to run a bar and get drunk every night for free. Believe me, I'm better off without them and their mid-life crises.'

I didn't just stop there. Not when I could say, 'Anyway, friends are the new family and Gustav and Harry who live in the flat next door come round once a month to force me to tidy up and eat some vegetables.'

'I can't really see the point of going to university,' I also said. 'I'm already my own lifestyle brand and I can just hire a business manager to take care of the number crunching. Anyway, what's the point of getting a degree *and* tens of thousands of pounds' worth of debt? Waste of time.'

I was being so objectionable and obnoxious and obstreperous and many other unflattering words that didn't begin with an o that I wanted to put down my chopsticks and slap myself around the face. From the frigid expression on Michael's mum's (sorry, *Kathy's*) face, I think she did too.

It wasn't until we were having pudding – a very disappointing fruit salad with Greek yoghurt – that I finally stopped talking, but Kathy wasn't done. 'So, how did you sprain your ankle?' she asked.

'Well, I had an argument with my bike and the ground,' I said quickly, but I wasn't quick enough to get in there before Michael.

'It was my fault,' he said right over me. 'I kinda threw Jeane off her bike.'

'Michael! Why would you do something like that?' Kathy demanded. 'That's not how you were raised.'

I shot Michael a reproachful look, because I didn't like the guy but he had to know there was a code that clearly stated that you didn't grass your peers up to their parents.

'It was an accident,' I insisted. 'Just a stupid accident. We were having an argument and—'

'An argument?' Kathy sounded like Lady Bracknell banging on about her handbag. She also seemed more aghast that her darling boy would get into an argument than push a defence-less girl off her bike. Though after five seconds in my company she'd probably realised that I was far from defenceless. I was entirely defence-y. 'That doesn't sound like you.'

'I do have arguments with people,' Michael said as he flushed with embarrassment. It was very entertaining to see him trying to pretend that he was controversial.

Despite the fact he had eyes that were the colour of black coffee and shaped like almonds (note to self: now that's a cake waiting to be baked), he was the Lees' blue-eyed boy. When Kathy hadn't been grilling me about my life choices, her and Mr Lee (who'd told me to call him Shen) had asked Michael all about his classes and his homework and if he'd read an article in the *Guardian* about last year's A-level results. He'd been reti-cent at first and kept shooting me these wary glances, but soon he realised that he had the advantage of being on his home ground and talked at length about current events like he was taking part in one of the school's deathly dull debating society assemblies. Snoozeville, but Michael's parents actually listened to what he had to say, eyes fixed on his face as they smiled and nodded encouragingly.

Even Melly and Alice gazed at Michael adoringly and pestered him with requests to play *Dance Revolution* and for big brotherly help on a school project about dinosaurs.

Michael Lee was the sun, moon and stars, maybe even the whole bloody solar system, as far as his family were concerned. No wonder he was so arrogant.

Still, I couldn't remember the last time the Smiths had sat down as a family to eat dinner, or even the last time I'd voiced an opinion that Pat and Roy had wanted to hear. But you couldn't yearn for what you were never going to get – you had to have your own dreams and inspirations, not live through other people, so I didn't envy Michael Lee because it seemed to me that if his parents had asked him to jump then he'd not only jump but promise to jump higher next time.

But right there and then they weren't asking him to jump but to pay for the damage that he'd done to my bike. 'Really, Michael, it's the very least you can do. I hope you've apologised to Jeane.'

'He has, countless times, and he's already offered to pay to get Mary repaired,' I said calmly, because it wasn't the awful calamity that Kathy seemed to think it was, even if it was very inconvenient. 'And I call my bike Mary after a famous woman explorer,' I added as she opened her mouth to bombard me with yet more questions. 'It's all sorted.'

'You'll also give Jeane a lift to and from school,' Mr Lee said mildly, but with an undertone to his voice that was far more intimidating than his wife's constant carping. 'That seems fair, doesn't it?'

'Of course I will,' Michael said, but I could see the panic in his eyes again and I certainly didn't want to spend quality time with him twice a day.

'You don't have to do that,' I assured him. 'I live right by a bus stop, which drops me off almost outside school and didn't you hear what I said before? With my crutches, I'm *so* getting a seat on the bus.'

'Don't be ridiculous,' Kathy snapped at me. 'We're very big on actions having consequences in this house.'

'But it was an accident and I was being beyond annoying. Your son doesn't usually inflict bodily harm on people. It was just a one-off.'

It was like trying to argue with a steel girder. Nothing I said could sway Kathy and Shen Lee and, half an hour later, Michael was driving me home with my crutches bashing him in the face every time he moved his head.

Now that the Barney and Scarlett business was settled, we had nothing to talk about.

'I'm sorry about my mum,' Michael finally said, as he turned into my street. 'It's very hard to say no to your own mother, isn't it?'

'Not really. I find it very easy to say no to mine.' I pointed at the other side of the street. 'Just squeeze in behind that white van.'

'So, what time do you want me to pick you up tomorrow?' Michael asked me in a resigned voice, as I unclipped my seat-belt.

'I don't,' I said shortly, as I tried to drag the crutches from the back seat. 'I can manage by myself perfectly well.'

'But I promised I would.' Michael got out of the car and walked round to open my door, like I'd lost the use of my arms as well as one leg. Though I wasn't the kind of feminist who started quoting from the SCUM Manifesto every time a boy held a door open for me, it bugged me. Like, he only did it to be a stand-up guy, not because he wanted to show me any common courtesy.

'Well, you can just unpromise.' I shoved the crutches at him and tutted furiously as he tried to take my arm and help me out of the car.

'I'm going to give you a lift whether you like it or not,' he said grimly, as he handed the crutches back to me. 'So, what time?'

'I don't like it at all so I'm not telling you a time and you don't know what number my flat is so you can't ring the bell and even if you stood outside and waited for me, you can't, like, physically put me in your car.'

'I bet I could,' Michael mused, eyeing me up and down as I adjusted the crutches and slowly and carefully stepped out on to the road. 'Look, Jeane, can you just be reasonable for once in your life? I made you fall off your bike and I've told my parents that I'll get you to and from school and that's what I'm going to do.'

'Look, Michael, I don't do reasonable. It doesn't suit me and what you told your parents isn't my problem. Just leave your house a little bit early and then don't come to pick me up. It will be our little secret.'

There was no point in arguing with me. Better people than

Michael Lee had tried and failed horribly. 'Fine,' he sighed. 'Fine. And I hope you *don't* get a seat on the bus because it will serve you right for being such a pig-headed, belligerent cow.'

'What*evs*,' I drawled and I wished I could flounce off but all I could do was hobble and shuffle away from him with my nose in the air, which really didn't have the same sort of vibe.

10

I could say that life went back to normal after Scarlett and me broke up but if I did then I'd be lying. Life wasn't normal. It was all wrong.

For starters, everyone knew I'd been dumped – even if they didn't know the painful and humiliating circumstances of my dumping. And everyone knew that Barney and Scarlett were seeing each other because they held hands at every opportunity. It was no surprise that loud whispers followed me around wherever I went.

I made a point of saying hello to Barney and Scarlett to show that there were no hard feelings and I was fine with it. But my ego was bruised and I spent a large part of each day with a churning in my gut and a feeling like I was something less than I used to be. I was also really irritable.

My extreme crankiness didn't have much to do with Barney and Scarlett, and a lot to do with Jeane Smith, because she'd got under my skin like a prickly heat rash. I did take some small comfort in knowing that I wasn't the only dumpee on the block, but at least I had my mates to whack me on the back and say, 'Plenty more fish in the sea, mate,' and, 'Her loss, Mikey,' and I had loads of texts from girls, including Heidi, saying that they were there for me if I needed to talk.

But Jeane ... Jeane, she had no one, and I felt sorry for her even though she didn't deserve any sympathy, especially when she'd execute a clumsy one hundred and eighty degrees on her crutches every time she caught sight of me. But I could tell she was troubled. She wasn't rocking the fluoro-prints for one thing – on Wednesday she was even wearing khaki and plum (it looked like purple to me, but on her blog she insisted it was plum, not that I check her blog every day but I'd just happened to be passing that morning), which had to be like wearing black in Jeane world. She was even keeping it kinda on the downlow on the interwebz. Instead of tweeting about cake, she tweeted about the various injustices being done to girls around the world. I'd never realised that girls had such a hard time, but they were being stoned and having acid thrown in their faces when they tried to access a proper education and pharmacists in small American towns wouldn't give them the morning-after pill and when Jeane mixed it up and posted photos of her glorious technicolour ankle, it was a welcome relief.

Then, on Friday, I felt better than I had done all week. There was a big party on Saturday night and I had a flirty text from posh Lucy, who went to the girls' grammar school, because:

I want 2 double-check that ur going 2 Jimmy K's par-tay & u & Scar r over. Her loss, my gain!

Posh Lucy was well fit, really outgoing, didn't wear weird clothes and was just what I needed to get my groove back. Even better, I got a call from the bike shop to say that Jeane's bike was ready to be collected. I'd pay for the repairs, hand over her boneshaker, then I'd never have to have anything to do with Jeane Smith ever again.

I didn't even care that I had to ask Scarlett to ask Barney to tell Jeane her bike was ready to be collected after school. I didn't have her phone number, no freaking way was I going to email her via her website, and I absolutely couldn't tweet her because she didn't know that I was the same @winsomedimsum who tweeted her links to pugs on surfboards.

So it was a huge shock after I'd just paid Colin, the bike repairman, sixty of my hard-earned pounds, to suddenly come face to face with Jeane as she limped through the door, minus crutches but with a big grin on her face. It disappeared as soon as she saw me.

'Why are you here?' she demanded. 'That wasn't part of the deal.'

'I couldn't pay until Colin knew exactly what needed doing,' I said huffily. 'Believe me, if you'd bothered to let me know what time you'd be putting in an appearance, I'd have kept well away.'

'If you'd never *thrown* me from my bike in the first place then neither of us would have to be here.' Jeane folded her arms. 'Go!'

Colin coughed pointedly and we both turned to look at him. He was in his fifties with tattoos over every inch of his body except his shaved head (I knew this because he was wearing shorts even though it was an icy-cold October day) and several facial piercings that looked painful. In short, he was intimidating, and you didn't want to be in the same place as someone intimidating when a shouty girl was accusing you of *throwing* her off her bike. 'Do you want me to take him round the back then, Jeane?'

I'd never known fear like it. I wanted to throw up, then fall to my knees and cry, 'Please, don't hurt me!' Fortunately I was saved by Jeane.

'Well, maybe he didn't *throw* me off my bike. Not on purpose anyway,' she conceded. 'You can still take him out back if you want though.'

'Now why would anyone want to do such a sweet little girl like you actual physical harm?' Colin asked, and he winked at me so I guessed we were cool and that I didn't have to fear for my personal safety. 'Anyway, I straightened out the wheel and I tweaked your gears and brakes and re-oiled the chain for you. Mary should be as good as new.'

Jeane sidled closer. Usually all I could see when she was near was whatever colour-clashing outfit she was wearing, but today it was a navy dress and mustard-coloured tights, which couldn't distract away from her pale face and the shadows under her eyes. She looked lost. She wasn't pretty, not even a little bit pretty, but she had a certain fire to her, except now it seemed as if it had sputtered and gone out.

After I'd got back from driving her home the week before, I'd been expecting a medium to heavy grilling from Mum about Jeane and any intentions I might have towards her, but she'd just shaken her head and said, 'That is one very troubled, very unhappy girl.'

I'd tried to laugh it off. 'She's a million times tougher than she looks.'

'No, she isn't,' Mum said simply. 'She's so brittle that one hard knock would shatter her.'

At the time, I hadn't paid much attention. Mum was reading Tolstoy for her book group and so I put it down to that. I've never actually read any Tolstoy but his books are long and full of people with confusing Russian names and Dad said that they were the reason Mum had been in a bad mood for weeks. When Alice had Crayola-ed the hall wall, I really thought Mum was going to put her up for adoption. But now as I watched Jeane climb on to her bike to see if the saddle needed adjusting, Mum's words came back to me.

I had lots of friends, both in and out of school. Jeane seemed to have a lot less, unless you counted the people who followed her on Twitter, and I didn't count them. Real friends were there for you and I could try to be there for Jeane. Not as a friend. God, no! But if people knew I was cool with her then they'd be cool with her too. It wouldn't take that much effort to say, 'Hello, how are you?' at school. I could do that.

'What are you still doing here?' asked a peevish voice and I realised that Jeane was trying to wheel her bike out of the workshop and I was standing in the way, possibly with a slack-jawed look on my face.

I got another black look as I held the door open for her, then, as she began to dump bags and belongings into basket and pannier, I had to ask the question that had been bugging me for days. 'If we take the fact that I *threw* you off your bike out of the equation, then why don't you like me?'

Jeane rolled her shadowed eyes. 'I don't have time for this.'

'C'mon, it's a valid question.' I rested my hand on the crossbar of her bike and she flinched even though she wasn't even *on* the bike yet.

She thought about it for all of three seconds. 'I just don't,' she said flatly, which was much worse than if she'd said it fiercely. 'Hard as it might be for you to understand, not everyone you meet in life is going to think the sun shines out of your arse so it's best you get used to it now.'

I decided to let that slide. 'But what specifically don't you like about me? Name one thing. No! Name three things.' If Jeane could only come up with one reason then it was just Jeane being Jeane, but if she had at least three believable reasons for hating my guts then those were areas that I needed to work on. 'What *is* the big deal? You don't like me either!'

'I do!'

'That's utter, utter crap and you know it,' she sneered.

'I don't *not* like you.' That wasn't what I meant. 'I'm open to the idea of liking you but you don't make it easy.'

'Why should I make it easy?' Jeane demanded. 'What makes you think that someone like *you* deserves to be friends with someone like *me*?'

I looked around slowly and deliberately. 'Yeah, because you have so many people queuing up to hang out with you.'

Jeane drew herself up to her full height, which actually wasn't very tall. 'Do you know how many followers I have on Twitter?'

I did know and I was one of them, but ... 'The internet doesn't count. I bet half your followers are middle-aged men with bad personal hygiene who live with their mothers and the rest of them are spammers who want you to click on dodgy links that will infect your computer with a virus.'

'No, they're not! They're real. Or most of them are. And just because you interact with people online doesn't mean that those friendships shouldn't be valued,' Jeane argued. 'It's the bloody twenty-first century.'

'And where were all your internet friends when you bust your ankle?'

Jeane practically howled in disbelief. '*I? I?* I didn't bust up my own ankle. You *threw* me off my bike!'

I wasn't sure how I'd gone from feeling sorry towards Jeane to baiting her into a full-on strop-attack. It was just she was so full of bullshit and someone needed to call her on it and ... and ... she reacted so beautifully. You just lit the fuse, stood well back and watched her explode. Except I'd forgotten to stand well back so now she was jabbing her finger in my general direction and with each fifth or so jab it would hit me in the chest. She could pack a lot of punch into one stubby index finger.

'Anyway, whatever,' I said in my slowest, drawliest, most bored-sounding voice. 'You bust your ankle and where were all your Twitter followers then? Did they rush around with bags of grapes and ibuprofen? And do they hang out with you when you're at school or do you have to go off by yourself into a little hidey-hole where you can do your knitting and generally act like a weirdo freak loner?'

'How dare you? How *dare* you? You know what? You think you're such a big man around school but these are the best days of your life. This is as good as it's ever going to get for you,' Jeane spat. 'You're just a big dumb goldfish swimming around in a fucking tiny pool but the pool is going to get bigger and bigger and you'll get smaller and smaller until you're just a minnow and while you're settling into mediocrity in your miserable, confined little life, I'll just be coming into my own. You might think I'm some weirdo freak loner but at least I'm not afraid of who I am.'

Her finger was like a branding iron, beating out a fierce, painful tattoo into my heart and the only way to stop it was to grab Jeane's wrist. Her skin was shockingly warm beneath my fingers and I waited for her to scream but she was looking at me with a confused expression on her face, eyes narrowed like she wasn't sure what I was doing or why I was doing it.

I wasn't sure either. But there was one thing she needed to know. 'I'm not afraid of who I am.'

She shook her head. 'You don't even know who you are,' she said in a much quieter voice, like she wasn't even trying to hurt me now and that it was the absolute truth. 'You just be what other people want you to be.'

Maybe I kissed Jeane because it made her shut the hell up. Or it might have been the easiest way to show her that I wasn't who she thought I was, that there might actually be some hidden depths to me after all. But I have a really horrible feeling that I kissed her because I wanted to.

One moment we were standing in the street, the bike between us, the next moment we were kissing. People always say, 'And then, like, the next thing I knew we were kissing,' and that never computed. Because there had to be a thing before the kiss. But this time there really wasn't.

It was me, *me*, Michael Lee, kissing Jeane Smith.

11

I kissed Michael Lee.

Four words I never thought I'd write. Four words that, in my wildest dreams (even wilder than the dreams I'd had the time I'd scarfed down a fudge brownie, which turned out to be packed with spliff as well as chopped-up dates), I could never imagine going together.

I don't even know why I kissed him. Maybe it was to shock him out of his sad, safe little life. To make him see that anything was possible. It certainly wasn't because I wanted to kiss him.

But I *was* kissing him and all I could think was, *My God, why am I kissing Michael Lee?*

And then I was like, *Oh. My. God! Why am I still kissing Michael Lee?* and I pulled away from him but I'll give him the benefit of the doubt and say that I think he was pulling away from me at the exact same moment.

I didn't know what to say, which never happens, because I always know what to say and Michael Lee was looking like Wile E Coyote in that split second after he's run off a cliff and realises that he's about to fall into a rocky ravine studded with cactuses. Sorry, cacti. In short, he looked like a boy whose entire belief system had just turned to dust and rubble.

We both stood there, not talking, just staring at each other. The not talking and the staring seemed to go on for several eternities and I wanted to look away but I couldn't. It was a relief when Michael Lee stopped looking at me in favour of fixing his eyes on the floor.

'Well, that was bound to happen,' I said calmly, because screaming hysterically wasn't going to erase the fact that we'd kissed. That I'd kissed Michael Lee. I couldn't help it – I wiped the back of my hand across my mouth. 'All that negative energy between us, well . . . it had to go somewhere.'

He frowned, then looked up to stare at my lips like he couldn't quite believe that two minutes before he'd had his mouth on them. 'Yeah, totally. Yeah. I mean, all that sniping. Had to end somewhere.' He shook his head. 'That was so weird.'

I nodded and tugged Mary out of his grasp. 'And at least you didn't throw me off my bike again . . .'

That wiped the frown off his face. 'For about the millionth time I didn't do it on purpose!' He was managing to talk in complete sentences again.

'I know. It was a joke. You do know what a joke is, don't you?' I mounted Mary and carefully steered her towards the kerb. My ankle seemed to be holding up all right. 'Anyway, it happened. It's never going to happen again and if you tell anyone, I'll deny everything.'

'Like anyone would even believe it,' Michael said. Then he ran a hand through his hair and ruined his faux-hawk. Annoyingly, being rumpled made him look very cute, though it wasn't the kind of cute that did it for me. 'You absolutely promise you won't tell anyone.'

'You really know how to win a girl's heart,' I told him, as I checked to see if there were any cars coming. I was as freaked out by the kiss as he was, but he didn't have to make it quite so clear that he was blates repulsed by the touch of my lips. 'But don't worry, your secret is safe with me.'

I pedalled off without a backward glance, even ignoring the twinge in my ankle because that wasn't important. What was important was getting as far away from Michael Lee as possible.

That was that. It really was. The days just flew by. I blogged, I tweeted. I trend-watched. I even hung out with Barney and Scarlett to show that the three of us were mature people (well, I already knew that I was a mature person, Barney has his moments and I don't think Scarlett will ever be mature, not even if she lives to be a hundred and five).

Barney made this big thing about the three of us having lunch together in the school cafeteria so everyone would know that all was cool and civilised between us. I think he also had this idea that he could gently ease me into mainstream society, like that was a big ambition of mine.

It didn't help that my lunch consisted of three cups of grainy vending machine coffee, a banana muffin and some Haribo Sour Mix. I'd stayed up until five in the morning working on a piece about youth tribes for a German magazine and I needed all the artificial stimulants I could get.

My knee kept banging against the table leg as Barney desperately tried to find something that the three of us had in common. Yes, Scarlett wasn't quite the insipid wretch that I'd originally thought but after she'd finished getting me up to speed on all the soaps, she had nothing else to say. Barney and I started talking about a Japanese graphic novel we'd both read but we had to stop after a minute because Scarlett didn't know what we were going on about.

It was agony and then Heidi/Hilda/whatever her name is and the rest of Scarlett's friends arrived and made it clear that the sight of the three of us together was causing them much amusement and they wanted to observe us at close quarters. I hadn't signed up to be observed at close quarters by the kind of people I usually U-turned in corridors to avoid.

'Well, this has been great, but I really do have stuff to do,' I said, standing up. I stretched my mouth into a smile, though it felt like a pained grimace. 'Thanks for getting me up to speed on *Hollyoaks*.'

Scarlett looked a bit pissed off at that, even though I hadn't meant to sound so bitingly sarcastic when I formed the words in my head. Wasn't much I could do about it though and it wasn't like Barney seemed that bothered. He was actually talking to her friend, Mads, like he and Mads had things that they could talk about.

It was all very strange, I thought, as I left the canteen and walked straight into Michael Lee. I found myself blushing, though generally, as a rule, I didn't blush. Blushing was for people with no backbone.

'Oh, hey,' he said in surprise and he was blushing too. 'How are you?'

'I'm fine,' I said, 'cause the Barney being friends with the pod people thing and then crashing into Michael Lee and having to remember the kissage made the bit of my brain that thought of tart replies completely malfunction. 'Actually, I've been meaning to, you know, come and find you.'

He stiffened. No, not like *that*. He tensed up and looked unhappy and suspicious like he knew that I just couldn't wait to ravage his poor, defenceless, innocent mouth all over again, which was so not the case. 'Why would you want to do that?'

'Because I have the crutches your dad lent me stuffed in my locker.'

Michael let out a sigh of relief. 'Right! OK! Do you want me to collect them now or wait 'til after school?'

'We should do it now,' I decided, because there was only ten minutes until afternoon lessons started and so I wouldn't have to hang around making painfully awkward conversation with him. I'd had my weekly quota of painfully awkward conversation.

Not a single word was spoken on the way to my locker. Michael Lee walked down one side of the corridor, I walked down the other side. Then he slouched against the wall as I opened my locker and braced myself for the deluge of crap that always fell out. Luckily, one of the things that fell out was a crutch.

'One down, one to go,' I said, as he picked it up and I began to try and extricate the other one while trying to prevent books and Tupperware and *stuff* tumbling to the floor.

'What exactly have you got in there?' Michael asked, peering over my shoulder to get a good look. 'Is that a *whole* jar of pick and mix?'

'No, of course not,' I said, yanking out the crutch with one hand and slamming my locker shut with the other. It was a three-quarters-full jar of pick and mix. I turned round and Michael was still looming behind me so we were suddenly *together*. Almost touching, just a pair of crutches coming between us, and I couldn't even work out how we'd kissed that first time because my mouth was on a level with the little divot between his top button and his Adam's apple.

So, in order for us to kiss, I'd have had to stand on tiptoe and Michael Lee would have had to stoop down, which suggested that it had been a mutual kiss. That there had been two willing parties and that was a theory that needed mulling. Much mulling. Like, even if I had been standing on the very tip of my tippiest toes there was absolutely no way I could get to Michael Lee's mouth unless he bent his head in much the same way that he was doing right now.

I think this time *he* kissed me because the only thing I was doing with my mouth was opening it to tell him to back the hell away from my personal space. It wasn't just a brush of his lips against mine, it was a proper kiss, firm but yielding, and instead of freaking out over the kiss, I was just being kissed, even thinking about kissing him back and then I heard the sound of voices, a loud thump of a door being slammed and the bell for afternoon lessons.

113

We leapt apart just a nano second before the corridor was invaded by Year 12s. I shoved the second crutch at Michael, who grabbed it from me then stood there opening and closing his mouth and generally acting like a gormless fool.

'Right, you've got the crutches,' I said sharply, because somebody needed to take control of this situation. 'There's absolutely no reason for us to have any more contact with each other.'

'Yeah, yeah. No reason at all,' he echoed, rubbing his chin. The tips of his fingers just grazed his bottom lip and I realised I was staring at his mouth as if it was the source of all comfort and joy.

He was staring at me too as if I was some new species of life that he'd never seen before.

'I'm going . . . now,' I said, and Michael opened and shut his mouth a few more times and when it became clear that no actual words were going to come out of it, I walked away.

12

The first kiss was a fluke.

The second kiss was obviously just to see if the first kiss really had been a fluke.

But there weren't any excuses for the kisses after that.

The third kiss occurred when Jeane just happened to be passing my car at the exact time that I was leaving early on Thursday afternoon, like I do every week because I have a free study period then. I'm sure she was meant to be in a lesson but she was walking across the staff car park towards me with a grim expression on her face and I put my bag down on the car bonnet so that when she did get to my side, I had my hands free to pull her close enough so I could kiss her.

The fourth kiss took place on the tiny twisty staircase that led from the second floor of the upper school to the Art studios in the attic. Jeane tended to camp out there during breaks when it was too cold and wet to skulk around the bike shed. I don't know how I knew that, I just did. No one else hung out there even though it was cosy and quiet – maybe it was because the entire school knew it was one of Jeane's special places and she'd kill anyone stupid enough to trespass with just a look.

When she saw me standing at the bottom of the stairs, she glanced up from her laptop then placed it a few steps above her and sat there with her hands in her lap, waiting for me. I sat on the step below her so we were almost the same height and it was a little awkward and neck-cricking but we kissed for a good ten minutes without any interruptions.

Jeane was the ninth girl I'd kissed but her kisses were nothing like the other eight girls' kisses. She tasted sweet and salty and she kissed like her life depended on it. She kissed me like I was going off to war or it was the end of the bloody world. There was no building up to it, no nibbling or nuzzling or clumsy introductory kisses – with her it was just BOOM!

Then the kisses would end in the same way they'd started. We'd break apart and put as much distance between ourselves as possible and we would never talk about what we'd just been doing. We never talked at all.

I didn't know if she was using me or I was using her. And I still didn't know why I was kissing someone I shouldn't have been kissing. I mean, she wasn't sweet or sexy or cool or any of the other qualities I wanted in a girlfriend. Obviously, I'd want to go out with someone who was good to look at, in the same way that if I had a choice of two shirts, I'd always pick the one that looked better.

It wasn't even like Jeane was secretly pretty. Though maybe

if you got rid of the horrible grey hair and the even more horrible clothes and the nasty shoes then she might be passably cute. Or even plain and ordinary, which wasn't as bad as, say, being ugly.

Whatever.

It was still all wrong and weird and I didn't know what I was doing and why I was doing it. All I knew was that it had to stop.

So, two weeks after the kissing had started and we were tucked away again on the stairs that led up to the Art studios, Jeane sitting on my lap because that was the most comfortable way for us to kiss, her short nails gently scratching the back of my neck as her tongue danced in my mouth, I was determined that we weren't going to do this any more.

I stopped kissing her and she sighed a little then slid off me on to the step and patted down her hair.

'We can't keep doing this,' I said firmly. I think it was the first thing I'd said to her in two weeks.

She didn't look surprised. 'I know,' she said, as she began to search through her tote bag. At all times she had at least two bags with her, plus books and folders. No one needed that much stuff.

'It's all this sneaking about and hiding from people,' I continued. 'It's doing my head in.'

Her face was as blank as a piece of white paper so I had no idea what she was thinking. 'What did you want to do about it then?' she asked calmly.

To stop this right here and now, both of us vow to never breathe a word of it ever again to another soul, and get on with the rest of our lives, I thought to myself. I cleared my throat.

'Well, maybe we could see each other outside of school. If you wanted . . .'

She actually had the nerve to smile. A small, triumphant smile that made me want to hurl myself down the stairs so I'd have amnesia and wouldn't be able to remember the moment thirty seconds before when I'd somehow asked Jeane Smith out on a date.

'I'll think about it.' She held up her phone. 'Give me your number.'

'Um, why?'

'Duh! So I can text you when I've decided what I want to do.' She raised her eyebrows at me. 'Unless you're having second thoughts because we could just carry on as we were, or, like, not. I don't mind either way.'

I wasn't going to have Jeane calling all the shots. 'Well, neither do I,' I burst out. I always ended up losing my cool with her. 'I mean, we could just not do this at all.'

'So, what do you want to do?' She sounded peeved, but not quite as peeved as she normally did, which was maybe a sign that she was as freaked out about our kissing sessions as I was.

'No way! If I say I do or I don't want to, you'll use it against me.'

Jeane put her hands on her hips. 'Why would I even do that?'

'Because that's what you do!' I rested my elbows on my knees. 'This is all some evil trick, isn't it? Has this been some psychosexual experiment for your blog? Will people leave mean comments about me?'

'Don't you think you're being just a little bit paranoid?' she asked sweetly. 'I don't diss people I know in real life on the internet, it's one of the cornerstones of my blogging philosophy. It goes against the whole spirit of the Adorkable brand.'

'Whatever!' She'd blogged about Barney so her philosophy didn't mean shit. Neither did Jeane's mistaken belief that she was building a geek master race in her spare time. 'This is all really messed up and—'

'I have Art in five minutes so please go and have your existential crisis somewhere else before Mrs Spiers and the rest of my class arrive.' She marched majestically up the stairs so she could sit on the top step.

'You can't blame me for not trusting you. I know you'd love to get one over on me.' Really, what other reason could there be for Jeane willingly kissing me? There wasn't. Not when she was looking as if she was going to march down the stairs again so she could knee me in the nuts.

'Excuse me! Excuse me! I *am* trustworthy, which you'd know if you knew a single thing about me instead of judging me on what other people say.' She twisted her face up until she looked like a gargoyle. 'Believe me, I am riddled with faults, but if you ask me to do something and it's something I want to do or you have a secret that needs keeping then you can trust me with your life.'

'Well, I'm sorry, it's just that you—'

'What did you think was going to happen here, Michael? Did you think I was going to *beg* you to keep doing this with me?'

How did she do it? I could be *so* sure that I was right then Jeane would blindside me and all of a sudden I was in the wrong.

'Why would *I* beg *you* when there are tons of girls who want to get with me? Pretty, non-stroppy girls who aren't such a bloody headache,' I told her furiously.

'Well, get with *them* then because I don't want to be part of this ... this freakshow any more.' Jeane rattled the studio door handle but it remained locked and the only way to end *this* and to stop an argument that I was never going to win was to get as far away from her as possible.

13

Kissing Michael Lee the first time was an accident. Kissing him the second time was just plain silly. And the times after that were sheer Oh-my-God-what-is-wrong-with-you-ness.

It was obvious it wasn't going to last but I never thought it would end with him calling me fugly and untrustworthy and just about the most evil, calculating person in the world. Like I would ever blog about what we were doing. Like I was *proud* of what we were doing.

I was meant to be working on a stupid seascape in Art because Mrs Spiers had said that if I didn't she'd fail me for that module. It really was the least of my problems but I was just in the right mood to paint a storm-tossed ocean with lots of greys and blacks and purples. I even added a little sailboat getting pulled under with a teeny-tiny little man onboard, and if he hadn't been so teeny-tiny then I'd have given him an Abercrombie & Fitch T-shirt and a faux-hawk because the teeny-tiny man was Michael Lee and the little sailboat was his miserable life, which was going to be nothing but a source of frustration and disappointment to him once he wasn't the most popular boy in school any more and was forced to join the real world.

Of course I couldn't tell Mrs Spiers that so I described my painting as a metaphor for the savagery of nature and how it would ultimately triumph over all the wrongs man had done. Mrs Spiers was really big on metaphor so she actually dared to pat me on the head and said that she expected great things from me this year if I kept up this standard.

Triple whatever.

I couldn't wait to get out of school, though I had to steel myself to go and unlock Mary in case Michael Lee was loitering around the bike shed because he wanted to hurl some more insults at me or, worse, somehow I ended up kissing him again. I'll say one thing for him, and only one thing: he was a really good kisser. That was a large part of the problem.

I've kissed seven boys and two girls and Michael Lee was definitely in the top three. He did this thing with my bottom lip and his teeth that made me want to squeal and swoon a little.

Anyway, he wasn't there, which was fine by me because it meant that the thing, the stupid thing that should never have started, was over. I didn't even cycle through the staff car park in case he was hanging around but took the long way down the grass slope and through the junior school.

It was cold with that crisp nip in the air that made me think of toffee apples and crunching through fallen leaves and mugs of hot chocolate and all the other things that were ace about autumn, but it was still light enough that I decided not to go straight home but huff and puff my way up the big hill, then up an even bigger hill until I was cycling to Hampstead and even then I didn't want to stop.

I love standing up on my pedals but keeping my body low so I can go extra fast and feel the breeze lift through my hair and all I am is the ache in my legs as I pedal faster and I don't have to think, I just am.

I cycled on to Regent's Park, craning my neck so I could see the giraffes through the canopy of plane trees as I whizzed past London Zoo and I thought about cycling right through the park but the sun was getting lower and lower, so I cycled back through Camden, slowing down to save my energy for the big steep hill that I couldn't avoid on the way home.

My legs were shaking as I walked through my door. God, the flat was such a mess. Normally I didn't mind the mess. Mess is a sign of a creative mind, after all, but right then it just seemed like one more aspect of my life where chaos reigned.

The fridge was another place where there was no order. There was also nothing in there for dinner and I'd spent my lunch-hour eating Michael Lee's mouth off his face, then two hours cycling around north London, so I was ravenously hungry. I couldn't even order a takeaway because a quick scavenge through bags and pockets and the back of the sofa only netted two pounds and thirty-seven pence. My debit card was somewhere in the flat, or maybe in my school locker, but right then it was lost to me.

Luckily I'm never more than five seconds away from some Haribo, so, ripping open a bag of Tangfastics, I switched on my MacBook and headed for Twitter.

 adork_able Jeane Smith
Sartre was wrong. Hell isn't other people. It's other people AND the complete absence of Pad Thai in my life right now. Please send food.

Immediately people began tweeting me pictures of Pad Thai and also cake, which was sweet but wasn't really helping the hunger pangs that the Tangfastics weren't doing much to quell.

 winsomedimsum is yum
@adork_able Sartre had nothing to complain about – he wasn't doing five A-levels or was related to my mother, as far as I can tell.

It was a tweet from a new follower of mine, @winsomedimsum. I mean, I had new followers by the hundred every day, more if I had something published or one of my tweets was retweeted by a celebrity, so I didn't take much notice of them and I very rarely followed back. But @winsomedimsum shared my love of weird foodstuffs and we'd just *connected*. And at least they weren't one of the fifty-seven tweeters to now send me a picture of Pad Thai.

adork_able Jeane Smith

People, please stop tweeting pics of food I can't have. Not that I don't appreciate the sentiment but it's making me cry actual tears.

adork_able Jeane Smith

@winsomedimsum I like to think that Sartre's mum was constantly getting on his case about leaving his gym kit lying about unwashed.

winsomedimsum is yum

@adork_able 'I don't care if you are writing about Existentialism, Jean-Paul, those clothes won't walk to the washing machine by themselves.'

I almost choked on a Tangfastic. This was what I loved most about Twitter: riffing on utter nonsense with a complete stranger who turned out to be on the same bizarro wavelength as me.

adork_able Jeane Smith

@winsomedimsum 'I'll give you Nausea, young man. Of course you're feeling sick with ten unwashed plates mouldering under your bed.'

That was the sum total of my Jean-Paul Sartre knowledge so I wasn't sure I was going to be able to come up with any more tweets about him.

winsomedimsum is yum

@adork_able You'd better amuse yourself
while I try to Wiki some more fun facts about
Jean-Paul Sartre.

adork_able Jeane Smith

@winsomedimsum I was just about to tweet
the exact same thing!

winsomedimsum is yum

@adork_able Must have been a bad day
though if you're channelling JPS (can't be
arsed to keep typing his name).

adork_able Jeane Smith

@winsomedimsum Not just a bad day, one of
the suckiest days.

Truthfully, it hadn't been that sucky. I'd actually bumped
into the postman for once, instead of making my weekly trek to
the sorting office with a shopping trolley to collect all my
parcels. In the post had been fanzines, a Pez dispenser I'd won
on eBay, two cheques, six bottles of nail varnish and a gingham
dress from my friend Inge in Stockholm.

Then I'd made it into school with enough time to bang out
half an English essay, got an email from a branding agency in
New York who'd asked me to be a keynote speaker at a conference confirming my FIRST CLASS travel details, and I'd
been on a two-hour cycle fest. It had been an awesome day. The

only blight in all the awesomeness had been realising that Michael Lee was every bit as evil as I'd suspected.

You shouldn't kiss someone just because they were a good kisser and ignore everything else about them, I told myself, but I'd been telling myself that for the last two weeks and I'd still found myself attached to Michael Lee's mouth.

My computer beeped and I realised I had another tweet from @winsomedimsum.

winsomedimsum is yum
@adork_able I promise it's not Pad Thai but thought this YouTube clip of dogs on skateboards might hit the spot.

It wasn't as good as dogs surfing because, quite frankly, what could be? Still, it was a close second and I forgot that I was hungry because there was an English Bulldog looking all kinds of happy on a skateboard.

I tweeted @winsomedimsum to thank them but they were nowhere to be found and none of my usual Twitter buddies were about and I didn't have any outstanding coursework or articles to write and there was nothing I wanted to Google and I could have written a blog post but I didn't feel passionate enough about anything to blog about it right there and then and mostly I just felt feh and meh and kinda blah. I had a sneaking suspicion that it was all to do with the argument I'd had with Michael Lee, but I couldn't allow myself to think like that, to give him that kind of power over me. I was much, much better than that.

I didn't know what to do with myself. Well, I did. I wanted to talk to Bethan because even when I didn't want to say what was bugging me, Bethan could always tell when I was bugged and she always knew how to chivvy me out of it. But Bethan was in Chicago and this week she was starting her shifts just as I was getting in from school so she wasn't even Skype-able.

There were people I could call, even Barney, but to admit I was furious because I'd let someone like Michael Lee use me and then discard me like a tissue stiff with dried-up snot (ewwww!) was not something I could do.

What I could do was put on Duckie really loudly and attempt to dance my way out of my existential crisis. It usually worked.

If you think I'm going to give you another chance
Hang around waiting until you ask me to dance
Then, baby, you're dumb, dumb, so very dumb

Not going to waste time baking a cake for you
I'm not going to put on my best dress for you
'Cause baby, you're dumb, dumb, so very dumb

The song descended (or should that be ascended?) into a cacophony of squalling guitars and a driving beat as Molly, the singer, shouted, '*Dumb, dumb, why are you so dumb?*' over the top and I shouted along as I jumped up and down on the sofa and actually it was all very cathartic until the song ended and I realised someone was banging on the door.

It was probably Gustav, my neighbour. We had an agreement about loud music, which stated quite clearly that after half an hour I'd give it a rest, but I'd been playing the same song over and over again so many times that I'd lost count.

I leapt off the sofa. 'I'm sorry,' I said breathlessly as I opened the door. 'I'll let you play awful dance music for an hour straight so we're even.'

'OK, good to know.' Oh, God, it wasn't Gustav, it was Michael 'dead man walking' Lee. I should have slammed the door in his face but what would be the point of doing that when I wanted to shout at him?

I hadn't had time to get the first, 'Just what do you think you're doing here?' out of my mouth when I registered that I could smell the siren scent of hot chips and Michael Lee was thrusting a tightly wrapped parcel at me.

'I'm sorry,' Michael Lee said quickly. 'I'm sorry that every-thing came out of my mouth wrong at lunchtime. And I'm sorry if I upset you and I'm sorry if I implied that I could do better because it's not about that and I thought I could make it up to you by, um, buying you dinner if you haven't already eaten.' He shoved the bag into my hands with more gusto so I was forced to take it. 'And generally I'm just sorry, OK? Except I'm not sorry for throwing you off your bike because I *didn't* throw you off your bike. It was an accident, I swear.'

There was so much information in that speech that I could only hit the highlights. Michael Lee was sorry for a whole slew of things that had hurt my feelings. He did sound as if all his sorrys were sincerely meant and he'd actually taken the time to wonder if I'd had dinner and then brought me food. Hot food.

It had been a long time since anyone had cared enough to make sure I had a hot meal inside me.

I could smell yummy chip-shop smells wafting out of the bag and it would be so easy to have it all be forgiven but I never did nothing nice and easy. 'How did you even find out where I live?' I asked as I stood my ground. 'And how did you get into the building?'

'Well, I had to do the whole ask Scarlett to ask Barney thing with this flimsy excuse about still owing you for the bicycle repairs and I was about to ring your buzzer but these two guys came out while I was standing on the doorstep and when I said I was here to see you, they let me in.' Michael frowned. 'One of them, I think his accent was German, said to tell you that you'd violated the loud music treaty and to expect payback.'

'Gustav, he's actually Austrian,' I mumbled, dreading the inevitable moment at some ungodly hour on a Sunday morning when he'd start blasting Deep House. 'He's like my gay dad.'

I stood there and Michael stood there, both of us very still, like we were afraid to make any sudden movements and it was really stupid after all that had happened not to step aside and say, 'Do you want to come in?'

14

I'd never seen anything like the inside of Jeane Smith's flat. It was like walking into one of those *Extreme Hoarders* programmes – everywhere I looked there were piles of crap.

Not actual crap but just mess, rubbish, junk. Like, I thought Hannah had been untidy because she was always starting projects and getting distracted halfway through so her bedroom was littered with abandoned collages and knitting and scraps of dressmaking material, but if you took Hannah's mess and multiplied it by a hundred, it still wouldn't come close to Jeane Smith's mess.

'Yeah, sorry about the clutter,' Jeane said, as she crunched her way over Jiffy bags, magazines, old pizza boxes and God knows what else into what I supposed was the lounge though it looked more like a shanty town after a tsunami had swept through it.

As Jeane threaded and weaved her way through to the sofa,

it was obvious that that was where she spent most of her time because that was where the rubbish reached critical mass. On either side of the sofa were stacks upon stacks of magazines and papers as if Jeane discarded whatever she'd finished reading and chucked it on top of the nearest pile.

The sofa was just about clear enough that she could throw herself down on it.

'Oh, let me make some room,' she said, and she scooped up magazines, envelopes, books and some empty sweet wrappers and simply threw them on the floor. It was one of the most shocking things I'd ever seen and it wasn't as if I'd led a very sheltered life, but you just didn't chuck stuff about. My mother would have expired on the spot from sheer disbelieving rage. I stood there, mouth agape, until Jeane looked pointedly at the space beside her and then at me. I began to carefully pick my way through the chaos.

Jeane began to unwrap all the steaming packages I'd brought her. 'I didn't know what you liked, but I figured most people like chips at the very least. You don't have to eat it all.'

'It's very kind. Let me know how much I owe you,' she said. It didn't suit her sounding all stiff and starchy like that, I thought, as I finally reached my destination and perched uncomfortably on the very edge of the sofa. It seemed inevitable that there'd be something gooey stuck to her cushions that would transfer itself to my jeans.

'You don't owe me anything,' I said, just as tightly. 'It's a peace offering to make up for behaving like a twat.'

'Yeah, but I couldn't ... Oh! You got me mushy peas? They're about the only vegetable that I actively like. And little packets of vinegar and ketchup? You rock at providing hot meals.' She gasped.

'Condiments can be tricky,' I muttered because I knew we were going to have to talk, really talk, and all this chat about food was just the warm-up act. 'Some people like vinegar on chip-shop chips, but some people are ketchup junkies.'

'See, I like them both equally. I couldn't decide between them. It would be like the *Sophie's Choice* of condiments,' Jeane burbled as she held aloft the plastic fork I'd also remembered. 'Look, y'know, thank you for this and, well, you know, I may have behaved like a twat too. Actually, I think I was behaving like a total arse, but your mileage may vary.'

I thought about it for five seconds. 'No, you're right. You were being a total arse.'

As soon as I said it, I wondered if there was going to be another temper explosion but Jeane just 'Hmm'ed and then she smiled around a mouthful of chips. 'I'm glad we've got that cleared up. Do you want to put the TV on or listen to some music because I'm starting to get really self-conscious about chewing loudly?'

She had this really complicated but cool set-up with a Mac mini wired up to her TV so I could whiz through her iTunes. I hadn't heard of a lot of the bands so I put her songs on shuffle. At least that way I wouldn't put something on which she'd only had in her iTunes as some kind of cool test so she could mock me mercilessly. I wondered why I cared if Jeane Smith mocked me mercilessly but apparently I did. I gingerly sat back on her couch and stared at her coffee table and the two MacBooks open and running, an iPhone, an iPad and three remote controls.

'It's so weird. I was on Twitter wailing about my lack of dinner options and then you show up,' Jeane suddenly said and my heart did this unpleasant stop/start thing. 'Are you on Twitter?'

The easiest thing would be to tell Jeane the truth. That, yes, I was on Twitter and actually we'd been sharing links of dogs doing extreme sports and had enjoyed several amusing exchanges about weird food and Jean-Paul Sartre. It would be so easy. 'I don't really get the whole Twitter thing,' was what my brain told my mouth to say.

I expected Jeane to launch into a passionate defence of Twitter and all who sailed in her, but she just shot me a smirky glance, then took a gigantic and enthusiastic bite of battered sausage. I had to look away.

And I hadn't lied. I still didn't get Twitter and if I told Jeane that I was actually @winsomedimsum, it would lead to yet another argument and for once we weren't arguing and it was kind of . . . nice. Besides, if (and it was a really big if) this thing with Jeane continued for a little bit, it was handy to be able to have a way to chart her moods so I knew when to stay away. If she was tweeting about food, puppies and general mundane trivia about her life, everything on Planet Jeane was good. But if she was tweeting about politics and feminism, retweeting mean things people had said about her or getting into pointless arguments, especially pointless arguments with minor celebrities, then I knew to avoid her.

Jeane seemed to think that we were done talking about Twitter anyway because she was rooting through the bag of chips for the crispy bits. 'Are you hungry? Do you want some of this? You'd better speak now before I scoff it all,' she said warningly.

I shook my head. 'Already had dinner, thanks.'

'So, does your mother know you're here?' She sounded amused like she already knew my mother's views on being out on a school night. Though, to be fair, I was allowed out until ten-thirty on school nights if all coursework assignments were complete and I remained in phone contact.

'Sort of,' I admitted. 'I said I had to help a school friend with a problem.'

'I guess I do go to the same school as you and I did have a problem in that I planned to go to bed without any dinner,' Jeane said, as she pushed away her half-finished chips. 'But we're not friends, are we?'

I glanced over at her. She was wearing a floral green blouse, a yellow cardigan, a grey pleated skirt, which looked like part of Melly's school uniform, and purple tights. 'No, we're really not friends,' I said.

'So it's a bit of a headspin that we keep finding ourselves with our tongues down each other's throats,' she continued. 'I mean, what's up with *that*?'

'Jeane!'

She swung her legs off the coffee table and stood up. 'If we can do it then we can talk about it and I think we need to talk about it.' She picked up what was left of her dinner. 'But first I'm going to put this in the fridge. Do you want something to drink?'

I didn't want anything to drink because I'd probably contract E coli or legionnaires' disease, but the kitchen was fairly clean and tidy because it was clear that Jeane didn't cook. In her fridge were bags upon bags of Haribo, tons of cosmetics ('They go on better when they're cold, and I kept treading on my favourite lipsticks') and a jar of pickled cucumbers.

Jeane didn't have anything to drink that wasn't water out of the tap but she did have disposable cups ('I don't do washing up') and she hauled herself up to sit on the kitchen worktop while I leaned against the sink and she was right, we probably should talk about this, but I wasn't even sure what I wanted to say. Even Jeane kept opening her mouth to speak then closing it again.

'The thing is, Michael,' she said eventually, 'the thing is that actually you're a really good kisser.'

'There's no need to sound quite so surprised,' I said, and it was hard not to smile. I nodded in her direction. 'You're not too shabby yourself.'

'Yeah, I do have mad kissing skills,' she agreed and this time it was absolutely impossible not to smile. All my other friends were so predictable. Like, I knew exactly what they were going to say before they even opened their mouths and with her, with Jeane Smith, every minute revealed another surprise.

'So, do we carry on with our mutual kissing appreciation thing?' she asked. 'A discreet little arrangement that no one needs to know about?'

I wasn't sure how I felt about that but mostly I think I was relieved. She was a really good kisser, but hanging out with her and having to listen to her diss all my friends, then have all my friends repeatedly ask me why the hell I was hanging out with her wasn't something I could deal with. Still, I couldn't exactly tell Jeane that.

'But if you wanted to hang out at school ... I mean, it's cool if you don't, but isn't it lonely ... that you're always on your own?'

She shook her head and smiled brightly. 'Not really. I hate school but I promised my parents that if they let me live on my own I'd do my A-levels.' She folded her arms. 'It's not as if I'm having any sleepless nights about all the crappy parties I don't get invited to and all the breaktimes when I could be sitting around talking shit about what was on TV last night. I get a lot of my Adorkable work done at school and, apart from Barney, I have *nothing* in common with anyone there so I'm much happier to hang out on my own. You really don't have to feel sorry for me.'

She was making out that she had it all going on but when you were seventeen, going to parties, even crappy ones, was fun, as was talking shit about what was on TV last night. It was what you were meant to be doing, not spending all your time working on a geek-centric media empire.

'Well, it still sounds kind of lonely,' I said and Jeane shrugged.

'It kind of is, and this may come as a surprise to you, but I'm not really a people person.' Jeane smiled at me, a slow, wicked smile, which made me like her a little bit more and also made me relieved that she did actually have a sense of humour. 'I know I hide it pretty well.'

'Well, at least you're a person,' I said. 'So that counts for something.'

'Yeah, at least I got it half right.' She fingered the end of one grey pigtail. 'So, please don't start paying me any attention while we're at school. I'd rather you didn't.'

Another wave of relief threatened to knock me off my feet but I reckoned one more token protest was industry standard. 'Yeah, but . . .'

Jeane held up one imperious hand. 'Honestly, I won't think any less of you if you ignore me at school. In fact, I'll think more of you.'

'So this thing, whatever this thing is, is just between you and me, and it's simply a kissing thing?'

'Well, kissing, and we already do quite a lot of touching but we can take the rest as it comes,' Jeane said. No one in my life was ever this direct. It made everything so much easier.

Anyway, we'd established some ground rules for the kissing and the maybe some touching so there was no good reason not to walk over to Jeane. For once, sitting on the kitchen counter as she was, our faces were level, which meant that I didn't have to lean down and she didn't have to crane her neck when I kissed her.

15

Over the next couple of weeks, I got used to kissing Michael Lee. I even moved on from being freaked out about kissing Michael Lee. Instead, I began to treat kissing Michael Lee as a special karmic reward. Instead of finding a fabulous dress at the very bottom of a basket of £1 T-shirts in a charity shop, or splurging on a box of macaroons from Maison Blanc, I treated myself to some serious kissage with Michael Lee on Monday and Wednesday lunchtimes, after school on Thursday, and we currently had a question mark against Sunday afternoons.

Whatever his other faults were, the boy knew how to kiss. And stroke. And touch. And *grind* just a little bit. Every time I saw his face with those wide-spaced almond-shaped eyes already closed and his pretty lips pursed in a perfect kiss-shape (and his cheekbones ... someone should write a poem about his cheekbones – oh, that's right, someone already has) coming towards me in pursuit of a kiss, all I could think was that this couldn't be happening to me. Because I was me and not even my mother (well, especially not my mother) could pretend that I was pretty or loveable or had a winning personality or was in any way the kind of girl who got the kind of boys that looked like Michael Lee. We didn't match, we weren't suited, and we didn't go together.

The rightness and the wrongness of it was all I could think about one Sunday morning about two weeks into our little kissing experiment when I should have been giving my full attention to dyeing my hair. I'd decided that the time had come to get rid of the grey. Now that my mousy roots were coming through, it looked all upside-down. Besides, I'd had grey hair for two months, which was for ever, and it was time for a change.

Ben had warned me that I needed bleach to get the grey out and he'd got me supplies from the hairdressing salon, as his boss had said that she didn't want me in her shop ever again. He'd also written a detailed list of instructions with lots of shouty caps about how the 'BLEACH CAN ONLY STAY ON FOR THIRTY MINUTES, JEANE, OTHERWISE YOUR HAIR WILL FALL OUT. ESPECIALLY AFTER WHAT HAPPENED LAST TIME. SET THE ALARM ON YOUR PHONE, NOW! HAVE YOU SET IT? GO AND DO IT.' Ben had only been working in a salon for ten weeks but he'd already become very, very dictatorial about haircare.

I tried to follow Ben's instructions but he wanted me to section off my hair and use tinfoil and in the end it was easier just to slap the bleach on and fashion myself a tinfoil turban after I set my phone alarm. The bleach stung my scalp and made my eyes water so it was very hard to watch a documentary about last summer's Rock 'n' Roll Camp for Girls. I'd run workshops on making zines and websites, and how to build up rock 'n' roll star-sized self-esteem. It had been a blast but I winced as I suddenly appeared on screen in a Wonder Woman T-shirt and started blathering on about being ... I don't even know what pearls of wisdom were falling from my mouth because all I could hear was my own drone of a voice. Even when I was really excited and I could tell that I had been really excited because I kept making jabbing motions with my hands, I sounded as if I was about to fall into a boredom coma.

I was saved from having to witness any more of my documentary fail by a bang on the door. I had ten minutes left before I could wash the bleach out, rinse my hair with some special gunk and then apply toner, so I needed to get rid of whoever it was. Though, as it was Sunday morning, it was probably God-botherers wanting to know if I'd accepted Jesus Christ as my personal Lord and saviour, which I *so* hadn't. Mrs Hunter-Down on the ground floor was always letting them in.

'Well?' I said as I opened the door, hoping that my scowl and my tinfoil helmet would make any evangelists think twice about giving me the hard sell, but I needn't have bothered because it was Gustav and Harry from next door and neither of them knew the meaning of the word no.

'New look for you, Jeane,' Harry boomed, as he pushed past me. 'Love it. Really brings out your blue eyes. It's your lucky day, we've got cleaning supplies and we're not leaving until we can see your carpet again.'

'It's not that untidy,' I protested, which was a shameless lie because even the area by the front door was littered with unopened post and flyers and takeaway menus.

'We've also brought vegetables,' Gustav said as he stepped through the door with a steely glint in his eyes. 'I am going to make you eat them and drink a glass of milk. You're at a crucial stage in your development when you need calcium.'

'I'm not going to grow any taller than this,' I cried, even though I knew it was useless. Gustav was Austrian and a personal trainer. Once he'd made his mind up about something, whether it was making me eat steamed broccoli (urgh, hack, hack, hack) or persuading lovely, smiley Harry, his Australian boyfriend, that they needed to come round and force me to throw out half my worldy goods, resistance was futile. 'Can there be chocolate powder in the glass of milk, Gustav? Can there?'

'That would be like letting you eat raw sugar,' Gustav said with a shudder, his muscles rippling in revulsion. 'We'll start here.' He thrust three bin bags at me. 'Recycling, rubbish and stuff that you absolutely can't live without.'

I knew from bitter experience that Gustav and I had very different ideas about the definition of stuff I couldn't live without. 'I hate you,' I told them both fiercely. 'I hate it when you do your gay dads routine.'

'Oh, secretly you love it,' Harry said, darting near like he was going to pick me up and swing me round, which he did occasionally, even though I told him it was demeaning and infantilising, which it was, even if it was also secretly thrilling. 'We'll put some Lady Gaga on to pass the time.'

'Yes,' Gustav added. 'It will be fun.'

It wasn't fun. Gustav wouldn't know fun if it came with a government health warning. And anyway, fun wasn't the right word to describe Harry trying to put all my Japanese style magazines in the recycling when he thought I wasn't looking and Gustav giving me a running commentary about mildew and mould and what they'd do to my pink, perfectly formed teenage lungs as he supervised me cleaning the shower stall.

Gustav refused to believe that my colour processing was at a crucial stage and wouldn't let me get the bleach out of my hair until the bathroom was squeaky clean. Even though I explained, through the medium of yelling, that he was condemning me to baldness the longer the bleach stayed on my head, he remained immoveable – quite literally, as he ripped me away from the showerhead. Gustav works out for a living and I don't so there was no way I could win. He also reminded me of several other times when I'd come up with similar excuses to get out of scrubbing the grouting. I was totes the girl who cried wolf.

Eventually the bathroom was deemed clean even by Gustav's ridiculously high standards and he gave me permission to wash the bleach out. By this stage it was rock-hard and it took both of us and the whole bottle of special gunk until my hair felt vaguely hair-like again.

'It's meant to be that colour, yes?' Gustav queried as he roughly towel-dried my hair. He probably wasn't as into the cleaning as he claimed he was, because he was more than happy to dump most of the heavy scouring on Harry while he helped me. 'It's very, er . . . what is the word?'

'I'm aiming for mid-blonde at this stage.' I sighed. 'Then we'll chuck on some toner and make it platinum.'

'Yes, well, it's always good to have goals,' Gustav agreed and when I tried to straighten up he kept his hand on my shoulder. 'No, stay there. I'll put this toner on for you.'

Normally I wouldn't let anyone boss me around the way that Gustav did but if it got me out of cleaning then it was a win. Especially now I was sure that Harry wasn't in the lounge and trying to throw out my precious, precious books and magazines and backs of envelopes where I'd written important things, but had moved on to the kitchen where he was bellowing 'Bad Romance' at the top of his lungs and there was no way that he would throw out my Haribo stash. Not if he liked living.

Although I was going to have backache from bending over so my head and shoulders were in the shower stall, it was quite nice to have Gustav's strong, muscly fingers working the toner in while he wittered on about his marathon training. Gustav actually flew to other countries to take part in marathons because he wasn't right in the head.

'The toner needs to come off now,' Gustav announced. 'This platinum blonde, did you have your heart set on it?'

'Kind of. Ben said it might take a bit more toner.'

'Maybe a *lot* more toner,' Gustav said, and he didn't sound very confident in my hair's abilities to reach the exact same shade as Madonna, Lady Gaga and Courtney Love back when she hadn't been quite so batshit insane as she was now. 'Still, is good to have goals.'

'Why? What colour is my bloody hair?'

'Back in Austria when I was a boy if I'd spoken to my mother all snappy like that she'd have washed my mouth out with soap.'

'What fricking colour is my hair, Gustav?' I demanded, wrenching myself free of his grip, drops of water splattering everywhere but mostly over Gustav, who moaned in protest.

Thanks to my earlier efforts with a damp cloth, the mirror was sparkling and there was nothing to dull the colour of my hair. My bright, fluoro, neon, is-that-the-core-of-a-nuclear-reactor-no-it's-just-Jeane's-head orange hair. I love orange as much as the next person, probably even more. I have a lot of time for orange. Orange tights. Orange jelly sweets. I have even been known, on occasion, to eat an actual orange, but on my head: no, no, a world of utter NO.

I have attitude in huge quantities but I didn't have the complexion and strong features necessary to carry off such a blaze of colour. Gustav certainly agreed with me 'You look like one of those troll dolls,' he mused. 'They were very big in Austria.'

'This is all your fault! If you'd let me wash the bleach off instead of making me clean then this would never have happened.'

'Oh God, what is that on your head?' Harry asked from the doorway and then he started laughing so hard that he had to sit down on the floor.

Even Gustav was smirking and there was only one thing I could do, which was grab my iPhone, take a scowling picture of myself and tweet my Twitter followers:

 adork_able Jeane Smith
Hair emergency! Already bleached & toned, can I put more dye on or do I have to shave it off?

I'd pretty much reconciled myself to a grade-one as Gustav began to assemble a foul-smelling broccoli bake, but Twitter came to my rescue. The general consensus was that I needed to buy some hair dye that was as close to my natural colour as possible, then set up a shrine to my favourite personal gods and pray for a positive outcome.

I was just on the verge of ordering Harry to leg it to Boots before it shut when I got a text from Michael: *Is it OK to come round or are you busy working on your masterplans for total dork domination?*

Just this once, I decided to let his snarking go unmentioned. It wasn't important. What was important was briefing him on the catastrophe that had befallen me and sending him a link to the hair dye he was going to purchase on the way over.

I tried to get rid of Gustav and Harry before Michael arrived but it proved impossible. Harry insisted that I went through all the piles he'd made and put at least half of them in the recycling and Gustav wanted to force-feed me green leafy things that he swore were vegetables but tasted like pond slime. As it was, when Michael knocked on the door, they were still working my very last, most tattered nerve, and sorting out the rest of the garbage sacks to be chucked down the rubbish chute.

'I'm in the middle of something,' I said to Michael as I opened the door. 'And by the middle of something, I mean planning the grisly murder of my two gay dads.'

Michael swallowed hard. 'If I've caught you at a bad time ...'

'We're just leaving,' Gustav snapped from somewhere behind

me, then he dared to shove me out of the door. 'After we see Jeane put at least five black bags down the rubbish chute.'

It wasn't as humiliating as, say, the time I turned up to DJ at a club in Shoreditch, misjudged the clientele and cleared the dancefloor three times by sticking on choons that were deemed far too tuneful to actually dance to. Goddamn hipsters.

Anyways, I could have done without an audience as I lugged seven (seven!) huge black sacks down the rubbish chute. Then I had to introduce Michael to Gustav and Harry. I hadn't been planning to, but Harry clamped his arm around my shoulders and said, 'So, Jeane Genie, are you going to introduce us to your little friend?'

I wasn't sure how to describe Michael to them. Gustav was ridiculously over-protective about gentleman callers. When I'd been seeing a French boy called Cedric (mostly because he was French and called Cedric), Gustav had come round at one in the morning and ordered Cedric off the premises, even though he was about six months too late to prevent the technical loss of my virginity. He'd even subjected Barney to his squinty-eyed, lock-jawed disapproval, though Barney had suffered a fit of the vapours just from touching one of my boobs over three layers of clothing.

Now he was staring at Michael with icy blue eyes like he'd recently seen his name on the Sex Offenders Register. 'This is Michael Lee,' I said. 'He's come round with hair dye so I can salvage the damage that's all your fault, Gustav. And Michael, this is Gustav and Harry who live next door and are the bane of my existence.' Attack is *always* the very best form of defence.

The three of them nodded at each other, then Harry drawled, 'Michael, what are your intentions towards our Jeane? I hope they're honourable.'

'Um, they're very honourable,' Michael muttered, holding a paper bag aloft. 'I really have brought hair dye.'

Gustav sniffed dubiously. 'It's a school night, so ...'

'It's five in the afternoon, Gustav!'

'... don't stay too late,' he continued. 'Harry and I are meant to be going out for dinner, though we're both exhausted. You're very tiring, Jeane.'

I pulled a face but decided to let that one slide. 'Thank you for bossing me to within an inch of my life,' I simpered, but the hug that I gave both of them was heartfelt. Not that I was appreciative of the enforced tidying or the ingestion of vegetables but I was glad that they cared enough to get all up in my domestic business.

Finally Gustav and Harry were in the lift and Michael was standing in my hall and blinking in wonder. 'You have floor,' he commented faintly. 'Actual floor and a sideboard.' He wandered into the living room. 'It's funny but the place looks much bigger now that it's not totally covered in pizza boxes and crap.'

He was right but the flat being bigger wasn't necessarily a good thing. 'So, hair dye?' I prompted and he threw the bag at me. I dropped it, retrieved it from the floor and pulled out a box of ash-blonde hair dye. It made my heart sink but girls with neon-orange hair couldn't be choosers.

'There's a disgusting vegetable bake in the kitchen if you want some,' I told Michael, but he shook his head and squinched up his face.

'Sounds delicious but I think I'll pass,' he said, and I wasn't sure if he was going to stick around or if I wanted him to but he gestured at the towel that was wrapped around my hair. 'Let's see it then.'

With a put-upon air I whipped off the towel.

'God! Wow! It's much brighter than I thought it would be.'

'Too bright.'

'You like things that are too bright,' Michael said, looking at the blue and white polka dot playsuit I was wearing with pink tights. 'It's almost the same colour as those tights that got ruined when I . . . when . . . you know . . .'

'When you *accidentally* tipped me off my bike?'

He nodded. 'Yeah, those ones.'

'Tights are one thing. You can take tights off, but I can't take off my hair and I'm not going to be in the mood to have bright orange hair every day,' I explained. 'Anyway, if you're staying, you can help me.'

Michael wasn't any help at all. He just sat on the edge of the bathtub and helpfully pointed out when I got splodges of hair dye over the white tiles I'd just scrubbed, but he did go out to get me a coffee while we waited half an hour for the colour to process and helped me wash all the murky brown-coloured dye out of my hair, though he did bitch about getting splashed. He even went to the kitchen to get me some Haribo as I deep-conditioned because my energy levels were flagging.

'Oh God,' he said when he returned with a bag of Cola Twists. 'Bloody hell, Jeane. You can't dye it three times in one afternoon. It will fall out.'

I'd been too busy towel-drying my hair to worry about the

colour but now I was seriously worried. I was one worry away from having a complete meltdown.

'Don't say that! Don't look at me like that.' His eyes were so wide with horror that I thought they might slip out of their sockets. 'It's brown, isn't it? A boring, muddy, drab, blah brown. Brown hair! I don't deserve brown hair.'

'Oh, shut up and stop being such a drama queen,' Michael snapped at me. 'Anyway it's not brown. You'll wish it was.'

I steeled myself to take off the sodden towel that I'd draped shawl-like over my head when Michael had started doing a good impersonation of the Harbinger of Doom. I turned to face the mirror, shut my eyes and removed my head covering. Then I opened my eyes and . . .

'Oh! Oh! Oh, well, it doesn't look *that* bad.'

Michael groaned as if he was in great pain. 'Your hair is the same colour as peach yoghurt.'

'Or apricot yoghurt.' I stared in wonder at my hair, which was a creamy, pastel orangey, pinky, peachy shade that I could totally work with. 'Now this is much better. This is a neutral.'

'In what world is *that* colour a neutral?' Michael demanded.

'In *my* world, boring boy,' I rapped back, but my heart wasn't in it. I much preferred to gaze at my new hair in the mirror. It looked kinda French and I decided that I might experiment with pinning it up and possibly investing in a tiara. And maybe a foofy skirt with another foofy skirt over it and why not a big flouncy net petticoat under both of them?

I love the endless possibility that comes from changing your hair colour. Now that I didn't have grey hair, I didn't want to dress like a little old lady any more but like a Fifties prom queen on mild-altering drugs. There was definitely a blog post in there: Hair or Flair – which comes first?

'I like it. I really, really like it,' I said decisively. Michael was still acting as if it hurt to look at me. 'At least you're spared the humiliation of being seen out in public with a girl with peach-coloured hair.'

'Well, there is that,' he agreed, and then he was by my side so he could run his fingers through my damp hair and I didn't know what this strange, intoxicating pull was but all he had to do was touch me and I began to wonder how long it would be before we were done with talking and could get to kissing. 'But I don't mind being with you in private.'

'That works for me,' I said, and Michael was staring at my mouth so I was self-conscious about how my lips moved as I was talking but I think he wanted to kiss me too. 'Shall we move this to the sofa?'

We'd never kissed lying down before, probably because usually we were either at school or there was so much stuff on the sofa that lying down wasn't an option. For once we weren't craning and stretching to kiss standing up, or bodies twisted at awkward angles to kiss sitting down, but lying on the sofa, legs tangled together, and we could concentrate on the kissing.

It was such good kissing that it deserved to be savoured. He tasted of tea and tangy cola sweets and every time we stopped kissing, because we needed that pesky thing called oxygen, Michael Lee would sigh. Sad-sounding sighs and I didn't want to think about why he might be sad so I'd kiss him again and because he was Michael Lee, he didn't freak out when he realised his hand was on my breast for the first time but kept it there. It wasn't just a motionless hand clamped to my boob either, he was stroking and pressing and finally unbuttoning my playsuit, which was sodden and chafing me from being continuously soaked with water throughout the afternoon.

But the stroking and the pressing and the unbuttoning all seemed a bit one-sided and what was the point of kissing Michael Lee on your sofa if you didn't get to see what all the fuss was about? What made the other girls short of breath and weak at the knees? Besides, I was only too happy to rid him of his American Eagle T-shirt, because his allegiance to faux-heritage American brands offended my eyes and my sensibilities.

Up until then I thought I was in control of myself and the kisses, but with all that caramel-coloured skin rubbing against me, it was impossible not to wriggle and writhe and maybe even shimmy until Michael's hand slid under my bra and I could feel his hard-on digging into me.

'I think we need to stop,' I whispered and I don't think he heard me because he was biting my ear and pushing against me, but then he stilled.

'We should stop,' he said and he rolled right off the sofa, and by the time I'd buttoned my playsuit back up he was sitting on the floor, back against the sofa, trying to reassemble his stupid hairdo. 'Sorry. Didn't mean to let things go that far.'

I wasn't sure what *that* was supposed to mean. Like, he was down with the kissing and the touching but he'd been repulsed by what he'd seen now that we'd moved on to partial removal of clothes? Or because he was the boy he got to make all the kissing-related decisions? Or that he was going to do a Barney and freak out about touching my breasts?

'You weren't the only one on that sofa,' I said, and he looked at me in surprise at my sharp tone. 'I was cool with it and when I wasn't cool with it, I decided it was time to stop. Please don't start having second thoughts while I'm in the same room because it makes me feel like shit.'

'I didn't mean it like that,' he said quickly, then turned round so I could see him looking all stricken and pained. 'Just we don't know each other that well and we don't know where this thing of ours is going and I don't want you thinking that I'm taking advantage of the situation.'

Michael was right – he didn't know me at all. 'You're not taking advantage of me because I won't let you,' I told him sternly. 'If you try something that I'm not down with then believe me, I'll make sure you get the message.'

'Yeah, well, I didn't mean that—'

'And same goes for you,' I continued, just so we were clear. 'If I bust out a move that you're not cool with, you need to tell me.'

Michael didn't say anything for a long time. Long enough that I started to freak out a little, then he smiled. 'You're not like any other girl I know.'

'So, is that a good or bad thing?' I asked slowly, though I wasn't sure that I wanted to know the answer.

'Most of the time it's more good than bad. And sometimes it's very, very good,' he said in a drawly voice and I swear he went a bit misty-eyed so I didn't need to carry on freaking out.

'OK then.' I settled back on the sofa and watched Michael as he absent-mindedly picked up the flyer that went with the DVD I'd been watching of the Rock 'n' Roll Camp for Girls.

'Isn't this the girl from Duckie? Polly . . . '

'Molly,' I corrected him and I had to bite my lip to stop myself from shrieking that Duckie and Molly were mine, all mine, and nothing to do with him. 'Her name's Molly.'

'Right, yeah. I heard some of their songs on 6Music, then I downloaded their album off iTunes. Did you know she used to be in The Hormones?'

It was kinda sweet but also very annoying that he was trying to bring me up to speed on the career of someone who I'd been on 'Hi, how are you?' terms with for the last three years, and after last summer when I'd hung out with her every day for a month and had even baked cupcakes with her and let her sleep on the very sofa that Michael and I had romped on, I could probably call her a friend. 'Yes, I did know that.'

'They're playing next Saturday. A whole bunch of us are going. Should be really good if you want to . . . ' Michael ground to a halt as he realised that asking me to go to a gig with a whole bunch of sad-sack people from school, who were only just jumping on the Duckie bandwagon even though they'd been going for years, violated the rules of our mutual privacy pact. 'So, yeah, should be cool.'

'Well, I'm going anyway,' I said casually, because it was better that I just told him, rather than him being caught by surprise and blurting something out and us getting discovered by half the school. I wasn't going to tell him that I was on the guest list though. It sounded way too much like bragging. 'Like, I'm going to shoot some interviews for the blog before the show and I'm meeting people there. Some of them I know from Twitter, so I guess they don't count as real people.'

'Jeane? Piss off.' Michael reached round to pinch my toe. 'Don't get all confrontational and belligerent with me because it doesn't really have any effect on me any more. Not now I've seen you getting proper told off by your two gay dads.'

I scowled at the back of his head. 'You tell anyone about that ...'

'You'll what? Call me out on Twitter? Write a mean blog about me? Then everyone will know our secret.' He turned round again. This time it was so I could get the benefit of his smug smile and it wasn't worth arguing about. Not when I planned to send him to the kitchen to bring me another bag of Haribo in the next ten minutes.

So, although it went against everything I believed in, I actually let Michael Lee have the last word.

16

I didn't see much of Jeane during the following week. She couldn't make any of our usual lunchtime sessions and on Thursday afternoon when I usually gave her a lift to a little backstreet five minutes from school so I could snog her face off (well, I had the last two Thursdays), she sidled up to me in the staff car park.

'Have to take a rain check, I'm afraid,' she announced cheerfully. 'I've got to go into town to pick up a video camera and my friend Tabitha has got a new consignment of vintage clothes and I've got first dibs.' She shook her head. 'Creating a new look is *such* hard work but maybe we can hook up over the weekend, but not Saturday. Anyway it's half-term next week so we can get together then, though I have to go into town for all the meetings I couldn't do because of school.' She finally paused to allow some air into her lungs and fix me with a fierce look. 'You're not really going to the Duckie gig, are you? It was just a wind up, right?'

Wrong. I'd bought my ticket *and* been charged an extra two quid for the booking fee. 'Yes, I'm going,' I ground out. 'You don't have a monopoly on the whole cool thing.'

She snorted. 'Yeah, right. Whatever. I'll see you around.'

I watched her pedal off, then stop to adjust her head covering. Jeane was yet to debut her peach-coloured hair because she wanted to assemble her new look first. In the meantime she'd wrapped a huge piece of brightly patterned material round her head and had got into a fight in English when the person sitting behind her couldn't see the whiteboard and Jeane had refused to remove her towering headgear.

In a way, you kind of had to admire her tenacity to go all out for the sake of her dodgy fashion choices and, in another way ... well, it had been a good two months with Scarlett before I realised I'd made a terrible mistake. With Jeane, it had only taken two weeks. Any fool could see (if they'd even known that we were 'together') that we were destined for disaster. Big, bad disaster. I didn't know when it would happen but I knew it would happen soon.

The feeling of impending doom was still there on Saturday evening when I met up with the gang in Nandos for some pre-gig peri-peri chicken. I was dreading going to the gig because Jeane would be there and maybe it would be obvious to everyone that we'd been getting off with each other whenever she could find a window in her busy schedule. Or I'd get dragged into some kind of Jeane-related drama. Or maybe she'd snub me completely, which would be for the best, but still the thought of Jeane giving me her most withering look (she could

157

kill an entire rainforest with one sweep of her lashes) was putting me off my double chicken burger.

Actually, that was a lie. What was putting me off my grub was Heidi, who kept rubbing her leg against mine in a really determined fashion as she tried to convince me to have everyone back to mine after the gig. Mum and Dad were in Devon to drop Melly and Alice off at the grandparents' for half-term week and weren't due back until late Sunday evening, but there was no way that I was going to invite a bunch of people over so they could drink themselves stupid, break stuff and vom.

'It's not going to happen,' I told Heidi for the fifth time but she just rubbed my leg harder and pouted.

'You're no fun, Michael,' she said and I caught the sideways look she gave Scarlett, who shrugged and raised her eyebrows so I guessed that Heidi coming on to me was sanctioned by my ex-girlfriend. Sometimes it seemed that we just all hung round in the same little group and swapped boyfriends and girl-friends. In fact the only new face in our crowd was Barney, which should have been awkward but wasn't.

He'd cut his hair so I could see his face, which was trained on Scarlett most of the time. They were a bit moony-eyed together but when he got the special salt on his chips, which she didn't like, he teased her out of her snit. Had to give the guy props for that. Then we realised that we'd both been at three of the same gigs in the last few months and maybe there was more to Barney than just someone who'd nicked my girl-friend.

It was natural to fall into step with him and Scarlett as we walked down the road to the venue, which was a converted ballroom. 'My grandparents did their courting here,' Barney confessed with a grin as we left the girls putting their stuff in the cloakroom and headed for the bar. Hanging over the dance-floor was the largest chandelier I'd ever seen, the stage had been set up at the far end and around the floor and tucked into little alcoves were tables and chairs.

Ant and Martin managed to grab a spare table while we got the drinks. The girls still weren't back – they'd probably gone to the loo to check the make-up that they'd checked ten minutes before in the Nando's loos. 'Right,' Ant said, lifting up his plastic pint glass of lager. 'Shall we neck these then start a mosh pit going?'

There were general murmurs of agreement but Barney shook his head. 'You can't. Not at a Duckie gig. It's a girls-only mosh pit.'

'Are you rinsing me?'

'Nope. There was a sign as we came in.' Barney spread his hands wide. 'If you try to get in the mosh pit you'll be pulled out by security. Actually, that's the best-case scenario.'

'What's the worst-case scenario?' I asked.

'You'll be savaged by hordes of moshing Duckie fangirls and be lucky to escape with your life,' Barney said. 'Anyway, it's kinda cool that the girls can dance and jump around without having to worry about some meathead trying to grope them, right?'

When he put it like that, it made perfect sense, but Martin just shook his head. 'Dude, you went out with that freak of nature for far too long.'

'She's not a freak of nature,' Barney snapped, his face

reddening. 'She's a bit ... well ... out there, but she's cool. Coolest person I'll ever know.'

It made me like Barney even more that he'd stick up for his ex. Not that Jeane needed anyone to defend her: if she'd been there and heard what Martin had called her, she'd probably have slapped him. As it was, Martin was backing down. 'Sorry, mate. It's just, like, wasn't she a bit much?'

'Oh, yeah. She was too bloody much,' Barney agreed with a faint smile.

We'd been there for twenty minutes now and all this talk of Jeane made me suddenly scan the room nervously, but all I saw were the girls coming towards us.

'OMG,' breathed Heidi as she plonked herself down on my lap. We were a couple of chairs short but she was coming on *way* too strong. Still, I couldn't push her off without causing a scene. 'We've just seen Jeane Smith. You won't believe what she's wearing.'

'And she's changed her hair,' added Mads. 'It's not grey any more. It looks like that Barry M nail polish you were going to get, Scar.'

Scar agreed that it was similar and then all four of them craned their necks and I followed their gaze to the merchandise stall where Jeane was standing with a little gaggle of girls around her.

She looked ... You know what? There aren't really any words to describe how she looked. Her hair was teased and back-combed and set off with a tiara and she was wearing a ballgown. Not a pouffy prom dress, but a humungous ballgown, which was bluey-green or one of those colours like turquoise or aquamarine that I'm not really sure about, and made out of some mysterious stuff like taffeta or shot silk or, well, recycled carrier bags. But what really looked different about Jeane wasn't that hair or the super-glam, over the top outfit, but the smile on her face.

Jeane looked happy, like she'd won the lottery and they'd transferred the cash into Haribo. I'd never seen her look like that. It suited her.

I tried not to keep sneaking glances at Jeane as she fussed around with a camcorder and interviewed people. When she wasn't doing that, she was totally working the room. Each time she took a step, she seemed to bump into someone she knew and would have to stop for hugs and kisses and excited chatter. It was a whole new side to her.

'Who do you keep looking at?' Heidi asked me crossly.

I turned my head away from Jeane so quickly I almost got whiplash. 'No one,' I muttered.

Heidi sniffed. 'FYI, if you're going to ask a girl to sit on your lap then it's blates rude to ignore her.'

'Don't remember him asking you to plonk your arse down,' Martin said, then they gave each other the stink-eye because there was history and all of Heidi's weight was centred on my right thigh, which was going numb, so I didn't even realise that Jeane was coming over until she was standing right in front of me.

'Scarlett,' she said. Scarlett looked at her warily. 'Scarlett, can I borrow Barney's brain for a second?'

'Well, yeah. Course you can.'

I forgot that sometimes Jeane could be thoughtful and

considerate. That instead of texting Barney and summoning him, she'd come over to a table of people she didn't like to check that it was OK with Scarlett before she thrust her video camera at Barney.

'It's on loan,' she explained, crouching down so she could point at the screen. 'And it's all digital and not like my clunky old one. I zoomed in and now I can't zoom out. What button should I be pressing?'

'I don't suppose you brought the instruction manual with you?'

Jeane rolled her eyes. 'Barney, why do you ask questions that you already know the answers to?'

Barney grumbled and gave her the finger but then he bent his head and studied the camera. Jeane swept a glance around the table then took out her phone and, I guess, decided to tweet this thrilling part of her evening. Then I felt my phone vibrate.

'Heidi, could you go and find a chair ... Or, look, have my chair.' She was forced to get off my lap as I stood up and retrieved my phone from my back pocket to read a text from Jeane.

Are u & Hilda/Heidi/whatever her name is together?
U should hv said

Really? *Really?* This thing between us was weird and freaky but it was still a thing and that meant I didn't do other things with other girls.

NO! I texted back. Wish Heidi would get the message.

But Jeane had tucked her phone away so she could crouch

down next to Barney. 'I don't care about auto-focus,' she told him. 'Just explain how to zoom.'

'But Jeane . . . !'

'Barney! I'm shooting vox pops, not recreating *Inception* shot for shot.'

They stayed in a huddle for a while, heads touching, not that Scarlett seemed to mind. She was talking to Mads and Anjula about taking a road trip to Brighton. Only Heidi kept glaring at Jeane's bent head.

'Why are you spazzing around with a camcorder?' she asked really aggressively when Jeane finally straightened up.

'Well, I'm asking girls and people who identify as girls what they like most about being a girl,' Jeane said flatly.

Heidi folded her arms. 'Why the hell would you want to do that?'

I had no idea why she was being such a bitch. Jeane didn't have time for anyone at school and they treated her a bit like a circus sideshow, but there was never open hostility. Not until now, anyway. Even Scarlett felt moved to mutter warningly, 'Hey, Heids, back off.'

'It's for a charity that works with young girls to promote self-esteem and body positivity,' Jeane explained. Her voice was so monotone that it was like listening to a Dalek. 'The video clips are going to be part of a viral campaign.'

'What*ever*. Sounds well boring,' Heidi drawled and I wondered if she suspected that there was something between Jeane and me, especially as she seemed to think she had a prior claim. But how could she? We'd been so sneaky. 'Your new look is, like, literally making my eyes bleed.'

Martin made a long-suffering face. 'What kind of bitchery is this, Heidi?' he asked. 'Are you on the blob again? Seems to roll round every week.'

Jeane didn't need anyone to fight her battles. 'I'll send you the link to the videos once they're online,' she told Heidi. 'They might help you with that insecurity that makes you lash out at other girls.' She held up the camera. 'Or you could do a vox pop. You might find it empowering.'

Heidi slunk down in her chair. 'I'm totes empowered,' she said sulkily. 'Anyway now that you know how to turn that stupid thing on, could you, like, go? We were having a private conversation.'

To their credit, Anjula, Mads and Scarlett all glared at her. 'We weren't,' Anjula said. 'Your dress is mad sick.'

Jeane shook out the folds of her ginormous puffy skirt and before she could say anything, or, God forbid, start bonding with my friends, a scruffy man in a suit and a pork-pie hat came hurrying over and suddenly burst into song . . .

'*Jeane, the low life has lost its appeal and I'm tired of . . .* looking for you everywhere!' he finished in a broad Mancunian accent then scooped her up in an enthusiastic hug. 'We're all upstairs on the balcony.'

'Hey, Tom,' Jeane said, struggling to free herself. 'I have to finish doing my interviews but I'll be up before Duckie come on.'

'Ah, that reminds me,' Tom said, tapping his nose as he pulled an envelope out of an inside pocket. 'Backstage pass and aftershow tickets, and Molly wants to know if it's still OK to crash on your sofa.'

Jeane pulled a face. 'As long as she doesn't start moaning about my housekeeping skills. She called me a dirty slut last time she stayed over.'

'Because she realised she'd been using an old pizza box as a pillow,' Tom said, and his arm was round Jeane's shoulders and she was being led away and when she turned and looked over her shoulder with a half wave, it could have been at any of us.

'That's Molly as in lead singer of Duckie Molly?' Mads asked. Everyone turned to look at Barney for clarification. 'Jeane's friends with Duckie?'

'I suppose. Molly does a rock 'n' roll summer camp for girls and Jeane ran some workshops for it.' Barney waved a hand dismissively. 'Don't start spreading it around or Jeane will kick my arse. She tries to keep her work stuff and her school stuff completely separate.'

Everyone nodded except Heidi. 'Why are we still talking about that horrible little troll? She made you cry, Scar, and she called you a retard.'

'Oh, we sorted all that out,' Scarlett said. 'And she was cool about me and Barney so stop giving her such a hard time.'

In the short while that she'd been going out with Barney, Scarlett had turned into a whole new girl. A girl who answered back and stood up for herself and a girl who was at least ten times the girl she was when she'd been going out with me, like I'd been holding her back or something.

'She's completely evil and she smells of dead people's clothes.'

'But, secretly, aren't you a little bit obsessed with her?' Mads asked. 'I always look to see what she's wearing every morning and, sorry, I'm kind of wanting to talk some more about her new look.'

'Me too,' Anjula said, switching her phone on. 'And now I'm kind of wanting to tweet about her being BFF with Duckie.'

'Oh God, I'm going if all you're going to do is talk about Jeane Smith for the rest of the evening,' Heidi snarled. I had to agree with her.

I was even thinking of pleading a headache and going home but then the first band came on and it was Barney's round and by the time the second support band came on, I was in a much better mood, though I could have done without Heidi clinging to me as we struggled through the crowd to get nearer to the stage.

Jeane hadn't replied to my text but she was tweeting throughout the evening and just as she told her followers:

 adork_able Jeane Smith
Here come Duckie sashaying on stage.
There's not many bands that sound like
Duckie. Come on, Molly, give it to us good.

Heidi tugged at my arm.

'Michael, we really need to talk,' she shouted as Duckie launched into their first song. 'Like, now!'

'Look, we'll talk after the gig.'

'No, now,' Heidi insisted, and when I turned to scowl at her I realised she was crying, or she was scrunching up her face, eyebrows almost touching, and her bottom lip was wobbling as if she was about to cry.

I had no choice but to leave the crowded dancefloor so we could find an empty table and listen as Heidi told me that: 'I thought we had something so why have you been harshing me all evening?'

Of course I denied all knowledge of harshing her and then I had to do the whole, 'We're good mates, let's not spoil that,' which Heidi wasn't buying. Then I said that I'd never really got over Hannah, which was true, and that I was still a bit wary after what had happened with Scarlett, which wasn't even a little bit true but by now Heidi had managed to squeeze out an actual tear, so I said that I didn't have time to get into a relationship because I needed to concentrate on my A-level studies, which was complete and utter bollocks.

Heidi brought the drama. We'd got off with each other maybe three times almost two years ago so she had no real reason to sob and pant and say that she was having a panic attack though it was the feeblest panic attack that this doctor's son has ever seen (and why have all the girls suddenly started having panic attacks and hyperventilating like it's the cool new thing?) but she went for it anyway. I had to go and get her some water and hunt down a paper bag. If I'd had even the tiniest bit of interest in Heidi then her antics tonight killed it stone-cold dead.

None of the crying had smudged Heidi's make-up but I'd just about calmed her down when the music stopped, the house-lights went up and apparently the show was over. As soon as the others emerged from the crowd, dishevelled, sweaty and glowing, Heidi started crying again. It was the kind of faux crying that Alice did when she'd been thwarted in her attempts to blag chocolate, but the other girls fell for it and there was lots of hugging and, 'Oh, Heidi's.

Predictably, Heidi stormed off and, with reproachful looks at me, Mads, Scarlett and Anjula stormed off after her.

'What was that about?' Ant asked.

'I hate it when girls get all pushy,' I said. 'Anyone would think we'd been together for five years and had a couple of kids from the way Heidi was acting like a total mentaller.'

'Aw, poor Mikey. It must be such an ordeal to have girls throwing themselves at you.'

'Piss off!'

Ant slung an arm round my shoulders. 'Shall we get a drink somewhere before we head off?'

I shook my head. The evening had been a total shambles so it was best to cut my losses before it got even worse. 'Nah, I'm going home.'

I started going home. I even made it to the bus stop when my phone beeped with a text message.

Hey. Aftershow at The White Horse. Meet me outside the M&S opposite or be incredibly boring instead.

It wasn't as if Jeane was drama-free but her dramas were completely different to other girl-related dramas and I couldn't justify it any further than that. Instead I was retracing my steps past the venue, taking a left, then a right, and there was Jeane standing outside Marks & Spencer with a smile on her face like she was pleased to see me.

17

There was something different about Michael Lee, I thought as he walked towards me. I couldn't quite put my finger on it, then he passed under a streetlight and he wasn't wearing one of his awful fake-distressed shirts with the logo of an over-priced US chain store on it. He was wearing a long-sleeved white tee with a green short-sleeved tee over it, leather jacket and skinny black jeans, and while his outfit was unimaginative and yawnsome, at least he wasn't going to completely show me up.

The other thing that was different about him was that he was smiling at me. Like he was pleased to see me. Totes bizarre.

When he reached me, I could tell that he didn't know whether a hug or a kiss would be appropriate given our unique situation. I saved him the effort by holding out my hand.

'Jeane Smith, pleased you could make it.'

He grinned. 'Michael Lee. I've heard a lot about you,' he

said as he shook my hand. 'Your tweeting of the show, by the way, was a lifesaver.'

'But you were there. You were experiencing Duckie in all their fully-faceted, physical glory,' I exclaimed as we crossed over the road. 'You didn't need to read about it on Twitter. Anyway, I thought you didn't do Twitter. Do you follow me on Twitter then?'

Michael's smile faltered. 'I said I didn't get Twitter, but I needed the distraction tonight – and your play-by-play tweets, because I didn't get to see much of Duckie,' he muttered. 'There was a thing with Heidi ...'

Michael possibly following me on Twitter to scrutinise my tweets and find out if I was talking shit about him (which I wasn't) didn't seem that important any more. 'A thing with Heidi? Oh, yeah?'

'Don't be like that,' he sighed, giving me a little shove so I nearly fell off the kerb. 'I've been getting it from her for, like, an hour at least.'

'Getting what from her?' I asked and I was pleased, for once, that my voice lacked any oomph because if it had, I was sure that I'd be sounding very wronged. Not that we'd discussed whether we were exclusive or not.

'OK, summer before last, Heidi and I snogged at, like, maybe three different parties and then I had a serious relationship with someone and then I was heartbroken and then there were some other girls and *then* I was with Scarlett. And now Heidi has decided that we're meant to be and when I didn't agree with her, she went all hysterical on me.'

'I hate it when guys say that girls are being hysterical just because they're daring to have feelings and emotions about stuff,' I pointed out, but Michael shook his head vehemently.

'No, she was proper hysterical or she pretended to be. I even had to find a paper bag because she said she was hyperventilating and she needed something to pant into.' Michael gave me a perplexed look. 'I didn't give her any encouragement so I don't know why she thought I was.'

'Well, objectively speaking, I s'pose you are a catch,' I sniffed. 'You're fairly easy on the eye and you're involved with stuff that people like Heidi seem to think is important and, well, you're popular.'

'You make it sound like those are all terrible things,' Michael snapped. He came to a halt. 'Look, Heidi made me feel like shit and now you're making me feel like shit all over again. I'm sick of it. I'm going home.'

Then he went and I was left gaping at the spot on the pavement where he'd been standing. I hadn't meant to make him feel bad about himself and anyway, he was Michael Lee. He was golden. He didn't ever feel bad about himself because, apart from huge amounts of parental pressure, his life was perfect. He was perfect.

The idea that he might not be quite as perfect as I'd thought was suddenly the most attractive thing about him and besides, I'd tried to do a nice thing by inviting him to the aftershow and now I'd ballsed it all up.

I had no choice but to run after him. However, I was far from perfect and running was yet another item on the huge list of things that I was rubbish at. There he was, striding down the road with his big, long-legged stride and covering huge amounts of ground while I hobbled after him but never seemed to catch up.

'Michael!' I was forced to shout. 'Please don't make me run after you. It's so clichéd and I have heels on and my ankle hasn't been the same since you accidentally threw me off my bike.'

That got his attention. I'd had a feeling it would. He turned round.

'Please come to the aftershow with me,' I wheedled, and it wasn't even as if I was too scared to go to a club on my own: there were going to be megatons of people I knew there. But none of them went to our school and, for once, I thought it'd be cool to do something together that didn't involve kissing or groping. 'There'll be free drinks and I'll introduce you to the band, not in a wanky, "Hey, I'm with the band" kind of deal but just, y'know, because I can. Come on . . .'

'Well . . .'

'But I'm not begging,' I added, just so we were clear on that point. 'So stop sulking and get your arse over here.'

'You really know how to make a winning argument, don't you?' Michael said when he reached my side.

'I bet you wish you had me in the school debating club,' I said as he fell into step beside me, and he stayed by my side without fidgeting or getting irritated as I had a long chat with Debbie, the girl on the door, about a hat she was knitting, and when we climbed the rickety staircase to the upstairs bar and I realised that pretty much everyone that I'd ever met in my entire life was in the room, Michael didn't get mad that I had to stop and talk to people.

Barney had taken months before he was properly house-trained and could make polite conversation with a total stranger and not tug at me and ask in a whiny voice how much longer I was going to be. Michael wasn't like that at all. He could talk to anyone, even Mad Glen, who I normally avoided because he was, well, absolutely bonkers. Word was that he'd done some dodgy E back in the nineties and he also had personal hygiene issues but Michael patiently talked to him about his crackpot conspiracy theories on 9/11 and the moon landings, then switched seamlessly to chatting about football with Tom, while I talked to Tabitha about the dress I was wearing that she'd sourced for me and why I still smelt of mothballs even though I'd sprayed a whole can of Febreeze on it.

I'll admit I was nervous when Molly and Jane from Duckie came over. I don't think there'll ever be a time when I'll get used to being hugged by a woman who's been my idol since I was eleven. I almost succeeded though.

'Love the new look,' Molly said, as she sat down in the empty chair next to me. 'It's a little bit Frenchy from *Grease* and a little, well, drag queen.'

I nodded happily. 'Not quite what I was going for, but I can deal.'

Molly fluffed up her honey-blonde hair. 'I miss dyeing my hair crazy colours but I don't miss my towels and pillowcases being stained pink. Anyway, wouldn't go down too well at work.' When she wasn't setting the world on fire through the medium of song or organising rock 'n' roll summer camps, Molly worked in a museum. 'I'll just have to live vicariously through you.'

'Even when I was going through my little old lady phase?'

'Yeah, that was an odd one.' Molly looked around then her gaze settled on Michael, sitting on the other side of me still talking to Tom about football, and stayed there. 'Oooh! Hello! This isn't Barney.'

Michael looked up and his eyes widened fractionally before he smiled. 'Nope, I wasn't Barney last time I checked. I'm Michael.'

'I'm Molly,' she tugged Jane over by her sleeve, 'and this is Jane. Jane, this is Michael, his status is yet to be determined.'

'He's my friend,' I said vaguely.

Jane smiled slyly and nudged me. 'Is he your special friend, Jeane?'

Michael and I looked at each other. I'm not sure what I was conveying through my eyes, possibly it was: 'Make me look like a tool in front of either of these women and I will kill you.' My telepathic skills weren't always that effective but he smiled again. 'Aren't all friends special?'

'Well, yeah, but some of them are more special than others,' Jane noted. 'Just how special are you?'

'Oh, Jane, we're all rare and unique snowflakes in our own way,' I said quickly. 'Stop trying to embarrass us.'

Jane thought about it. She was the most beautiful person I'd ever seen in real life. Like nineteen-forties-Hollywood-siren beautiful, which she totally played up with her Marcel-Waved hair and perfect winged liquid eyeliner, so it only seemed right that she was in a band. I knew that during the daylight hours she was a counsellor for youths with alcohol and substance addiction, but I didn't like to think of that side of Jane. When

I did think about it, I had a fuzzy notion that she probably just intimidated the youths into not ever binge drinking or scarfing huge amounts of class-As again under pain of death. She was that type of person; a pretty bloody awesome type of person.

'OK,' she decided. 'As we're probably going to have to book a room at the Jeane Hilton, I'll stop teasing. So, what did you think of the show?'

She knew what I thought of the show because I'd been watching from the side of the stage and jumping up and down and squealing all the way through the set. Basically, this was Michael's real test. He was going to try and bluff his way through a review of the show and Molly and Jane would know, because people in bands have a sixth sense about that kind of thing, and it would reflect very badly on me. Normally I didn't care what people thought of me but this was Jane and Molly, my two honorary badass older sisters, so actually I did care very much.

I held my breath as they both stared at Michael. I could almost hear the gears in his brain shifting.

'Well, I didn't get to see much of the show,' he admitted, to my surprise. 'You were about halfway through the opening number when I got dragged into a drama that lasted for the whole set and both encores.' His shoulders slumped. 'What I could hear over the crying and the shrieking sounded good, though. Really good. I mean, I love the CDs but bands always sound better live.' Michael rubbed his chin. 'Apart from Justin Bieber, he's always going to sound shit, isn't he?'

It was exactly the right thing to say and neither Molly nor Jane seemed to mind that Michael had missed witnessing them in all their splendour. Instead Jane called over their friend Kitty who looked just like Justin Bieber, then we talked to her and two hours passed in a blur of drinking and chatting and at one stage Michael even danced with me to old skool hip hop. It wasn't any kind of dancing that could actually be defined as dancing but at least he tried. Barney and just about every other straight boy I knew would rather have an enema than be seen dancing.

At precisely two o'clock, the lights came on and I had to prise the soles of my shoes off the sticky floor and think about going home. Michael had barely touched me all evening, but once he'd pulled on his leather jacket, he took my hand and then he held it. My hand tucked into his like it belonged there. Again, totes bizarre, but kinda nice. My hands were cold but his were warm and I'd forgotten my gloves so it worked out very well.

It occurred to me that Michael and I had never been out on a Saturday night together because that was what regular couples did and whatever we were it certainly wasn't regular.

'Don't take this the wrong way,' I said, which showed that I was maybe a little bit tipsy because normally I wasn't bothered if he did take things the wrong way, 'but don't you have a curfew? I mean, most people living with their parents do.'

Michael gave me a bit of eyebrow action at the suggestion that he was still completely parent-whipped, but I'd met his mother and she was a woman who'd have no patience with her beloved son arriving home at all hours.

'Not so much on Saturday nights.' Michael looked at his watch – he was the only person I knew who wore one. 'Though if they weren't in Devon, I think coming home at past two would really be pushing it.'

'Even at the start of half-term?'

'But, Jeane, it's my crucial A-level year,' he said in a high-pitched voice that *did* sound a bit like Kathy Lee. 'You need at least eight hours' sleep every night and don't forget to let the cat out.'

'So, um, do you want to share a cab or come back to mine for a bit?' I asked hesitantly, because I'd been so busy lately that we hadn't had a chance to get together. And by get together I really meant kissing each other until breathing became an issue.

Michael squeezed my hand a little tighter. I squeezed him back. 'I really do need to let the cat out, but you could come back to my house. It's clean, for one thing . . .'

I stopped squeezing and scowled. 'My place is clean. I spent *hours* this morning tidying up and I even vacuumed and did the recycling without Gustav and Harry coming round and standing over me.'

'Yeah, but did your place have a supermarket delivery in the last twelve hours and a dad who went to Chinatown yesterday and came home with two boxes of cakes?'

'Well, no,' I admitted. 'No, it didn't.'

'So, come back to mine. For cake and, y'know, whatever.'

It sounded like a plan. A plan whereby I'd stuff my face with cake, then get down to a whole lot of whatever. 'Fine,' I said, pulling him towards the exit. 'Let's try and find a cab.'

18

I couldn't believe I was holding hands with Jeane in public, on a street corner, at nearly 2.30 in the morning, and that she was coming back to my house that was free of parents and annoying little sisters.

As Jeane peered up and down the road for a vacant black cab, the streetlight caught the angles in her face and she looked almost beautiful. Well, no, not beautiful, but exotic. Like she was a bird of paradise or a rare flower that didn't belong on a damp, grey London street on a damp, grey London night.

'Hey, take a picture, it lasts longer,' she said when she caught me staring at her but she didn't sound like she minded.

There were no cabs to be found and just as we were about to walk up to the main road, someone called Jeane's name and we turned round to see Molly and Jane and a couple of randoms hurrying towards us.

'So, we're all right to sleep at yours then?' Molly asked as she drew level and Jeane went from holding my hand to not holding my hand and stepping away from me. 'You don't mind?'

'Of course I don't,' Jeane said and I didn't know why I suddenly felt furious. Compared with coming back to mine for Chinese buns and a grope and grind session, hanging out with Molly Montgomery was always going to be the better deal. Always. 'And before you start bitching, it's beyond clean. My dad's coming to London for a visit so I've been up to my elbows in hot soapy water for most of the day.'

'I'm glad to hear that because last time I stayed at yours, I swear I got scabies,' Jane said with a shudder.

Molly smacked her. 'You great fat liar,' she gasped. 'You were allergic to that body lotion that smelt like Toilet Duck.'

'I still say it was scabies,' Jane insisted. 'I hope you remembered to vacuum the sofa as well as the floor.'

'Any more backchat and you can sleep in your van,' Jeane said. 'And I guess we can stop looking for a cab,' she added to me.

I nodded. There wasn't much else I could do. It wasn't the end of the world that she was heading home with her cool friends and I was going back to an empty house on my own. Her kisses were pretty good but I could live without them.

Duckie's van was parked in the next street. Jeane and I climbed into the back and I spent the next ten minutes with a drumstick poking me in the arse and having to cling to the wheel arch as Jane took the corners too fast. Even though Jeane had told me that she was a total straight-edge who didn't drink or do drugs, Jane still drove like she was under the influence. When we reached the Broadway, Jeane started to give her directions to my place as she fished around in her tote bag.

I wasn't paying much attention because ... well, because I was sulking and I was cramped and uncomfortable and I was thinking about the bacon sandwich I was going to have when I got in, then Jeane pulled out her keys and tossed them to Molly. 'You remember the address, don't you?'

'Yeah,' Molly said. 'It's saved in my phone so I can use Google Maps to take us the rest of the way.'

Jeane leaned forward. 'Just drop us off by that postbox,' she said, as, with a terrible grinding of the gears, Jane pulled into the kerb. 'Leave my keys under my doormat and I'll buzz someone to let me in.'

There was a collective snort of disbelief. 'Don't be a twat,' one of the other girls said. 'Anybody could pick them up.'

'Remind me to never ask you to join my Neighbourhood Watch scheme,' Molly said. 'Let's meet for lunch tomorrow before we drive back to Brighton and we'll have a ceremonial handing over of the keys.'

It took another five minutes to sort out the details of the lunch and finally we were clambering out of the back of the van.

'Help yourself to anything in the fridge, but if you finish all my Haribo I'll kill you,' Jeane called out before she slammed the van door shut. She turned to me with a satisfied smile. 'Well, at least we saved on taxi fare.'

I was more relieved that she was walking up my drive than I would have thought possible. 'You could have hung with them if you'd wanted,' I said as I unlocked the front door.

'But we'd already made plans,' Jeane said, as if the plans had been carved into tablets of stone. 'And besides, five people all wanting to use my bathroom at the same time? No, thanks!'

The house was cold and silent and I couldn't quite believe that my mum wasn't suddenly going to come flying down the stairs and berate me for breaking my lax Saturday night curfew and grounding me until my A-levels were over. But she was still in Devon so I made Jeane a cup of tea and it turned out that she fancied a bacon sandwich too.

She swung herself up on the worktop, still wearing her quilted gold jacket, which looked like it was made out of an old dressing gown, and watched as I cut slices from a loaf of sourdough bread and shoved them in the toaster, then heated oil in the frying pan.

'When I was six I decided to become a vegetarian because I made the connection that Sunday roasts were actually cute little chickens and lambs and stuff,' Jeane suddenly said. 'My mum is so hippy dippy that she had to go along with it. Anyway, I was vegetarian for five whole days but on Saturday morning my dad always made bacon sandwiches and when he and my mum told me I couldn't have one because bacon was meat and I was a vegetarian, I got so mad that I didn't talk to them for two weeks.' She gave this odd snuffly laugh and shook her head. 'My mum thought I'd lost my voice until she realised I was still talking to my sister Bethan.'

'God, when I was six, I was more interested in Pokémon than the environment,' I said as I turned each rasher and jumped back as I was splashed with spitting fat. 'We were living in Hong Kong then and you could get really cheap knock-off Pokémon stuff that my mum refused to buy because she was convinced they were made of toxic materials and had bits of metal and glass poking out of them. Apparently one time I lay down in the middle of the street and had a complete fit because she wouldn't let me have a furry Pikachu.'

Jeane stretched out her legs and grinned. 'What did your mum do?'

'She stepped over me and carried on walking down the street.' I could still remember the stickiness of the hot pavement under my fists and the smell of ginger and chillies and scallions from the noodle shop and that moment of defeat when I finally picked myself up and raced after my mother. 'It's very hard to get one over on my mum.'

'Really? I find it very easy to get one over on mine,' Jeane said, her voice as tart as lemon juice.

'What about your dad?' I asked tentatively. 'You said you were going to see him later on in the week.'

Jeane pulled a terrible face; eyes screwed shut, mouth and nose disappearing into a painful pucker. 'God, my parents are two of the least interesting things about me.' She tore off sheets of kitchen roll as I turned out the light under the bacon. 'I'd much rather hear about Hong Kong. How long did you live there?'

It was late and we were both tired and cold, so even though my mother would have had a fit if she'd known that I was taking a girl into my room and shutting the door, even worse that I had hot, smelly food in my room, we decamped to my attic bedroom. Jeane kicked off her shoes and curled up on my bed as she demolished her bacon sandwich like she hadn't had a decent meal in weeks. In fact, knowing her preference for living on jelly sweets and coffee, she probably hadn't. Then she sipped her tea as I told her about living in Hong Kong and our tiny apartment on Pok Fu Lam Road and how while my dad was working at Queen Mary Hospital and my mother at the Consulate, I was looked after by May, my Chinese nanny, who'd put chicken soup in my sippy cup and take me to the playground just down the street. I told her about the weekends when we'd go to Victoria Harbour to look at the boats and how there were so many skyscrapers that looking up made you dizzy. That English rain didn't even begin to compare with the black rainstorms of a Hong Kong spring and that the humidity later on in the season felt as if you were being slowly stewed.

I told her about the flower market and the bird market and the market that just sold goldfish and how, as a special treat, my parents would take me to Tai Yuen Street, which had nothing but toy shops and stalls selling all kinds of brightly coloured, flashing, whirring, beeping toys and our holidays on Lamma Island and I thought Jeane was asleep as her eyes were shut and her limbs swathed in aquamarine shot silk and taffeta and bright pink tights were relaxed but when I stopped talking, her eyes snapped open. 'Don't stop,' she said.

'But there's nothing much else to tell,' I protested with a laugh.

'It sounds amazing,' Jeane sighed, and it wasn't one of her world-weary, God-can-you-really-be-such-a-massive-tool? sighs. This sigh was full of wonder. 'It's definitely been added to my list of places I *have* to visit.'

I wanted to know what other countries were on her must-see list, but before I could ask her, a massive yawn that went on for a long, long, long moment overtook me and once I'd stopped, Jeane started yawning.

'I'll leave you to get some shut-eye, then, shall I?' I started to scramble off the bed, but Jeane caught my hand.

'Shut-eye? Are you, like, fifty?' she asked mockingly. 'Where are you going to sleep?'

'I can sleep in the spare room.' I pulled away from Jeane but she didn't let go. 'What?'

'You could sleep in here, if you wanted,' she said slowly.

My throat suddenly closed up. 'With you?' I croaked.

Jeane smiled. 'Yeah, unless that would make your head explode?'

It did feel like my head was exploding a little bit, because the sight of Jeane lounging on my bed like a beached mermaid was mind-bending enough but the thought of Jeane *in* my bed, with me in my bed as well, possibly doing things that two people sharing a bed did, was making the parts of my brain that deal with logic and reason short-circuit.

'Just to sleep or, er, not sleep?' I clarified, because Jeane expected me to be all open about sex and establishing personal boundaries and—

'Oh, for God's sake, Michael, we're both consenting adults.'

'You're not an adult, you're only seventeen.'

'In the eyes of the law, I've been legally able to have sex for fifteen months,' Jeane informed me. 'Even though I'm not legally able to vote, buy alcohol and I can't stand for Parliament until I'm twenty-one, though I have way more sense than most of our elected representatives. Anyway I'm not talking about some non-stop shagathon, I'm talking about us sharing a bed and maybe moving things forward a little bit so we *get off* as well as getting off with each other.' I hadn't thought that Jeane knew how to blush but her face was as red as her lipstick, which even a doorstep of a bacon sandwich and a mug of tea hadn't dislodged.

What she said made perfect sense. After all, our post-school make-out sessions usually ended with me going home to relieve some of the pressure with my left hand and a couple of adult-orientated websites that I always cleared from my browser history two minutes after the deed was done. Yeah, it was Jeane who had got me into that state but the idea that Jeane could help me out of that state too hadn't really dawned on me.

'Are you sure that's what you want?'

'Well, I was pretty sure but your utter lack of enthusiasm is a real mood killer,' she said. She flopped back on the bed with a sulky-sounding huff. 'Let's just go to sleep, shall we? It's late and it won't be long before we need to get up and go and meet Molly and the others, OK?'

'If there was a world record in annoying someone, I think I'd have smashed right through it 'cause you're always annoyed with me about something, aren't you?'

'Not *always*,' Jeane conceded. 'Lately there have been huge periods of time when you haven't annoyed me at all. I think that's called progress. Now we've cleared that up, can we have some shut-eye or whatever the completely old-timer expression was that you used? Forty winks. Up the stairs to Bedfordshire. Sleep, let's do it.'

Nothing was ever that simple with Jeane. She insisted on seeing my entire T-shirt collection before she found one that she'd deign to wear and she took ages to clean her teeth and then I made her go and take her make-up off because I didn't want

185

to wake up with glitter, mascara and lipstick all over my pillowcase, and I didn't think Mum would be too impressed either.

Once she had a glass of water and the radio set on a low volume and was on the left-hand side of the bed, because 'I'm left-handed so *of course* I need to sleep on the left,' I was finally allowed to turn off the light.

I wasn't feeling even remotely like doing anything that would lead to mutual orgasms until Jeane rolled over.

'There's not much point in sharing a bed if we're not going to cuddle,' she announced, though I'd never in a million years thought that she'd be a snuggler. 'You probably take hugging for granted. Like, if your little sisters want to hug you, you probably wriggle and complain, but I live on my own and I don't get to have much in the way of hugs and you have very good arms, Michael.'

Oh God, now, if it was possible, I felt the least sexy I'd ever felt, as if Jeane had magicked away my dick and turned me into a gigantic teddy bear. And now I felt sorry for her too because she had Cuddle Deficiency Syndrome and generally feeling pity towards someone didn't make me want to bust out my best moves. But I did have good arms (I did fifty press-ups every morning) and I could give her a hug.

'Come here then,' I said gruffly, to prove she hadn't totally de-dicked me.

Jeane came willingly. She settled into my arms with a happy sigh and her head fitted neatly under my chin. She wriggled to get more comfortable and I could smell the scent of her perfume, which always reminded me of freshly baked cakes, and her legs were soft and smooth as she shifted against me and just like that I was hard.

19

Once Michael finally got into bed and snapped off the light after wasting loads of time doing God knows what in the bathroom and then traipsing downstairs to get me a glass of water that I didn't want and refusing to let me sleep in a ratty old school T-shirt of his – apparently it had sentimental value so I had to choose something else – anyway after all that, it took me all of five seconds to decide that his bed was my third favourite place in the world.

Michael's bed was firm and big and warm and his bed linen was clean and crisp, which mine never was even when I did get round to changing it. And he was in the bed next to me, all big and firm and warm too so I wanted to be wrapped up in him instead of his duvet.

It's not easy to ask someone to hug you. It makes you feel vulnerable and needy when you spend most of your life pretending to the world, and yourself, that you're neither of those two things, but as soon as I managed to choke out a request to be held, Michael didn't take the piss or get huffy, he was just holding me.

I think that he's even better at cuddling than he is at kissing and we just fit together in a way that we never normally did. I wound myself around him and in that moment I just wanted to be closer still, even if it meant climbing inside him like he was a sleeping bag, which actually doesn't really work as an analogy and makes me sound like some kind of sick serial killer who likes to wear my victims' skins.

As soon as I snuggled in closer, it was obvious that Michael had gone from nought to raging boner in the space of a second. It wasn't because I was oh-so-sexy with my face bare of glitter and my peach-coloured hair, which was all tangles and hairspray. It wasn't me. I had nothing to do with Michael's erection. He was an eighteen-year-old boy sharing a bed with a girl. It would have been weird if he didn't have an erection.

His whole body, not just his penis, stiffened. 'Sorry,' he mumbled as he tried to put some distance between us.

'Would it be better if we spooned instead?'

'No,' Michael said shortly, then he shoved me away and rolled on to his back. Even in the dim light, I could see his clenched jaw. 'Sorry.'

'It's all right.' Maybe I should have been freaking out or insisting that it would be better off if I slept in the spare room, but the truth . . . the truth was that now I was in the mood. The feel of *it* pressing into me was the same feeling I got when I was getting ready to go out and almost falling over myself in a delicious, shivery mix of anticipation and excitement. It was the same feeling I got just as one of my favourite bands came on stage or I was in a club and a tune I loved began to play. It was a feeling that made me itch inside my own skin and it was a feeling that made me inch across the bed so I was pressed up against him.

'Jeane,' he said in a warning. 'Just don't, OK?'

'Oh, are you nearly asleep then?'

'What do you think?'

'Well, I think neither of us are going to get much sleep right now and I also think that I could, like, help you out.'

He didn't say anything and I thought I'd shocked him, because I tend to do that. Not just with Michael but with pretty much anyone who can't deal with being honest and admitting that you have wants and needs and desires and all those other fun things.

'Is this some new plot to mess with my head?' Michael asked hoarsely. He had the most appalling trust issues.

'Rather mess with something else,' I said, and before he could demand an explanation I decided that show was a million times better than tell and I smooshed even closer so I could kiss him.

It was like kissing a plank of wood. Or it was for about five seconds and then Michael groaned and turned over so he could kiss me back with a lot more fierceness than usual. My hand snaked under the duvet and I'd barely got it inside his shorts before Michael groaned, like the other groan had just been the warm-up act, and it was game over. Move it along. Absolutely nothing to see here.

I tried my hardest not to 'Ewww' as I carefully removed my sticky hand and held it in the air so I didn't get any stuff on the duvet cover.

'I'm sorry about that,' Michael mumbled. 'Um, it's been a while. Well, not a while but a while since somebody else ... you know. I mean, what I'm trying to say is—'

'I get it,' I said quickly, but I was talking to myself as Michael had already scrambled out of bed and was halfway out of the room. Then he stuck his head back round the door.

'Tissues. Bedside table,' he flung at me, then disappeared.

Of course he had a box of tissues by his bed. He was a boy, after all. Though some boys I knew just had loo roll. I wiped my hand clean, peered under the duvet to make sure there was no damp patch, and, by the time Michael returned with a hangdog expression and a fresh pair of pyjama bottoms on, I was snuggled under the quilt again and attempting to look completely unfazed and non-judgey.

'Sorry,' he said again, as he got back into bed.

'Honestly, it's fine. It happens,' I said, because it did, though it had never happened with me before. 'Stop wigging out about it.'

'I'm not wigging out about it. Actually, I am.' Michael sighed. 'And you got, like, about one minute of kissing in the end?'

It hadn't even been a minute. More like twenty seconds, but it seemed rude to point that out.

'You can make it up to me some other time.' I snuggled down like I was ready to go to sleep, though after all the excitement and the build up and the total let-down I was wide awake and likely to stay that way for ever.

'What about I make it up to you now?' Michael suggested and I'd have totally called him on such a cheesy line but he was already kissing me.

Sometimes when he kissed me, he made me feel like such a girl and this was one of those times, and I was kissing him back but sighing a little and stroking the back of his neck where the skin was so soft that it made me want to cry a little, which makes no sense but it was late and I was so tired that I wasn't tired any more and I was a little sad.

'How far do you want to go?' Michael asked me as he kissed my neck.

'All the way to happyland,' I replied, grabbing his hand and putting it exactly where it was needed.

I didn't really have to do much after that, just hum in approval every time Michael hit the right spot and soon I didn't have to hum any more because his fingers were right *there*.

'It kinda takes me a while,' I whispered, when he asked me for the fifth time if he was doing it right. 'Just be patient, I'm almost there.'

He didn't talk any more after that, just kept kissing me, until I couldn't kiss him back any more because I was wrenching my head back and gasping and spluttering and babbling a whole lot of nonsense, the general gist of it being that if Michael stopped what he was doing then I'd murder him. Even when I was in happyland, I was still belligerent.

And the other thing was that after the first time I could always go again, and Michael was hard and he kept grinding into my hip without even realising. Or maybe he did know but wasn't as unshy when it came to talking about it as I was.

Besides, it was obvious he knew his way around the main attractions and responded well to instruction so it seemed a pity to let this unique set of circumstances go to waste.

I didn't just blurt it out, which was a first for me. Instead we kissed for a bit and I was still in the mood. Also Michael was still with the grinding and the gritting of his teeth and just as I was about to ask if he wanted to be taken out of his misery, he put his hands on my hips to stop me from moving.

'Shall we ... like, we could do what we just did but together, or do you thinkitwouldberushingitifwehadsex?' That was how he said it, one long clump of words all stuck together, his voice breathy and shrill. I hadn't expected him to be the one to ask first. 'Is it bad that I asked? Am I pressuring you?'

'Like you could even try,' I scoffed, kissing away any sting left by my words. 'And no, I don't think it would be rushing things. After what we've just done, actual sex is only going a little bit further.'

It was a very important step in a relationship, but we weren't exactly boyfriend and girlfriend, and it wasn't going to make much difference if we did have sex. It wasn't as if having sex meant we were committing to anything more than, well, just having sex with each other.

Michael agreed with me. 'Cool,' he said, as he leaned over and opened the nightstand drawer. 'Condoms.'

I peered over his shoulder to see more foil squares than even the time I'd gone with Ben to the sexual health clinic, because he had a rash over his bits from going commando while wearing very tight skinny jeans, and the nurse had totally thought we were sexually active with each other and had given us a carrier bag stuffed full of Durex. As Ben said, she obviously had the worst gaydar in the world. Maybe Michael had been to see the same woman.

He grabbed a couple and handed them to me. I shoved them back at him. 'You do it,' I demanded.

'You're such a control freak that I thought *you'd* want to do it.'

'I've only ever put one on a banana in Sex Ed,' I admitted reluctantly. 'The other times the guy I was with did it, but thanks for making me feel *so* special at a time like this.'

Michael grinned and it seemed right that even though we were both naked and in bed together, we were still bickering. We argued; it was our thing.

'Luckily, I've put them on other things besides bananas,' he said slyly and I had to kiss the smug smile off his face because he didn't look at all pretty like that.

There was more kissing, a lot more kissing, a short pause while Michael took care of business and then ... Michael was on top of me and then with a bit of adjusting and some tense whispering, which is never that sexy, he was inside me and I was like whoa! Because no matter how many times I've done it (and I haven't done it that many times), the moment that you begin to do it, really do it, is always a shock. And it always feels weird and you want to freak out because when you think about it sex is strange. Even the concept of sex is strange. And all these things are rushing through your head and it's a bit awkward and uncomfortable and sometimes it never stops being awkward and uncomfortable but this time as I frowned and panicked and wondered if someone who occasionally shopped in the children's department was mature enough to be having of the sex and if this would change everything between me and Michael and if it would be a good change or a bad change and once we'd had sex maybe I wouldn't see him for dust, which would mess with my head, Michael stopped what he was doing so he could kiss me very gently on my scrunched-up forehead.

'Hey, Jeane,' he murmured. 'Are you going weird on me?'

'I'm not going weird, I've been weird all my life,' I stated, and Michael smiled and he kissed me again and I could feel every molecule and atom and neuron that made up my being stop having a tizzy and settle back down and I could move again and wrap my arms and legs around Michael and kiss him back. And actually sex wasn't always that strange. Sometimes it could be pretty awesome.

It didn't quite get to awesome this first time with Michael but that was all right, although he was a total boy about it.

'But you did come, right?' he said after he'd come because sex, like life, is usually easier for dudes. "Cause we can go again if you give me a few minutes or I could, you know, sort of, like, *help*?'

Sometimes he was the dictionary definition of a nice boy and maybe if we carried on doing it and sex still didn't get to be pretty awesome, I'd take him up on the offer, but, right now, I was mellow and relaxed and I didn't really need anything else but to burrow deeper under the covers and destroy Michael's faux-hawk with my fingers. It was so stiff with hair product that even two orgasms hadn't been enough to diminish it.

'Look, I didn't come but if I had a problem with that then you'd be the first to know,' I said as I ruffled his hair. Even though I was only touching his scalp, I could feel his entire body tense up. 'It was our first time and first times can be a bit odd so don't get in a strop about it.'

I kissed his furrowed brow, which was a good indication of just how mellow I was. Normally I'd have told him to stop whining and, if he didn't, I'd have totally kicked his arse.

'But I thought it was good,' Michael complained. His eyes widened. 'Wasn't I any good?'

'You have mad skillz,' I told him, which was the truth. Michael had taken time and effort and had done something with his fingers that in the normal way would have had me shrieking and promising to buy him a pony. 'Now shut up. This is supposed to be a time for quiet reflection.'

20

I'd never known her so quiet or so still. So quiet and still that she didn't seem like Jeane at all, but some other girl with peach-coloured hair. It was because I'd been a crap shag. I'd been all wham bam, thank you, ma'am, and the only reason why she wasn't kicking me out of bed was because it was my bed and her bed was occupied by members of Duckie.

I couldn't understand it because I'd paid a lot of attention to her clitoris as I'd been instructed by two of the other girls I'd slept with. I hadn't had performance anxiety either, although I'd been worried that once Jeane was naked I wouldn't fancy her. She was kind of chubby but a bit flat-chested out of her clothes, and that shouldn't have been sexy, but it was. Maybe it was because Jeane's clothes were so hideous that looking at her naked was the better option.

Or it might have been because Jeane was comfortable with her own body. Not once did she moan about her thighs or her pot belly or about how fat she supposedly was like every other girl I knew, even the really skinny ones because they wanted you to say, 'Oh, fat? I think what you meant to say is that you're really fit.' That wasn't Jeane's style and anyway her skin was soft and smooth and I liked that she had proper muscles in her arms and legs. Sometimes when I'm with a girl, even just hugging a girl, they can feel so fragile and frail that I'm frightened of breaking them.

Not Jeane. A weapon of mass destruction couldn't break Jeane, but she hadn't come and I knew she was going to put me through hell for it. I knew it and I was dreading it and she was stroking my hair and kissing my face and I knew that the minute I relaxed she'd probably do something evil to my nutsack.

'Please, Michael, stop angsting about my non-orgasm,' she said with an irritated edge to her voice. 'I was close and then I wasn't. It happens. It's not, like, an exact science. Like, sometimes when I'm doing it to myself, my timing goes all wrong.'

'It does?' I managed to spit out because my mind had just gone into a tailspin at Jeane's casual reference to the fact that she masturbated. I mean, I know that some girls do, but generally they don't talk about it.

'Course it does. And, seriously, you were good. Much, much better than I expected you to be.' I think I was getting used to Jeane now because I didn't automatically take offence when she insulted me. 'If you tell me that Scarlett gave you tips on that thing you did with your index finger, my world might end.' Jeane looked like she was going to cry. 'I'll have to bake her some cookies.'

'It's all right. Your world still exists. I didn't sleep with Scarlett and please don't tell me that Barney taught you that thing you do with your tongue.'

'As Barney leapt about a foot in the air if I even tried to French him, of course not.' Jeane's hands stilled. 'I wonder if Scarlett and Barney will ever have sex, like, with each other? Who would make the first move? I'm sure they haven't even kissed yet. It will be *decades* before they can even muster up the courage to grope *under* the clothes. So, anyway, if it wasn't Scarlett, who did teach you your moves?' Jeane asked, while I was still reeling from the thought of her masturbating and then Barney and Scarlett having sex. Jeane was right. They'd probably be getting their telegrams from the Queen for hitting the big one hundred before they got down to getting down. But now Jeane had moved on to my sex life and I knew she wouldn't move away from my sex life until I told her everything.

I sighed. 'Well, my first sex girlfriend ...'

'A sex girlfriend? What the what, Michael?' She chortled with glee. 'Sex girlfriend!'

There was nothing for it but to pinch her arse so she'd shut up, although she bit down hard on my earlobe in retaliation. 'OK, the first girl I had sex with was when I was fifteen and it was Ant's older sister so I didn't go out with her properly but she'd get me on my own or drag me off at parties to have her way with me and bark orders at me when I wasn't doing it to her exact specifications.' I thought back to the fraught but exhilarating two months I'd been Daria Constantine's sex slave. 'Actually you and her have a lot in common.'

'She sounds excellent,' Jeane said. 'Who was your next girl-friend?'

'Well, I was so scarred by my experiences with Daria that I didn't have sex with my next girlfriend,' I lied, because that hadn't been the reason why Hannah and I hadn't slept together. What we'd had had been so perfect, so intense, that sex would have got in the way. Just kissing her had been enough and I didn't want to tell Jeane that because she wouldn't get it and she'd mock me. There might have been times when I probably needed the piss taken out of me, but not when it was to do with Hannah. 'And then I went on a fort-night's lads' holiday to Magaluf after GCSEs and I hooked up with Carly from Leeds.'

Jeane nodded. 'And the next night you hooked up with Lauren from Manchester and the night after was Heather from Basingstoke and—'

'Do you want to hear this or are you just going to keep inter-rupting with a whole lot of bullshit that isn't even close to the truth?'

She opened her mouth then closed it again, and settled back down with her head nestled in the space between my head and my shoulder. 'Sorry, I'm shutting up now.'

'Yeah, for all of one minute.'

'Five minutes, tops,' Jeane corrected. 'So, right, Carly from Leeds?'

'Well, we met on the first night and I liked her and she liked me so we decided that we might as well stick together, instead of going out every night and shagging random, um, randoms because we'd had too much booze. And before you ask, yes, we're still in touch and have both vowed that we'll never have sex on a beach ever again.'

'Why?'

'One word: sand. What happened to shutting up?'

Jeane mimed zipping her lips together, but nudged me to continue.

'And then there was Megan, who was my girlfriend before Scarlett. Went out for about eight months and, well, we did it a lot. Like, all the time.'

'Oh, are your parents the kind of parents who are cool about giving you your own space and being respectful of your burgeoning sexuality?' Jeane asked. 'Because I have to say that your mum really didn't strike me as being one of those kinds of parents.'

'Well, she's not, especially when she caught me and Megan going at it.'

'She didn't?' Jeane breathed, as she struggled up on one elbow and nearly broke one of my ribs in the process. 'What did she do?'

'Gave me an excruciating speech about sex and respecting women and every week she returns my laundry with condoms stuffed in the pockets of all my jeans,' I told Jeane, who gurgled. 'But seriously, I'd go to Megan's house after school every day and we'd work our way through her parents' porn collection and their instructional sex DVDs. Y'know, like, *The Lovers' Guide To Sexual Positions*. One of them was even in 3D.'

'You are *so* making this up,' Jeane said crossly.

'I am *not*,' I insisted as crossly. 'You wait. Just you wait. You'll see.'

'What*ever*. Is that meant to be a threat or a promise?'

'Bit of both,' I said, and I was starting to get really tired. Truthfully, I wasn't starting to ... I *was* tired. It was almost dawn o'clock and I'd been up for twenty-four hours, two of which had been spent playing a really rough game of football and there'd been the scene with Heidi and I'd come twice and I was ready for sleep. But when I looked down at Jeane she was wide awake and barely blinking.

'Aren't you tired?'

She shook her head. 'Nah, I've got my second wind and anyway, I've trained myself not to need that much sleep. But I know you're not as evolved as me so if you want to bed down that's cool.'

'I'm all right,' I said through clenched jaw as I stifled a yawn. 'So, how about you? Where did you learn your moves?'

Jeane began to talk and it was as if her one-note voice was the aural equivalent of a sleeping pill and my eyelids began to droop down and I'd drift off but the more Jeane got into her stride, the more animated she became. She'd wriggle and fidget and dig me with her elbow and I'd drift back into consciousness.

So, from what I could gather, her previous sexual encounters had been with:

1. David, who blogged about books and was a committed Christian. Jeane was only fifteen and he was only sixteen and wrestling with his faith so they didn't go all the way but went about three-quarters of the way for a few months. Then they started to have lots of

arguments about how organised religion was just an evil conspiracy to keep women down, 'and in the end, I told him that he had to choose between me and Jesus and he totes chose Jesus.'

2. Jens was the editor of some Swedish lifestyle magazine who Jeane met at a conference for Free Thinkers, Radicals and Next Big Things. 'Wanky, I know, but it was a week, all expenses paid, in Stockholm.' So, Jens, who was twenty-seven and should have known better than to glom on to a girl eleven years younger than him, spent most of the week hanging out with Jeane and they shopped for bright orange tights together and went to see modern art and dined on moose burgers and at the end of the week when the conference decamped to a cruise ship to tour Sweden's archipelago, Jens very kindly took Jeane's virginity. 'I thought it was cool,' she mused. 'He was Jens and I was Jeane and he was really handsome. Swedish men are total foxes. They all look like Eric from *True Blood* and sometimes I am that shallow. And yes, he was older than me but I figured that I was going to have sex sooner or later so I might as well have it with someone who was stupidly good-looking and knew what they were doing. It was, like, twenty-four hours of sexual boot camp.' I was wide awake at this point and could see Jeane shake her head sadly. 'I didn't get to see the archipelago though. I never left Jens's cabin.'

3. Ben, fashion student and part-time hairdresser, who Jeane had picked up at a craft fair because he was

wearing a *Little Monsters* T-shirt. They got off with each other for two months until Ben decided that he preferred boys and they parted on good terms. Or Jeane said that they had but as he was the one responsible for her hair being iron-grey I wasn't quite sure that I believed her.

4. Cedric, French, taught Jeane about Anaïs Nin, good coffee and eBay France, before he went back to Marseilles to finish his degree in Advanced Pretentiousness.

5. Judy, who played roller derby, and then I was all *Judy?* JUDY?

I'd come out the tunnel of tiredness into being teeth-clenching, eye-popping awake with no hope of sleep, and Jeane telling me that one of her past hook-ups was called Judy was like having icy-cold water flung in my face. 'Are you bisexual?' I asked, because that was something she might have thought to mention. 'Are you into girls? What's the deal with Judy?'

Jeane looked perturbed like she had no idea why I was acting as if she'd started speaking in tongues. 'Dude,' she said. 'Dude, your voice is getting so high that it's making my ears hurt.'

'Are you generally into doing it with girls as well as boys then?' I asked, as if my voice breaking had never happened.

'Well, see, it's like I *really* like Haribo but then occasionally I'll be in the newsy's and I'll think, Hmm, maybe I could fancy some Maltesers for a change. So, I have the Maltesers and they're all right but they don't really hit the spot and I couldn't have them every day like Haribo,' Jeane finished with a pleased smile like comparing sexual orientation to sweets made perfect sense and in a weird kind of way it did.

'So, there was Judy, but it turned out she was a total player and when I stopped seeing her, I saw Barney and we never did anything but kiss and that is all the people who I've had fun and not-so-fun sexy times with.'

Apart from the Swede, who sounded like a total paedo skeeve, it wasn't such a bad list and I realised there was no need for me to start feeling insecure that she preferred older men or girls. Jeane wouldn't have been here if she hadn't wanted to be and although the sex was an exciting, new development, it wasn't like we were going to stay together for ever. We were just a chapter in each other's sexual histories.

Jeane settled back down in my arms and even made a snuffly little noise as if she hadn't quite trained herself to do without sleep. My hand crept up to stroke the back of her neck and as I began to knead the ginormous knot I found there, Jeane's limbs slackened and the half of her body that was sprawled on top of mine seemed to get heavier.

'That hurts,' she muttered. My hand stilled. 'I didn't tell you to stop.'

I kneaded and massaged and stroked until the knot was gone and Jeane was breathing evenly and deeply and I thought she was asleep.

She wasn't. Just as I was about to turn out the bedside lamp she curled herself tighter into me and raised her head.

'Michael, will you ... when my dad turns up on Friday to take me out to dinner and give me a hard time about my lifestyle choices . . . it would go a lot better . . . ' Her eyes were almost crossed with the effort of getting the words out, then she collapsed back on my chest. 'No, it doesn't matter. Forget it.'

For one moment it crossed my mind that this whole thing, the sex, had been a cunning way to get me onside so she could introduce me to her dad. Then it wouldn't matter that she lived on jelly sweets and black coffee and handed in all her coursework late and didn't sleep enough, because she had to be doing something right if she was going out with someone like me. Not to be big-headed or anything, but on paper I'm pretty much a textbook-perfect boyfriend. Textbook best mate. Textbook son. I'm whatever people expect me to be.

Then again, Jeane was the only person in my life who didn't expect me to be a perfect anything. And she was always honest with me, brutally honest, and she had many faults but sneaky ulterior motives weren't one of them. If she wanted something from me then she'd come right out and ask me, except when the thing she wanted was too hard to put into actual words. I got that because I was starting to get her.

'Did you want me to come and meet your dad then?' I asked gently. 'Safety in numbers and all that?'

I thought she was asleep until she kissed my bicep, which was the bit of me that was nearest to her mouth. 'It will be torture *and* we'll have to go to a Garfunkel's. He's freaking obsessed with the free salad bar.'

'That's all right. I like salad. Besides, you've met my parents. Meeting your dad would be payback.'

'You don't have to . . . I mean, I don't expect you to, it's not like we're dating and it's time to meet my dad.'

'Yeah, I know, but if you want me to then I will.'

There was another pause. Jeane kissed my bicep three more times and then actually nuzzled my arm with her cheek. 'Yeah, I do want you to.'

I didn't even realise that I'd been tensing up until she said that. I untensed. 'OK. Cool.'

'Cool,' she said. 'Now will you shut up so I can get some sleep?'

21

It was only now, now that we'd got down with our bad selves, that I was forced to admit that I had a HUGE crush on Michael Lee. It sort of happened about ten minutes after he woke up the next morning. I'd already been up for *hours*, or minutes if we're going to be technical about it, and was perched behind his desk as I uploaded the photos I'd taken the night before to my Flickr, when he sat up, stretched, then stared at me like he wasn't sure why I was in his bedroom. It was interesting to watch the recall of last night's events play out on his face and when he reached the end, it seemed as if it was only sheer force of will that stopped him from pulling the covers over his head.

'Oh. Hey. Right. So, how are *you*?' he mumbled.

I was tempted to describe a burning sensation and a terrible itching in my lady garden just to wind him up, but that would have been mean. Also untrue. And he'd been all kinds of lovely the night before and had even offered to come and sit next to me and partake of all the salad he could eat when my dad rolled into town, so I just smiled at him.

'I'm fine, better than fine,' I told him, and, if possible, he looked even more panicky, like he was having a serious case of regrets and that he'd never meant *any of it* to happen. There was only one way to find out.

'Look, Michael, can we not do the awkward morning-after thing? We're both better than that but if you think it was a terrible mistake and actually someone slipped a date rape drug into your lager last night then just say and we'll pretend that it never happened and we can go back to how we were, or we can go further back than that and just pretend the other one doesn't exist? OK?'

'How can you be so … so like *you* this early in the morning?' he grumbled.

'What can I say? It's a gift.'

Michael scratched his head, then cautiously touched the tufts of hair that were in serious disarray. 'For the record, I don't regret last night. Well, apart from the bit when you didn't get your happy but I did.'

I hadn't expected to feel quite so relieved. 'Oh, I remember feeling fairly happy.'

Then Michael smiled. It was a slow, sexy smile, and with him sitting in a rumpled bed with rumpled hair and his muscles rippling in a pleasing manner, he looked like a model in an aftershave ad in a men's style magazine and I finally got what all the fuss was about. It wasn't the pretty. It wasn't his join-the-dots cool. It wasn't his being good at everything. It was because he was ridiculously sizzling hot and I was *so* glad that

I wasn't the type of girl who simpered or blushed or giggled, because I'd be doing a sickening combination of all of those three things.

'What time do we have to meet Molly?' he asked, as he settled back on his pillows and folded his arms.

I checked the time on my phone. 'In about two hours, just as we're ready to leave, she'll call me and say that she's only just got up and can we put it back by an hour?'

'Three hours, then? Well, I could get up and make us some coffee or you could get back in bed and we can do something about the happy you didn't have?' The slow, sexy smile got leer-shaped. 'What do you fancy?'

If I'd worn glasses I'd have pushed them up my nose, but I settled for a prim look. 'Coffee, please,' I said, because I knew it would make him stop leering. It did. He pouted instead and I was laughing as I wrenched myself away from my various Mac devices and leapt on to the bed so I could pounce on him.

That set the tone for the rest of the week. We weren't at it all the time. I had to work on my presentation for the New York conference and write something for the *Guardian* and take a lot of meetings in Shoreditch and Michael's parents were around and he was boringly fixated on coursework and dull admin work for his mum and dad to get money to buy stuff, but, apart from that, we managed to get together to do IT. Doing it. Seems so weird that you could classify the things we did with each other and how they made us both feel with a mere one-syllable, two-letter word. It.

Anyway we did the amazing, transcendental, life-affirming it every chance we had, which wasn't as often as we wanted because it wasn't as if Michael could stay over. He did vague up the idea of telling his mum and dad about us but before I could list the three hundred and fifty-seven reasons why that would be a bad idea, Michael decided he wouldn't.

'She'd be bound to mention it when one of my mates was round mine and we're still keeping this on a strictly need to know basis, right?'

I nodded. 'Right, and people who go to our school don't need to know about us.'

But there was one other person who was going to know about us, whether he liked it or not, and that was my dad. But as my dad was in his sixties and mostly lived a long way away and only used the internet to hook up with women at least twenty years younger than him who had a thing for ageing, alcoholic Lotharios, it didn't matter.

And even though the week had turned out to be one of the best weeks in recent memory, the threat of my dad's visit hung heavy in the air, like the scent of wet dog.

Roy, my dad, was due to come round at 4.30 on Friday after-noon. We weren't meeting Michael until seven at the dreaded Garfunkel's. Given that it would take half an hour to get there, that was two whole hours spent in the company of a man with whom I had nothing in common apart from a microscopic shred of DNA. Sometimes I wondered if we were genetically related but, as Pat absolutely wasn't the type of woman to play away from home (during my facts-of-life talk she'd told me that she found gardening far more fulfilling than sex) and Roy and I both had identical crooked middle fingers on our left hands, I had to accept the cruel hand that fate had dealt me.

By 3.45, the flat was gleaming. Well, it was tidyish by my standards but probably not by Roy's standards – he might have liked his drink but he wasn't one of those sloppy drunks, which would have made my life a lot easier. He could take half an hour to lay a table. One Easter Sunday, there had even been a ruler involved.

Anyway, I'd filled the fridge with nutritious food, quite a lot of it green and not Haribo-green either. Not that I was going to be eating any of it. I'd also given myself a makeunder. I wasn't getting rid of my peach-coloured hair, not for no man or paternal signifier, but I'd toned down the technicoloured splendour of my ensemble. Normally I wore what I wanted, but Roy was allegedly my father and he paid the service charges on the flat and the utility bills and put some money into my account for housekeeping, and in return I went to school, did my coursework like a good little girl and when he rolled into town for a visit, I tried to give every appearance that I could live a successful, independent life free from the parental yoke. Part of that was not letting my freak flag fly quite so high, which was why I was wearing a matching jumper and cardigan, a silver lamé twinset that I'd found in a charity shop, a red knee-length circle skirt and shoes that didn't look like an old lady had worn them first.

Even so, when I opened my front door and Roy saw me, his face dropped. Like he'd had an idea of me in his head that was prettier and smilier and just a lot *less* than I actually am and, as usual, I'd disappointed him before I even opened my mouth.

'Oh, hey, Roy,' I said, and his face dropped a bit more. My dad looks like the human equivalent of one of those really jowly dogs, so he always seems fairly morose, but when I'm with him it gets more pronounced, especially as I refuse to call him Dad. I mean, he's not really my dad. He kind of stepped back from that role a long time ago and I don't live with him, I don't speak to him much, he wouldn't dare give me a curfew and he doesn't help me with my homework, so why should I call him Dad?

Anyway, I let Roy gingerly wrap one arm round me in an awkward hug, and kiss my forehead, and then I ushered him into the flat and bringing up the rear was his latest woman. To be fair, it was the same woman he'd turned up with three months ago, so it was obviously serious. I couldn't remember her name, but then Roy said, 'You going to give your Auntie Sandra a kiss?'

He always talks to me either in a patronising voice like I'm seven or in a bluff, blustery way like I'm a proper adult and should act like one. I still wasn't going to give Sandra, who was smiling nervously at me, a kiss. I settled for a half-hearted wave and led them into the lounge.

They both looked round and I knew they weren't seeing the several metres of floor – not heaped with *neat* stacks of magazines – that I'd actually vacuumed. Sandra was looking at the exact spot on the sideboard where I'd set up the DustCam and when I graciously offered them a cup of tea and went to the kitchen, she ran her finger along the mantelpiece and showed the grimy evidence she'd uncovered to Roy.

It was excruciating but familiar. I gave Roy a tour around the flat so he'd know I hadn't moved in a family of meth-heads or illegal immigrants. I showed him some coursework, though he and Sandra were very dismissive of my seascape. 'You should have painted the beach at Margate,' Sandra said, pursing her lips. 'You get a lovely vista there.' Then I gave him the pile of envelopes from boring places like British Gas and he wanted an explanation of how long I had the central heating on for every day.

When it was 6.30 and I'd told Sandra for the fifth time that I didn't want to change and, yes, really, this was what I was going to wear for dinner, I hustled them out of the flat. We had to take public transport because Roy would want a drink, more than one drink, so he used the time to grill me about Michael.

'How old is he? Where did you meet him? What's he doing his A-levels in? Has he applied to university? What do his parents do for a living? Oh, so they're not short of a bob or two?'

'What does this Michael do in his spare time?' Roy asked as we got out at Leicester Square tube station. In all his years of going to Garfunkel's, Roy had decided that the one on Irving Street had the cleanest loos, friendliest staff and best-stocked salad bar. There was probably a spreadsheet involved. 'Does he have the same hobbies as you?'

This was Roy-speak for, 'Is this boy, who may or may not be trying to impregnate you, the same kind of weirdly dressed weirdo with weird pastimes as you?'

'He's just a friend,' I kept grimly repeating. 'A friend who, by some strange accident of birth, just so happens to be a boy.'

It occurred to me as we finally reached Garfunkel's that Roy had asked far more questions about Michael and his likes and dislikes and future career trajectory than he ever asked about mine.

The object of Roy's curiosity was hovering at the entrance to the restaurant. His face lit up when he saw us, because it was a freezing cold November night and Michael always turned up for everything at least ten minutes early and we were five minutes late. I wanted my face to light up too because, honestly, I was so pleased to see someone who wasn't Roy or Sandra. I settled for gently punching him on the arm instead.

'Michael, this is one of my secondary caregivers, Roy, and this is Sandra, Roy's special friend,' I said by way of introduction. 'Roy, Sandra, this is Michael, who's not, repeat not, a special friend. Just an ordinary friend.'

I squeezed Michael's hand as he held the door open for us to show that he wasn't just an ordinary friend and I was fudging the truth for appearance's sake and, actually, to save him a world of trouble. He caught my eye and pulled a face but I wasn't sure if he was annoyed with me or if he already realised that he was in for one of the most tedious evenings of his life, free salad notwithstanding.

There was a lot of fuss before we could sit down as the first table was too near the toilets and Sandra couldn't sit with her back to the room because it made her feel dizzy but she did need to be able to see out of the window because she got 'a touch claustrophobic', but eventually we were all seated. Michael and I had our backs to the restaurant because we didn't suffer from claustrophobia and Sandra and Roy were sitting opposite, a gin and tonic and a large whisky in front of them.

They both kept staring at Michael and I hoped Roy wasn't going to say something really tactless like, 'Are you sure you don't want to go to a Chinese restaurant?' For real. Once

Bethan was seeing a black guy, shock horror, and Roy actually asked him where he was born and wasn't happy when Martin said, 'Chalk Farm.'

Thankfully that didn't happen tonight and Michael wasn't wearing his low-slung jeans that showed his boxer trunks to the world. He was wearing his dark blue jeans that stayed on his hips with a blue and white check shirt and his grey hoodie. Not the most exciting outfit in the world, but it was parent- and girl-friend-of-parent-friendly and so was Michael.

He politely answered all of Roy's questions, giving the answers that we'd already run through, but Roy had only just asked Michael what his projected A-level grades were when Sandra tugged on Roy's sleeve.

'I think we should go to the salad bar now,' she said urgently, her head swivelling in that direction. 'They've just restocked.'

It shouldn't have been possible for two old people to move so fast. One minute they were sitting there, the next they were on the other side of the restaurant. I rested my head on Michael's shoulder for the briefest of moments.

'Oh, poor Jeane, has it been awful?'

'It's been the absolute awfullest,' I replied. 'And I'm pretty sure I'm going to have to eat some salad.'

Michael grinned, though there was nothing to grin about. 'If you eat all your salad then I've got you a special treat for later on.'

'I thought you had to go home,' I groused, because even though it was half-term and there were no school nights during half-term, Michael wasn't staying over. It was stupid. He was eighteen. Legally he was allowed to stay over without his parents' consent, or he could simply lie and say he was at a friend's house, but he was too vanilla. 'They'll go up for at least two more salad refills and we'll be here for *hours* and then there won't be time for you to give me a special treat.'

I had no idea why Michael was still grinning. 'I'm not talking about *that*,' he said prissily, as if I had to beg and plead and cajole in order to be able to have my wicked way with him, which, not even. 'I came up here early so I could go to Chinatown to get some stuff for my dad and visit my favourite Chinese bakery.'

'Oh! Did you get the buns with the red sticky paste in them?'

'I might have done.'

'You know, if I did proper boyfriends and you were my proper boyfriend then you'd be, like, the god of proper boyfriends,' I managed to spit out, because props were due. 'I'm sorry I dragged you into this.'

Michael nodded. 'If I'd known I was expected to bring my driver's licence and last three report cards, I probably wouldn't have agreed to it, but, hey, free meal!' He frowned. 'Is it free? Should I offer to pay my share?'

'No! We're not here of our own free will and if Roy expects us to pony up then I'll pay for your dinner. It's the very least I can do.' I glanced over to the salad bar where Roy and Sandra were deep in conversation over their heaped bowls. 'You know, it's not too late. You could still make a run for it and I'll cobble together some story about how you were taken ill or you had a sudden emergency and had to take your pet rabbit to the vet.'

It was Michael's turn to punch me on the arm. 'Lame. Very lame.'

'Well, I'm stressed out and I stayed up all night cleaning and tidying. I haven't even had a little bit of sleep and I can't think on the fly when I've had no sleep at all.'

Everything that came out of my mouth was one gigantic whine but Michael was still sitting there next to me, knee brushing against mine. All large and solid and calm so I had to blink and shake my head because it made me wonder exactly why he was sitting there next to me.

22

Jeane's dad, Roy, was the saddest looking man I've ever seen. I don't mean sad like in saddo, though he was wearing a really tragic cardigan and shirt and tie combo. I mean sad as in he looked like something terrible had happened to him at some stage in his life and he'd never got over it.

His lady friend, Sandra, also seemed to have suffered great misfortune. She twitched and fidgeted and smiled apologetically every time she spoke. Really, neither of them were that bad, even though they kept bombarding me with questions, but I think it was because they didn't know how else to keep the conversation going.

Jeane wasn't quite as snippy as usual. She didn't even explode when she was told to go and put more salad things in her salad bowl instead of just bacon croutons and pineapple pieces. She'd also made an effort not to look like too much of an eyesore. Yes, she was wearing a glittery silver jumper and cardigan but at least they matched and probably most girls wouldn't have worn a red skirt with yellow tights and black and white lace-up brogues (she insisted they were something called saddle shoes) but Jeane wasn't most girls.

The second round of drinks arrived and as we waited for our main courses Sandra started talking to me about her ex-husband and how all he'd left her with was a mountain of debts and a peptic ulcer. As Sandra talked, I watched Jeane and Roy.

He'd say something. Jeane would reply with an answer so curt, it was almost, but not quite, downright rude. She also kept glancing down at her salad bowl suspiciously as if it might suddenly leap up and attack her. The lights glinting off the silver cardigan gave her face a ghostly hue and there was Roy with his tie and his comb-over and his sad, sad face and all I could think was, how could you two be blood relations? How could you have lived in the same house for sixteen years? How is it possible that you're even sitting at the same table in Gar-funkel's?

Just then Jeane glanced up from her salad bowl and caught my eye. I'd never seen her look so lost before. She looked as sad as Roy and for a moment I was tempted to grab her and rush her to a place where she could sparkle and be gobby and eat huge quantities of Haribo.

'This is hell,' she mouthed at me. 'Can we do a runner?'

I was definitely thinking about it but then our main courses arrived. There was a moment's excitement when it looked as if they'd forgotten Sandra's mashed potatoes but it was all sorted out so the four of us could eat our dinner in a tense silence.

As soon as the waiter swooped down to take away our empty plates, Jeane was on her feet. 'I need a wee,' she yelped, snatching up her bag and galloping for the Ladies'. I knew for a fact, like I knew exactly how many goals Robin van Persie has scored for Arsenal in his career, that she was going to channel her anguish into a tweeting frenzy. I gripped my dessert menu as if it were a life belt and smiled wanly at Roy and Sandra.

'I don't understand it,' he said. 'She barely touched her omelette.'

'Well, maybe she was full up after her salad,' I said, though Jeane had only eaten the bacon croutons.

Roy shook his head. 'She loved coming to Garfunkel's when she was little. I've never seen a child so excited at the thought of a chocolate sundae.'

Jeane was still that girl. Some of her happiest moments were spent watching bad TV and rooting through a bag of sweets, but I don't think Roy had seen that girl in a long time. Still, he ordered her a chocolate sundae and when she finally returned to the table she gave him a thin-lipped smile and said thank you, even though normally if anyone had ever tried to order for her she'd have spat out a ranty lecture about the complex, conflicted relationship girls had with their bodies and food and possibly something about patriarchy.

I thought I hated at least half of the bits that made up Jeane but I hated this sad-faced, quiet bit of Jeane the most. When she sat down I couldn't help myself and I surreptitiously took her hand and gave it a comforting squeeze and the worst thing was that she let me.

'So, Jeane, we were thinking, Roy and I, that you might like to spend Christmas with us?' Sandra ventured timidly, as Jeane ate her chocolate sundae with all the enthusiasm of a girl who was working on a chain gang. 'There's a lovely family moved into our apartment complex, they're coloured even though they're German but they're very nice, and they have two daughters about your age that you can play with.'

Jeane didn't say anything at first because she was struggling to scoop out a piece of chocolate brownie from the bottom of her sundae glass.

'Now, I know you think the Costa Brava isn't the most exciting place in the world but it will be nice to spend Christmas together,' Roy said as he rubbed his hands together nervously. 'I've got an old portable TV in the spare room so you can watch your programmes.'

'That sounds nice, it really does,' Jeane said in a voice that was flatter than Holland and I *knew* her now and the angrier Jeane was, the flatter her voice got, like she didn't dare to let any emotion break through because then she might start screaming or doing something else that she'd normally think was totes uncool. She hadn't actually told me this but by this stage I'd had plenty of field experience. 'Ordinarily I would love to come but Bethan's coming back to London for Christmas.'

'Well, it would be lovely to see both of you,' Roy said gamely. 'Might be a bit of a squeeze but you and Beth could share the spare room and—'

'Yeah, it's just, like, we've already made plans 'cause Bethan could only get a few days off work and I've already booked us

Christmas dinner at Shoreditch House. It was very expensive,' she added with a frowny significant look. 'But it was really sweet of you to offer. Maybe I could come for a really quick visit in the New Year.'

It was obvious that Jeane had no intention of doing any such thing but we all nodded and then Jeane pulled out her phone and began to type furiously. A second later my phone vibrated and under cover of the table, I read her text:

God, how much longer is this torture going to last?

Not much longer by the look of things. Roy signalled for the waiter and asked for the bill, then pulled a buff-coloured envelope out of the inner pocket of his anorak. 'It's a shame about Christmas.'

Jeane sighed. 'Honestly, Roy, after six hours tops you'd be wanting to kill me, you know you would.'

'Why can't you make more of an effort to be normal? It would be so much easier for everyone,' Roy said, shaking his head, and still Jeane didn't lose her temper, though she was gripping her extra-long sundae spoon so tightly I was surprised it didn't snap. 'Now, do you have a thing that takes copies of photographs and puts them on your computer?'

'You mean a scanner, right?'

'Is it a home photocopier, Roy?' Sandra butted in and I actually *heard* Jeane grit her teeth.

'I've got one,' she properly snapped for the first time that evening. 'What do you want scanned?'

'I had to sort through some boxes I had in storage . . . now that Sandra has done me the kind honour of moving into my apartment with me ...' Several very long-winded moments later, Roy finally handed over the envelope, which contained family photos. 'I'm sure your mother would like copies. So can you turn them into photos once you've copied them?'

'Yeah, sure, or I could just email them to you or put them on Flickr,' Jeane suggested to Roy's blank face. 'Look, I'll email them *and* print out copies on photographic paper – I'll put them in the post with the originals.'

'They might get lost that way, dear.'

'That's why I'm going to send them special delivery, Sandra,' Jeane said in her flattest, dullest voice yet. It was official. She'd met the end of her tether, which was why she was standing up, then taking hold of the sleeve of my shirt so she could yank me to my feet too. 'Thanks *so* much for dinner. It's been *great* catching up, but Michael and I have to go now.'

I think Jeane put Roy and Sandra out of their misery too because they didn't pretend that they wanted to linger over coffee or see Jeane before they went back to Spain. Roy didn't even stand up or make any attempt to give Jeane a goodbye kiss or a hug. He just nodded at her and said, 'Let us know if you change your mind about Christmas. Have to be in the next week or so because we might go away if you're not coming.'

Jeane didn't comment but her jaw was working furiously as she gave a mock salute then marched out of the restaurant. She was halfway up the street before I managed to catch up with her.

'Are you all right?' I asked pointlessly, because it was obvious that Jeane and all right weren't on speaking terms.

'I'm fine. Why wouldn't I be fine? My dad came to town and took me out for a free meal. End of. I've got absolutely nothing to complain about.'

'That's weird 'cause you kinda sound like you're complaining.'

'Look, Michael, I know we have this whole thing where we bitch and take the piss out of each other but I'm really not in the mood right now,' Jeane said. She came to a halt. '"Happy families are all alike; every unhappy family is unhappy in its own way." I come from the unhappiest family since records began.'

I knew from when Mum's book club tackled *War and Peace* that when someone starts quoting Tolstoy they're not in a good place. But the thing was that I didn't know how to get her to a good place.

'Come on, let's just go,' Jeane said.

'We could go and see a film if you like, or there might be a band on or—'

'Let's just *go*.'

We got the tube in silence. Waited for the bus without speaking. I could feel Jeane's unhappiness as if it was a person coming between the two of us, wrapping us up in its misery. Jeane stared at the bus timetable, her lips moving soundlessly, arms folded, and suddenly I felt angry.

I'd given up a night to meet her dad and she hadn't even said thanks. I'd let myself be interrogated and eaten food that I didn't really like and had been there for her and now she was giving me the silent treatment. I wouldn't have done half that shit for a real girlfriend.

The bus arrived. It was a ten-minute bus ride back to our nabe and I knew that by the end of the journey I had to break up with her. For the sake of my sanity and, more importantly, my reputation, because the way things were going, Jeane was going to infect me with dork disease. Like, I hadn't even thought that tonight's outfit was too awful even though Jeane was wearing a cardie and a jumper made out of scratchy silver material and a clashing red skirt – the more time I spent with her, the more immune I became to the hot mess that she looked. Not even a hot mess, which implied some kind of hotness, just a mess.

I watched resentfully as Jeane marched up the aisle of the bus, then, just as she was about to sit down, she turned and smiled at me. It was a weak, lopsided smile and whatever hell I'd been through tonight, it had been worse for Jeane, but she was still colossally self-involved and she still could have said thank you. Instead, surprise, surprise, she'd pulled out her phone and her fingers were flying over the screen.

I sat down in the seat in front of hers and thought about how to break up with her. It would probably have to be via text message as it was the only way I was sure of getting her attention, and, as I thought it, I was pulling out my knackered old BlackBerry and surrpetitiously checking Jeane's Twitter timeline.

 adork_able Jeane Smith
I've seen hell and it looks a lot like the salad bar in Garfunkel's.

adork_able Jeane Smith
You can never go home again. Fo sho.

adork_able Jeane Smith
They fuck you up, your mum and dad. They
may not mean to, but they do . . .

adork_able Jeane Smith
They fill you with the faults they had. And add
some extra, just for you . . . Way over-
identifying with Philip Larkin tonight.

adork_able Jeane Smith
I heart Chinese buns stuffed full of red bean
paste and people who buy me Chinese buns
stuffed full of red bean paste.

I could feel my anger starting to recede, become fuzzier and
indistinct, and then Jeane suddenly leaned forward and softly
(and unbelievably) kissed the back of my neck. I almost shot
a metre off my seat and was frantically trying to shield my
phone from her when she did it again. Kissed the back of my
neck again.

'That meal would have been about eleventy billion times
more excruciating if you hadn't been there,' she whispered. 'I'm
going to do something AMAZE-ing to make it up to you. Not
sure what, but it will knock your socks off.'

Sometimes it was impossible to stay mad at Jeane. 'My folks

drove to Devon today to spend the weekend there before they come back with the little sisters,' I informed her.

'Did they? How interesting.' I could feel her breath warm on my nape. 'Are you suggesting what I think you're suggesting, Michael Lee?'

'Well, I don't have football practice tomorrow so I could come back to yours, but my house has a fully stocked fridge and I know I won't end up with congealed Haribo stuck to my socks when I walk across the room.'

Jeane rested her arms on the back of my seat. 'That only happened the one time, but you kind of had me at fully stocked fridge. Can we go to mine first so I can pick up some stuff?'

'Yeah, sure.' Her hand fleetingly stroked the side of my face and it made me feel shivery, the good kind of shivery. 'You know we're not meant to touch in public. People might see.'

I thought I heard her giggle, though usually Jeane didn't do giggling. 'There's no one on the bus in the right demographic to recognise us, and, even if they did, we can just deny everything.'

She was right. It wasn't important. What was important, as I pointed out, was that, 'When you have a meal, even a three-course meal, that you didn't enjoy, you're as hungry as if you hadn't eaten anything.'

'It's probably something to do with the brain and its pleasure receptors. You should ask Barney, he loves shit like that.'

'Are you hungry, too? 'Cause I think Mum made some shepherd's pie for me before she left.'

Jeane pressed her face right up against mine. 'I'm bloody *starving*.'

23

Usually when I have a fit of the sullens, it can be days, even weeks, before they disappear, which is why I try to avoid situations that might make me get my mope on. But, somehow, Michael always managed to head my mope off at the pass.

Like, he seemed to instinctively know that I couldn't handle being on my own after a parental visit and, after going to mine to pick up pyjamas, toothbrush and a hundred other things that I couldn't do without in a twenty-four-hour period, I was sitting on his bed eating home-made shepherd's pie and watching an *Inbetweeners* repeat. Even though we had the whole house to ourselves, I much preferred Michael's room.

It was all odd angles from being up in the rafters and it was *so* tidy. So neat. So ordered. It wasn't even like his mum fussed and nagged at him to get it that way. I had seen, with my very own eyes, Michael get me some of the guest towels (guest towels, I mean, what the hell?) and neatly fold them up before he placed them on the bed.

In deference to my emotionally fragile state, he didn't try to kiss me, when normally we'd have been mucking up the perfect millpond-smoothness of his duvet within five seconds. He was quite happy to eat his shepherd's pie and pretend that he was riveted by my insightful analysis of *The Inbetweeners* and where it fitted into the canon of dorks on TV. He even agreed, without too much nagging, to let me use his scanner because I wanted those photographs dealt with right away.

Michael hovered for a while to make sure my hands were clean before they went anywhere near his pristine keyboard but once he was satisfied they were spotless and I wasn't trying to look at his browsing history to see what porn he was into, he left me to it and started playing *LA Noire*.

I found that I didn't really have to look at the photographs if I placed them face-down on the scanner and unfocused my eyes so they appeared on the computer screen as flesh-toned blobs. I was almost done when Michael nudged the back of his desk chair with a foot.

'The least you can do is show me some pictures of you as a kid.'

'Dream on, dreamer, never going to happen,' I said as I clicked away.

'There is no way that anything your parents made you wear could be worse than what you actually choose to wear now,' Michael insisted, and when I turned round to give him my most withering glare, I realised he'd snuck up behind me. 'Come on, Jeane, there has to be at least one photo of you either in a nappy or naked on a fake sheepskin rug. It's the law.'

'We weren't a taking-photos sort of family,' I said, which was the truth. Or it was the truth by the time I came along. 'Besides, these photos were all taken before I was even thought of.'

'You sure you're not just saying that because when you were a small child you loved nothing more than dressing up in princess outfits?' Michael said, as he rested his chin on my shoulder, which was very annoying.

'Do you really think I was that kind of little girl? FYI, I had my own home-made superhero costume for this character I invented called Awesome Girl,' I admitted. In a cardboard box somewhere in the depths of my flat were the badly drawn comic strips I'd written for Awesome Girl and Bad Dog, her trusty canine companion. Pat and Roy had been vehemently anti-television so I'd had to make my own fun.

My trip down memory lane, and Awesome Girl and Bad Dog's successful campaign to rid the world of vegetables, abruptly came to an end when Michael poked me in the ribs. 'You owe me! Your dad actually expected me to tell him how I was going to repay my student loans that don't even exist yet.' Michael sounded like he was getting properly annoyed now.

'God, there's nothing to see.' I highlighted all the pictures I'd scanned and with a few more clicks I had a slideshow. 'That's Pat and Roy with Bethan in utero, Bethan, Bethan, Bethan, Pat, Roy and Bethan and . . .'

'There!' Michael said triumphantly, pointing to the next slide. 'Jeane as a baby. I knew there had to be photographic evidence.' He shoved his face right against mine. 'My, what chubby cheeks you've got.'

I shoved him away. 'That's not me,' I said shortly. 'It's Andrew and, well, I'd call him my older brother but he died long before I was born so it always seems weird to call him my brother.'

Michael opened his mouth but then he didn't say anything as I showed him the rest of the photos, which consisted of Bethan and Andrew in a series of vile eighties outfits, so vile that even I couldn't find any redeeming qualities in them. Then there were the pictures that explained why these photos had spent so many years stuffed away in an envelope, unseen: Andrew getting paler and more fragile, mustering up a wan smile for the camera, and then his eleventh birthday, his last, in a hospital bed surrounded by helium balloons and ominous-looking hospital equipment. I think he'd died a week or two later but I was a bit fuzzy on the details.

'Shit, Jeane, I'm so sorry. I wouldn't have started cracking jokes if I'd known,' Michael said heavily, and I could feel him looking at me, really staring. 'Are you OK ... I mean, having to go through these photos?'

'Well, yeah ...' I shrugged. 'Of course it's sad that he died. It's, like, awful, but I wasn't there. It was something that happened to my family though I don't think the three of them ever recovered from it. Maybe Bethan did, but then again I don't think she'd be working seventy hours a week as a paediatric resident if her older brother hadn't died of a rare form of leukaemia when she was seven.'

'Your dad, he just seems so *sad*. Has he always been like that?'

Most anybody else would not want to be asking questions about this because it was awkward and deeply personal but Michael didn't seem to get it. And I realised that I'd never talked about this, about Andrew, with anyone. Occasionally, Bethan would tell me a story about Andrew, but if I started asking her questions – Did you fight with each other? Was he scared of the dark? Were Pat and Roy different, then, like, were you all happy before he got ill? – we'd never get very far because Bethan would start to cry. Even though it had been over twenty years ago, she'd cry these awful stomach-wrenching sobs like it had happened only yesterday.

So, I'd never talked about Andrew before because I always felt that his death hadn't anything to do with me. Though really, when you thought about it, I wouldn't be here if it hadn't been for him.

'Yeah,' I replied at last. 'He's always been like that. Pat, my mother, she's like that too, but more snippy.'

Michael sat down at the foot of his bed and I swung round the chair so we were facing each other, because I had a feeling that we weren't done talking about this.

I was right.

'It couldn't have been much fun growing up in a house where everyone was sad all the time,' Michael remarked casually, and maybe if he'd been firing questions at me and implying that my mum and dad had fucked me up Philip Larkin-style, I'd have got all defensive and huffed and flounced and maybe even stormed out, but he wasn't and I didn't.

'It wasn't like they walked around crying and going on about how sad they were,' I explained. 'It was more like they weren't *there*. Like, they were kinda absent. Which was fine by me. I'm pretty much self-made.'

'Well, I did half suspect that you were raised by wolves,' Michael said with a tentative smile. 'Wolves with a liking for sweets.'

'Don't get me wrong, there's lots and lots of people who had worse childhoods than mine, but ...' I faltered because some stuff was hard to say, even if you thought about it a lot or tried really hard not to think about it at all.

Michael took my hand and traced circles on my palm. 'But what?' Then he lifted my hand so he could kiss the spot where his fingers had been, and I wondered if Scarlett had had rocks in her head because when it came down to who was the better boyfriend, Barney or Michael, then Michael won every time in every category. Except Barney outshone him when it came to playing *Guitar Hero* (seriously, he was a demon on that thing) and taking my computer apart and putting it back together in the space of a weekend so it ran faster, better and with less of a whirring noise. 'You can tell me stuff, Jeane. I'm not going to tell anyone.'

I nodded. He did have a point and it wasn't like he had any secret recording equipment – at least I didn't think he had.

'The thing is, right, really they should have got divorced after Andrew died. Apparently it happens a lot when a couple loses a kid. It doesn't bring them closer together; it tears them apart. There's been surveys done and everything.' I didn't bother to point out that I'd spent hours reading up on the subject. 'But anyway, Pat and Roy didn't take that option. They decided that having another child would take the pain away, like when your dog dies and you get a new puppy a month later. Except they didn't get some cute smiley baby that filled them with a renewed sense of purpose, they got me, and then they were stuck with each other for another eighteen years ...'

'Well, yeah, but it wasn't eighteen years, was it?' Michael pointed out. ''Cause you're only seventeen now and you said that you started living here with your sister when you were fifteen so your parents must have split up around then.'

'I was getting to that part,' I said, and I was proud of that part because it proved that I had more common sense than the two adults that were meant to be bringing me up and doing a pretty poor job of it. 'It was a Sunday and Bethan was on nights so she was sleeping all day and Pat was working on her MA in Advanced Tree Hugging and Roy was drinking in his shed at the bottom of the garden and when Sunday dinner was finally ready, vegetarian spaghetti bolognese, because Pat thinks red meat gives you bowel cancer – in fact she thinks everything gives you every type of cancer there is – I realised that it was the first time all weekend that any of us were in the same room at the same time. God, I'm rambling like a rambling thing, aren't I?'

'It's OK,' Michael said. 'I'm used to your run-on sentences now. So, right, you're all eating veggie bolognese, then what happened?'

'Nothing much, except I said there was no point staying together for my sake when my mental well-being would probably be improved if they just split up.'

Michael looked horrified, especially when I giggled, but it wasn't a callous giggle, it was more a giggle as I remembered telling them about the audacious plan I'd hatched to become legally emancipated from them.

'Of course they told me not to be so ridiculous and that everything was fine, but it so obviously wasn't, and, after three months of hard campaigning, they came round to my way of thinking.'

'Because in the end it's easier to give in to you than to keep saying no?'

'Something like that,' I agreed, because that was always my MO. If reason didn't work, I usually found that repetition and volume did the trick. 'Anyways, they got a divorce, sold the house, bought the flat for me and Bethan to live in and Pat went off to Peru to work on her PhD and Roy buggered off to Spain to open a bar. So by the time Bethan got a fellowship to study in Chicago, it was too late to change things.'

Michael was still looking horrified and a lot like he felt sorry for me, when there was no reason. 'You poor—'

I clamped my hand over his mouth. 'Poor nothing.'

Michael swatted my hand away with annoying ease. 'Sorry, but it sounds like a pretty shit childhood.'

'Whatever. I doubt I'd be quite as awesome as I am today if I hadn't learnt from an early age that I was the only person I could rely on. Though maybe I was just born dorky and proud of it. Who knows? Everyone has some trauma growing up, don't they?'

Michael shook his head. 'I'm pretty much trauma-free.' He pursed his lips as he thought hard about any trauma he might have known. 'Well, apart from being an only child for ten years until Melly rocked up. That was a shock after being top dog for so long.' His face brightened. 'I suppose the weirdest thing about our family is that biologically Melly and Alice are twins.'

'How can they be, when Melly is seven and Alice is, what, five?'

'I don't know all the details but Mum and Dad had problems after they'd had me so they went through IVF, froze some of the spare embryos, had Melly, defrosted the rest of the embryos and then there was Alice.'

'I still don't understand how that makes them twins,' I argued, and if Michael had been trying to distract me from my own woe-is-me-ness then my God it was working.

'No, neither did Melly when Mum and Dad told her and they got into a whole thing about sperm and eggs, which just confused her even more, and then Alice wanted to know why she'd been stuck in a freezer for two years.' Michael choked back a laugh. 'I caught the pair of them standing on a chair rooting in the freezer to see if there were any more tiny babies in test tubes hiding behind the fish fingers.'

I couldn't help it, I giggled, though I forced myself to stop as soon as was humanly possible. 'I guess if that is your closest brush with a childhood trauma then at least it was a nice sort of trauma. Well, that and the fact that your mum and dad are kind of hands-on with the whole parenting thing.' I shuddered. 'Now that would be something I totes couldn't deal with. I much prefer Pat and Roy's benign neglect.'

'I think we're about to have another argument,' Michael announced, sitting up straight. I dreaded what he was going to say next. Normally I loved a good argy bargy but I was too wrung out for any more bickering.

'Why?' I asked suspiciously.

'Because, actually, my mum and her overprotective parenting style is looking bloody good right now.' He sounded so amazed that he might actually have lucked out in the mum department that I started giggling again. 'What's so funny?'

'You are,' I told him, sliding off the computer chair so I could slide on to his lap and push him down so he was lying on his back and I could pin his arms above his head. 'Everything shows on your face. I always know exactly what you're thinking.'

'No, you don't,' Michael said grumpily as he made a token effort to free himself. He wasn't even *trying*. 'I do have some mystery.'

'You don't. You really don't.' I gasped slightly because now Michael was *trying* to break free from my puny hold. 'You have zero mystery. Besides, mystery is totes overrated.'

Sure, Michael might have had a few issues courtesy of his control freak mum and his insane need to be liked by everyone, but he was pretty much an open book. Not even a book with a lot of long words.

'You're such a bitch sometimes,' Michael grunted as he flipped us so he was on top and I was squirming on the bottom. 'You don't know everything. Like, you don't even know what I'm thinking right now.'

But I did. He was holding me down with his body and I was wriggling to get free and it was suddenly *very* obvious exactly what he was thinking about. I didn't need to say anything; I just smiled knowingly. And, yes, I knew exactly what the next words out of his mouth were going to be.

'Well, apart from *that*, I bet you don't know what I'm thinking about.'

'How much you'd like to kill me at this particular point in time and how did you ever get mixed up with a mixed-up girl like me blah blah bloody blah,' I said in a singsong voice.

He kissed me then and his kisses chased the last of my blues away and he'd been solid and dependable and rock-like and utterly boyfriend-able during the evening's awfulness with added bits of awful. Instead of winding Michael up, I should have been thinking of ways to repay his kindness.

Then Michael stopped holding me down and just held me and his kisses got sweeter and fiercer and it was all I could do to kiss him just as fiercely and payback was going to be impossible until, as Michael tore his mouth away from mine so he could get some air, I had my best idea ever.

'Come to New York with me!' I panted. 'My treat!'

'What?' He tried to kiss me again, but I warded him off. 'Come on, give me another kiss.'

'No kisses right now. I'm serious. I'm speaking at a conference in New York in a fortnight and you're *so* coming with me.'

Michael shook his head. 'I am so *not* coming with you. New York in two weeks' time? Are you freaking crazy?'

'Never been saner. Come to New York! It will be fun!'

I was laughing. Michael was laughing too, even as he shook his head. 'No!'

'Yes!'

'No!'

'Yes! You know that secretly you want to.'

'No! Never! Not in a million years. Now shut up and kiss me or go home.'

I kissed him, but we weren't done with the conversation. I knew that within twenty-four hours, Michael would come round to my way of thinking. People always did.

24

'Michael, you're coming to New York. End of. I swapped my business class seat on Virgin Atlantic for two premium economy ones. Does my sacrifice mean nothing? Does it? What kind of unfeeling brute are you?'

I thought Jeane was being her usual melodramatic self when she'd claimed that she'd badgered her parents into getting a divorce but after five days of being badgered, pestered and nagged, I was beginning to believe her.

I'd told Jeane that there was no way, not even if the Rapture was imminent, that my parents would let me go to New York with her for the weekend. Never even mind taking the Friday off school – I might just as well ask if I could go to the moon. I had to ask my parents' permission before I took something from the fridge.

Of course when I'd told Jeane this, after paraphrasing so I didn't sound like a complete loser, she'd looked appalled.

'For God's sake, why can't you just lie to them like a normal teenager? I'll *tell* you what to say. It's not rocket science, Michael.'

I'd often wondered how Jeane managed to run her dork empire when her life was so chaotic and disorganised until she emailed me a bullet-pointed action plan.

Your New York Checklist

1. Tell your parents that you're going to look at a university over that weekend. You must have an older friend who managed to get on to a degree course. Pretend you're going to stay with him. Have checked your timetable, you hardly have anything on Friday – just Comp Sci and Maths. Quelle boring.

2. I also need to register you for the conference. TBH, most of the other speakers will probably be deathly dull. But I won't be deathly dull, I promise. I will do exciting things via the medium of PowerPoint and video.

3. You can't take liquid in large quantities in your hand luggage so you'll have to put your hair gunk in your suitcase. Or better yet see if you can manage without it for a weekend. I'm not sure that strange cockscomb thing usually seen on middle-aged lesbians is going to cut it in New York. Just saying . . .

4. I need your passport deets for the ticket. Also what kind of meal do you want? I thought I'd mix things up and go for the kosher option.

5. You need to log on to this website and fill in a US visa

waiver form NOW. It has to be done at LEAST three days
before you enter the States, otherwise you'll either be put
on the first plane back to London (can you say 'expensive'?)
or be arrested at gunpoint, possibly with the assistance of
some snarly dogs, and detained in an illegal aliens prison-
type place (which would be a major bummer).

6. You also need to call your mobile phone company and get
them to turn off your voicemail. Also, turn off international
roaming on your phone otherwise it'll cost you £££££££s.
Don't worry, I'll remind you at half-hour intervals until you
do it.

7. I'm sure there was other stuff you need to do. I'll get back
to you.

Now it was eight days until Jeane jetted to New York and
she'd redoubled her efforts. Her efforts had been pretty non-
stop anyway so redoubling them meant there wasn't a spare
moment when she shut up about bloody New bloody York.

'Don't you want me to go because I actually want to go, not
because you've nagged me into going?' I asked Jeane.

We were in the stationery cupboard tucked away at the back
of the upper school basement. I don't know where Jeane had
got the key from and I also never knew that the school had so
many hidden spots where we could sneak away for a kiss and
a cuddle. It was only ever a kiss and a cuddle (and maybe a
little unbuttoning) on school premises, but today Jeane had
lured me to the cupboard under false pretences.

We'd only had ten minutes of kissing before she pushed me
away and started on her New York nagathon.

Now she swung herself up on a broken filing cabinet and gave me a stern look. 'I don't care what makes you go to New York, as long as you go. Why are you being such a drag about this? It's so boring.'

'If I'm so boring then you won't want me tagging along for three days.'

'I didn't say *you* were boring, I said *the situation* was boring, and technically it would be four days, but that's all right. Just tell your parents that you're coming back from seeing your old football-playing friend at his place of higher learning really early on Monday morning and you'll go straight to school.' She tilted her chin defiantly. She never tilted her chin in any other way. 'Really, what could be simpler than that?'

'Open heart surgery would be simpler. Have you met my mother?'

Jeane grumbled something under her breath and pouted. Some girls broke your heart when they pouted but Jeane just looked bad-tempered and sulky. 'We both know that you're going to give in eventually sooner or later and it would be much more convenient for me if it was sooner.'

I took a step towards the door. 'One more word about New York and I'm out of here.'

'But secretly you'd love to go to New York with me, wouldn't you? Just admit it.'

This time I took three steps towards the door. 'I've had enough of this.'

'OK! OK! I promise I won't talk about you-know-what for a whole ten minutes.'

'You can't go ten seconds without talking about it.'

I turned round to see her pouting again. 'I can if you're kissing me.'

And when she put it like that, and there was still a good half hour before afternoon lessons and I'd already bolted down my lunch, kissing Jeane was much more fun than storming off in a huff.

Sat on top of the filing cabinet, Jeane was taller than me for once, which made for an interesting adjustment as I had to stretch to reach her mouth and she wrapped her legs, adorned in red and blue striped tights, around my chest to pull me in closer. I didn't even care that one of the drawer handles was digging into my stomach.

'You're such a pretty boy,' Jeane whispered and I should have been offended and pulling away because, Christ, no boy wants to be called pretty, but she sounded, I don't know, wistful and like she was completely down with the whole pretty thing, so I let it go just this once.

Jeane shivered when I kissed her mouth. Then I kissed a path along her cheek, pausing to nip her earlobe before I started kissing her neck. She always smelt so good, of figs and vanilla and baby lotion, particularly this spot where her pulse thundered away and she was extra ticklish so it always made her squirm and giggle.

'You're so cute when you're like this,' I told her and she dug her knees into my ribs.

'Piss off. I am *not* cute. Cute is not what I aim for.'

'Tough. You're cute. Deal with it.'

'Oh, shut up and kiss me.'

I was just shutting up and kissing her when I thought I heard something outside, but I'd just succeeded in undoing the third button on Jeane's dress so I wasn't really paying attention, especially as she was wriggling to get even closer to me.

But I was definitely paying attention when the door handle rattled and I heard Barney say, 'Sometimes she hides out in here. She has a secret stash of Haribo tucked away in a box of A3 paper. Oh! Door's unlocked.'

Jeane and I were still pulling away from each other as Barney, closely followed by Scarlett, burst into the cupboard and they both said, 'What the . . . ?' in perfect unison, which would have been funny if Jeane didn't still have her legs wrapped round me and her dress unbuttoned and my hoodie and jumper were slung over a broken fan.

It was the most awful silence I'd ever known. It felt as if it lasted for centuries, but it was only about a minute until Jeane had done up her dress, folded her arms and said, 'Well, this is awkward.'

Barney looked at me, then he looked at Jeane, then he looked at me again. 'What is going on? I mean, *why*? Like, you two? This is *so* weird.'

'It's not *that* weird,' I snapped as I retrieved my jumper and pulled it over my head because Scarlett had averted her eyes and I wasn't sure if it was because she'd seen me and Jeane pretty much having sex with most of our clothes on or she was still as disturbed by my body as she had been when we were dating. 'We go to the same school and we live in the same area and we're kinda the same age. We have loads in common.'

'We have *nothing* in common,' Jeane piped up and crushed that little bit of my ego that had remained intact despite her best efforts to destroy it. 'Michael thinks I'm a bossy, badly dressed freakazoid and I think he's just a pretty face and not much substance. What we're doing doesn't mean anything and if either of you tell anyone about this ...' She paused. 'You know how I've made you cry twice in English, Scar?'

Scarlett nodded. She still hadn't regained the power of speech and my ego was now officially dead, no hope of a cure. Jeane was such a bitch.

'Well, I can make you cry like that every day for the rest of your school career,' Jeane continued. 'I don't want to but I will if I hear any talk that links me and Michael. If I even *hear* us mentioned in the same sentence. Got it?'

'Like anyone would ever believe it,' Scarlett gasped. 'I saw it with my own eyes, and my brain ... I can't deal with this.'

None of us could deal with it. Barney was glaring at Jeane because she'd been mean to Scarlett. Scarlett was glaring at Jeane because she'd just been threatened and I was glaring at Jeane because she had zero respect for me. And have I mentioned the fact that she was a bitch?

Jeane wasn't glaring at anyone. She swung her legs and seemed as if she was deep in thought. Suddenly she looked up, yelped, then jumped down from her perch.

'Barnster, you're a genius!' she exclaimed as she dropped to her knees and started rummaging among the dusty boxes. 'I'd totes forgotten I had some Haribo tucked away in here. I missed lunch and I'm *ravenous*.' She pulled out a bag of sweets. 'Though what I was thinking when I bought Milky Mix, I don't know. Not Haribo's finest moment.'

It was classic Jeane. Create a diversion. Go off on a tangent.

Be kooky. That way everyone forgot why they were mad at her – Scarlett was actually digging into the bag of Milky Mix that Jeane proffered.

I started to laugh. Jeane drove me mad and there were lots of times that I didn't like her very much but she was the one part of my life that never went to plan and I knew then that I would go to New York with her, not because she'd worn me down but because it would be fun. Jeane was really good at making me have fun.

'I don't know why you're laughing,' Barney grumbled, because he was still mad at Jeane. 'None of this is funny.'

I wondered if Barney still had a thing for Jeane, but he probably didn't because he grabbed Scarlett's hand and started walking her to the door. 'If you make Scar feel even a bit sad, there's going to be trouble,' he warned in a very un-Barney-like way.

'It's OK, Barns, I can look after myself,' Scarlett said, which was patently not true. 'Anyway, I'm not going to say anything. Not because I'm scared but because I don't want to think about what I've just seen ever again.'

And with that they were gone and it was just Jeane and me left. She was doggedly chewing on her Haribo, which were no substitute for a lunchtime sandwich, and she held up her hand to indicate that she wanted to speak once she was done masticating.

'I don't think you're *just* a pretty face,' she said eventually. 'I know there's more to you than that but I could hardly tell Barney and Scarlett that. It would make things even more complicated. It's best they think it's just to do with our hormones.'

'Oh, so I do have some substance then, do I?' I asked, because this was as close as Jeane would ever get to an apology and I was determined to drag it out for as long as possible.

'I just said so, didn't I?' She held up a thumb and a forefinger, a tiny gap between them. 'About this much, I reckon.'

'At least I have style,' I said teasingly. 'And by the way, Pippi Longstocking called, she wants her DNA back.'

Jeane put her hand to her heart and pulled a face. 'Ouch. First, I don't look anything like Pippi fricking Longstocking and, hello! The guy who buys all his clothes from shops that pipe out foul-smelling perfume and don't do real people sizes is dissing *my* dress sense? I don't think so.'

'Sorry that my clothes cause you so much pain. Probably best if we keep on pretending that we don't know each other in New York – that way if we bump into someone you know, I won't cause you any embarrassment.'

'Oh, I'll just say that you're my special-needs cousin or something,' Jeane assured me, and I waited while she rewound what I just said, played it back and then went all googly-eyed and gormless.

Jeane Smith. Speechless. God, I was *good*.

She pointed at herself, then at me, with one shaking finger.

'Yes, Jeane. You and me go to New York together,' I said slowly and loudly as if she wasn't very bright and English wasn't her first language. Her facial expression, caught somewhere between glee and a scowl, was one of the funniest things I'd ever seen and I started laughing again.

I laughed until she stamped on my foot.

25

I'd half wondered if he'd back out at the last moment or confess everything to his parents, but, at 2 p.m. on Friday, Michael was sitting next to me on the Virgin flight from Heathrow to JFK, and, once they'd done the safety announcement and we were taxiing down the runway, he turned to me with a grin that made my heart genuinely skip a beat, though normally my heart doesn't do stupid stuff like that.

'Oh my God! I'm going to New York,' he said. 'It didn't seem real before but now we're about to take off, I'm getting proper excited.'

'Hallelujah,' I said. 'Because mostly you've been stressed out about the whole thing.'

'Yeah, well, you've been making me stressed out. Even after I said I was coming you still kept sending me those checklists.' Michael pulled a crumpled piece of paper from his jeans pocket. 'I could have worked out how many pairs of socks I needed for four days all by myself, you know.'

He had a point but I was used to my peer group being as flaky as a bag of sliced almonds. 'I can't help it. I micro-manage and then that way when something goes wrong I know that it wasn't my fault.'

'You call it micro-managing, I call it being really, really bossy.'

'Potato, potarto, my friend.' I hoped that he wasn't going to be like this in New York, picking at me the whole time, but then Michael nudged my arm and gave me another of his pretty smiles.

'Anyway, I'm trying to say thanks for all this. Like, for asking me to come with you, and we'll have to find a sweetshop so I can repay you in candy. It's the very least I can do.'

'You don't have to do that,' I said quickly, although I was already mentally adding Dylan's Candy Bar to the detailed itinerary I'd already compiled. 'The trip was *my* thank you for helping me to deal with all that family crap of mine.'

'Well, whatever . . .'

'Yeah, whatevs . . .'

There was a lurch as we left the ground and no matter how many times I'd flown I couldn't unclench until I was sure we were properly airborne and weren't suddenly going to plunge to our deaths. I was so tensed up that I didn't even realise, until there was a ping and I went to unfasten my seatbelt, that Michael had been holding my hand the whole time.

So we flew over the Atlantic for about seven hours. Michael watched three films and I ate Haribo and worked on my presentation. When it was time to give my speech, I'd appear to be winging it when, in reality, I'd rehearsed it so many times that I was word-perfect and didn't even need to look at my notes. I'd throw in a few ums and ahs because nobody likes a smartarse seventeen-year-old, and I probably would fall over my sentences at the start from nerves but then I planned to be funny and insightful and the voice of my generation, which wasn't difficult as my generation was woefully inarticulate.

Eventually we disembarked and started walking through miles and miles of corridors, until we were standing in the queue to have our passports checked. It was then that Michael started to get very antsy at the thought of having his fingerprints scanned and his photo taken.

'But why?'

'To make sure that you're not a member of Al Qaeda or on any no-fly lists,' I hissed.

'Of course I'm not,' he whispered back. 'Do they keep our information?'

'Well, of course they do.' I had no idea whether they did but then Michael shuddered and light dawned. 'I promise they're not going to phone your parents to tell them you've entered the United States.'

'I know that,' Michael said huffily, then he sighed. 'On one level I know that but on another level, where I've never lied to my parents on this kind of scale before, I expect vengeance to heap down upon me.'

'You're not taking drugs or binge drinking or committing random acts of violence so vengeance doesn't even come into it,' I said, as we reached the top of the queue and a customs official gestured to a booth. I tugged Michael with me. 'It will all be good. Now shut up and let me do the talking.'

It was another hour before we'd been reunited with our luggage, gone through 'Nothing to declare' and were in the back of a proper yellow New York taxi cab. There was absolutely no way I could have got us to our hotel via the subway and not ended up detouring via The Bronx.

By now it was almost six and night had fallen as we travelled through the urban sprawl of Queens. Then we were on the BQE and when we looked out of the window, across the river, we could see the island of Manhattan all lit up and glittering like some futuristic mirage on the horizon.

'Wow,' Michael breathed. 'New York. It looks magical.'

It wasn't quite so magical having to sit in rush hour traffic but finally our cab was weaving through the narrow streets of the trendy Meatpacking District and pulling up in front of the Gansevoort Hotel. Before I'd even paid the driver, one of the doormen was getting our luggage out of the boot and we were ushered into the hotel which was all glass and tubular steel and luxurious in a sleek, modernist way that was exciting but also really scary, especially when Michael was in a leather jacket, hoodie and jeans and I was wearing a pair of golfing shorts over pink woolly tights and a faux-fur leopard-print anorak.

The receptionist, who looked as if he modelled for *GQ*, didn't blink an eyelid but checked us into a junior suite, handed me a pile of conference-related bumph, a wad of phone messages and our room key. Five minutes later we were standing in the sitting room of our suite staring wide-eyed around us at the huge plasma TV and the breeze machine and the Andy Warhol

Marilyns on the wall and the view. Oh, the view! Skyscrapers and neon as far as the eye could see.

'Oh my God. Oh my God. Oh my God.' It was all Michael could say. 'Oh my actual God.'

'God had nothing to do with this,' I said, and he looked at me with awe and wonder in a way that no one had ever looked at me before.

'This conference, Jeane, is it a really big deal?' He gestured at the splendour of our surroundings. 'Are you a really big deal?'

'Well, I know a lot of stuff and I'm good at talking and theorising about the stuff,' I explained, because I could hardly start banging on about how I was reckoned to be an innovator and a one-girl zeitgeist and the queen of the outliers, which was how the conference organisers had described me in their publicity material.

'Look, it's just a bunch of people who are doing new things in their fields. Like, there's some social network people from Palo Alto and fashion designers and a graphic artist from Tokyo and this guy who's big in molecular gastronomy and a science dude and we're talking to this audience of corporate suits and venture capitalists about the future. I'm going on at the end like a palate cleanser to represent for the kids, you know?'

Michael shook his head. 'I didn't really understand any of that. So, like, they're paying for all this, the conference people?'

'Well, yeah! You don't think I'd spend weeks working on a presentation out of the goodness of my heart, do you? Damn right they're paying me.'

'They're paying *you* as well as the flights and the hotel room and . . .' He trailed off and collapsed into a leather armchair.

This wasn't the time to tell Michael that I was getting paid ten thousand of our English pounds and was generally considered to be something of a bargain on the conference circuit. His mind, it would be totes blown – besides, it was tacky to talk about money. So I just crouched down in front of him and put my hands on his knees.

'Are you tired?' I asked. 'It's about midnight English time.'

'I'm too wired to even think about going to bed.'

'And are you hungry?'

Michael shook his head. 'They kept thrusting food at me on the plane.'

'Right, so you don't want to sleep and you don't want to eat and if we stay here you'll keep saying "Oh my God" under your breath in a really annoying way, so let's go out and explore New York.'

I expected protests because Michael seemed so far out of his comfort zone that he might as well be on the moon, but a smile slowly appeared on his face.

'Can we go on the subway? And can we get a ginormous pretzel from one of those street carts and, oh! I want to take a picture of the Empire State Building all lit up, not that I can show it to anyone, because nobody else knows that I'm here.'

'That's all doable,' I agreed, standing up so Michael could get out of the chair, but he caught hold of my hand and lifted it to his mouth so he could press a kiss to the backs of my knuckles.

'Thanks, Jeane, for all of this, I really mean it,' he said earnestly.

'Oh, don't be so wet,' I complained, pulling my hand free.

'Come on, chop-chop, and put a proper jacket on. It's cold out there.'

We did as much of New York as it was possible to do in five hours. I took Michael on the subway to the South Street terminal so we could get the free Staten Island ferry and see Ellis Island and the Statue of Liberty en route, before we headed back to Manhattan.

Then we subwayed up to Herald Square and Macy's and I introduced Michael to Old Navy, which was way cheaper than his beloved Abercrombie & Fitch. He was so excited about his super-sized pretzel that he didn't mind that every time we took the subway I managed to get on the wrong train or the wrong line or the wrong platform. New York is very hard to navigate. Yes, I know it's on a grid but I can only work with left and right, not east and west, and using Google Maps was eating my iPhone battery so we jumped in a cab and headed to Chinatown so we could have dim sum served by fabulously rude waiters.

'They're even ruder than the waiters in London,' Michael announced with glee as we cracked open our fortune cookines. He read his message and sniggered. 'I can never tell if these things are deeply significant or randomly selected by a fortune-cookie message-generating algorithm.'

'Let me see.'

He handed over a tiny piece of paper that proclaimed: *You will stumble on to the path that will lead to your happiness.*

'Well, you're sitting in a dim sum bar in Chinatown, New York, and you look pretty happy to me so maybe there's some truth in it,' I said lightly, but I felt a surge of pride. Michael's current happiness was entirely my doing. I had made him happy, which was not something that I usually excelled at. I was good, really good, at all kinds of things but not making other people happy.

'What does yours say?' Michael asked.

I unrolled the little slip of paper and although it was randomly selected by a fortune-cookie message-generating algorithm, when I saw the words my heart jolted like when you dream that you're falling: *Don't cry, life is pain*.

'It says, "you are destined for greatness,"' I lied, though it wasn't really a lie because I *was* destined for greatness. I mean, obviously. I screwed up my fortune and signalled the waiter for our bill.

'Oh, come on, I showed you mine, aren't you going to show me yours?' Michael complained as I tried to catch someone's eye. All the waiters were pointedly ignoring me so I had no choice but to stand up and wave my arms around while shouting, 'Can I have the cheque, please?'

It was super-late, almost midnight, which meant it was almost five in the morning back in London, and Michael's voice sounded tetchy the way it always did when I kept him up long past his bedtime.

There was only one thing that shifted his mood when he was tired and cranky. I lowered my lashes and looked at him. 'I'll show you mine when we get back to the hotel,' I said, and he perked up instantly because I wasn't talking about anything that came in a fortune cookie.

26

When I woke up at 8.30 to my first New York morning, Jeane was already awake and bashing away at her laptop. There were three empty coffee cups next to her and it looked as if she'd stripped the minibar of all its snacks.

'How long have you been doing that?' I asked as I struggled into an upright position.

She barely glanced up from the screen. 'A while,' she mumbled. 'I'm meeting the conference coordinator and the tech guy in half an hour to go through my stage specs and everything's going wrong.'

Jeane was still in her Bikini Kill T-shirt and polka dot sleep shorts and her hair, which she'd subjected to a lavender rinse the week before, looked as if it had been caught in a wind tunnel. Her eyes were swollen and red too like she'd decided that she didn't need to sleep, even though not sleeping made her really snippy. Then she'd drink tons of coffee and get really hyper. It was going to be a very long day.

'Is there anything I can do to help?'

'Hang on,' she said, and typed even faster. Then she frowned and stopped. 'Can you ring room service and ask them to send up a vat of very strong coffee and their most sugarific pastries?'

Jeane had explained last night that everything was comped, from the cab fares to the hotel room to the contents of the mini-bar to room service ('as long as we don't go mad and start ordering, like, six bottles of champagne and caviar and lobster and stuff'), but even so it made me feel uncomfortable. The woman who took my order was really nice but I half expected her to suddenly say, 'You're eighteen, I refuse to let you order room service. Don't be so ridiculous!'

Not that Jeane noticed. In fact, she didn't notice anything until the coffee and pastries arrived and she finally smiled at me. And when I helped her fix one of the slides in her PowerPoint presentation, which wasn't doing what she wanted it to, she even gave me a hug.

'Right, I'm done,' she said, as she saved the document five times just to be on the safe side. She picked up one of the fluffy robes that the hotel had provided. 'I'm going to do my sound-check. I'll be about an hour, OK?'

'You're going to meet them in a dressing gown?' She was already walking to the door with her laptop tucked under her arm and looking at me as if I was the unreasonable one.

'Well, *yeah*. The conference doesn't start for another hour and a half and it's not like I have time to change.'

She slammed the door behind her and was back in the time

it took me to sulk, have a thirty-minute power shower that was one of the single best experiences of my life, brood, look up places for brunch on the internet, and I'd just finished the long process of getting my hair just right when Jeane returned with the most ferociously furious look on her face that I'd seen yet and that was saying something.

'How did it go?' I asked dutifully, even though I was dreading the rant that was sure to follow. She could rant for hours and I was really hungry and it would be much better if she could get washed and dressed and then I'd let her get her rant on halfway through brunch.

She held up her hand. 'Don't. Even. Ask.'

'Oh, it couldn't have been that bad,' I insisted cheerfully, but she just rolled her eyes and slammed the bathroom door behind her.

She was in there for ages so I had plenty of time to realise what a bad idea this trip had been. Not just because of the web of lies I'd had to spin to get here but because I was at the tender mercy and mood swings of a girl who spent seventy-five per cent of our time together arguing with me.

I couldn't do what I did when she was getting on my nerves back home, which was to leave her to get on with it while keeping a close eye on her Twitter feed until I knew she was over her snit. I was stuck with her.

Oh God.

Jeane was still pretty tight-lipped when she emerged from the bathroom an hour later. She was back in the fluffy towelling robe but her lilac-tinted hair was pinned up and she'd applied full make-up, glitter all over the show, bright red lipstick and thick, winged eyeliner. She completely ignored me as she began to rummage through her unpacked suitcase for something Day-Glo and mismatched to wear.

'Do you want to get some brunch?' I asked. I already knew the answer would be no but I wanted to remind her that I was still there in the room, breathing the same oxygen as her.

'I can't. I have to attend the morning session of the conference,' she muttered. 'I did tell you.'

'Well, you kinda didn't.'

'Yeah, but you should have realised. I mean it's just, like, *rude* if I don't.' She looked up from her suitcase to glare at me more effectively. 'You don't have to though. You can go out and get lost on the subway trying to find the Empire State Building if you want. I don't care.'

'I get that you're nervous, I really do. I feel the same way when I'm taking part in a debate at—'

'This is *nothing* like debating capital punishment with the sons and daughters of Tory scum from the posh school at the other end of the borough and I am *not* nervous. I've appeared at *hundreds* of conferences. Hundreds.' She jabbed a finger in my general direction. 'Look, you have to leave now. You are doing my head in.'

'I'm doing your head in? I don't know why you even wanted me to come to New York with you—'

'Neither do I!' Jeane contorted her face into a grimace so twisted it looked as if it was causing her a thousand immense agonies. 'Just . . . GO!'

I went. It wasn't exactly a hardship. It was exciting. I had all of New York City to myself and it looked just like it did in the movies, steam rising up from the manhole covers, the streets stretching towards the horizon and on this cold, crisp day, the sun glinted off the skyscrapers and yellow taxi cabs hooted and everyone I walked past had an American accent and when I went into Starbucks to get a cappuccino and a muffin the barista really did ask me, 'How *you* doing?'

Also, the subway was really easy to use. Like, super-easy. New York's laid out on a grid and most lines went uptown or down-town and a few went crosstown. It was simple: any fool could figure it out. I went to Central Park, which was pretty much a big park, and then I walked up to The Museum of Modern Art because I felt like I should do something cultural, even if I did spend most of my time in the gift shop. After that I jumped back on the subway and went to Dylan's Candy Bar, because the interwebz said it was the best sweetshop in New York.

I owed Jeane candy – not that she deserved any, but I couldn't wait to see the sheepish look on her face as she stumbled through an apology when I presented her with a great big jar of sweet and sour mix and chocolate-dipped jelly beans. But mostly I wished Melly and Alice were with me because they would have both thought they'd just died and gone to sweetie heaven.

I bankrupted myself loading up on lollipops and Pez sets and gummy bears and Wonka chocolate bars because they were both obsessed with *Charlie and the Chocolate Factory*. My allowance was dependent on doing chores and admin work for the parents, and I was going to have to put in overtime so I could afford Christmas presents. It wasn't like I got paid to bore on about all the crap Jeane liked to bore on about.

It was lunchtime so I decided to head back to the hotel to dump my stuff and see if there were some leftover pastries from Jeane's breakfast that I could eat – I was now too broke to even hit up Burger King. Unfortunately, when I got back to our suite, it was a pastry-free zone, and though the minibar had been restocked, I was damned if I was going to make any dents into Jeane's bill. As it was, I was probably going to sleep on the couch tonight.

Not sure what to do next, I drifted back down to the lobby. I found myself following the signs that pointed to the conference and, when no one stopped me, I wandered into a little ante-room where there was a lunch buffet set up. Score!

I walked casually over as if I attended conferences all the time, grabbed a plate and quickly started to fill it with sushi. Then I swiped a bottle of Coke and was about to scurry for the safety of our suite when a woman rushed over. She was dressed all in black and had her hair cropped in a severe cut that matched the equally severe expression on her face.

There was nothing I could do except dredge up some rusty Cantonese if need be and pretend that I had no idea what she was talking about, but she was already looking down at her iPad. 'You're Jeane's guest? Michael Lee? Did you know you've already missed the morning session?'

'Oh, well, I didn't know that.'

'And you've missed the breakout sessions over lunch too,' she continued accusingly. 'And you're just about to miss the start of the afternoon schedule.'

She was already hustling me into the conference room, one steely hand at the small of my back, and she stayed standing over me until I sat down and then finally she left. She was back one minute later though, like she knew I was planning to make a run for it, and shoved a glossy folder and a neoprene duffel bag at me, then stood right by the door. At least it was warm and I'd got to keep my sushi and when the mean woman stopped glaring at me I could have a little sleep.

But it turned out that conferences on The Future is NOW! were really quite interesting. Who knew that? Not me.

First, a man and woman from a global trend agency, wearing matching nerdy glasses, talked about how they sourced and tracked trends and used the information to help businesses develop new products. Like, one of their scouts might find some kids who'd set up their own club in east London and dressed like nineteen-forties gangsters who sold nylon stockings on the black market. Then, in Berlin, there might be other peeps dressing like the swing kids of forties Germany who were obsessed with American jazz and refused to join the Hitler Youth. And *then*, in Tokyo, there might be a DJ mixing old Benny Goodman arrangements with breakbeats. They'd take all this information and present it to their clients and, two years later, there'd be lots of forties-influenced fashion and Make Do And Mend posters all over the high street.

Then there was a scientist guy. Considering he was talking about scary, mutant, drug-resistant superbugs and had all these great slides of people with their faces eaten away, he could have gone big with a *28 Days Later* scenario. He didn't. He just droned on and on. Scary-Haircut-Lady was still glancing over at me so I didn't dare to even take too long to blink in case she thought I was snoozing and came over to shout at me. Simply to kill time and to show there were no hard feelings, I texted Jeane to wish her luck. She texted me back immediately:

It's bad luck to wish someone luck. Everyone knows that.

I hated her so much right then.

Thinking of all the reasons why I was hating on Jeane was a great way to spend the next half hour, until two guys with hair just like mine, wearing jeans and T-shirts, bounded onstage. They worked in Palo Alto, in California, also known as Silicon Valley. It was where Google, Facebook and Twitter had all started and, as they began to talk about the artificial intelligence product they were developing, I finally sat up and began to pay attention. I even took notes as they described how their technology could be used in everything from computer gaming to microsurgery. They were so into their work and made it sound so cool (and they had a rock-climbing wall in the middle of their office) that I wanted to abandon everything to fly to San Francisco and beg to be their tea boy.

They loped offstage and the emcee returned. 'We've all been looking at ways in which the future is already here,' he said. 'And now we're going to end with a remarkable young woman who's so beyond the future that she's been described as "a zeitgeist in the form of a teenage girl".'

I didn't know whether to sit up or slink down in my seat, as the guy continued singing Jeane's praises. No wonder she was so up herself.

'Jeane will be talking to us about the future that will be mapped out by her teenage peers, the Echo Boomers of

Generation Y. I was chatting to Jeane during one of the break-out sessions and asked how she'd describe herself in one sentence and she said, "The *Guardian* thinks I'm an iconoclast, my half a million Twitter followers think I should spend more time linking to YouTube videos of cute puppies and my boyfriend thinks I'm an idiot.'" He paused to let the laughter die down but I wasn't laughing. I was mortified. I'd never called her an idiot and I'd never given her permission to say I was her boyfriend and there was a camera crew filming this and what if it ended up on the internet and someone recognised me and put two and two together and came up with not just four but the proof that I was Jeane's boyfriend?

By the time I'd finished seething, Jeane had stumbled out onstage and now I was cringing in horror. I'd got used to how she looked, but now it was as if I was seeing her for the first time and I could *hear* people laughing at her. It was no surprise. She was wearing her silly greeny-blue vintage prom dress, which she'd since told me was actually seafoam, with a black sequinned evening cape, big clunky motorcycle boots and on her head was a turban. Not a turban like the one Hardeep's dad wore, but a red velvet hat that really posh old ladies might wear once the Alzheimer's began to kick in. I couldn't believe that I was actually hitting that.

She stood at the front of the stage doing this really weird thing with her feet, tripping over her boots and crossing her ankles, so there was a very real possibility that she might crash to the ground. Her head was bowed and it didn't look like she was going to do anything but silently freak out.

Then Jeane raised her head and smiled slyly. 'Listen, it's

OK,' she said conspiratorially. 'Ninety-nine-point-nine per cent of teenagers don't dress like me. Their loss, I reckon.'

This time when people laughed it was with her, not at her, and Jeane smiled again and clicked on her first slide.

GENERATION Y BOTHER?
The revolution will probably not be televised, unless you subscribe to the premium channels, but I bet I can find one million people to 'like' it on Facebook

'So, welcome to Generation Y. Please keep your arms inside the car and don't feed the animals. My name's Jeane and I'll be your guide as I tell you about the strange beast called the teenager. Their thoughts, their dreams, their passions, their ambitions and why they make a good case for bringing back National Service.

'Because Generation Y are everything you feared. They're everything your worst nightmares conjured up.

'They're lazy, apathetic, unoriginal, scared of innovation, scared of difference, just plain scared.

'They binge drink. The confuse sex for intimacy. They definitely couldn't tell you the capital cities of more than five countries. And they really think that Justin Bieber is the Second Coming.

'Only fifty per cent of Generation Y own more than two books and, yes, they listen to music, but they download it from the internet because content is free, yo. Want, take, have is their battle cry.

'Ladies and gentlemen, this is my generation and my generation is royally screwed up.'

THE TEENAGER IS DEAD, LONG LIVE
THE PRE-TWENTY-SOMETHING
Gucci dresses and drop top compressors,
Gen Y want everything and they want it NOW!

'My generation were raised, not by actual parents, but by *Sex and the City* and *Big Brother*.

'They want labels, they want logos. Louis Vuitton and Chanel, preferably, but Abercrombie & Fitch and Hollister will do as long as they're selling us a lifestyle based on nostalgia for a world we've never known.

'But what Generation Y really want, more than they even want an iPhone, is to be famous. Proper famous. Red carpet famous. Known only by your first name famous. Each one of them knows that they're a special little snowflake and they deserve everything that goes with fame, which is free clothes, flash cars, skipping to the front of the queue outside some expensive nightclub and being whisked straight to the VIP room where an endless supply of champagne awaits them.

'How they get famous doesn't matter. They'll date, or ideally marry, a footballer or win *The X Factor* or a TV modelling show. Everyone tells them that they're amazing and talented and beautiful and, God, if that big-haired, binge-drinking bint from *Jersey Shore* can become a mega-celebrity, why can't they?

'So, to recap. Generation Y. Shallow. Narcissistic. Self-involved.

To paraphrase Oscar Wilde, Gen Y knows the cost of everything and the value of nothing.'

STRESS PUPPIES
Why burnout is the new black

'But the thing is, unless they do get hurled into the arms of that bitch called fame, the future for Gen Y is pretty damn bleak. They're the first generation who will earn less than their parents. They're the first generation who won't be expected to better themselves by going to university, because what's the point in running up thousands of pounds or dollars in debt for tuition fees and student loans when there's little chance of being able to find a job at the end of it?

'So, quite frankly, who wouldn't want an easy route to fame and riches if the alternative is working in a call centre or asking people if they'd like to supersize their order?'

SO IS THIS THE DEATH OF
TEEN REBELLION?

'Nuh-huh. Not even a little bit. I said that teenagers don't dress like me. They don't think like me but, hey, I'm an early adopter. Where I lead, about two years later, everyone else follows. I joined Twitter when it was just one man and his dog and I was the first girl in my school to wear tights and open-toed sandals and so I honestly believe that what I'm telling you today is slowly percolating into the brains of my peer group and in the next couple of years will come to pass.

'If I think it, then it will happen.

'And what I think is that we're slowly rejecting your mass-market, consumerist culture. We're rejecting you because you want to co-opt our youth. We don't want you buying clothes from the same shops as us. We don't want to watch the same TV programmes that you do. God, we really don't want our mothers banging on about how hot that bloke from *Twilight* is. But it's really, really hard to find our own identity when there's no such thing as teen culture any more, because everything has already been done.

'Long, long ago, there used to be an underground scene of kids making music and art and running clubs and doing what they loved and languishing in obscurity because it would be years before anyone outside their little cliques would catch on. But now we have the internet and within five minutes any new scene has been TwitPicced, debated on Gawker and by the end of the month it's on the front pages of the *Daily Mail*.

'And that's why I started Adorkable. Adorkable was a blog for all the weird, wonderful and really random things I was into but very quickly Adorkable became a mission statement, my USP, a call to arms. And, yes, it's evolving into a lifestyle brand and, yes, I make money spotting and reporting on street trends, but the core ethos behind Adorkable is actually about celebrating a teen culture that hasn't been created by big corporations so they can sell us a whole bunch of crap that we don't need or want.

'Adorkable is about ripping the logos off your clothes or inking them out with Magic Markers.

'We're sending letters and mix CDs to each other in the post.

'We'll run our own bake sales, rather than gorging on your overpriced Krispy Kremes, thank you very much.

'We don't want your fast, sweatshop fashion, we'll learn to make our own clothes.

'We don't want music with Simon Cowell's grubby finger-prints all over it. If we can't make it ourselves, we'll rediscover the joy of old records that never made it to the mainstream.

'But more than anything, we don't want the tiny, miserable futures that the government and our parents have mapped out for us. We'll live our own dreams.

'So, Adorkable isn't just about me any more. Adorkable is a freeform, loose-knit, organic network of like-minded souls who might get pushed to the ground for the way we think and the way we look and because we're not afraid of who we are, but my God we're looking up at the stars.'

GENERATION Y NOT?
Tomorrow is here today

'But enough about me. I'm getting paid to talk about my generation and I have been kinda harsh on them. So, despite the fact that I despair every morning when I walk into school and I want to shake people and scream in their faces and force them to *feel* something, there are times when I'm proud to be a member of Generation Y.

'Over the last couple of years in Britain there have been cuts to the health service and cuts to education and many, many other cuts that hurt the most vulnerable and needy members of our society. It made me very angry and I wrote impassioned blog posts and even went on BBC radio as part of a panel discussion and got very shirty with a cabinet minister. Then a really big demonstration was planned. I leafleted the entire school, though I wasn't sure why I was bothering because everyone thought that politics was beyond boring.

'On the morning of the demo, I went to school. Then, at twelve, in the middle of a Business Studies lesson, I stood up and told Mr Latymer, our teacher, that I was now leaving school to go into town and protest the erosion of my civil liberties. To be honest, I could have just waited until the lunch bell but quiet women rarely make history.

'Then, as I started to leave, two boys who've never even spoken to me stuck their hands up and said they were leaving to join the protest too. One by one, everyone stood up in an "I am Spartacus" style and marched out of school with me, texting as they went, so by the time we got to the yard there were hundreds of teenagers assembled. I thought it was just an excuse to head to Starbucks, but, nope, they were bloody angry about having their rights to free education and healthcare snatched away and they were coming into town with me and if they got to shout rude things at a policeman, then, hey, added bonus.

'So, they came, they marched, they took photos of themselves marching and posted them on Facebook, we almost got kettled and the next day they went back to ignoring me and I went back to looking down at them, but it was one small step for Generation Y.

'And as the recession continues and our prospects look bleaker and bleaker, I'm excited. I look to the past to see what our future will be like. And in times of economic hardship and harsh governments, of pointless wars and mass unemployment, there was pop art and there was punk, there was hip hop and grafitti, there was acid house and riot grrrl.

'There was art and music and books that could bring you to your knees with their utter perfection. Because, when everything else is gone, all we're left with is our imaginations.

'So, you know what? I'm not ready to write Gen Y off just yet and neither should you, because I think we're going to grow up just fine. Yeah, it pains me to admit it, but the kids are all right.

'I was going to punch the air at this point but now I think it might come across as a little cheesy, so I'm just going to fold my arms behind my back to let you know that I've finished.'

27

Applause.

People were clapping but my body was still clenched painfully tight because maybe the clapping meant nothing more than, 'Thank God that weird girl has finished yammering and we can go to the bar.'

But they were still clapping and now people were rising to their feet, not to leave but to clap harder, and when I made my eyes focus everyone seemed pretty happy. I think this is what they call a standing ovation.

Oh yeah, Jeane, you've still got it. Like there was ever any doubt.

Then John-Paul, the host, strode on stage and I had to take questions from the audience, which all came down to the same thing – how can we sell our products to your generation? – and I was all like, have you not listened to a single word I've been saying?

Finally some snooty-looking hipster commented that I wasn't really a typical teenager and I said, 'Well, duh!' then I realised that probably wasn't the most tactful response. 'That's the whole point. I'm among them but not of them, thank the Lord.'

Then I was done. John-Paul was happy. Even Oona, the really grumpy woman who'd organised the conference, seemed happy. When I walked into the green room, I had to pose for pictures with the other speakers and string whole sentences together even though the tension and the adrenalin were starting to slowly drain away so all I was really capable of doing was grunting and maybe drooling a bit.

I looked across the room as this really boring scientist guy was talking to me about really boring science stuff and saw Michael being pushed through the door by Oona. He didn't look very pleased when he first caught sight of me. I shrugged and pulled a face to say that how I'd behaved before the conference couldn't be held against me because I'd been stressed up the wazoo.

Michael's telepathy skills had to be getting better, because he started to smile. As he came closer his smile got broader and then he actually picked me up and twirled me around even though I thumped his back and threatened to kill him.

'You were amazing,' he yelped, once he'd put me back down. 'Seriously. I didn't like all that "Gen Y, they're rubbish and they just want to be famous and God help us if there's a war" and I was really pissed off about you going on about logo T-shirts yet *again*, and then you did this complete one-eighty about how no one is going to put us in the corner and we're going to overthrow capitalism and I might even have got a little choked up.'

'Really?' I asked doubtfully. ''Cause that wasn't *quite* what I said.'

'For absolute reals. And, hey, guess what?'

Michael grabbed my hands and gave them a little shake and now I was over my conference-sponsored angst, his enthusiasm and gushing and utter approval was kind of infectious like nits and I was smiling too and entwining my fingers around his. 'I don't know. What?'

'I walked out of school and went on that demo! I mean, I'd thought about it but I didn't have the guts but when I saw Year 11 marching down the corridor, I just walked out of Maths and half the class followed me.' Michael beamed. 'I was never sure how we all suddenly decided to go on the protest, but I should have known you were behind it. It had you written all over it.'

'To be fair, I think it was more a kind of mass hysteria thing, like—'

'Oh, please, you know that modesty doesn't suit you,' Michael snorted. 'Anyways, it was fantastic. At one stage someone let me shout into a megaphone. It was one of the best experiences of my life – to feel like I had a say in my own future, you know?'

I did know and then Michael was hugging me again, really hard. 'When you were up on that stage,' he said, right in my ear, 'I was so proud of you I could have burst.'

'That would have been really messy,' I said, or I choked out because I had this massive lump in my throat. I didn't know why Michael being proud of me seemed more important than getting a standing ovation or an editor from *The New York Times* asking if they could quote from my presentation or John-Paul and Oona checking my availability for a conference in Tokyo. *Tokyo!* But Michael was proud of me and he couldn't stop smiling at me and he was still holding my hand and nothing else seemed to matter that much. Except one thing.

'Look, I'm sorry I was such a witch this morning.'

Michael nodded. 'So are you going to admit that you were nervous?'

My hard exterior was already shot to pieces what with the extended hand-holding, but it was a point of principle. 'I wasn't nervous. I was stressed.'

'What*ever*. It's the same thing.'

'It is not. Being stressed has a totally different energy to being nervous,' I insisted. 'But anyway, I'm sorry, and I'm also sorry that I'm going to drag you to the post-conference party in one of the bars upstairs. It'll probably be an ungodly bore but we can duck out after an hour.'

Michael grinned. 'Free drinks and food in some swank bar with wall-to-wall hipsters that we can laugh at? I'm all over it.'

Three hours later we were sat on a leather bench in a corner of a bar that was really a glass-enclosed garden. It had slate floors, wrought-iron chairs painted black, blue and purple, and was lit with huge red lights dangling down from the ceiling.

I'd kicked off my boots so I could tuck my legs under me and had made the discovery that scallops wrapped in Japanese bacon were my new favourite things to eat. I was washing them down with a cocktail called a Peachy Lychee, which was meant to have vodka in it, not that I could taste it, peach schnapps and lychee juice. They were very moresome.

When I wasn't stuffing my face or drinking, my head rested

on Michael's shoulder as we took pictures of ourselves on my iPhone. 'This hardly even looks like you,' I told Michael as we scrolled through the photos. 'It's just your left nostril and your mouth. Pity, though, it's a great one of me.'

'Well, in that case, if you want to post it to your Twitter then that's OK,' Michael said amiably. He was still in a ridiculously good mood and we hadn't argued for at least an hour, which was a personal best. He'd wanted to circulate but I'd pointed out that if you stayed in one place then, sooner or later, everyone that you wanted to speak to would drift over. Eventually Adam and Kai, two guys from San Francisco who were doing something with artificial intelligence and hundreds of thousands of dollars in start-up capital, had indeed drifted over. While I guzzled down Peachy Lychees, the three of them had had a conversation about human genomes and DNA and *Grand Theft Auto* that had slid right over my head so I'd amused myself by taking pictures of Japanese canapés and posting them on Twitter, and then they'd offered Michael an internship in Palo Alto next summer. Ever since then I could do no wrong in Michael's eyes.

Mind you, he had been knocking back sake, even though it tasted rank. I don't think either of us were in our right minds because there'd been a lot of tension and then the hyper good mood that comes when the tension goes away and a lot of alcohol and there had also been a lot of snuggling and nuzzling and maybe even a bit of snogging in between visitors to our table. All these things added up to my judgement becoming as cloudy as the sky on a cold, damp November day. I'm just saying.

What I was saying then was, 'So it's OK to post this photo on Twitter?'

'Who cares?' Michael waved his hand languidly about to show how much he didn't care. 'I think most people are on Facebook, not Twitter.'

Soon Twitter would be overrun with the suburban hordes LOLZ-ing and PMSL-ing all over the place but I was pretty sure that no one at school followed me on Twitter and we were just talking about a picture of me looking adorbz and his nostril and mouth. I posted it on Twitter, then Michael, not to be outdone, faffed about on his ancient BlackBerry, and then we could get back to snogging until the waiters brought round more bacon-wrapped scallops.

28

On the six other occasions when we'd slept together, I don't think Jeane actually slept. She always had her eyes glued to some kind of electronic device as I fell asleep. Then, when I resurfaced hours later, she was already scanning through her blog feed.

But when I woke up at eight on Sunday morning, Jeane was fast asleep. And she was sleeping *hard*, lying on her side, clutching the quilt tightly to her. She hadn't taken her make-up off the night before so there was glitter and black smudges all over the pillow and she was snuffling gently. It was the stillest she'd ever been and I didn't have the heart to wake her.

Though there had been a few incredibly bitchy put-downs in her speech, generally Jeane had rocked it right out of the park and she'd introduced me to the two guys from the artificial intelligence start-up in San Fran and demanded that they gave me an internship. Besides, she'd been knocking back these gross peach-flavoured cocktails all night whose main ingredient was vodka. I'd switched from sake to soft drinks so I could keep an eye on her but it had turned out that Jeane was a happy, sweet drunk and the least I could do was let her sleep off her drunken stupor.

I got up, showered, dressed, and, when she still showed no signs of waking up, I quietly slipped out of the room and walked around the Meatpacking District. All the stores were shut but a roadsweeper was getting rid of the Saturday night debris from the pavement, or sidewalks, whatever. Even though it was freezing cold and I could feel the wind whipping through my T-shirt, shirt and hoodie, tables were being set up outside restaurants and people were already queuing for first service.

I stopped at a coffee shop to get Jeane something sugary and a triple-shot espresso with the last of my dollars, then hurried back to the warmth of our suite. As I shut the door, Jeane's eyes fluttered open and she slowly sat up. She was still wearing her prom dress because we hadn't even done more than kiss last night. Or if we had then I'd fallen asleep before it got interesting. Maybe that was why she was scowling.

No, it was just a yawn. 'What time is it?' she croaked.

'Nearly ten,' I said, and she flopped back on the pillow with a tired groan. 'I've been up for a while but I didn't want to wake you.'

Jeane grunted something unintelligible but I saw her nose twitch. It was bizarre: one hand groped in the direction of the coffee I was holding as the other one reached for her iPhone.

I didn't even try to talk to her until she'd gulped down her caffeine and checked her email, by which time she was upright, vaguely alert and maintaining eye contact. 'Right, so, let's head to Brooklyn for brunch,' she said. 'Shall we cab it?'

'Couldn't we have brunch around here? I saw a nice place a couple of blocks away.' It was too cold to go far and I wasn't sure what time we needed to be at the airport, but Jeane just snorted.

'Blocks? Dude, you're talking American!' She snorted again. 'I said last night that it would be *really* lame to come all this way and only leave Manhattan to go to and from the airport. And you agreed!'

'I have no memory of that.'

'Well, you did have a lot of sake and you were falling asleep as I was telling you about how amazing the thrift shops are in Brooklyn. In fact you said, "Shut up, I'm trying to sleep."'

That wasn't quite how I remembered it. 'I only had two sakes.'

'Er, yeah, and about four bottles of beer,' Jeane said, as she scrambled out of bed, but she didn't seem to mind that I'd fallen asleep while she was talking or that I'd been drunk. Allegedly drunk. Because I hadn't actually been drunk. Anyway, *everyone* knows that American beer hardly has any alcohol in it.

By now Jeane was walking across the bed but instead of jumping off the end like she usually did because she couldn't just get out of bed without acting like a freak, she stopped, her eyes wide.

'What's that?' she asked, pointing her finger at the desk. 'Did you do a trolley dash or something?'

I followed her gaze to where my many bags from Dylan's Candy Bar were piled on the desk. 'No, I just bought candy like a normal person.'

She clutched a hand to her heart. 'Is it all for me?'

'Well, they didn't have any Haribo ...'

'God, what kind of one-horse town is this?'

'But I managed to find stuff that would appeal to someone with an obsession for chewy jelly sweets.'

I could see that Jeane was trying, unsuccessfully, to quirk one eyebrow. She settled for a smirk in the end. 'I don't know why you're sounding like my obsession is a bad thing. It's a very, very good thing.'

'It will rot your teeth.'

'Not if I brush and floss a couple of times a day.'

Sometimes there was no arguing with Jeane and though she wasn't a morning person, she was still in a good mood from the triumphs of yesterday so I decided not to push it.

'Anyway, most of it's for you and the rest is for Alice and Melly ... oh, shit!'

'Why oh, shit?' Jeane bounced into a sitting position and patted the spot next to her. 'What's up?'

'I can't give them sweets I bought in New York, can I?' I sat down and let Jeane rub my back. Her hand kept going over the same spot again and again like she was trying to wind me but I did appreciate the effort. 'I'm not meant to be in New York. I'm meant to be in Manchester.'

Jeane was silent for a second. 'Just say that there was an amazing American sweetshop in Manchester and you got them stuff there. You are *so* bad at lying, Michael.'

Jeane had a point. 'Well, you're good enough at it for the both of us.'

She beamed at me. 'I really am, and you bought me candy and if I didn't have morning mouth and coffee mouth and really need a wee, I'd kiss you right now.'

It was past one before we arrived at the Greenpoint diner where Jeane had decided we were going to brunch, because she'd spent over an hour getting ready and had then wasted valuable time begging me to change my outfit.

'But Michael, nobody wears skinny jeans any more,' she pleaded. 'Especially not with a tartan shirt. The grunge revival is over.'

I'd refused to listen and when we arrived at Café Colette in Greenpoint, which apparently was even more achingly hip than Williamsburg, which was way more cooler than New York, practically every guy in the place was wearing skinny jeans and a tartan shirt. They also all had hair that looked like it had been cut with a rusty pair of garden shears, so I was easily ahead on points.

There was a line out of the door and I was all for finding somewhere else to have brunch, but Jeane was insistent that we had to wait in line. She was also insistent that brunch was her treat and she paid the cab fare and even though she was getting all her expenses back, it made me feel weird. Not just weird, but like we weren't on the same level. OK, there were times when it felt like Jeane wasn't even on the same planet as me, but back home we went to the same school, walked down the same streets, raided each other's fridges, but here it felt like Jeane was the one with all the power. I knew I should be more enlightened and cool about her mighty girl power, but I wasn't. No matter how hard I tried.

'Hey, you're holding up the line,' Jeane suddenly said to me and I realised that we'd actually made it inside the diner and there was only one party in front of us.

Jeane's phone started beeping as we were finally led across a chequerboard floor to one of the tables for two that were lined up against the back wall. I looked around with interest at the other brunchers and the big old-fashioned counter opposite, but Jeane was glued to her phone.

'I've had, like, fifty emails in the last ten minutes,' she muttered. 'And on the day of rest too.'

I picked up a menu, keen to explore the brunch options. Maybe this would be my opportunity to try bacon with maple syrup, but then Jeane suddenly looked up from her phone and yelped like she was in pain.

'What? What's the matter?' I asked, as the two girls on the next table glared at her.

Jeane looked around the café wildly. Then she pointed at a rack of newspapers by the door. '*The New York Times*,' she rasped like she was a hardened forty-a-day smoker. 'Have they got *The New York Times*?'

As she was paying for, well, everything, the least I could do was get up and fetch her the paper.

She snatched it from me without even a thank you and started rifling through it. 'Boring. Boring. Economic downturn. Universal healthcare. Blah blah bloody blah. Oh my days! I do not believe it. Pinch me.'

I was kind of tempted but I leaned over and tried to look at the newspaper upside-down. It wasn't difficult because even upside-down the huge photograph of Jeane taken onstage the day before was instantly recognisable.

'*Smells Like Jeane Spirit.*' I read the headline out loud. '*Meet the English teen who's turned dorkiness into a lifestyle brand.*'

Jeane blinked slowly and put her hands on her cheeks, which were bright red.

'Wow,' she said. 'Oh. Wow. I emailed them my speech after the conference but I didn't think they'd run it so soon. Or just run it as, like, a feature in its own right. Jeez Louise.'

'*The New York Times,*' I said slowly. I was pleased for her, really I was, but somehow I couldn't make my voice sound pleased. 'So, is that a pretty big deal?'

'The biggest.' Jeane stared at the photo of herself with a rapt expression like she'd never seen her own face before. 'It's a total game-changer.'

I didn't even know what that meant. It sounded like the kind of bollocks people spouted on *The Apprentice* just before their arses got fired, but Jeane wasn't even waiting for my reply but was tracing her fingers over the page and it was only when someone came over to take our order that she reluctantly tore her gaze away and deigned to look at the menu.

She didn't say a single word to me for the next half hour. I didn't even know that Jeane could go that long without talking. She just sat there in her plaid golfing shorts, a *Thundercats* T-shirt and an orange cardigan, and, instead of eating a proper breakfast, munched her way through a baguette heaped with Nutella and cream cheese held in one hand while she replied to emails with the other.

I had ceased to exist. In fact, I started to wonder if I'd become invisible until my phone started to ring. At least there were still people who wanted to talk to me, even if that person was actually my mother.

To be honest, it was a relief to have an excuse to leave the table. There were too many American accents within earshot for me to take the call anywhere else but outside.

'Be back in five,' I told Jeane, who didn't look up or nod or in any way acknowledge that she knew I was still there.

29

I couldn't believe it when Michael just got up and, like, left. This was the biggest day of my life. The most amazing thing that had ever happened to me and I'd been lucky enough to have quite a few amazing things happen to me over the last two years, but this was the most amazing thing yet. It was totes AMAZE-ing and Michael couldn't even be bothered to say, 'Well done,' or, 'Hey, congrats.'

He'd been in a mood ever since we'd arrived in Greenpoint. Probably because he'd wanted to stay in Manhattan and do something naff and touristy like have brunch at, I don't know, The Four Seasons. But the first evening in New York, I gave him the tourist experience, and yesterday I'd been stressed like I'd never been stressed before and so I wanted half a day to scout round Brooklyn and photograph interesting-looking people and check out the vintage shops, so sue me.

There were times when Michael could be kind and

considerate and the head boy of my heart and then there were other times when he could be an absolute dick. He also wasn't back in five, so after twenty minutes of having to sit on my own and getting too many coffee refills because there was still a massive queue of people waiting for a table and they were all staring pointedly at me, I paid the bill and went outside to find Michael squatting against a wall and still on his phone.

I stood over him with my hands on my hips until he looked up. 'My mum,' he mouthed. 'She knows I'm in New York.'

Whoop-de-do. So he was in New York and not in Manchester. He'd get grounded and suffer a very boring lecture about responsibility and not telling lies and being a role model to his younger sisters. It was hardly a matter of life and death. Perspective: he really needed to get some.

I didn't have a chance to tell Michael that because he was *still* on the phone and furrowing his brow and saying he was sorry again and again and acting like he had the weight of the world on his shoulders. Which, not even.

Eventually he finished, slowly stood up and hunched his shoulders inside his hoodie. 'I am in so much trouble,' he said in a forlorn voice. 'You put a picture up on Twitter of us last night, didn't you?'

'*What?*' I snapped. I hadn't even checked Twitter this morning – I'd been too busy emailing Oona who was anxious to lock me down for the Tokyo conference. 'As if I'd do anything as stupid as tweet a picture of the two of us *together*, never mind in New York. Why would I even do that?'

'I don't know, why would you?' Michael snapped back, and then he went into a long convoluted story about how Sanjit, the friend he was meant to be staying with at Manchester University, had a sister the same age as Melly and this stupid little sister had had a sleepover and when Michael's mum had collected her from said sleepover at some horribly early hour and asked after Sanjit, *his* mum said he was in Leeds to meet his girlfriend's parents.

By then, it was before dawn o'clock New York time, so when his parents couldn't get hold of Michael, they went on the internet and somehow found this alleged picture.

I pulled out my phone and went on Twitter myself to see this famous photo and when a blurry image of me alongside Michael's nostril and pouty mouth showed up, the events of last night slowly came back to me. Well, some of them did.

'I was drunk! Look! I couldn't even spell Gansevoort properly and *you* said it was OK to post the picture. Oh! Oh! Some moron retweeted it. Why would they even do that?'

'I don't know!' Michael ground out. 'Why do you have to tweet every single last thing that happens to you?'

I ignored him as I clicked to see who'd retweeted it. It was a follower of mine called @winsomedimsum.

winsomedimsum is yum
My girl & my left nostril RT @adork_able NYC, baby! At the Gansevort with ML. Peachy Lychees all round!

It took me all of five seconds to make the connection. @winsomedimsum had an encyclopaedic knowledge of Chinese cakes, overidentified with Jean-Paul Sartre's imaginary harping, bossy mother and always knew when I was down, even if I kept my tweets upbeat, and sent me links to dogs doing extreme sports.

Winsome-bloody-dimsum was Michael and I was going to end him.

'You! This is you!' I spluttered, as I waved my phone in his face. 'Have you enjoyed fucking with my head, have you?'

'What are you talking about?' Michael grabbed my wrist to still it so he could see what I was thrusting at him. 'Oh.'

'Don't even try to deny it.' I wrenched my hand and my phone free. 'You said that you weren't even on Twitter!'

Michael shifted uncomfortably. 'Well, what I actually said was that I didn't get Twitter.'

'I think you got it just fine. Was it funny to completely play me? Did you tell all your friends so you could have a good laugh at how you duped me? How you took me down a few pegs?'

'It wasn't like that,' Michael protested. His face was flushed and he pulled at the collar of his shirt like it was choking him. I wished it was. 'I hardly knew you when we first started talking to each other on Twitter—'

'You knew me enough to keep pestering me at school about Barney and Scarlett and you knew me well enough when you were having sex with me, but you didn't think to mention it when we were tweeting each other,' I spat at him. 'It's a total invasion of my privacy.'

'It's not. It's a public forum and anyway, it was the internet. It wasn't real. You're not the same person on the internet as you are in real life and—'

'Yes, I am! I'm like the most optimum version of me. And,

like, the internet is my happy place. I take a leap of faith that the people I interact with are as honest as I am—'

'That's ridiculous! We've been through this before. Everyone pretends to be someone they're not online. They have, like, an internet persona.'

'So who are you, then? The person I tweeted who was actually a great fat liar—'

'None of the stuff I tweeted was a lie—'

'Or are you Michael Lee, creepy cyber stalker, who used all the information I posted online for his own evil ends?' I asked, and I wasn't even being needlessly dramatic. For once. I hated the thought that Michael had pored over my tweets, looking for clues, trying to sniff out my weaknesses and maybe if he'd revealed himself sooner, it wouldn't have made any difference to the things we'd tweeted each other, the tweets that I'd thrown out into the ether, but now I'd never know. He hadn't given me that choice.

'You shouldn't put stuff up on the internet if you don't want people to find it,' Michael insisted doggedly, instead of apologising profusely, dropping to his knees and begging for my forgiveness. 'You uploaded it for people to see, so I don't get what the problem is. OK, maybe I should have come clean, but—'

'There's no maybe about it! It's not just about you tweeting me under false pretences. I've told you things that I would never put on the internet, I confided in you, I trusted you . . .' I had to break off because my voice was thick with tears even though I was determined I wasn't going to cry. I wasn't going to be one of those girls and I wasn't going to cry over a boy. 'And all that time, you were being completely deceitful.'

'You're overreacting about this, Jeane,' Michael said, and he was sounding all clenched and long-suffering about it, like it wasn't important when it so was and actually I was reacting just the right amount. 'And I don't really need you yelling at me right now. Kind of in a pretty bad situation in case you hadn't noticed.'

I stamped my foot then. 'You are not in a pretty bad situation, Michael,' I hissed. 'The worst that will happen is that your parents might stop your allowance and ban you from going to New York for three years. You're a fricking legally responsible adult, why don't you start acting like one? And when you're done with that, maybe we can go back to talking about me.'

Michael didn't even get angry. He just looked bemused, as if my pain and suffering hadn't even registered. 'We do nothing but talk about you.'

'Oh, excuse me for being excited about being in *The New York Times*. I'm sorry if that cramps your style. God, you just can't handle the fact that I'm not happy to simply study for my A-levels and work on my university applications like all the other boring teenagers that you hang out with. You can't even be pleased that I'm in *The New York Times*!'

'Of course I'm pleased for you but this is about the fiftieth time that you've mentioned it and it's getting a little boring.' Michael sighed, completely interrupting my flow even though I'd barely warmed up. 'Anyway, I don't get what the big deal is. You're always in the papers. You're their go-to girl whenever they need a gobby teenager with a hell of a lot to say for herself.'

I stamped my foot again and flailed my arms for good

measure. 'I am *so* much more than that. You wait. I can do TV if I want to. I've got three production companies *begging* me to take meetings and a publisher who wants me to write a book. And why shouldn't I have my own column in a newspaper? I've got plenty to say and I'm going to say it on behalf of the dorks and the geeks and the nerds and the disenfranchised, because we don't want to be co-opted by the mainstream. We want it on our terms and nothing and no one, not even—'

'Oh, for God's sake, Jeane, will you just shut up?' Michael suddenly shouted. Really shouted. Up until then, I'd been doing all the shouting. 'What you're doing doesn't really matter. Yeah, it's cool that you're getting to do all this stuff, but you *have* got A-levels coming up and pretty soon you won't want to dress the way you do and you'll realise that you need to tone everything down because you're not going to get into university or find a job or proper friends unless you stop with this whole stupid dork business.'

I didn't say anything because I couldn't make my mouth work and words come out of it. I'd shown Michael parts of my life that I'd never shown anyone else and not only had he betrayed me by violating my Twitter feed with a fake identity but he'd thrown it all back in my face like I'd given him a grubby pair of pants for his birthday that I'd found under my bed. It wasn't at all like what had happened with Barney. Yeah, I'd taken him to roller derby and made him listen to Kitty, Daisy and Lewis, but I hadn't ever let Barney see the dark heart of my dorkiness.

'It's not stupid,' I said tightly, shivering as the wind whipped around me. 'It's what I am. Nothing else matters. Not A-levels

293

or going to university or getting a job. This *is* my job, this is what defines me. If I died tomorrow then at least I'd have done something with my life. Left something behind so people would know that I'd existed. Adorkable is all I've got.'

'No, it's not all you've got,' Michael said, taking the three steps that placed him right in front of me. He was trying to do this piercing thing with his eyes, like he was all perceptive and shit. 'Look, we've both behaved like twats and said things we shouldn't have, but you've still got me. I'm not going anywhere.'

God, he just didn't get it. He didn't get me and I was stupid to think that he ever had. 'I haven't got *you*. I don't want *you*, not after what you've done. And I don't need a boyfriend to validate my existence because I can validate myself.'

'If you just cut all this out, things wouldn't be so hard,' Michael said forcefully, as if he'd given the matter a lot of thought. 'And maybe if you didn't try so hard to be different and not fit in then I wouldn't be embarrassed to be seen with you. I could make life easier for you.'

'What a load of hetero-normative crap!'

'What does that even mean?'

'It means that I'm not going to give up my dreams just so I can be a B-list character in your movie. You want to know what your problem is? For once in your life you don't get to be the centre of attention and you can't stand it, can you?'

'And your problem is that you can't bear to act normal, because when you take away your ugly clothes and all the long words and all the wacky shit that you think makes you different, you're actually left with not much – just a girl with a serious personality disorder.'

The hipsters and the cool mums and dads with their little off-spring called stupid names like Demeter and Minnesota queuing in the freezing cold to get a table for brunch all stared at us as we shouted at each other and I really felt like nothing special then. I was just a stupid girl wearing stupid, mismatched clothes, yelling at a boy who I didn't match with either.

That was all Michael Lee was – just a boy – and I had to take away any power that he thought he had over me. Bring him down to size so he felt as small as I did.

'Why don't you just piss off back to your mum and dad so they can take away your TV privileges and send you to bed without any supper?'

'And why don't you piss off back to your festering pit of a flat and eat yourself to death, you absurd media creation?' Michael shot back and it killed me, literally killed me to let him have the last word, but there was a cab with its light on and the only way to flag it down was to run across the road and, again, literally kill myself in an effort to get it to stop.

Much as I would have liked to have never ever seen his face again, by the time I was back at the Gansevoort, I realised that I couldn't abandon him. I wasn't sure he even had the subway fare and I had our plane tickets so I was forced to text him to tell him to meet me at JFK.

He was there waiting by the premium economy check-in when I turned up, dragging a luggage trolley behind me. I hated him, I did, I did, but my heart gave this happy little skip because it wasn't used to hating him yet. My head was made of much stronger stuff.

He looked at me sheepishly as he took his bag off the trolley.

'Hey, Jeane . . . I know I should have told you about Twitter, but the longer I left it, the harder it was . . .' he began, but I ignored him and marched to the check-in counter. I knew that I had to keep being strong. I was going places and you travelled faster if you travelled alone.

'We absolutely don't want to sit with each other,' I told the check-in attendant. 'I'll pay to upgrade my ticket if I have to.'

'Unbelievable,' Michael hissed, but he couldn't cause a scene because it was an airport and he'd be carted off on suspicion of being a total terrorist.

So I was whisked off to the safety of the business class lounge and, though our eyes briefly met as I boarded the plane first, soon I was tucked away in my own suite with a big table so I could switch on my laptop and start making lists and plans. Adorkable was getting a major upgrade and I wasn't going to let the haters stand in my way.

30

♥ Michael Lee has changed his relationship status from It's Complicated to Single.

adork_able Jeane Smith
Taking a Twitter break to sort out several
things made of awesome. Feel free to TwitPic
me cute puppy shots though.

Dear Michael

As discussed, this is your schedule for the next month. We will revisit this topic when you break up for Christmas and after you've had time to reflect on the poor choices and decisions you've been making.

Mum and Dad

Monday to Friday

7.30: Feed cat. Help with breakfast, clean up from breakfast.

8.30 – 4.45: You will go directly to school, you will stay at school. If you have a free period, you will go to the library to study. After school you will come straight home.*

5.00: Help Melly and Alice with their homework, start on dinner, feed cat.

7.00: Load dishwasher, then you will study at the kitchen table. As we agreed, you will not have access to TV, games console, iPod, and we have removed the AirPort card from your laptop.

If you don't have any school work, there is plenty of admin work you can be doing for Dad.

10.30: Lights out!

- Monday – school council
- Tuesday – football practice
- Wednesday – debating society
- Friday – football practice

* Have thought long and hard about allowing you your extra-curricular activities but for the sake of your university applications have decided to let them stand.

Saturday

7.30: Feed cat. Help with breakfast, clean up from breakfast.

9.00 – 12.00: Studying.

12.00 – 1.00: Lunch.

2.00 – 5.00: Football match.

6.00 – 7.00: Dinner. Clean up after dinner.

7.00 – 10.00: You can either watch a family-orientated DVD with us or read a book. Your choice.

11.00: Lights out!

Sunday

7.30: Feed cat. Help with breakfast, clean up from breakfast.

9.00 – 4.00: Family outing.

5.00: Help Dad make Sunday roast.

7.00: Clean up after dinner.

8.00: Get stuff organised for school.

9.00 – 10.00: Study or read.

10.30: Lights out!

To: bethan.smith@cch.org
From: jcastillo@qvhschool.ac.uk
7th December 2011

Dear Ms Smith

I'm writing to you as regards Jeane Smith. Our records show that you are your younger sister's guardian, though I understand from Jeane's form tutor, Ms Ferguson, that you are currently working in the States and that both your parents are also residing abroad. However, I must inform you that Jeane has been absent from school for the last three weeks and has not completed her coursework for this period either.

Every effort has been made to contact Jeane via phone and email, as her future at the school and her plans to take AS-levels next year are now in serious jeopardy. I have no other option but to contact you and ask that you make Jeane aware of the potential seriousness of her actions.

While there have been siginificant issues with Jeane's conduct and behaviour, her academic record is excellent and I am confident that the school can offer her support and solutions so she can resume her studies. I would be more than happy to discuss matters with you over the phone, if you would like to call me.

When you do talk to your sister, can you ask her to contact either myself or Ms Ferguson so we can set up a meeting in order to resolve whatever issues are affecting Jeane?

I look forward to hearing from you and hope we can work together to reach a positive outcome on this matter. Yours truly

Jane Castillo
Deputy Headteacher

Michael! How f-ing long r u being punished 4? We miss U! Heidi x

Long boring story. Might get time off 4 gd behaviour Xmas hols. Michael

So wt went down? Ppl say U got Dorkface preggo!!!!!! That U eloped to NYC!!!! Were U C-ing her? H x

J & I were just mates. But she's totes insane. C'mon! Dunno why ppl have to spread rumours. M

Totes! Ppl be haters! Will set things str8. But Y R U grounded? Is ridic! Ur 18.

Working on Cambridge applic & got caught drinking. So ridic!

U don't even hang out with us @ skool. Every1 misses U. Not just me. But espesh me!!!! Will think of sumthing spesh 2 do when ur free. H xxxxx

OK. Have 2 go. C U tmrw @ skool. M.

OK babes. Luv U. H xxxxxx

THE MOST DORKTASTIC BLOG ENTRY IN THE HISTORY OF BLOGGING, YO!!!

Hello! *Hola! Buenos dias! Guten tag!* Insert greeting in the language of your choice!

So, hey, how have you been?

Rumours of my untimely demise have been greatly exaggerated. I'm still alive and I'm approximately a gazillion times more dorky than I was last time we spoke because – drum roll, please, maestro – Adorkable is going multi-platform, global and coming right at you!

I mean, I could have carried on blogging and vlogging and tweeting about all the cool random stuff I love in the scant moments I have when I'm not studying for my AS-levels, but really! What's the point of being stuck in a classroom with twenty-nine dead-eyed, soulless anti-dorks that I have nothing in common with except my age? There is no point. Not when I can be using my time and my energy to spread the message that the geeks will inherit the earth.

So, I've spent the last month taking so many meetings that I now break out in hives at the sight of a tray of flaky pastries or a flipchart, but it was worth it (even though I can never knowingly eat a pain au chocolat ever again). OK, buckle up, and I'll take you on the guided tour.

Adorkable – the TV show

Next year I'm filming a documentary series for Channel 4. I'll be exploring what it means to be an outsider in this crazy consumerist cookie-cutter world that we're forced to live in. I'll be hanging out at Molly Montgomery's (from Duckie and my all-time girl hero) Rock 'n' Roll Camp for Girls. I'll be going to Tokyo to hunt down a box of green tea Kit Kats and spend time with street photographer and all-round goddess Keiko Ono. Oh, the places I will go: Sweden, Brazil, America – even China if we can cut through swathes of red tape.

Adorkable – the book

I've also signed a two-book deal to write about vampires. Ha! As if! But I am writing two books. The first one will be called *Adorkable – How I Became Queen of the Nerds* and it's part manifesto, part memoir, part rant. It will have photos and recipes and also a comic strip. I have no idea what the second book will be about but let's not tell my publisher that.

Adorkable – the column

The *Guardian* will be publishing eight hundred words from me every Friday. I will pontificate on how cupcakes took over the world, if puppies are the new master race, why the education cuts are an ideological ploy to keep us down and, oh, all the other things I love to pontificate on.

Adorkable – the website

Yes, I already have a website, but this will be a proper website that has a bit of money behind it so you don't have to just sit and watch my DustCam for hours on end. I have so many amazing friends with amazing talents so Adorkable.com will be a place where they (and I hope YOU) can showcase your awesomeness. It will have articles and films and puppies and it will be a place full of love and snark.

Adorkable – on tour

I'm doing a lot of public events next year. Like, a lot, a lot. Some of them will be academic conferences but I'm also partnering up with a charity to go into schools and youth clubs to run workshops on self-esteem and empowerment. OMAG! So excited about this but also kind of terrified.

So, there it is. I have a nagging feeling that I might be selling out, but the way I see it is that there should be someone like me representing. Call me misguided, but I believe I've got some important things to say that people need to hear and if I can take an hour of screentime or a book sale away from the Snookis and the Jordans, then that has to count for something.

Right, I'm climbing off my soapbox now. There has to be a clip of a puppy doing something adorbs on the internet that I haven't yet seen and I feel duty-bound to find it.

Laters, 'taters, Jeane x

31

I hadn't even started to find any new puppy videos when my Skype icon throbbed into life and I automatically turned on my webcam. Then I slid off my chair and crouched under the table in case it was someone I really didn't want to talk to, until I heard a familiar voice say, 'Jeane the Bean, where are you?'

It was Bethan! I shot up, banged my head and sat down again, hand massaging the sore spot on my temple. I didn't have time to deal with a spot of brain damage.

'Look at you in your hospital scrubs like you've just walked off the set of *Grey's Anatomy*,' I said cheerfully.

Bethan was perched on the sofa in the living room of her Chicago apartment. She looked tired and her blonde hair was scraped back in a tight bun, but then she gave me a daft little wave and a goofy grin and I did the wave and grin back and I felt like I'd come home.

'I just read your blog so I know that you're still alive,' Bethan said dryly. 'Thank God for that!'

'But every time I've tried to Skype you, you were curing sick kids,' I reminded her. 'And if you will live on another continent then it just makes everything more complicated.'

'True,' Bethan conceded. 'Little kids do have a nasty habit of falling out of trees and getting diseases, but hey, Jeane, Mum and Dad have been trying to get hold of you, I've had emails from your form tutor and your deputy head ... what's going on? You can't just stop going to school.'

'Well, I kinda can and I have,' I said calmly. What's done was done and there wasn't anyone who could do anything about it. 'Look, I could spend another eighteen months in school being forced to paint seascapes and write essays about *The Fountainhead*, neither of which are going to give me important life skills, or I could be making a real difference to people's lives. There's no contest.'

Bethan sighed and pushed back the hair that was escaping from her topknot. 'But we had a deal. The four of us agreed that you could live on your own as long as you fulfilled certain promises. Like eating three proper meals a day and keeping the flat tidy and *staying in school*.'

'But—'

'And you still have that stupid DustCam and the amount of tweeting you do about Haribo makes me think you're not getting your five a day and now it turns out that you've decided you don't need an education.' She sighed again. 'This is not cool, Jeane.'

'I am keeping the flat tidy,' I protested. 'Look!'

I turned the laptop round so she could get a sweeping panorama of the lounge, which was blates tidy. I was fed up with *certain people* acting like I didn't live in the real world and couldn't cope with real world stuff, which was, like, so not true. Anyway, in the real world, people had cleaners. So, I'd hired Ben's mum's cleaner to come round once a week. Lydia was from Bulgaria and she was scarily obsessed with vinegar and how it could obliterate most household grime. She was also just plain scary and shouted at me if I didn't tidy up before she arrived.

'Well, it looks OKish, and what about the eating of fresh fruit and veg?'

I stuck my tongue out at her. 'Rome wasn't built in a day, you know.'

'Jeane, you promised you'd do your A-levels. You actually promised.'

Bethan in guilt-trip mode was awful. She'd get this sorrowful, disappointed note to her voice, which always made me feel terrible.

'Bethan, don't be mad at me,' I pleaded. 'I have all these amazing opportunities that won't be there if I wait until I've done my A-levels. It's all good – I get to travel the world and do interesting things and have experiences and write books and get paid stupid amounts of money.'

'You're too young! No one is looking out for you and, God, this is all my fault. I should have stayed in London and forgot about the fellowship because—'

'No! You deserved the fellowship and you got to follow your dream and now I'm getting to follow mine. There's nothing to feel bad about.'

'There are so many people who must be taking advantage of you ...'

I loved Bethan. I loved her more than all the Apple products and Haribo and fab second-hand dresses in the world, but when she was being all earnest and pained, it killed me.

'No one is taking advantage of me,' I told her. 'I'm not stupid. I talked to people like my friend Molly, who got taken for a ride by her record company when she was my age, and I signed with a really reputable talent agency and I have an accountant and a lawyer. I'm even VAT-registered. Everything's fine, Bethan. Really, really fine.'

'Oh, Jeane ...' Bethan looked like she was going to cry. 'None of this is fine. Things shouldn't have turned out like this.'

'Things have turned out just great and if you're still pissed off with me when you fly over next week, I'll let you spank me. You can even pretend to send me to my room if it will make you feel better.' At least that made her smile, even if it was a pretty sad smile. 'Actually, is there anything you want me to add to my Christmas shopping list? Maybe another yule log and more mince pies? You can never have too many mince pies. We usually have a six-a-day habit by Christmas Eve, don't we?'

I expected the mention of mince pies to perk Bethan up where all else had failed, but she slumped on her beige sofa. 'Oh God ...'

'Why oh God? Have you developed a fatal allergy to mince pies?'

Bethan looked to her right and said something that I didn't catch and then Alex, Bethan's boyfriend, who was almost rippling with as many muscles as Gustav and wanted to be a neurosurgeon when he was all grown up, sat down next to her.

'Hey, brat,' he said. 'How's tricks?'

'Hey, Mr Apple Pie, Bethan's mad at me, can you tell her to stop because it's beyond boring?'

Alex took Bethan's hand and they nudged each other a bit and whispered until I had to rap my knuckles on my monitor to get them to stop.

Bethan took a deep breath. 'Well, do you want the good news or the bad news?'

I knew right away that the bad news was far going to outweigh the good news. It always, always did. 'Bad news, please.'

They both glared at me. 'You've got to have the good news first,' Bethan said.

'Fine, whatevs. Hit me up,' I said impatiently.

Bethan held up her hand and I waited for the good news and I waited and then I waited a little longer. 'Can we hurry this up, please?'

'Look at my sodding hand!' Bethan demanded. 'Third finger.'

I squinted at the screen and on her finger was a ring. Possibly a diamond, though it could have been cubic zirconia. 'Um, are you engaged?'

Alex beamed the smile that was a credit to his orthodontist. 'I asked Beth last weekend and she agreed to make an honest man out of me. How do you feel about having a brother-in-law?'

Honestly, I wasn't sure how I felt. I guess I was pleased for them. But Alex was American and Bethan was British and when her residency at the hospital was over, they were going to have to make a decision about which continent they were going to live on. I mean, I liked being independent and that Bethan could only breathe down my neck via Skype, but she wasn't meant to stay away for ever.

I managed to plaster a smile on my face. 'Hey! Yay! That's great news. I'm *so* pleased for both of you and, Alex, if you don't get on my case about eating vegetables then I'm happy to offer you the position of my brother-in-law.'

This time Bethan smiled like she almost meant it. 'There's something else,' she said. 'No easy way to say it so here goes: I'm pregnant.'

'Oh, wow! Right. Is that why you're getting married?' I asked baldly.

'Part of the reason, but mostly because I love this big old lughead,' Bethan said, rubbing Alex's crew cut while he beamed toothily at me. 'And, well, there's a whole immigration issue so it makes sense to get married before the baby's born.'

There were so many questions that I should have been asking, like when was it due and did they know what sex it was and did they have any names picked out, but I couldn't ask them because I was sure that as soon as I opened my mouth, I'd say something awful. Something like, Why the hell would you even want a baby? Aren't you worried that it will get ill like Andrew? And aren't you scared that you won't love the baby like Pat and Roy never loved me? So, why the hell are you actually keeping it?

How could I say any of that? My smile was slipping and before it fell off my face altogether, I managed another, 'Yay.'

'It's a shock, isn't it?' Bethan asked me gently.

I nodded. 'Yeah, I'm kind of processing. So, was that the bad news?'

'Oh, Jeane! You have *such* a dry sense of humour.' I'd never heard anyone guffaw before, but Alex was doing it right now. 'Of course it's not bad news. We're both so excited – it's just that, well, it's good news when we needed it. My mom's really sick.'

'Oh! I'm so sorry to hear that.' I was and I meant it. 'Is there ... like, will she get better?'

Alex's smile dimmed and he shook his head. 'She's got about three months, though she reckons she's determined to see her first grandchild.'

Life sucked sometimes. It wasn't enough that parts of it could be really good, like winning-the-lottery good – something equally bad had to happen just to keep you in your place. 'I'm so, so sorry. It's not fair, is it?'

'Really isn't,' Alex agreed, and he looked at Bethan and she looked at him, then she turned her head to me and I saw tears trickling down her face.

'I know it's all horrible but the baby is a good thing,' I told her. 'You have to focus on that.'

'Oh, Jeane, I can't come home for Christmas,' she blurted out. 'I just can't. It's Alex's last Christmas with his mum and we're having to get married really, really quickly and there's so much stuff to arrange and as it is I'm working twelve-hour shifts. Please don't hate me!'

'I don't. I never, ever would,' I assured her. 'There's nothing you could do that would make me hate you.'

'Even when I tell you that we tried to get you on a flight to

Chicago, even if it meant having to stop over in Canada, but everything's booked up?' Bethan sobbed. 'Will you spend Christmas with Dad? Please! I can't bear the thought of you spending Christmas on your own.'

'Jesus! I'd rather spend Christmas on my own than with Roy and Sandra! They'd probably book Garfunkel's for Christmas lunch,' I shrieked, and it wasn't even a joke but Bethan giggled and sobbed at the same time.

'Jeane, I feel bloody awful about this, but the wedding's probably going to be in January and—'

'So I'll see you in January and, just so you know, any vile bridesmaid's dress you pick out for me in puce-coloured satin, I'll probably love. Just don't make me wear anything ... *tasteful*.' I gave a mock shudder and Bethan and Alex both laughed. 'You're not to worry about me because I can crash Ben's family's Christmas dinner or my friend Tabitha always has an open house for anyone who's at a loose end. Honestly, I'll be fine.'

'I hate myself for this.'

'Bethan, it's very boring when you're being all self-effacing so please don't,' I drawled, and I could feel all the disappointment and the bitterness welling up inside me and I had to swallow it down like bile because I'd been counting the days until Bethan rocked up in the Arrivals hall at Heathrow and I could hug her very, very hard and have her all to myself for a whole week. She was never going to be all mine again. I'd come way down on the list after Alex and the new baby. 'Stop crying, it can't be good for the sprog. It will come out with a really mopey disposition.'

'Oh, shut up,' Bethan sniffed but she got the tears under control and we chatted for a few minutes about the awesome Christmas present she was going to buy me and how they shouldn't have a stodgy boring fruitcake at their wedding because no one actually liked it, before they had to go.

As I finally started to trawl through YouTube for puppies or anything that would make me smile, I knew that I'd been right to leave everything behind in pursuit of my dreams. Adorkable made me part of something and without Adorkable I had nothing.

32

And then on the morning of Christmas Eve, after I'd made Mum and Dad approximately two hundred and thirty-two cups of tea as part of my penance and the week after I'd been to Cambridge – and, though I didn't want to tempt fate, the professor who'd done my final interview had shook my hand and told me that he looked forward to seeing me in September – I was given an early Christmas present.

The Wi-Fi was reinstalled (I didn't have the heart to tell them that I'd hacked into the router whenever I'd wanted to go online), my PS3 was ceremonially reinstated and so were iPod, TV and car keys.

I had my freedom back. I also had three hours to finish buying Christmas presents before I met up with the gang for lunch. 'If you're taking the car then please only have one drink,' Dad said as the entire family trooped into the hall to wave me off.

'Taking the bus. There'll be nowhere to park,' I said.

'And don't forget to buy tinfoil,' Mum reminded me, and we were back to normal. There had been about a fortnight of only speaking when I was spoken to, but as the Cambridge interview got nearer, Mum and Dad had needed to speak to me frequently about mock interview questions and did I know who was interviewing me and should I buy some of his books to be properly prepared and so it went on.

But now Mum pecked me on the cheek and Dad smiled when he saw Alice and Melly clinging to my jeans. 'Have you got our list?' Melly asked me yet again. 'Percy Pig, not Peppa Pig. That's very important, Michael.'

'Be home in time to watch *The Muppet Christmas Carol*. We're making special Muppet cupcakes,' Alice added. Mum shuddered as she contemplated the havoc they'd wreak in the kitchen. I was still grinning as I walked to the bus stop.

Because I wasn't a girl and because I'd done most of my gift-buying when I was 'allowed' online, I was done in three hours. An hour of that was spent in Claire's Accessories being elbowed, kneed and punched by tween girls who'd all inhaled too much glitter. Laden down with bags, I turned up at the gastropub owned by Ant's dad.

I was trying to fight my way through the crowd at the bar when Heidi suddenly appeared and threw her arms around my neck. 'Michael! I'm so glad you could make it,' she said, and then she kissed me. Like, on the lips, because she'd obviously decided that the 'Thanks, but no thanks' speech I'd given her at the Duckie gig had just been me playing hard to get. 'Oh! Look at all your bags. You got a little something for me in there?'

I managed to shake her off before she strangled me. 'Depends on whether I got you for Secret Santa, doesn't it?' She pouted and I could tell she was about to slip her arm through mine, but I did a nifty sidestep and turn, spotted our table and left Heidi teetering after me in her nosebleed-high heels.

'I saved you a seat,' she called, but there was an empty chair next to Scarlett so I threw myself on to it and shared an eye roll with her and Barney.

During the weeks of the 'Go directly to school and do not pass Go' regime, which I still think was an overreaction because it wasn't like anyone died and Mum has been boring all her friends about my ninety-nine-per-cent-confirmed internship in Palo Alto, I only got to hang out with my friends at lunchtime. But mostly, I'd hung out with Barney and Scarlett.

I mean, they already knew about me and Jeane so they hadn't driven me to the edge of despair by bombarding me with questions and asking me to confirm the rumours that Jeane was pregnant/had emigrated/been expelled. Even though Scarlett had been dying to know what had really happened and would look at me with a really perplexed expression on her face, then frown and squint, but as soon as she opened her mouth, Barney would glare or nudge her and once he'd even thrown a Cheesy Wotsit at her when she'd uttered the words, 'So, you and Jeane . . .'

But when it became obvious that Jeane wasn't coming back to school and that I was beyond fed up with people wanting to talk about her and that things hadn't just ended badly, it had actually been the worst break-up in the whole history of break-ups, Barney and Scarlett had been there for me in a low-key, low-maintenance kind of way. Scarlett wasn't half so whiny and hair-flicky now that she was with Barney, and Barney, well, I think I'd definitely call him a mate. He was funny and we talked about computers and *Star Wars* while Scarlett painted her nails. I think Jeane and I had brought out the worst in them, but together they were way, way more than the sum of their parts.

Now, they both smiled and Scarlett launched into a long story about her cousin walking out of her part-time job in Claire's Accessories because the high-pitched screaming had perforated her eardrum and Barney wanted computer advice, while Heidi kept pouting at me from the other end of the table and clamping her elbows to her tits to give herself a cleavage.

Eventually everyone was assembled, food and drink were ordered, crackers were pulled and we started on Secret Santa. I'd got Mads, which had been a major bummer because we were only meant to spend a fiver and Mads didn't do budget. 'I might only be able to afford Topshop, but in my dreams I'm wearing Chanel,' she was fond of saying.

I'd had to go to Cath Kidston to pick up Mum's present and had bought Mads a pair of hairslides with little Scottie dogs on them. They were cute. All girls liked cute. Fact. Well, girls that weren't hell-bent on imposing their own warped notion of cute on the rest of the world anyway.

I realised my mistake as soon as Mads opened the present. Mads didn't really do cute either, unless cute came with the Chanel logo on it. Mad's anticipatory smile faded, then returned, twice as wide but half as bright.

'How sweet,' she exclaimed, in much the same way as she'd said, 'How gross' when she'd tried Dan's Bloody Mary. 'Very sweet.' She looked around the table with narrowed eyes. 'OK, so who was my Secret Santa?'

I timidly raised my hand. 'If you don't like them, I'll give them to one of the brats and you can have cash instead.'

'Don't be silly,' Mads said, holding the hairslides to her heart as if I was about to snatch them back. 'I *do* like them. They're very, um, quirky.'

'Yeah, they are,' Dan said. He smiled slyly. 'The kind of thing that if, say, you were porking Jeane Smith, which apparently you're not, you'd give her as a Christmas present.'

'Arsehole,' I said, because he was. 'Please credit me with some taste. I'm not boffing her. Never was.'

'Not any more anyway,' he muttered, and I clenched my fists but didn't react because if I started hurling swears and getting angry then Dan would get the reaction he wanted and everyone would think I had something to hide, so I waited a moment and gave myself enough time to come up with a crushing response. 'Maybe it's because you're not getting any that you're so obsessed with my sex life.'

'Hey! Nothing wrong with my sex life.'

'Does bashing one out every hour count as a sex life?' Ant drawled and we all groaned. I thought the subject was now closed. I was wrong.

'Come on, Michael, just admit that you were seeing her,' Mads said. 'And that you *did* go to New York with her and that you were absolutely definitely one hundred and ten per cent snogging her at the Duckie aftershow party at Halloween because my cousin's best friend's older sister hangs out with the Duckie crew and she said that she saw you and Jeane there and that there were pictures of you making devil's horns with Molly and Jane on the band's Flickr.'

'I'm not admitting anything because it's not true,' I insisted.

Dan actually clapped his hands together in glee because he had a mental age of ten. 'Ha! Two negatives make a positive!'

'No, they don't, and anyway—'

'But is she preggo? How can it even be possible that someone would want to have sex with her? Urgh, does not compute. But is that why she's left school?' Heidi asked sulkily. 'Because she's totes totes *totes* been expelled. For real. That's what I heard.'

'She's *not* pregnant,' Scarlett said sharply. 'She's left school because, because she's ... What is she doing, Barns?'

'Preparing for total dork domination,' Barney said. 'TV show, website, book, public speaking engagements and jumble sales.'

'Barney's helping to build her website.' Scarlett announced proudly. 'At the moment he's working on this animation of Jeane as a superhero. It's really cool. Even though Jeane would make a rubbish superhero. She'd be far too bossy in a crisis situation.'

'I don't even believe it,' Heidi snapped. 'She got expelled because she never does any work and she argues with the teachers and there's no way that Michael would ever have sex with her because she dresses like a total pikey and she's *fat*.'

I could have cried tears of sheer joy when I saw two waiters coming towards us. There was a flurry of black pepper and

Parmesan, then the conversation moved on to other things. The other things were who was seeing who, who was breaking up, how we were going to fill the gaping chasm in our lives now that *The X Factor* had ended, and what everyone was getting for Christmas and how much it cost. Weren't there other things, important things, we could have been discussing? It didn't necessarily have to be about workable solutions to ending world hunger but something more challenging than how 'blates rigged that show is, I can't believe a single word that comes out of Louis Walsh's mouth'.

'Buck up, mate,' Barney whispered, and I realised I was slumped in my chair with a scowl on my face. All that dorkside crap must have slowly permeated my skull, like dripping water carves fissures into rock, because I was sitting here thinking about how dull my best friends were and how they all dressed the same and thought the same and all the girls pretended that they didn't want pudding for five agonising minutes until they decided that it was all right to have pudding as long as everyone else did and it was so predictable and boring that I wanted to shout at them, so it was probably just as well that my phone rang.

It would be my mother calling to see if I'd remembered tinfoil but really calling to check that I wasn't drunk or in a foreign country.

'I've had one lager,' I said, answering my phone without even checking to see who was calling. 'And, yes, I will remember to get tinfoil.'

There was no reply, just this muffled snorting, and I realised it probably wasn't my mum because the person calling was crying and when my mum cried, which wasn't very often, it was mostly silent crying.

I held my phone away from my ear and all it helpfully said was 'Unknown Caller' because I'd deleted her number from my address book but even though she was crying and not saying anything, I knew it was Jeane. I just knew.

33

And then it was Christmas Eve and the world went silent and still.

Well, no, that was a total lie. Not silent. Not still – especially at eight in the morning when I was making my way back from an all-nighter in Shoreditch and decided to pop into the supermarket and get my Chrimbo comestibles ahead of the rush.

It turned out that the rush had got there first. Seriously, what was wrong with these people? It was Christmas Eve and they had nothing better to do with their time than get up, get dressed and go shopping.

At least I hadn't been to bed yet and was still in the gold Lurex and taffeta ballgown I'd worn to dance to breakbeats and dubstep in a derelict mini-mart. Doing your Christmas food shop on the way home had a completely different vibe to getting up at dawn o'clock to do your Christmas food shop in tracksuit bottoms and hoodies.

Anyway, it was a bad scene. Everyone was shoving and a woman with two small children in tow actually called me a bitch when I snagged the last tub of brandy butter and someone else grabbed hold of the back of my fun-fur coat to yank me away from the tins of Roses. I'd been in more civilised mosh pits. And of course I couldn't find a cab or my Oyster card so I had to walk home in the bitter cold with four bags of heavy shopping (who knew sweets, cakes and tortilla chips could weigh so much?) in shoes that hadn't been worn in very well by their previous owner.

The light on my landing was broken and I knew the caretaker was away until New Year so I had to wrestle with my bags and my keys in near-darkness, but eventually I was home.

Home.

It felt like I hadn't been home for days, weeks even. The flat was just somewhere that I passed through to get clean clothes, charge up iPhone, iPad and MacBook and maybe sleep for a few hours, because honestly the last month had just been a blur.

My days usually started with a breakfast-meeting, then more meetings, then a lunch-meeting. Editors, agents, TV executives, publicists, sales and marketing, they all needed to sit down for 'face time'. In the afternoon, once America had woken up, there would be conference calls and then maybe I'd head to the web company in Clerkenwell who were helping me build adorkable.com, or the production company in Soho who were making my documentary series.

I should have hated it but I didn't. It was a kick to spend every day talking to people who listened to what I had to say.

Usually, I had to work really hard to find people outside of Twitter who got where I was coming from, but now I'd found those people.

OK, they were all at least ten years older than me, but I've always known that I was way more mature than my immediate peer group. I also relished the complete lack of eye-rolling when I was sounding off about something. In fact, I was positively encouraged to sound off, but it was quite exhausting having to sound off for hours at a time and people always looked a little disappointed when I wasn't sounding off, like I was a performing seal or something.

So, after a long day of sounding off, I needed to kick back in the evenings. Luckily, there was always something to do. It was the run-up to Christmas so there were parties and drinks and bands playing their last gigs of the year and special club nights and lots of alternative Christmas dinners with friends who wouldn't be in London for the holidays. Even Ben was being dragged off to the wilds of, well, Manchester for a big family Christmas at his nanna's.

But now it was Christmas Eve and the mad merry-go-round I'd been on had stopped, but that was all right. Because I totes needed time to regroup. And it was really just as well that Bethan hadn't been able to come home because, apart from heading out to Tabitha and Tom's open-house Christmas tomorrow (note to self: order a minicab), I was going to stay in and work on the first draft of my book.

It was going to be fun. Just like the old days. I'd camp out on the sofa in my PJs eating things with lots of sugar in them, watching every single musical that the TV schedules had to offer and banging out one hundred thousand words on the Life and Times of Jeane Smith and how the world would be a totes better place if everyone was a bit more like me, yo.

There wouldn't be any more meetings or parties but I was still going to be very busy. Being busy was what was important 'cause if I wasn't busy and I wasn't focused then my mind started to wander and it always wandered in the same direction and it wasn't a direction where I wanted my mind to go.

Being busy was the key. So, although I'd had, like, no sleep, I decided that I wasn't going to go to bed but get to work. If I went to bed, I'd wake up in a few hours' time and then I'd stay awake all night and although I was fine about being home alone and I had stuff to do and lots and lots of things to eat, being wide awake in the wee small hours of Christmas morning would make anyone feel a little mopey, unless they were waiting up for Father Christmas. Whatever.

The weird thing was that the flat didn't really feel like home any more. It was so tidy. Lydia, my cleaner, had pitched an absolute fit after her first session and had forced me to buy all these shelving units with ridiculous names and pretended not to understand when I protested about the IKEA-isation of the domestic sphere. She also pretended not to understand when I said it wasn't working out and that maybe I didn't really need a cleaner. She tidied everything. Cleaning was her crack. She even went into my sock drawer (not that I'd ever had a sock drawer before, but she'd decided that each specific type of clothing should have its own drawer) and paired them all up.

As I unpacked the shopping, I noticed that she'd even touched my Haribo and arranged them in neat rows in the fridge. Unfortunately, she hadn't noticed that I was out of milk and bought me some, but I didn't have the energy to go out again and get shouted at by people who had full-on trolley rage.

I just pulled off my clothes and took great delight in throwing them on the bedroom floor because Lydia had gone home to Bulgaria until the third of January, put on some pyjamas and sat down to write.

It took a while to get going but soon I was engrossed and only getting up to make another cup of black coffee or go to the loo – though I'd also forgotten to buy loo roll but I improvised with a packet of Hello Kitty hand tissues that I found in a handbag. Anyway I wrote three chapters about my formative early years, glossing over anything to do with Pat and Roy because being raised by them had been boring enough: no one wanted to read about it too.

I'd just finished summing up the amazing adventures of Awesome Girl and Bad Dog when I realised I was squinting at my laptop screen because the daylight had disappeared and the room was in darkness. I had a cramp in my right hand and an ache in my neck from hunching over my laptop. I also felt thoroughly ooky, the way you did when you'd stayed up all night and it was now four in the afternoon and you still hadn't had a shower.

I would feel tons better once I had a shower and possibly had a home-cooked meal inside me. Or a meal cooked by my local Thai takeaway place – they always seemed very friendly, homely even, when they answered the phone. But my need to be clean was even greater than my need to stuff prawn Pad Thai into my mouth.

When I staggered into the bathroom to turn on the shower, I realised that I'd also forgotten to get shampoo, but I was sure I had some little bottles that I'd nicked from various hotel bathrooms. I'd hunt for them while I waited for the shower to heat up. Except when I tried to slide back the shower door it was alarmingly wobbly and then it stuck, leaving a gap so small that I couldn't even squeeze myself into the cubicle.

Lydia had obviously done something, because as well as getting up in my grill about my standards of cleanliness she was always breaking stuff as she charged around the flat with a damp cloth in one hand, dragging the vacuum cleaner behind her.

For one moment the enormity of not being able to get in the shower seemed almost too enormous, but that was just ridic. It was a fricking shower door and I wasn't going to let it get the better of me. I would simply use some common sense and, if that failed, brute strength.

First I squirted some body lotion along the bottom of the door to get things going but it didn't make one bit of difference. Then I tried to close the door, but it was stuck fast, and then I took a deep breath, tensed all my muscles and shoved the door as hard as I could. I didn't just shove, I kind of hefted it too – actually I don't know exactly what I did but the door lifted off its bottom track and it was really, really fucking heavy, and I was trying to get it back in place and not have it land on top of me or take half the bathroom tiles off with it but I couldn't and I was gripping it so tightly that I bent back one of my fingernails and I had to use my whole body just to prevent it crashing to the floor when it slid out of my grasp.

'Could be worse,' I muttered out loud. It really could. Nothing was broken, though my hands were stinging like I don't know what.

So then I couldn't take a shower because the shower door was currently propped against the cubicle but I could ask the caretaker to come up, except he was in Scotland and Gustav and Harry were in Australia and Ben was in Manchester and Barney was with Scarlett and what was the point of having all these people to help me build a lifestyle brand and half a million followers on Twitter when it was Christmas Eve and I couldn't have a shower and there was no one to remind me to buy milk and shampoo and toilet roll because I was all on my own?

The buck stopped with me.

And being alone and being lonely were two different things but they felt exactly the same: they felt *horrible*. Christmas Eve was like Sunday evening but to the power of a gazillion, then tomorrow it would be Christmas Day and being alone and being lonely would feel even worse and I'd probably left it far too late to book a cab to take me to Tabitha's anyway.

I realised I was crying, though generally, as a rule, I didn't do crying. I couldn't see the point. It didn't achieve anything. It wasn't useful and it just made me feel worse.

Made me feel so helpless that I was reaching for my phone to call the one person who I tried not to think about because if I did they'd be the only thing I could think about. We hated each other now and we hadn't talked in weeks but I knew, I just *knew* that if I asked him to come round, to make the loneliness stop, to fix my bloody shower door, he'd be there.

For me.

34

'What's up?' I asked, not unkindly but not like we were cool and she could just call me whenever she was feeling a bit down.

'I'm sorry,' she spluttered. 'You were the last person I wanted to call, but I've called everyone else and you're the only one left. The only one!'

OK, you'd have to be made out of concrete not to feel something when someone you'd had some of your best and worst times with was crying their eyes out and you didn't know why.

'What's the matter? Are you all right?'

'No. Nothing's right and I don't know what to do.' She ended the sentence on a wail then she was crying too hard to talk.

'Do you want me to come round?' I asked, but I was talking to dead air because she'd rung off, and, without thinking about it, because if I stopped to think about it then I'd be staying where I was and ordering a coffee, I stood up.

'Got to go. Tinfoil emergency,' I said, digging out my wallet. 'Shall we call it twenty quid for my share plus tip?'

'Don't go,' was the general theme. Along with 'Get the sodding tinfoil from the yellow shop that never closes,' but it wasn't as simple as that. It never was with her.

It felt strange to be walking along Jeane's road again, standing in her doorway, ringing on her bell and shouting, 'Jeane? It's me,' into her intercom. She didn't reply but buzzed me in, and she was waiting in the darkened hallway, the only light coming from the open door of her flat, when I got out of the lift.

I'd forgotten how small she was. She was wearing purple pyjama bottoms with slinky black cartoon cats on them and a huge fuzzy jumper. Her hair was white, which didn't suit her face, which was red and swollen like she'd been crying for ages. I hate it when girls cry. It's so unfair.

'I didn't expect you to come round,' she said in a choked voice, like air wasn't coming out of her windpipe. 'You didn't have to.'

'Well, you sounded like something awful had happened and you shouldn't just buzz people in. I could have been a homicidal rapist murderer.'

Jeane sniffed. 'Aren't homicidal and murderer kind of the same thing? Like, you can't have an unhomicidal murderer.'

'You could if they didn't mean to commit murder. Like, if it was a crime of passion or something,' I decided, and Jeane nodded tiredly like she couldn't be bothered to argue out the details and that's when I realised that something was really wrong: arguing out the details was as natural to Jeane as breathing oxygen. And also, she looked awful. Not the kind of awful that had anything to do with her lack in the pretty department or because she dyed her hair unflattering colours or because she dressed like a lady clown; it was another kind of awful.

Her face, the bits of it that weren't red or blotchy, was the colour of putty and she was slumping rather than standing up straight, her arms wrapped tightly round herself. She oozed defeat and I didn't know why because it sounded as if everything in her life was just fine. She was taking over the world, one dork at a time.

'I shouldn't have called you,' she said. ''Cause now that you're here it's awkward and you're going to yell at me for totally overreacting and I really can't handle being yelled at right now.'

'Tell me why you called and I'll decide if you were overreacting.'

Jeane traced a pattern on her hall carpet with her toe. 'I probably was overreacting.'

Absence hadn't made my heart grow fonder. It had made it grow a lot more exasperated. 'Jeane!'

'OK, OK,' she grumbled, and I followed her into the flat with slight trepidation as to what terrible thing had sucked all the ornery out of her. Maybe Roy and Sandra had popped round with a Christmas card and Jeane had bashed in their skulls with a potato masher.

'Place looks tidy,' I remarked as I glanced into the lounge. 'Really tidy. What's up with *that*?'

'I got a cleaner,' Jeane said. 'She's Bulgarian and she shouts at me and she made me buy a new vacuum cleaner and she keeps breaking stuff. She broke my favourite mug and my second-best keyboard because she cleaned it with a wet cloth and today she did something to the shower door and it wouldn't budge and then it came off.'

'What came off?' I asked because I wasn't really following any of this.

'The shower door,' Jeane said, and as she showed me into the bathroom she burst into tears again.

Without wanting to get too tech-y about it, Jeane's shower cubicle had a split door on runners, so you slid one half of the door behind the other to get in the shower. Or you did when it wasn't propped up against the other door.

'It's not worth crying about,' I told Jeane, but she shook her head and shrunk back against the sink like I was going to slap her and tell her to stop being so hysterical. I wasn't but I did think about it for a second.

Instead I peered into the shower cubicle to look at the top and bottom tracks, then I looked at the top and bottom of the forlorn shower door. 'See this thin bit? It slots into the groove on the track.'

'No shit, Sherlock.' Jeane was obviously going to be no help.

With a deep breath I took a firm hold of the shower door, tensed my muscles and lifted. Nothing happened. I tried again and maybe managed to lift it a centimetre away from its resting place.

'How the hell did you even manage to shift this? It weighs a bloody ton.'

Jeane was crying harder now and, yes, she was totes overreacting.

'I'll go next door and see if Gustav and Harry are in. There's no way I can do this by myself.' Jeane was saying something but it was too distorted by snot to decipher. 'What? What are you trying to say?'

'They're not there! They've gone to Australia to see Harry's family and the caretaker's gone to Scotland and everybody else who lives here is either away or very old, apart from the woman below me who *hates* me 'cause she says I slam doors and Ben's family are in Manchester and Barney's even weedier than I am and everyone is busy with Christmas crap and Bethan was meant to be here for Christmas but she's not because she's pregnant and she's getting married and her boyfriend's mum is dying so she had to stay in Chicago.' Jeane's face was bright red. It was brighter than red. Someone would have to invent a new shade of red to describe the colour her face was. She took a deep, shuddering breath. 'There was nobody else I could call and everyone has families and places to be and stuff to do except me because I haven't got anybody. I'm all on my own and it's Christmas Eve and I can't even take a sodding shower even though I've been working for eight hours straight because the sodding shower door is broken and no one even cares.'

'Oh, Jeane, I care,' I said, and it wasn't just because it was the only thing I could say in the circumstances. In that moment when she was shaking and crying and sounding more desperate than I'd ever heard anyone sound, I *did* care. How could I not?

'No, you don't,' she said and she cried even harder.

I hated seeing her like this. Jeane was tough and strong and she could blag her way to New York and persuade people to give her TV shows and book deals. She wasn't defeated by a broken shower door. She was better than that.

Jeane didn't seem to think so when I tried to give her a rousing pep talk, and when I went to hug her she shied away from me and I didn't know what to do to make her feel better or get the shower door back on its runner, so I did the only thing I could do.

I phoned home.

When my dad arrived, Jeane was still crying, but just to mix it up a little she was lying in a miserable heap on the bathroom floor.

I'd explained to Mum on the phone that she was having some kind of psychotic break, though Mum had said that still wasn't a good enough reason to stop me being grounded. Then I'd said that I hadn't had too much to drink and they'd said nothing about how seeing Jeane would violate the terms of my parole.

Thankfully there'd been a cupcake crisis and she'd put Dad on the phone and now he was here in Jeane's bathroom and squatting down on the floor in front of her with a damp flannel.

'You'll feel much better once you've wiped your face,' he said in the same tone of voice he used when Alice had fallen off her bike or Melly was throwing a wobbly about her spelling homework. It worked on Jeane, too. A small hand came out of the Jeane-shaped ball to take the flannel and the sobs muted down to hiccups. Eventually she sat up and pushed the hair out of her eyes.

She'd have melted the stoniest, steeliest heart. Even Mum would have stopped calling her 'that girl' and made her a cup of tea, but Dad just took off his coat, hung it on the towel rail and rolled up his sleeves. 'OK, Michael, let battle commence with this shower door.'

It took nearly an hour until we finally admitted to ourselves and to Jeane (who'd been dubious about our chances from the start) that the door was not going to be returned to its rightful resting place.

'It seems too big to slide into the tracks,' Dad said with a bemused expression on his face. 'I'm very sorry.'

'That's OK,' Jeane said dully. 'Thanks for trying though.'

There was an awkward silence because our work here was done, or not done, and now there was no reason to stay.

'Are you going to be all right, Jeane?' I asked.

I thought she was going to assure me that she'd be, 'Just fine, don't you worry about me,' but she just swallowed hard.

'Well, you can't stay here with the shower door like that,' Dad said firmly, like the untethered door might attack Jeane while she slept. 'My parking voucher runs out in ten minutes so run along and pack an overnight bag.'

'I can't do that,' Jeane said. She sounded appalled, which was a lot better than when she'd sounded catatonic. 'I can't just rock up uninvited.'

'I'm inviting you,' Dad said calmly. 'Come on, let's go.'

I wasn't too thrilled about this turn of events but the thought of leaving Jeane on her own to lie in a crumpled sobbing heap on her bathroom floor wasn't too appealing either.

'There'll be cupcakes and *The Muppet Christmas Carol*,' I said cajolingly. 'You love the Muppets.'

'I do,' she agreed, and she slowly turned to pick up her toothbrush.

35

'I'm really sorry to turn up like this,' I said when Michael's mum opened the door and found me outside, like a parcel that had been dumped there without a 'Sorry we missed you' card stuck to it. Michael and his dad had gone to the off-licence and had left me to fend for myself with a cheery, 'It's OK, we phoned ahead!' It really wasn't OK though. 'And I'm very sorry about the whole New York thing.'

She gave me a long, hard look. I much preferred Michael's dad. He was so Zen that I always felt as if a little of his inner chi was rubbing off on me, but his mother made my hackles and the hair on the back of my neck rise.

'You'd better come in,' she said, and though I didn't normally care what anyone thought of the way I looked, I wished I wasn't wearing my cat pyjama bottoms and my faux-fur leopard-print anorak and bunny slippers. I also wished that crying hadn't left my face so swollen that it felt as if someone had been using it as a punchbag.

I hesitated and she sighed, 'You're letting the cold air in,' and I had no choice but to walk through the door. Well, I did have a choice but I didn't fancy walking home in my bunny slippers.

'I really am sorry about everything,' I said again. I wasn't sure I was *that* sorry, but I couldn't face having to go back to my empty flat. I was sick of my own company. In fact, I hardly knew myself at the moment because myself didn't usually cry for hours and hours. The last time I'd cried had been on the final day of Rock 'n' Roll Camp when we'd had an impromptu singalong to 'Born This Way' and then it had been mostly happy tears that had lasted the time it took to scrub at my cheeks before anyone could see. I'd certainly never cried for hours before and never over an annoying but not that serious domestic mishap.

But I had to admit that maybe the reason I'd had a meltdown wasn't just about the shower. I think the shower door was, like, a metaphor. It represented everything that was bad. Yeah, there was good stuff but there was also a lot of bad stuff and it went deep and it hurt, so standing in Michael's hall on Christmas Eve in my pyjamas and clutching an overnight bag as his mother looked at me like I'd tracked dog shit into her carpets was still better than being at home.

'Never mind what happened a few weeks ago,' she said. 'It's in the past and in the present is a hot bath and a cup of tea.'

I nodded and followed Mrs Lee into the kitchen where she put the kettle on. I mentally prepared myself for twenty minutes of tea-drinking and stilted conversation and a bit of glaring, but then the lounge door swung open and two little heads peered round it.

'Oh! It's you!' Then both Michael's little sisters, in matching fairy outfits, were suddenly in the kitchen and clambering all over me.

'We're dressed up in case we bump into Father Christmas!'

'We've made him Muppet cupcakes!'

'Why is your hair white? Did someone give you a nasty shock?'

'I have bunny slippers just like yours! I'm going to put them on so we can be slipper twins!'

''Cause it's Christmas Eve we're having sausage, beans and chips for dinner *and* we're allowed to eat it in front of the TV.'

'*The Muppet Christmas Carol*! It's our favouritest ever, ever, ever film!'

'Apart from *Toy Story 2*! Do you like *The Muppet Christmas Carol*?'

That was how they talked, with an exclamation mark tacked on to the end of every high-pitched sentence. It was funny and exhausting.

'Of course I like *The Muppet Christmas Carol*,' I said, and unbelievably Michael's mum caught my eye as she peeled potatoes and smiled at me. 'It's a classic.'

We then had a fierce debate about our favourite Muppets because they weren't happy when I chose Gonzo. I had both of them pleading the case for Miss Piggy when Michael and his dad came back with a crate of bottled lager and a couple of clanking carrier bags.

Michael nodded at me coolly. 'You all right then?'

'Yeah,' I said. His mum and dad were joking about how much longer they could last before they cracked open the wine and Melly and Alice were having a pointless argument about how many cupcakes they could eat before they vommed and as Michael reached across his mum to start putting lager in the fridge, she stroked his arm, just this brief, fleeting gesture that he didn't even notice, and though I'd been an outsider all my life, I'd never felt quite so outside as I did at that moment.

'Is Jeane staying for dinner?' Melly suddenly asked.

'Yes,' Mrs Lee said firmly. 'She's staying the night.'

Melly and Alice shared an evil smile. 'When Katya's brother's girlfriend sleeps over they share the same bed,' Melly announced, accompanied by much nudging and giggling. 'Is Jeane going to share Mich—'

'No!' I burst out. 'Never in a million years.'

'Jeane's not my girlfriend,' Michael snapped. 'And it's rude to ask personal questions.'

'But you didn't let me finish asking a personal question so really I haven't been rude.'

'Anyways, you *were* girlfriend and boyfriend,' Melly said with a glance over at her parents, who were having a tense conversation about goose fat. ''Cause Mum said you were after you ran away to New York and then Michael was all punished and he was in a really, really, *really* bad mood. He said it was his Cambridge interview but that was *ages* ago and he's still been in a really, really, *really* bad mood.'

This was all . . . interesting. I hadn't missed Michael at all, or I hadn't let myself miss him what with being so busy and the

341

fact I'd stopped going to school so I didn't have to look at his cheekbones and his almond-shaped eyes and that pout of a mouth that was currently a tight slash on his face, or seen his lithe, lanky body loping about. It was very easy not to miss someone when they weren't in your life, but maybe he'd missed me. A little bit. Or else he was still angry and resentful at all the horrible things I'd said to him in New York. Also I'd told him to fuck off when we landed at Heathrow and he'd tried to help me with my bags. You couldn't really come back from that.

'If I was in a really, really, *really* bad mood, Melly, it was probably because I have two really, really, *really* annoying little sisters,' he said, and they both huffed in sheer outrage.

'You are bad and mean and I'm going to spit on your cupcakes,' Alice said just as Mrs Lee emerged from the fridge.

'I know two little girls who may get sent to bed without any dinner or any cupcakes,' she said sternly, and it was impossible to have a pity party when a five-year-old and a seven-year-old were throwing a strop. If Michael wouldn't even look at me then that was fine. I could deal with that. I'd have my bath and some dinner and then I'd go home.

The only reason I didn't go home was because I fell asleep halfway through *The Muppet Christmas Carol*. I was stuffed full of food and cups of tea and had Melly and Alice wedged on either side of me as we shared a big armchair, and one moment Miss Piggy and Ebenezer Scrooge were throwing down, the next I was being woken up by Mrs Lee who put me to bed in the spare room. She even tucked me in. No one had tucked me in since ... well, I couldn't remember ever being tucked in.

During the night I was joined by Melly and Alice who'd got up because they thought they'd heard reindeer, had eaten all the chocolate coins in their stockings and thought I might like to watch cartoons, but when they realised I didn't, they got into bed with me and I started to tell them a story about Sammy, the rock 'n' roll squirrel, and they fell asleep, which was just as well as I had no idea where I was going with Sammy.

And so it came to pass that Mr and Mrs Lee weren't woken up at five on Christmas morning but got to lie in until 8.30, and if Mrs Lee had been harbouring any lingering ill will to the horrible girl who'd kidnapped her son, it was all gone.

It might have been the thirteen hours of almost-uninterrupted sleep or yesterday's crying jag or just having a chance to recharge my get-up-and-go but I was anxious to get up and be gone. I didn't want to intrude on all their family traditions. Besides, Michael couldn't bring himself to look at me or even talk to me much beyond passing me the sugar bowl without being asked, because he knew that I needed at least three sugars in my coffee.

'You're very welcome to stay,' Shen said. And Kathy – I felt like I should call her Kathy now, instead of Mrs Lee – nodded. 'We have so much food in the house, we'll be eating savoury snack selection boxes until Easter.'

'I'm going round to my friend Tabitha's later,' I explained. 'I said I'd help her make sausage rolls.'

I had trouble making toast so my sausage-roll input would mostly be as an observer but it made it sound like I was all involved in someone else's Christmas, and, as it was, Kathy already had the turkey in the oven, Shen was peeling potatoes

343

and Michael was doing something to a mound of Brussels sprouts so I was only going to be in the way.

'You're going round for Christmas lunch, then?' Kathy asked and I snorted, I couldn't help it, because Tabitha never got up when it was still technically morning and she'd already told me her Christmas dinner would involve whatever she and Tom could get in Lidl half an hour before it closed on Christmas Eve.

'Well, not lunch, but an early dinner and I never ordered a cab so I'll have to cycle to Battersea and—'

'Then you *have* to stay for lunch,' Kathy said firmly. 'End of discussion.'

'But I have—'

'I thought we were already finished talking about this. If you want to be helpful, you can go and entertain Melly and Alice so they stop coming in here every two minutes to ask when we're going to open presents.'

Kathy Lee was good – really good, with the steely voice and determined glint in her eye, and I couldn't imagine why she wanted me to stick around but she already had her hand on my shoulder and was steering me towards the living room, but not before I saw the grimace on Michael's face, like my continued presence in his life and in his actual house was causing him immense physical pain.

I didn't want to stay. Not just because being in the same room as Michael was like having my fingernails, toenails, teeth and nose hairs pulled out slowly one by one, but because I couldn't deal with their happy families bullshit. Except it wasn't bullshit – they *were* a happy family.

While they were opening presents, I took a diplomatic bath so it wouldn't be embarrassing that I hadn't got them anything and vice versa, but when I came downstairs again, Melly and Alice insisted that I have a pair of fairy wings and an Etch A Sketch from their combined haul, and there was also a Cadbury's selection pack and a vanilla-scented candle because Kathy and Shen were the kind of parents who always had spare presents lying around for any last-minute guests. Michael only gave me another pained look as I helped to lay the table.

It was just your regular, run-of-the-mill, bog-standard Christmas dinner. We pulled crackers and put on our paper hats and groaned at the bad jokes in the crackers. There was an argument over who had the last pig in blanket and the home-made cranberry sauce ran out pretty quickly because the girls slathered their entire plates with the stuff.

They were all proper Christmas traditions but then, when I thought about it, I realised they were other people's Christmas traditions. Apart from last year when Bethan *had* come home and we'd cooked a small but perfectly formed Christmas dinner and spent the day watching my MGM Musicals box set, our family Christmas traditions had sucked.

Pat and Roy would get us up really early. Not so we could open our Christmas presents but because Christmas dinner was at noon sharp. Then I'd get left with the clear-up while they took Bethan and went to put flowers on Andrew's grave at a green burial ground in Buckinghamshire with a wild cherry tree and an environmentally friendly bench next to his plot. They never asked if I wanted to go with them, so I'd get left behind with a mound of dirty plates and a box of Quality Street.

Then, when they did get back, Roy would disappear to his shed and Pat would go to bed with a terrible headache and Bethan would hang out with me but she'd usually end up crying. And that had been our family Christmas tradition. Then I thought about how this would be the first Christmas that no one went to visit Andrew's grave – last year Bethan had driven up on Boxing Day – and that made me feel depressed in a way that not even each of the Lees making a wish over their first spoonful of Christmas pudding had.

Everyone said that friends were the new family, I'd even written a blog about it, but as I sat at the Lees' dining room table with cracker debris all around me and Melly and Alice treating us all to a rousing chorus of 'Jingle Bells', I knew I'd been totes wrong.

Friends shouldn't be the new family. Your family should be your family and friends got sewn into the fabric of your family life. It was only people who didn't have a family or had a crappy family who needed friends as a substitute. And then there were people who didn't have a family and really, when you thought about it, didn't have friends either.

This had nothing to do with Michael Lee sitting across the table from me, not looking at or talking to me as I didn't look at or talk to him right back, OK? I wasn't even angry with him any more, though I was still a little bit fumy about the Twitter thing and also the thing about him not being able to deal with my success. But now I was starting to wonder if it wasn't that Michael couldn't deal with my success but that he couldn't deal with *me*, because I was a hell of a lot to deal with.

I sighed and Kathy gave me a look. Not one of her old 'God, I wish they'd never banned corporal punishment in schools' looks but one of her new 'Oh, poor little Jeane' looks.

'Everything all right?' she asked with a little head tilt to show that she was there for me and, oh no, now I wanted her to be there for me. I barely recognised myself.

'Everything's great,' I said with huge amounts of false enthusiasm and I was saved from having to go into details about just how great everything was by my phone beeping. It was a text from Tabitha.

We're awake! Get your arse over to ours. I have a rolling pin with your name on it. Tab xxx

It was no wonder I was having a deep crisis of faith. I'd been spending far too much time with the Lees and that was why I was suddenly hankering for all this happy families nonsense. How could you hanker for what you'd never had? It was pointless. I'd feel much better when I was back with my own people.

Kathy and Shen and even Melly and Alice were very reluctant to let me go, whereas Michael grunted something and went to load the dishwasher as I said my goodbyes and promised faithfully to call and let them know when I got home that night, and if I did want to stay over for a few days that was all right too, though Kathy's elderly aunt was coming over on Boxing Day and, according to Melly and Alice, 'She smells of actual wee.'

They even made noises about giving me a lift home, but I insisted frequently and a little forcefully that I was fine walking and finally, eventually, at last the front door was opened and I was free.

36

It was 6.30 on Christmas Day evening and I wasn't sure if I was going to have another mince pie, throw up or fall into a food coma.

I was lying on the living room floor, back propped against the sofa where Mum and Dad were snuggling, even though they'd been told repeatedly to stop because parental PDAs were revolting. I had a Melly and an Alice cuddled up on either side and we were watching the *Doctor Who* Christmas special. All five of us were still wearing our paper hats and I'd hidden the last three roast potatoes at the back of the fridge to eat later.

God, I love Christmas, I thought, and then my brand new iPhone beeped.

I had an email from Jeane and just like that my warm fuzzies went cold and I really thought I was going to puke. An email from Jeane felt like getting followed round a store by the security guard. It gave me a sense of foreboding and even though I hadn't done anything wrong (or I thought I hadn't, but it was hard to tell with Jeane), I immediately felt guilty.

Because, yeah, she was all me, me, me all the bloody time, but now I was starting to realise that the reason she was so self-involved was because she had nobody else in her life to get involved with. She shouldn't have to deal with broken house stuff – I didn't even know how to put the washing machine on – and she shouldn't have been on her own on Christmas Eve. And, yeah, I should have come clean about who I was on Twitter and, oh God, I suppose I should have admitted that I was jealous of how she was doing amazing things with her life when I didn't even know how to put the washing machine on.

It still didn't make it any easier to have her in my house, sucking up to my parents and my little sisters and looking all wan and fragile. I was still pissed off about how she'd behaved in New York but I didn't want to be pissed off with her any more and so, even though I could have left the message unread and gone back to the Daleks, I decided to read it and then send her back a friendly but not *too* friendly reply.

Hey Michael
I never got to say Happy Christmas to you, so, hey, Happy Christmas and all that stuff. Are you lulled into a sense of false security with my unexpected festive felicitations? Probably not, so it's better if I just come out with it.
    I'm actually at my flat – Christmas dinner at Tab's never happened because Mad Glen and his alcoholic mate Phil came to blows over some fake After Eights from

Lidl so Tab and Tom had to take them to A&E and the thing is that actually I WOULD love to stay over at your place for a few days. Like, your mum and dad both offered repeatedly and I think your mum and I are SO over the New York business and Melly and Alice are totes my spiritual twins.

This is not some cunning ploy to worm my way back into your good graces or, like, your pants. I know that we're over and even when it was ongoing we both knew it was doomed. That's OK. I'm cool about that. I'm even cool about you because I know I'm impossible. I do know that, Michael, and I know you're not cool with me. You can hardly bring yourself to look at me or talk to me, though I do appreciate you coming round when I lost it over the shower door.

So if the thought of me spending maybe two or three days at your place is going to be too awkward then please say. I will understand. Or, like, I'll TRY to understand (I plan to be big with the empathy next year).

Do let me know if you could bear to have me around. I promise to be on my best behaviour, though that isn't saying much.

Jeane

She was right. She was impossible. Impossible to say no to, because Jeane was seventeen and she was on her own and it was Christmas and even though I don't think I'll ever stop being a little bit mad at her, she didn't deserve to be on her own at Christmas.

I turned my head and winced as I saw Mum and Dad nuzzling.

'Can you stop that?' I waved my phone. 'Had an email from Jeane. Her Christmas dinner got cancelled and she wants to know if she can come and stay for a couple of days.'

It would have been all right if Dad had groaned and Mum had said, 'But I only offered to be polite,' but Mum was already getting up. 'I'll make sure she's got clean towels. Will you go and pick her up, darling?'

I wasn't sure which darling she was referring to but Dad was levering himself up off the sofa and Melly and Alice were asking if they could come with him because, 'We really want to see the shower door and do you think Jeane might have different-coloured hair?' and even if I had minded – and, well, I did a little bit – I was totally outnumbered. I emailed Jeane back.

It's OK, Dad and the brats will be there to pick you up in a bit. I hope you like cold turkey 'cause that's all we're going to be eating for the next few days.

An hour later Jeane was in the house, laden down with a Fortnum & Mason's hamper, a present from her agent which she re-gifted to Mum and Dad, and a heap of brightly coloured crap for the girls (she was always being sent heaps of brightly coloured crap by PRs who wanted a mention on her blog): hair-slides to toy robots to mounds of sweets that sent them into ear-splitting squeals of delight. There was nothing for me but as she was ceremonially escorted by Melly and Alice to the spare bedroom to unpack, I checked my iPhone (I'd been checking it every five minutes since I set it up), there was an

352

email from iTunes to let me know that Jeane had sent me a £100 gift card.

> I couldn't help but notice that your email came with the tag 'sent from my iPhone'. This should get your apps collection off to a good start.

Even though she'd only had an hour to pack, she'd used part of that time to write me a long, detailed list of all the apps I *had* to buy.

> But not *Angry Birds*. Please don't be that predictable.

It wasn't like she was magically forgiven or that I wanted to start something up again that I never should have started in the first place, but I couldn't fault Jeane's generosity. Even during that argument on a street corner in Greenpoint, even though she'd hurled insults at me, not once had she reminded me that if it hadn't been for her I wouldn't have been standing on a street corner in Greenpoint in the first place.

And when I thought of New York, I remembered that I had a ton of sweets bought at Dylan's Candy Bar, which Jeane had stuffed in my bag when she'd packed for me. I could give them to her as a Christmas present, but it was very hard to find a good time to hand them over.

The first evening Jeane crashed out ridiculously early again and on Boxing Day she was more interested in helping Mum concoct huge turkey sandwiches smothered in chutneys, pickles and other condiments. When Great Aunt Mary arrived and

Alice point-blank refused to go near her (which was perfectly justified because she smelt like she'd been left out in the rain), Jeane took the girls to the park with their new scooters.

Then when she got back, she bonded with Great Aunt Mary over her pink rinse and once Great Aunt Mary had been ferried back to Ealing and Mum had spritzed a whole can of Febreeze over the armchair where she'd been sitting, she and the girls and Jeane commandeered the sofa and started watching musicals. Proper old musicals in glorious technicolour where everyone kept breaking into these big song and dance numbers about having a night on the town and singing in the bloody rain. It was horrible. Usually, Melly and Alice counted as one person and the sexes were evenly represented, but with Jeane in residence the power balance had shifted and Dad retreated to his study to watch a documentary about leprosy and I lay on my bed playing *Angry Birds* until I couldn't see straight.

So Jeane stayed out of my way and I stayed out of hers until the next morning when Melly and Alice were off to an all-day birthday party and Mum and Dad were braving the sales to buy a new washing machine.

'I filled up your car with petrol the other night,' Dad said as we were finishing breakfast. 'Why don't you and Jeane go out somewhere?'

'Oh, that's all right,' Jeane said through a mouthful of toast and jam. She had let Melly and Alice do her hair, which now had at least twenty clips and bows in it. 'I can amuse myself for a few hours.'

'It would be nice if you two did something,' Mum said with a pointed look at me. 'And it would be really nice if you stopped playing that bloody game with the pigs and the birds and the incessant noise, Michael.'

I looked at Jeane who looked back at me with a blank expression and then we both looked at my mother who had her 'My word is law' face on and half an hour later we were in my car.

'So where do you want to go?' I asked Jeane politely, because she was *so* in with my mother I'd be in trouble if I were rude. Not that I was going to be rude but the whole thing was weird. And Jeane was being weird. Not once in the last thirty-six hours had she lectured anyone on obscure girl groups or the God-like genius that was Haribo and I didn't want to talk about what had happened with us or what was going to happen with us because we'd start arguing and so I didn't know what to say to her.

'You don't have to take me anywhere,' she said as she crossed her arms. 'Like, you could take me to a café and I could hang out there for a couple of hours and no one would ever know.'

Then I'd have to find another café to sit in for a couple of hours in case Mum and Dad came back early, which was just stupid.

'Look, we can handle spending some time together, can't we?'

'Well, yeah, we should be able to, but it's going to be hard when you're not really talking to me,' Jeane said calmly.

'No, you're not talking to *me*,' I said, and I wished I didn't sound so sulky.

'I didn't think you wanted me to talk to you.'

I didn't know what I wanted any more except not to get tied up in one of Jeane's conversational knots. 'I'm starting the car now. Where shall we go?'

'I suppose we could go to the seaside. Going to the seaside in winter is quite cool, though everything will probably be closed,' Jeane mused. Inevitably she started doing something with her iPhone, then she switched on the Sat Nav I'd inherited from Dad, who'd got a swizzy new one for Christmas. 'How does this work? Do I just put in a postcode?'

'Yeah.' I took my eyes off the road long enough to jab at it then watched Jeane tap in a postcode. 'Where's that?'

She frowned. 'I'll tell you when we get there. It's not going to be the funnest road trip ever but it can be your Christmas present to me.'

'I didn't get you a present because I didn't know my parents were suddenly going to adopt you! I still have the sweets I bought in New York, I've been waiting for a chance to give them to you.'

'It wasn't a dig and I did ask you before I turned up.'

'I could hardly say no.' I glanced over at Jeane. She was sitting there with her arms tightly folded and her lips moving silently. I swear she was counting up to ten so she wouldn't start shouting at me. 'I really don't mind you staying over. I just don't understand why you'd want to and, to be honest, that whole scene with the shower door freaked me out.'

'Yeah, that scene with the shower door was quite an epiphany,' Jeane said unhelpfully and then she started asking me questions about Cambridge and if I was going to do the internship in San Francisco and when the Sat Nav told me to take the next exit off the motorway, I realised that we'd managed a whole hour of not arguing.

Jeane asked me to stop at a garage, then got back in the car with a bag of Haribo Starmix and a bunch of flowers. 'Are they for my mum?'

'Nope,' she said, and I waited for her to start asking me questions again but she just stared at the route on the Sat Nav. We were only a couple of miles away from our destination and I still wanted to know where we were going, but she didn't seem to want to tell me.

Take the next left. You have arrived at your destination, the Sat Nav informed me as I pulled into a cemetery. The sign said it was a green burial ground but it looked like a cemetery to me.

'What are we doing here? Are your grandparents buried here?'

Jeane shook her head. 'Andrew. I told you about him.' She unbuckled her seatbelt. 'Though now that we're here I realise I don't have a clue where his grave is. We're looking for a bench and a wild cherry tree. Do you know what a wild cherry tree even looks like?'

It was freezing cold with a damp, vicious wind rolling in from the open fields and the ground squelched underneath our feet as we peered at gravestones. They weren't laid out in neat rows but dotted randomly about. It was nice, I suppose, that each grave had its own space and they weren't all crammed together, but it was still depressing to be wandering around a graveyard, even if it was an ecologically aware graveyard.

Eventually we found the right grave, after we'd done a complete loop and were almost back at the car. I stood to one side as Jeane crouched down and wiped at the stone with the sleeve of her fun fur anorak.

ANDREW SMITH
1983 – 1994
Cherished son, beloved brother, taken too soon.
Rest with the angels, our brave, beautiful boy.

There was a wooden bench under a tree, possibly a wild cherry tree, which I sat on as Jeane removed a desiccated bouquet from a vase on the plinth of the grave and arranged her own flowers in it. Then she stayed squatting for several long moments, which must have been hell on her knees, until she slowly straightened up and walked over to me.

'I realised that this was the first Christmas that no one had visited his grave,' she said, as she sat down next to me. It was even colder now, a seeping wet cold that felt as if it were burrowing into my bones, and Jeane was shivering so I put my arm round her, not in a copping-a-feel kinda way but more like a boy-scouts-who-huddle-together-for-warmth-when-they-get-separated-from-the-rest-of-the-troop-on-an-Outward-Bound-course kinda way. She immediately huddled against me. 'The only person who could come this year was me.'

'Does it make you sad?' I asked curiously, because she didn't seem sad so much as thoughtful.

'This place isn't exactly a laugh riot, but it is a nice place to come so people can feel close to the people they've lost.' She wrinkled her nose. 'Though, really, you shouldn't *have* to drop everything to come here to remember someone. They're either dead and that's it, or if there is some kind of afterlife then they're always with you.' She nodded her head in the direction of the grave. 'I mean, that's just his bones, it's not him.'

'Oh, Jeane, Jeane, Jeane ...' I said and I honestly didn't know what else to say. 'Something is really wrong, isn't it?'

'It really is but I'm going to make it right,' she said. 'Because I don't want to die and have no one to visit my grave.'

'You're not going to die,' I said and I tried to make it sound like a joke, but now I was worried that she was suicidal or something.

'Well, of course I'm not going to die,' she said with a touch of the old scathe back in her voice, which was a relief. 'Unless I get mown down by a bus, I plan to be around for ages, but I don't want my life to be long and lonely and the way I'm going, I *will* be lonely. No, worse than that. I'm going to be alone.'

'You won't be alone. You have loads of friends who—'

'People I know off the internet,' Jeane reminded me dryly. 'Michael, even my own parents don't love me.'

'But they do! They're your mum and dad, they have to.'

'Just 'cause they're *supposed* to doesn't mean they do,' Jeane said. 'And, yeah, I have friends, but I spent Christmas Day with your family who barely know me and the one invite I did have got cancelled because of a fight between a middle-aged man who went menty after doing too many drugs and his alcoholic perv of a friend. That's not cool. And the night before, when the shower door broke, I thought: I'm seventeen and I'm all on my own and it's just too much responsibility. I kid myself that I'm fine and I'm coping but my life is just a flimsy façade held together with Haribo and Pritt Stick. When I really needed help, there was no one to call.'

'You called me,' I told her. 'Or was I the last resort?'

'The very last of my last resorts but I think I knew, deep down, that you'd come, even though you hate me right now.'

I tightened my arm round her. 'I don't *hate* you. You're not my favourite person in the world but maybe you're starting to grow on me again.'

'Yeah, like a fungal infection.'

'You're not *quite* that bad,' I said, and Jeane looked up at me and grinned. 'And you're only focusing on the bad stuff because it's Christmas and when you feel crap at Christmas it's a special, powerful feeling like crap. There's loads of good things happening for you. The TV show and the book and the website – that will teach me not to call you an absurd media creation.' I took a deep breath. 'I'm sorry about that, by the way, and all the other things I said.'

Jeane bit her lip and stared down at the ground. 'Well, thanks for apologising, and I'm sorry that I said ... well, *hurled* loads of insults at you, but pretending that you didn't know me on Twitter, that was not cool.'

I wriggled a bit and hoped that Jeane would think that I was trying to get more comfortable rather than squirming in shame. 'I know, but honestly, it didn't start as some evil scheme to get one over on you and you were so much nicer to me on Twitter than you were in real life. Then when we started to hang out and stuff, you were still much nicer to me on Twitter than in real life. Like, you were less adorkable and more adorable. And it's like I said at the airport in New York, I'd let it go on for so long that, in the end, I couldn't tell you that we were Twitter friends.'

She didn't say anything for a long time. I wasn't quite sure if she'd even understood what I was trying to say but then Jeane 'hmm'ed and almost giggled.

'I suppose I can relate to that,' she said at last. 'About being more adorable than adorkable, I mean. It's why I'm quitting all that. I've decided I'm not doing Adorkable any more. Not the book or the TV show or any of it. I'm going to give the money back or something.'

'What the actual fuck? Are you *mad*?'

'I don't want to be Adorkable any more. I don't want to be a dork. I want to be like everyone else instead of pretending that it's OK to exclude yourself and that everyone else is wrong because they like all the same things and they dress the same way. I'm meant to be preaching to people about how cool it is to just be yourself but really what I mean is that it's only cool to be how I want you to be and what do I know about anything? I know *nothing*.'

'You know lots of things, Jeane. That speech you gave at the conference was amazing. One woman sitting in front of me was *crying*.'

'Well, she probably had her own stuff going on,' Jeane argued. She struggled to sit up straight instead of leaning into me and I felt cold without the warmth of her body against mine. 'I'm so hostile that I'm pushing people away even when I want them to be close. Like you. It doesn't matter if you have stupid hair and you wear those overpriced poseurish clothes—'

'What were you just saying about how you were going to stop making snap judgements about people just because they don't dress in a Jeane-approved fashion?' I asked her tartly and she huffed and flounced where she sat. I think Melly and Alice were rubbing off on her.

'That's my point. Despite your lamentable personal style, you are actually capable of independent thought and you know loads of interesting things about computers and Hong Kong and artificial intelligence and your parents are cool and it was right that you didn't want to lie to them, but I only ever see things from my point of view and my point of view is seriously deluded. I just want to be part of the world instead of looking down on it the whole time and that's what I'm bloody well going to do.'

I could hear what Jeane was saying. I even agreed with some of it. She was always banging on about people being shallow and how they shouldn't judge other people for being weird or different when Jeane was the most judgemental person I had ever met. But Jeane *was* weird and different and, if there were absolutely no witnesses, I'd have to admit that her weirdness and her difference was what I liked most about her.

'I wouldn't do anything rash,' I advised her. 'I mean, you're obviously feeling a bit raw right now but you can still do Adorkable and go on about jumble sales and all that other crap.'

'I can't. It's wrong. It's not me. I don't want to buy my clothes at jumble sales any more. I want to buy them from Topshop.'

I couldn't help it. I started to laugh because only Jeane could be so unintentionally funny when she was trying to be deathly serious. I wasn't that surprised when she hit me, though she apologised because, 'I'm not going to hit other people when they disagree with me any more. I'm going to be so easy to get on with that they won't even disagree with me.'

It made me laugh even harder. I stood up. 'You can't change who you are. Being argumentative is hardwired into your DNA.'

'You wait,' she muttered darkly, standing up and following me to the car. 'On the way back let's stop somewhere so I can buy a pair of jeans.'

I'd always thought the oddest thing about Jeane, and this was really saying something, was that she didn't possess a single pair of jeans.

'You might want to ease yourself in gently,' I said, as we reached the car. 'Start off with a pair of coloured jeans. Maybe orange ones?'

'Blue jeans,' Jeane said firmly. 'And I need to get some hair dye too.'

Every time I thought I'd got the laughter under control, it would bubble back up, so in the end Jeane was forced to sit on her hands so she wouldn't be tempted to hit me again.

37

THAT'S ALL FOLKS!

You know how I'm always saying that Adorkable is about following your own path in life and cocking a snook (though I've never actually known what a snook is or how to cock it) at mainstream fashion, whether it's the clothes you wear or the music you listen to or the thoughts you thunk?

Yeah. That.

Well, I take it all back. Every single last word, comma, semi-colon and full stop.

I denounce dorkiness. Dorkiness and I have broken up. We've decided to divorce due to irreconcilable differences.

Does dorkiness automatically make you a better person? Does being touched by the hand of dork turn your life into puppies and rainbows and instant happiness? Does dorkiness keep you warm at night or make you cookies or give you a back rub when you're feeling down? No, it doesn't. And I've been doing myself, and you, a disservice by claiming that it's OK to be different. Maybe it is and maybe it's not, because you (by which I mean me) become so obsessed with being different and not fitting in that you push away anyone who tries to get close.

Really, what's the point in having half a million people following your tweets and being the teen queen of the blogosphere when it's Christmas Day and I'm so knee-deep in loneliness that I had to throw myself on the mercy of strangers?

It turned out all right, the strangers were very welcoming, but I've been forced to take a long hard look at myself and where I'm going. It's become clear that my final destination is mad old lady with a thousand feral cats and my only human interaction will be with the person who delivers my Meals on Wheels.

I really don't want my future to be like that, so I'm shutting up shop.

Down with dorkiness, I say! Here's to crossing over to the darkside. Except it doesn't feel like the darkside. It feels like I'm moving towards the light.

So, this is me, Jeane, signing off.

Over and out.

End message.

38

So it turned out that being normal was great. It really was. It was just *so* easy. Why had no one ever told me this?

To start with I dyed my hair brown, much to Melly and Alice's disgust (they even threatened to throw me out of their special club, The Melly and Alice Club, which I'd been inducted into with great ceremony). I packed away all my multi-coloured polyester dresses and Day-Glo tights and I went to Hollister and Abercrombie & Fitch and American Apparel to buy tight stretchy clothes in navy, grey and black, which were actually perfectly all right colours because they went with everything. I was eating three proper meals a day, some even contained vegetables, going to bed at a proper time and getting up nine hours later, and I even took all the shouty girl groups and boy groups and obscure film soundtracks off my iPod and was listening to chart music. I'd also unplugged myself from the internet. No blogging and no tweeting. I was living in the moment, man. I was just, like, *being*. And without all my Adorkable extra-curricular activities, I had so much spare time. Loads of it! I hardly knew what to do with myself.

I did take Melly and Alice to the cinema to see a film. We were meant to see the latest Pixar but it was sold out so we watched a film about princesses. I suppose that was actually quite hard because it was a really shit film, and instead of sitting there and composing a blistering blog about forcing antiquated notions of gender and sexuality on small girls and how pink needed to be reclaimed as a colour that had nothing to do with princesses or fairies before it was lost to us for ever, I just had to sit there and try really hard to keep my blood pressure at manageable levels. But when the film finished, Melly and Alice both thought the main princess was stupid and she should have just rescued herself instead of singing sappy songs until the prince came along to save her, so it was all good.

Yeah, being normal was the way forward and I loved having all this me-time to give myself facials and watch back-to-back episodes of *America's Next Top Model* and *My Super Sweet 16*. I even did some heavily supervised cooking that didn't involve putting leftover takeaway food in a microwave to heat up.

It was a whole different Jeane. An adorable Jeane, if you will.

'You can't keep this up for ever,' Michael said to me on the fourth day of my new exciting life as an ordinary, regular, run-of-the-mill girl. 'You're going to crack. I'll be amazed if you can last another week.'

'I'm not going to crack. I love the new me,' I said as we

loaded the dishwasher after dinner. We'd finally seen off the last of the turkey and were now working through a massive ham that hadn't been cooked on Christmas Day because there'd been no room for it in the oven.

I'm not entirely sure but I could have sworn I heard Michael mutter, 'Well, I don't think much of the new you.' But when he straightened up from rearranging the cutlery that I'd shoved into the dishwasher in a more ergonomic fashion, he had a bland smile on his face. 'All I'm saying is you can't pretend to be normal. You either are or you aren't and *you* aren't.'

'That's where you're wrong. Like, if I pretend to be normal then eventually it won't be pretending, it will be just what I do.'

'Except anyone else wouldn't think of it as *doing* normal, they'd just *be* normal.' Michael grinned again, because he thought the whole thing was just a joke and not a big life-changing transformation. I kept catching him giving me these odd, expectant looks, like he thought I might suddenly rip off my new clothes to reveal a fluorescent catsuit and shout, 'Psych!' as loud as I could.

Considering that he'd always complained about the way I dressed and got really, really pissed when I was lecturing him on sexual politics or the history of Haribo, I'd have thought that he might have been, well, more attracted to the new me. Now there was nothing embarrassing about me, and I would no longer lose eleventy billion cool points by going out with Michael, it would make perfect sense for us to get back together again.

I had lots of free time to devote to a boyfriend and if I was going out with Michael Lee, holding hands with him in public, then the whole world would be able to tell that I was just a normal girl going out with a normal boy. Move along, nothing to see here. Except, now that I was doing normal, I was forced to admit that I was plain and ordinary-looking while Michael was still exotically handsome, and last time I checked he was still the centre forward on the football team and head of the student council so in a normal world that made him completely out of reach.

It was a timely reminder that normal wasn't always going to be such a breeze.

'This New Year's Eve party tonight, just so we're both clear, we're not going to it together,' Michael said, just in case I wasn't up to speed on that point. 'Not as a couple, just as mates, so I can properly introduce you to all my friends that you've looked down on for years and you can start to become socialised.'

I counted to ten. I'd been counting to ten a lot over the last few days. 'OK. I'm going to get changed. I think I'm ready to wear my new jeans outside the house.'

Two hours later I was ready to rock this joint. Or go to Michael's friend Ant's New Year's Eve party. My brown hair was freshly straightened. My make-up was light and tasteful and I'd applied two coats of brown mascara (I hadn't even known that mascara came in brown) to make my eyes look less piggy, and I was wearing a black top, my skinny dark blue jeans and black suede high heels. No corsages pinned in odd places. No glitter. No animal-prints. I was going to look the same as all the other girls, though there was just one problem . . .

'I didn't think denim would chafe so much,' I said to Michael as I hobbled along beside him. High heels that hadn't been worn in by a previous owner then donated to the jumble really hurt my feet. 'Jeane in jeans. It would make a great photo essay for my blog, except I don't do that any more.'

'I think there are plenty of normal people who blog,' Michael said as he relieved me of the big Tupperware container I was holding. To show just how friendly and likeable I was, I'd made some cheese straws to share with my fellow partygoers. Also, Kathy had cut me off from the TV after I'd watched six episodes of *America's Next Top Model* back-to-back. 'Though I suppose once you get near a computer you might relapse and start going off on one about how wearing jeans is actually part of a global conspiracy to make everyone wear denim and look exactly the same.'

'Piss off!' I snapped, before I could stop myself.

'I thought normal Jeane wouldn't be quite so hostile. Guess I was wrong,' Michael said. He'd never given me such a hard time, even when we were sleeping together and giving each other a hard time the rest of the time. 'Probably best you get it out of your system before we get to the party.'

I couldn't wait to get to the party, but it was only because my heels hurt more when I was walking on hard, unforgiving pavements. As soon as we got to Ant's house and I was on thick carpet, they were bearable and I could prepare for the ordeal that lay ahead. I wasn't sure what I'd expected apart from the music stopping and everyone turning round to stare at us as I walked in with Michael Lee, but it wasn't like that at all.

Everyone ignored me. Everyone!

Whereas Michael was being hailed on all sides like he'd just come back from fighting on the frontline of a ferocious overseas conflict. He'd only seen his friends a few hours before when I'd been baking my cheese straws and explaining to a select committee that comprised Melly and Alice why I should still be allowed in The Melly and Alice Club, but his friends were all like, 'Dude!' and, 'What took you so long to get here?'

'You know Jeane from school,' Michael kept saying, but everyone shook their heads or said, 'Right, yeah, Jeane,' as if they didn't have a freaking clue who I was.

I shuffled into the kitchen to deposit my cheese straws and when I looked around Michael had disappeared. Probably couldn't wait to exchange flirty talk and saliva with Heidi/Hilda/whatever her name was, who texted him about fifty times a day.

I grabbed a paper cup of white wine and positioned myself in a prime spot by the mantelpiece in the front room, so I wasn't in the way of anyone dancing and I could see everyone who came in and smile at them in a welcoming, inclusive way. Like, 'Hey, look at me being all approachable and smiley. Come on over and say hello.' Except no one came over to say hello apart from bloody Hardeep who's been in the same Business Studies class as me for the last four years.

'Hardy, it's Jeane,' I kept saying, but he was blathering on about football and all kinds of other crap and I knew I could shut him down in ten seconds but I had to stand there with a frozen smile on my face until he said, 'Well, Jane, been nice talking to you, I'm going to get another beer.'

I stayed by the mantelpiece for another half hour. My old life might have been lonely but apart from when I was at school, I'd never had to be in close proximity to such a lot of imbeciles. I actually saw two boys doing the whole 'pull my finger' routine. Jesus wept.

Eventually, when I could feel my blood rising and counting to ten wasn't really cutting it, I tottered into the kitchen, skirting around the sobbing girl who was being comforted by her friends ('He's a total dick who thinks with his dick'), opened the back door and staggered out into the garden.

It was freezing cold. I could feel my skin shrinking as I shivered on the decking. It was even too icy for any smokers to want to brave the elements so I was free to let rip – it didn't count if there was no one to hear me.

'O M actual G, why are my generation such a bunch of moronic idiots without an original thought in their heads? Why? For the love of God, why? And actually, Hardeep, if you'd looked at my face instead of my non-existent tits you'd have realised that it's Jeane standing in front of you. Yes, Jeane! The Jeane who once hit you over the head with her Business Studies textbook when you said that women needed actual balls to run a FTSE 500 company, and, by the way, Hardeep, the only reason that you don't believe in climate change is because you're too stupid to understand it!'

I felt a little bit better. But only a little bit. Besides, I had a lot more ranting to get out of my system.

'Also, school colleagues of mine, grinding up against the buttocks of a member of the opposite sex is not dancing. Technically, it's sexual assault and—'

'Jeane? Is it Jeane?'

There was a light hand on my shoulder and I nearly screamed. I also nearly fell over as I whirled round and saw

Scarlett standing behind me with a little group of her friends. Girls. I think they went to our school, but quite frankly by this stage everyone looked the same to me. 'It is you!'

'Who else would it be?' I snarled because I was in full-on grrr mode. She backed away and I held up my hand. 'Hang on!' I counted to ten, twenty, thirty ... 'OK, sorry about that. Hi, Scarlett. How are *you*? Love what you're doing with your hair.'

'Are you on drugs? Did someone spike the punch?' Scarlett asked tremulously. She waved a hand in front of my face. 'What have you done to yourself?'

'I haven't done anything. Well, apart from a makeunder,' I said. 'I've stopped doing that whole dork thing. I'm like everybody else now.'

'Yeah, you sure about that?' Scarlett was very snippy now she was dating Barney. And Barney had never been snippy until he started dating me. My influence spread far and wide, which was why I'd had to call time on my pernicious ways before I turned everyone snippy.

'Yes.' I struck a pose. 'Say hello to the new Jeane. Jeane version two-point-zero, if you will.'

Scarlett shared a look with her friends. A smirky sort of look. 'Not sure I really get the new Jeane,' she sniffed. 'I think I preferred the old Jeane.'

'You hated the old Jeane,' I reminded her.

'I didn't ... I don't. OK, the old Jeane was super-scary but she wasn't that bad.'

'Yes, I was. I was very bad,' I insisted.

'Not when I got to know you properly and you put me in touch with my inner feminist warrior.'

373

I sighed. 'But you're only one person, Scar. The only person who didn't actively hate old Jeane.'

'Not the only person,' one of her friends said. 'Everyone loved having you in their class because you argued with the teachers when they were being arseholes.'

By now the decking was filling up. A group of smokers had decided to brave the Arctic conditions and Barney had come out to find Scarlett, so there was a small circle of people around me who were all nodding and talking. Not at me, not at new friendly Jeane, but about how they liked old dorky Jeane and her stand-offish ways.

A boy who I was sure I didn't know pointed at me. 'What's with the new image? Seeing what you were wearing was the highlight of my morning.'

'Yeah, if I didn't see you at school before Registration, I used to go to your blog to see what your outfit of the day was,' someone else said.

'And your Twitter. Like, you'd already have sent fifty tweets and posted a few links before I'd even had my first cup of coffee. When are you going to start tweeting again? You always find the best links, like that one with the kitten riding the Roomba.'

They were screwing with me. Now I looked all meek and unassuming they thought they could take the piss. 'I happen to know that I'm only big on Twitter in Japan and America. Oh, and parts of Scandinavia.'

Barney was trying to take a hit on a joint. He wasn't very good at it and he gave up so he could say in a very long-suffering way, 'Jeane, how could you not know that there are a group of Year 10s that everyone calls The Jeanettes because they all dress just like you, except none of their mums would let them dye their hair grey?'

I shook my head. 'This is precisely why I had to change so I could stop being some kind of freakshow for everyone else's entertainment.'

Scarlett actually put her arm round my shoulders and gave me a comforting squeeze. 'You're not a freakshow. You're just, well, eccentric. Sometimes in class when you were going on about something that I didn't even understand, I used to think that it was a bit like going to school with a younger version of Lady Gaga, though you did draw the line at walking around in just your underwear.'

I didn't want to be apart, I wanted to be a part of them, but they were standing in a semicircle around me, looking at me but still not accepting me, and I didn't know what else I could say to persuade them.

It was a relief when Michael stepped through the back door. 'What's everyone doing out here? Ant's about to fire up the *SingStar*.'

'Stick up for me here, Michael,' I begged. 'Will you tell your friends that I've renounced my dorky ways?'

'We've been through this a hundred times already.' He sighed. 'Being an obnoxious, badly dressed pain in the arse is who you are, not a lifestyle choice. It's not something you can renounce.'

'No, I can. I take my dorkdom back. I don't want it because one day I won't be a dork, I'll just be a mad old lady wearing weird clothes who yells at small children for pushing in at the bus stop.'

'You yell at small children for pushing in at the bus stop now.'

'But I have to start fitting in, before it's too late. Look, I'm wearing jeans!' I shouted, slapping at my denim-clad thighs.

'They don't suit you,' Michael said, and I knew he was about to start laughing at me *again* but he didn't. Instead, right in front of everyone, all his friends who thought he was the coolest thing in the whole world ever because their parameters of what was cool were actually very, very narrow, he kissed me.

He kissed me so long and hard that it would have been blates rude not to kiss him back, and after five minutes I guess everyone became acclimatised to the sight of Michael Lee and Jeane Smith kissing because I was dimly aware of them beginning to complain about the cold and they drifted back indoors.

Once they were gone, we could really start to kiss properly.

'I can't believe I'm saying this but I miss old Jeane so much,' Michael said when we finally broke apart and sat huddled together on the garden wall. 'You're a dork, Jeane, deal with it.'

'Old Jeane wasn't very loveable, though, was she?' I asked and wished I hadn't because it wasn't like I was expecting any great declarations.

'She had her moments,' Michael decided, and we sat there in silence for a while, until he started giggling. 'And her huge fanbase is in pieces.'

'What? You mean those half a million Twitter followers who don't even know me?'

'They might not know you but they seem to be missing you,' Michael said. 'The internet's gone into mourning at Adorkable's untimely demise.'

'Look, I get that you're trying to make me feel better by cracking a few funnies but it's not helping,' I said, and I couldn't bear to talk about this *again*. Not if kissing Michael might be back on the agenda, because I'd really really missed his kisses.

But Michael ignored me when I leaned in for another smooch. He pulled his iPhone out of his back pocket because he checked it every five seconds. It was very annoying. Even I never used to check my phone that often.

'Look!' he demanded, thrusting the phone in my face. 'Look! Over ten thousand people have liked a Facebook page called "Bring back Adorkable and reinstate Jeane Smith as Queen of the Interwebz."'

I went to snarl something sarcastic but actually nothing sarcastic came to mind. It was kind of sweet. 'Well, that doesn't mean anything.'

Michael nudged me. 'Go on, check your email or Twitter, or go on YouTube, because I bet some new puppy videos have gone up over Christmas. You know you want to.'

'Oh my God, you're like a skanky drug dealer trying to give me the first few rocks of crack for free,' I snapped. 'I'll only mean to check my Twitter for five seconds and the next thing you know I'll have started a heated debate about the inherent evil of Haribo's Fried Eggs and got into a fight with an old *Big Brother* housemate.'

As I was talking I was logging into Twitter, Michael peering over my shoulder as I clicked on my replies feed.

> @adork_able Where are you? I'm suffering puppy links withdrawal.

@adork_able Come back, Jeane. The world is a cold lonely place without you.

@adork_able I dork, therefore I am. Isn't that what you always said? Don't leave us!

@adork_able Every time you tweeted it might not have meant much to you, but it always made me feel less alone.

It went on and on, until I couldn't get my replies feed to load because there were too many tweets for it to handle. And the really weird thing was that since turning my back on dork, I'd gained over ten thousand new followers, though that might have had something to do with a link to a *Guardian* article about me and something called blogger burnout.

'See? It's not just me that misses the old Jeane,' Michael said. He stroked his fingers through my hair. 'I miss your horrible experiments with hair dye. I miss the clothes that smelt of old lady. I miss y—'

I pulled away from him, because his touches were making me come undone and I wanted to be whole. 'This is really nice that people miss me, but they're not real. It's not real. It's just the internet.'

'I know,' Michael said soothingly, like he was just humouring me. 'But you're on a roll now. You might as well check your email.'

He had a point. It couldn't do any harm. Besides, I might have a message from Bethan or from a Nigerian government minister who wanted me to send him my bank details so he could transfer a million quid into my account.

I had over thirty thousand new emails in my inbox. In fact, for five minutes I couldn't even get into my email as my inbox was full. Who knew that was even possible?

I didn't know where to start so I looked in my Friends folder, which was where messages from people I knew in real life went. There were messages from Bethan, Tabitha and Tom and even Mad Glen. Scarlett, Barney, Ms Ferguson, Gustav and Harry and Ben and Ben's mum and all of Duckie and an email from Molly that began –

> Oh, Jeane, my honorary little sister
> I don't know why you're hurting but I want to make it
> better. Get yourself on a train to Brighton where there will
> be tea and cake and the *My So-Called Life* box set and a
> big, squidgy hug waiting for you.

I wasn't crying. I wasn't. It was cold and my eyes were watering, which was why Michael was brushing the tears from my cheeks. I say tears, but there were only about three of them.

But then I started opening random emails from people I didn't know. Not people from real life but people from the internet.

> I'm fourteen and I had no friends because I'm a dork. I
> used to spend all my time sitting in my bedroom planning
> what my life would be like when I was old enough to leave
> home and try to find people who were like me.

But then I found you. I read your blog and I realised that it was OK to not fit in. That it was OK to be odd and a bit weird and to be a dork, because my dorkiness was something special. And then I followed you on Twitter and you tweeted me back and I followed other people who followed you and they were a bit like me and then I did what everyone told me not to do: I met people off the internet in real life! I found friends who accepted me for who I am and are a bit weird like me. We meet up to go to jumble sales and we share a Tumblr but mostly we laugh and don't feel alone any more and it's all because of you.

Hey Jeane
Not sure if you remember me but I met you last summer at Molly Montgomery's rocking Rock 'n' Roll Camp for Girls. You did this amazing talk about empowerment and self-esteem and you made us share the most hurtful names we'd ever been called then reclaim them by Magic Markering them on to our bodies as tattoos.

My word was 'Fat' and this is a picture of the beautiful tattoo I had done for Christmas.

I don't think of fat as an insult any more but as a powerful statement of who I am, to let the haters know that they can't touch me.

Just wanted you to know that you helped me loads and that everyone at Rock 'n' Roll Camp had an out of control girl crush on you.

Jeane!

I read your blog about trying out for roller derby and you
inspired ME to attend a training session with my local
team.

I'm now a proud member of the Blackpool Brawlers
and we all love you. Come to Blackpool and let us take
you out for chips and a go on the waltzers.

Dear Jeane
Every time you post a blog, you change someone's life. I
promise you.

You changed mine.

It was message after message from people that I'd never met.
People that I'd never even tweeted or mentioned in a blog. But
they all had something in common: they all insisted that even
though we'd never been in the same room together, I was their
friend. They were my friends. That the whole point of the internet was so that people like us could find each other and
Adorkable was the Sat Nav that guided them towards all the
other dorks and freaks and outsiders and loners and that none
of us were on our own. Together we were strong. And if that
wasn't enough to convince me, there were also offers of spare
rooms, muffin baskets and someone even wanted to give me an
actual live puppy.

'Well, I suppose this is something to think about,' I said
slowly. My voice was very croaky as it was taking a super-
human effort not to burst into tears. 'What was that you were
saying about most of the people I knew on the internet being

weird middle-aged men who live with their mothers or spammers who just—'

'OK, I'll admit that maybe I was wrong,' Michael muttered. He gave me one of his penetrating looks, which I was sure he practised in front of the mirror while he was taking ages to do his hair. 'Maybe I've been wrong about a lot of things.'

I blinked. 'I'm sorry. I didn't quite catch that. Did you say that you were wrong?'

Michael nudged me so hard that I almost fell off the wall. 'I said that *maybe* I've been wrong, but you've been wrong too. God, you've been wrong to the power of, like, a billion.'

I couldn't believe I was arguing with Michael Lee again. I'd missed it so much. I'd missed it even more than I'd missed his kisses.

'Yeah, but you were just one of the many people who repeatedly told me that life would be much easier if I wasn't so different.'

'No one but you forced you into a pair of skinny jeans,' Michael snapped back at me. 'But you know what? Your experiment with being a normal girl has just proved to me that I don't like normal girls. I like girls who are different and make me see the world in a way that I've never seen it before. And it isn't just a bunch of freaks off the internet, who I still reckon are probably weird middle-aged men who live with their mothers, who care about you. There are actual real people in the actual real world who care about you too. Like, say, Melly and Alice.'

'I love Melly and Alice. I'm totally going to raise them in my image,' I said, as Michael shuddered at the thought. 'And, well,

I think your mum and I have reached an understanding, haven't we?'

Michael shuddered again. 'She was making noises about asking you to come and live with us.'

Now it was my turn to shudder. 'God, I don't think things are that bad.' I shot him a sideways look. 'But, well, coming round for dinner a couple of nights a week and staying over occasionally might be cool. When I'm not busy with Adorkable stuff – if I decide that I'm going to do the Adorkable stuff, that is,' I added, even though it was a forgone conclusion. Every bit of me was longing to go Adorkable again.

'I've been thinking about that,' Michael said. 'Like, if you had the whole Adorkable thing going on and the support of a good man behind you – that's me, by the way – Jesus, I think you'd probably be able to take over the world in about six months tops.'

He had a point. I'd always been really goal-orientated but there was so much more I could achieve if I didn't have to waste so much time being angry. 'Well, the world does need changing, doesn't it? And as long as you don't get any funny ideas about being the power behind the throne, then maybe we could work something out,' I told him, and I felt strange. Like I wanted to run around the garden and maybe try a cartwheel. And I wanted to laugh out loud and have Michael pick me up and spin me round really, really fast until I thought I'd throw up. I wasn't entirely sure but I think what I was feeling was sheer, unbridled happiness.

'More of a silent partner, then?' Michael suggested and I pretended to think about it, until he looked a little annoyed. 'Come on, Jeane. This last week, haven't I shown you that it was the dorky Jeane I wanted? J'adork – you can write a whole blog about it. You can even post my picture if you think you can live with the shame of dating a boy who has stupid hair and wears clothes that are mass-produced and sold in major chain stores. I'd do pretty much anything for you.'

I narrowed my eyes. Thank God I still hadn't lost that little trick. 'Anything?'

'Pretty much anything. Trips abroad without parental permission might still be a little tricky and I'm going to dress how I want and do my hair in its usual awesome style,' he said. 'Apart from that, yeah, anything.'

It was what I'd been longing to hear. I jumped up from the wall and grabbed his hand. 'Great! Then take me back to yours so I can get out of these jeans, because for every second that I wear them I can feel my powers draining away.'

And he did.

J'ADORK

I'm back! I'm back in dorkdom. Did you miss me?
I hope you did because I missed me and I missed you, too.
I was wrong, OK? And I hate to be wrong but I could no
sooner stop being a dork than I could stop breathing or
eating a bag of Haribo every day or seeing an abandoned
mitten on the pavement and taking its picture to post on
Twitter.

But I needed to screw up in a big, dramatic, throw-all-my-
toys-out-of-my-pram way to realise that what I created with
Adorkable has taken on a life of its own. When I started
blogging, it was because I had no one else to talk to about
the ace new band I'd discovered or to see how splendid my
new frock was or to test out my theory that cats are evil and
want to control us with subliminal messages cunningly
disguised as a cute meow.

I never imagined that I'd find even three people who were
on my level, never mind finding you. All of you. Yes, even
you at the back. But I still convinced myself that I was on my
own, that the people I knew on the internet were just people
on the internet and certainly not friends.

My definition of a friend was someone you could call at
three in the morning to say that you couldn't sleep because
the very fabric of your life was precariously held together

385

with thumbtacks and they'd be at your door within five minutes with a tub of ice cream and a lovingly compiled mix CD. By that definition I didn't have anything even close to a friend.

So, I had this HUGE meltdown and tried to turn my back on dorkdom. I even dyed my hair brown and bought a pair of jeans. I wanted to fit in and it was a disaster. Also, it was very, very boring. I've been to a dark place, my friends, and what pulled me out of it was realising that no matter how much I thought I was pushing people away, there were people who wanted to be close to me, if only I'd let them. Even people I went to school with – like, how weird is *that*?

But mostly there was you guys, and I hope we're still cool because I can't do Adorkable without you and I think Adorkable is too important to lie dormant in a dusty corner of the internet. Not all of us want to conform to the narrow definitions of what it means to be a girl or a boy or a teenager or gay or straight. I know this because I know *you*.

We're the lucky ones; we've found each other. Adorkable gives a voice to anyone who's sat in their bedroom or on the sidelines or is trying so hard just to fit in. But guess what? You don't have to fit in. You don't have to be anyone else but who you really want to be. Sometimes we forget that there's no law that says you have to be what other people expect you to be.

Dorkdom isn't something you can choose. It's something you are. But instead of dividing the world up into dorkside and darkside, I've realised that we all have a little bit of dork inside us.

So, yeah, I'm back and I'm adorkable all the way. I don't know how to be anything else. But as well as being adorkable, I'm going to strive to be more adorable so you'll love me more than you ever thought possible.

This is my pledge to you. All dork. All of the time.

Jeane x

dork face

Acknowledgements

Samantha Smith, Kate Agar and the team at Atom for making me feel so welcome in my new YA home. My wonderful and wise agent, Karolina Sutton, Catherine Saunders and all at Curtis Brown.

I'd also like to thank Hannah Middleton for bidding so generously on the Authors for Japan auction to win the chance to have a character named after her and Keris Stainton for organising the auction.

Props are also due to Lauren Laverne, Emma Jackson and Marie Nixon for being in Kenickie when they were teenagers and providing the soundtrack for this book and to Miss Hill, my English teacher who got me through my GCSE, and always forgave me for being a gobby, obstreperous girl because she could see something in me that I couldn't see myself.

Sarra Manning is an author and journalist. She started her writing career on *Melody Maker*, then spent five years on legendary UK teen mag, *J17*, first as a writer, then as Entertainment Editor. Subsequently she edited teen fashion bible *Ellegirl UK* and the BBC's *What to Wear* magazine.

Sarra has written for *Elle*, *Grazia*, *Red*, *InStyle*, *The Guardian*, *Sunday Times Style*, *The Mail on Sunday's You*, *Harper's Bazaar*, *Stylist*, *Time Out* and *the Sunday Telegraph's Stella*. Her bestselling YA novels, which include *Guitar Girl*, *Let's Get Lost*, *Pretty Things*, *The Diary of a Crush* Trilogy and *Nobody's Girl* have been translated into numerous languages.

She has also written three grown-up novels: *Unsticky*, *You Don't Have to Say You Love Me* and *Nine Uses for an Ex-Boyfriend*.

Sarra lives in North London and prides herself on her unique ability to accessorise.